**“Do you kn[illegible]?”
he asked.**

“Doesn’t matter, [illegible] led the gun from b[illegible] her through the window. “It’s ready to go. All you have to do is pull the trigger. Aim for the largest part of a person.” He saw her cringe. “You can do this.”

She nodded, a determined look settling on her features.

He gave her a smile, then pulled off his glove and reached through the broken window to touch her face with his fingertips. She closed her eyes, leaning into his warm palm. Tears beaded her lashes when he pulled his hand away.

"Do you know how to shoot a gun?" he asked.

"Doesn't matter," he added quickly as he pulled the gun from behind him and handed it to her through the window. "It's ready to go. All you have to do is pull the trigger. Aim for the largest part of a person." He saw her cringe. "You can do this."

She nodded, a determined look settling on her features.

He gave her a smile, then pulled off his glove and reached through the broken window to touch her face with his fingertips. She closed her eyes, leaning into his warm palm. Tears beaded her lashes when he pulled his hand away.

CHRISTMAS AT CARDWELL RANCH

BY
B.J. DANIELS

All the characters in this book have no existence outside the imagination of the author, and have no relation whatsoever to anyone bearing the same name or names. They are not even distantly inspired by any individual known or unknown to the author, and all the incidents are pure invention.

First published in Great Britain 2013
by Mills & Boon, an imprint of Harlequin (UK) Limited,
Eton House, 18-24 Paradise Road, Richmond, Surrey TW9 1SR

ISBN: 978 0 263 90380 5

46-1113

Harlequin (UK) policy is to use papers that are natural, renewable and
recyclab[illegible] The
logging [illegible] al
regulati[illegible]

Printed [illegible]
by Black[illegible]

USA TODAY bestselling author **B.J. Daniels** wrote her first book after a career as an award-winning newspaper journalist and author of thirty-seven published short stories. That first book, *Odd Man Out*, received a four-and-a-half-star review from *RT Book Reviews* and went on to be nominated for Best Intrigue that year. Since then, she has won numerous awards, including a career achievement award for romantic suspense and many nominations and awards for best book.

Daniels lives in Montana with her husband, Parker, and two springer spaniels, Spot and Jem. When she isn't writing, she snowboards, camps, boats and plays tennis. Daniels is a member of Mystery Writers of America, Sisters in Crime, International Thriller Writers, Kiss of Death and Romance Writers of America.

To contact her, write to B.J. Daniels, PO Box 1173, Malta, MT 59538, USA, or email her at bjdaniels@mtintouch.net. Check out her website, www.bjdaniels.com.

In memory of Rita Ness, who will always be remembered as the bright ray of sunshine she was. She is dearly missed.

Chapter One

Huge snowflakes drifted down out of a midnight-blue winter sky. Tanner "Tag" Cardwell stopped to turn his face up to the falling snow. It had been so long since he'd been anywhere that it snowed like this.

Christmas lights twinkled in all the windows of the businesses of Big Sky's Meadow Village, and he could hear "White Christmas" playing in one of the ski shops.

But it was a different kind of music that called to him tonight as he walked through the snow to the Canyon Bar.

Shoving open the door, he felt a wave of warmth hit him, along with the smell of beer and the familiar sound of country music.

He smiled as the band broke into an old country-and-western song, one he'd learned at his father's knee. Tag let the door close behind him on the winter night and shook snow from his new ski jacket as he looked around. He'd had to buy the coat because for the past twenty-one years, he'd been living down South.

Friday night just days from Christmas in Big Sky, Montana, the bar was packed with a mix of locals, skiers, snowmobilers and cowboys. There'd be a fight for sure before the night was over. He planned to be long gone before then, though.

His gaze returned to the raised platform where the band, Canyon Cowboys, was playing. He played a little guitar himself, but he'd never been as good as his father, he thought as he watched Harlan Cardwell pick and strum to the music. His uncle, Angus Cardwell, was no slouch, either.

Tag had always loved listening to them play together when he was a kid. Music was in their blood. That and bars. As a kid, he'd fallen asleep many weekend nights in a bar in this canyon listening to his father play guitar. It was one of the reasons his mother had gathered up her five sons, divorced Harlan and taken her brood off to Texas to be raised in the Lone Star State.

Tag and his brothers had been angry with their dad for not fighting for them. As they'd gotten older, they'd realized their mother had done them a favor. Harlan knew nothing about raising kids. He was an easygoing cowboy who only came alive when you handed him a guitar—or a beer.

Still, as Tag watched his father launch into another song, he realized how much he'd missed him—and Montana. Had Harlan missed him, as well? Doubtful, Tag thought, remembering the reception he'd gotten when he'd knocked at his father's cabin door this morning.

"Tag?"

"Surprise."

"What are you doing here?" his father had asked, moving a little to block his view of the interior of the cabin.

"It's Christmas. I wanted to spend it with you."

Harlan couldn't have looked any more shocked by that—or upset.

Tag realized that surprising his father had been a mistake. "If this is a bad time…"

His father quickly shook his head, still blocking the door, though. "No, it's just that…well, you know, the cabin is a mess. If you give me a little while…"

Tag peered past him and lowered his voice. "If you have someone staying here—"

"No, no, it's nothing like that."

But behind his father, Tag had spotted a leather jacket, female size, on the arm of the couch. "No problem. I thought I'd go see my cousin Dana. I'll come back later. Actually, if you want, I could get a motel—"

"No. Stay here. Bring your stuff back later. I'll have the spare room made up for you. Your uncle and I are playing tonight at the Canyon."

"Great. I'll stop by. I haven't heard you play in a long time. It'll be nice."

Tag had left, but he was still curious about his father's female visitor. He knew nothing about his father's life. Harlan could have a girlfriend. It wasn't that unusual for a good-looking man in his fifties.

Tag tried not to let Harlan's reaction to him showing up unexpectedly bother him. Determined to enjoy the holiday here, he had made plans tomorrow to go Christmas tree hunting with his Montana cousin Dana Cardwell. He'd missed his cousins and had fond memories of winter in Montana, sledding, skiing, ice-skating, starting snowball fights and cutting their own Christmas trees. He looked forward to seeing his cousins Jordan and Stacy, as well. Clay was still in California helping make movies last he'd heard, but Dana had said he was flying in Christmas Eve.

Tag planned to do all the things he had done as a boy this Christmas. Not that he could ever bring back those family holidays he remembered. For starters, his four brothers were all still in Texas. The five of them had started a barbecue joint, which had grown into a chain called Texas Boys Barbecue.

He would miss his brothers and mother this Christmas, but he was glad to have this time with his cousins and his dad. As the band wound up one song and quickly broke into another, he finished his beer. He'd see his father back at the cabin. Earlier, he'd returned to find the woman's leather jacket he'd seen on the couch long gone.

Harlan had been getting ready for his gig tonight, so they hadn't had much time to visit. But the spare room had been made up, so Tag had settled in. He hoped to spend some time with his father, though. Maybe tomorrow after he came back from Christmas tree hunting.

As he started to turn to leave, a blonde smelling of alcohol stumbled into him. Tag caught her as she clung to his ski jacket for support. She was dressed in jeans and a T-shirt. Not one of the skiers or snowmobilers who were duded out in the latest high-tech, cold-weather gear.

"Sorry," she said, slurring her speech.

"Are you all right?" he asked as she clung to his jacket for a moment before gathering her feet under her.

"Fine." She didn't look fine at all. Clearly, she'd had way too much to drink. "You look like him."

Tag laughed. Clearly, the woman also didn't know what she was saying.

She lurched away from him and out the back door.

He couldn't believe with it snowing so hard that she'd gone outside without a coat. Hesitating only a moment, he went out after her. He was afraid she might be planning to drive herself home. Or that she had been hurrying outside because she was going to be sick. He didn't want her passing out in a snowdrift and dying of hypothermia.

Montana was nothing like where he lived in Texas. Winter in Montana could be dangerous. With this winter storm, the temperatures had dropped. There were already a couple of feet of snow out the back door of the bar before this latest snowfall. He could see that a good six inches of new snow had fallen since he'd arrived in town.

He spotted the woman's tracks in the snow just outside the door. As he stepped out to look for her, he saw her through the falling snow. A man wearing a cowboy hat was helping her into his pickup. She appeared to be arguing with him as he poured her into the passenger seat and slammed the door. The man glanced in Tag's direction for a moment before he climbed behind the wheel and the two drove off.

"Where did she go?"

He turned to find a slim brunette behind him. "Where did who go?"

"Mia." At his blank expression, she added, "The blonde woman wearing a T-shirt like the one I have on."

He glanced at her T-shirt and doubted any woman could wear it quite the way this one did. The letters THE CANYON were printed across her full breasts with the word *bar* in smaller print beneath it. He realized belatedly that the woman who'd bumped into him had been wearing the same T-shirt—like the other servers here in the bar.

"I *did* see her," he said. "She stumbled into me, then went rushing out this door."

"Unbelievable," the brunette said with a shake of her head. Her hair was chin length, thick and dark. It framed a face that could only be described as adorable. "She didn't finish her shift again tonight."

"She wasn't in any shape to continue her shift," he said. "She could barely stand up she was so drunk."

For the first time, the brunette met his gaze. "Mia might have had one drink because a customer insisted, but there is no way she was drunk. I saw her ten minutes ago and she was fine."

He shrugged. "I saw her two minutes ago and she was falling-down drunk. She didn't even bother with her coat."

"And you let her leave like that?"

"Apparently her boyfriend or husband was waiting for her. The cowboy poured her into the passenger seat of his pickup and they left."

"She doesn't *have* a boyfriend or a husband."

"Well, she left with some man wearing a Western hat. That's all I can tell you." He remembered that the blonde had been arguing with the man and felt a sliver of unease embed itself under his skin. Still, he told himself, he'd had the distinct feeling that she'd known the man. Nor had the cowboy acted odd when he'd looked in Tag's direction before leaving.

"Lily!" the male bartender called. The brunette gave another disgusted shake of her head, this one directed at Tag, before she took off back into the bar.

He watched her, enjoying the angry swing of her hips. Then he headed for his father's cabin, tired after flying all the way from Texas today. But he couldn't help thinking of the brunette and smiling to himself. He'd always been a sucker for a woman with an attitude.

LILY MCCABE CLOSED the front door of the Canyon Bar behind the last customer, locked it and leaned against the solid wood for a moment. What a night.

"Nice job," Ace said as he began cleaning behind the bar. "Where the devil did Mia take off to?"

Lily shook her head. It was the second night in a row that Mia had disappeared. What made it odd was that she'd been so reliable for the three weeks she'd been employed at the Canyon. It was hard to get good help. Mia Duncan was one of the good ones.

"It's weird," Lily said as she grabbed a tray to clear off the tables. In the far back, the other two servers were already at work doing the same thing. "The man who saw her take off out the back door? He claimed she was *drunk*."

James "Ace" McCabe stopped what he was doing to stare at her. "Mia, drunk?"

Lily shrugged as she thought of the dark-haired cowboy with the Texas accent. Men like him were too good-looking to start with. Add a Southern drawl… "That's what he said. I believe his exact words were 'falling-down drunk,'" she mimicked in his Texas accent. "Doesn't sound like Mia, does it? Plus, I talked to her not ten minutes before. She was fine. He must have been mistaken."

Admittedly, she knew Mia hardly at all. The young woman wasn't from Big Sky. But then most people in the Gallatin Canyon right now weren't locals. Ski season brought in people from all over the world. Mia had shown up one day looking for a job. One of the servers had just quit and another had broken her leg skiing, so James had hired Mia on the spot. That was over three weeks ago. Mia had been great. Until last night when she'd left before her shift was over—and again tonight.

"Well, tonight was a real zoo," Reggie Olson said as she brought in a tray full of dirty glasses from a table in the back. "The closer it gets to the holidays, the crazier it gets."

Lily couldn't have agreed more. She couldn't wait for Christmas and New Year's to be over so she could get back to her real life.

"Did Mia say anything to either of you?" she asked.

Reggie shook her head.

Teresa Evans didn't seem to hear.

"Teresa," Lily called to the back of the bar. "Did Mia say anything to you tonight before she left?"

Teresa glanced up in surprise at the sound of her name, her mind clearly elsewhere. "Sorry?"

"Someone's tired," Ace said with a laugh.

"More likely she's thinking about her boyfriend waiting for her outside in his pickup," Reggie joked.

Teresa looked flustered. "I guess I *am* tired," she said. "Mia?" She shook her head. "She didn't say anything to me."

That, too, was odd since Teresa was as close to a friend as Mia had made in the weeks she'd worked at the bar. Lily noticed how distracted the server was and wanted to ask her if everything was all right. But her brother was their boss, not she. His approach during her short-term employment here was not to get involved in his employees' dramas. Probably wise since once the holiday was over, she would be going back to what she considered her "real" life.

"Maybe you should give Mia a call," Lily suggested.

Her brother gave her one of his patient smiles, looked up Mia's number and dialed it. "She's not home," he said after he listened for a few moments. "And I don't have a cell phone number for her."

"If she left with some cowboy, she must have a boyfriend we haven't heard about," Reggie said. "He's probably the reason she was drinking, too," she added with a laugh. "Men. Can't live with them. Can't shoot them."

Ace laughed. "Reggie's right. Go ahead and go on home, sis," he said when she brought up a tray of dirty glasses. "The three of us can finish up here. And thanks again for helping out."

She'd agreed to help her brother over Christmas and New Year's, and had done so for the past few. Since it was just the two of them, their parents gone, it was as close as they got to a family holiday together. The bar was her brother's only source of income, and with this being his busiest time of the year, he had to have all the help he could get.

Ace had learned a long time ago that if he didn't work his own place, he lost money. With Lily helping, he didn't have to hire another server. She didn't need the money since her "day" job paid very well and working at the Canyon gave her a chance to spend time with the brother she adored.

"I *am* going to call it a night," Lily said, dumping her tips into the communal tip jar at the bar. Her Big Sky home was a house she'd purchased back up the mountain tucked in the pines about five miles from the bar—and civilization. The house had been an investment. Not that she could have stayed with her brother since he lived in the very small apartment over the bar. Christmas would be spent at her house, as it was every year.

When she'd bought the house, she'd thought Ace would move in since her real home and work was forty miles away in Bozeman. But her brother had only laughed and said he was much happier living over the bar in the apartment.

Lily loved the house because of its isolation at the end of a road with no close neighbors—the exact reason

Ace would have hated living there. Her brother loved to be around people. He liked the noise and commotion that came with owning a bar in Big Sky, Montana.

But as much as she yearned to go to her quiet house, she couldn't yet. She wanted to make sure Mia made it home all right. Mia lived in an expensive condo her parents owned partway up the mountain toward Big Sky Resort.

Lily noticed Mia's down ski jacket where she'd hung it before her shift, her worry increasing when under it she found Mia's purse hanging from its shoulder strap. She left both there, thinking Mia might return to retrieve them. As she went out the back door of the bar, she saw that it was still snowing. She glanced toward Lone Mountain, disappointed the falling snow obliterated everything. She loved seeing the mountain peak glistening white against the dark winter sky. It really was a magnificent sight.

Thinking of the skiers who would be delirious tomorrow with all this fresh powder, she had to smile. She understood why her brother loved living here. The Gallatin Canyon was a magical place—especially at Christmas.

The Gallatin River, which cut through the steep, granite bluffs in a breathtaking hundred-mile ribbon of river and winding highway, ran crystal clear under a thick blanket of ice. Snow covered the mountains and weighted down the pine boughs, making the entire place a winter wonderland.

Before the ski resort, the canyon had been mostly cattle and dude ranches, a few summer cabins and even fewer homes. Now luxury houses had sprouted up all around the resort. Fortunately some of the original cabins still remained and the majority of the canyon was national forest, so it would always remain undeveloped.

The “canyon” was still its own little community made up of permanent residents as well as those who only showed up for a week or two in the summer and a few weeks around Christmas and New Year’s for the ski season.

Outside, her breath expelled in cold white puffs. She hugged herself as she looked through the driving snow and saw Mia’s car. Mia was always so protective of her car. It seemed strange that she would leave it. But if she really had been drunk… Maybe she was planning to come back.

Who had she left with, though? Some cowboy, the Texan had said. That, too, didn’t sound like Mia, let alone that the cowboy had “poured her into the passenger seat.”

Everything about this felt wrong.

Unable to shake off the bad feeling that had settled over her, Lily headed for her SUV. The drive up to Mia’s condo didn’t take long in the wee hours of the morning after the bars had closed. There was no traffic and few tracks in the fresh snow that now blanketed the narrow paved road. Her windshield wipers clacked noisily trying to keep up with the falling snow, and yet visibility in her headlights was still only a matter of yards.

Lily was used to driving in winter conditions, having been born and raised in Montana, but just the thought of accidentally sliding off the road on such a night gave her a chill. Why hadn’t she told her brother where she was going?

She’d heard tomorrow was supposed to clear, the storm moving on. With a full moon tomorrow night, maybe she would go cross-country skiing. She loved skiing at night in the moonlight. It was so peaceful and quiet.

Through the falling snow, she got glimpses of Christmas lights twinkling on the houses she passed. She'd already done all her Christmas shopping, but she was sure her brother would be waiting until the last minute. They were so different. She was just thankful they were close in spite of their differences, even though Ace was always trying to get her to loosen up. He saw her orderly life as boring.

"You need to have some fun, sis," he'd said recently when he'd given her a ski pass and the ultimatum that she was to use it on her day off. "It will do you good."

She didn't need Ace to tell her what else he thought would do her good. She'd forbidden him to even mention her former fiancé Gerald's name. Not that it often stopped him.

Distracted with her thoughts, she saw that she'd reached her destination. But as she pulled up in front of Mia's condo, her earlier bad feeling turned to dread.

Mia's front door stood open. A drift of freshly fallen snow had formed just inside the door.

Chapter Two

The hair stood up on the back of Lily's neck as she got out of her SUV and walked toward the gaping front door.

"Mia?" she called as she carefully peered in. She could hear music playing inside the condo. Mia's unit was on the end, and it appeared that whoever was staying in the adjacent one wasn't home.

Lily touched the door. It creaked the rest of the way open. From the doorway, she had a view of the stairs. One set went up, the other down.

"Mia?" she called over the music. No answer as she carefully stepped in.

She'd only gone a few steps up the stairs when she saw what appeared to be a fist-size ball of cotton roll across the floor on the breeze coming in the open door behind her.

One more step and she saw dozens of white balls of cotton. Her heart began to pound. Another step and she saw what was left of the living room sofa cushions.

The condo looked as if it had been hit by a storm that had wreaked havoc on the room. The sofa cushions had been shredded, the stuffing now moving haphazardly around the room. Lamps lay broken in pieces of jagged glass shards on the wooden floor. A chair had been turned over, the bottom ripped out. Nothing in the room looked as if it had weathered the storm that had blown through here.

Who would do such a thing? Why would they? Lily fumbled out her cell phone as she backed down the stairs, her heart hammering against her rib cage. What if whoever had done this was still in the condo?

"I need to report a break-in," she said the moment she reached her SUV and was safely inside. She kept her eyes on the open doorway. When the dispatcher at the local marshal's office answered, she hurriedly gave her name and the address.

"Is the intruder still there?"

"I don't know. I only went just inside the door."

"Where are you now?"

"I'm outside. I don't know where the owner of the condo is. I'm worried about her."

"Can you wait in a warm place?"

"Yes. I'm in my vehicle and watching the condo."

"Please stay there until law enforcement arrives."

MARSHAL HUD SAVAGE was on duty when the call came in. He'd just been up on the mountain on a disturbance call. All day he'd felt as if he were moving in a fog. A cop friend of his from the academy had been killed two nights ago. He was still in shock.

Paul Brown's death, on top of what had happened to Hud's family last spring, had left him shaken. In April, he'd let a dangerous woman come into his home. Hud's wife and children had almost been killed.

He was a *marshal.* He should have seen what was right in front of his eyes. He would never forgive himself. Worse, the incident really had him questioning if he had the instincts anymore for this job.

When he'd heard that his friend Paul had been murdered just forty miles away in Bozeman, he'd been ready to throw in the towel.

"I'm running scared," he'd told his wife, Dana.

She'd hugged him and tried to persuade him that none of what had happened to their family was his fault. "I was the one who was so excited to have a cousin I'd never met come stay with us. You saw that I was happy and ignored things you wouldn't have under any other circumstances."

"I'm a *marshal,* Dana. There is no excuse for what happened last April. None."

Now as he turned into the condo subdivision in the pines, he tried to push everything but this latest call out of his mind. More and more, though, he wasn't sure he deserved to be wearing this star.

As he pulled up, a young brunette got out of her SUV and stood hugging herself against the cold snowy night. A break-in this time of year was unusual. Normally this sort of thing happened during off-season when there were fewer people around.

"Are you the one who made the call?" he asked as he got out of his patrol pickup.

She introduced herself as Lily McCabe.

"Ace's sister," he said with a nod.

"Sometimes I forget how small a community Big Sky is," she said, not looking in the least bit happy about the prospect that everyone knew her business.

Gossip traveled fast in the canyon. Hud had heard something about Ace's sister being left at the altar. He couldn't imagine any sane man leaving this woman.

"Wait in your vehicle while I take a look inside," he told her. But as he headed for the open front door, he saw that she was still standing outside as if too nervous to sit and wait.

At the door, he pulled his weapon and stepped in, even though he doubted the burglar was still inside. The condo had been ransacked in a way that surprised him. This was no normal break-in. Nor was it a simple case of vandalism. Whoever had done this was looking for something and was determined to destroy everything in his path if he didn't find it.

He moved carefully through the upper floor, then the lower one, before he returned to the woman waiting outside.

"Is she…"

He shook his head. "No sign of anyone. I've called for backup. Until they get here, can we talk in your vehicle?"

She nodded and climbed behind the wheel. She'd left the SUV running, so it was warm inside. He couldn't help noticing how neat and clean the interior was as he pulled out his notebook. "Whose condo is it?"

"I don't know their name. Mia told me that her parents own it. She is the one who's been staying here."

"Mia?"

"Mia Duncan. She went to work for my brother at the Canyon three weeks ago. I'm here helping out over the holidays, as you apparently know."

He nodded. He'd heard Ace's sister had bought a house about four years ago up the mountain—about the same time her brother had opened the Canyon Bar.

"Were you meeting Mia here after work?"

Lily shook her head. "She left before her shift was over. I was worried about her, so I decided to drive up and check on her."

"Did she say why she left?"

"No. That's just it. She didn't say anything. One of our patrons saw her leave with a man. The patron said he thought she'd been drinking."

He sensed that she didn't see how any of this helped and hated talking about Mia behind her back. "Could the man she left with have been a boyfriend?"

"She'd said she wasn't seeing anyone, but I can't swear to it."

"Did this patron describe the man he saw her leave with?"

"Just that he was wearing a cowboy hat and driving a pickup."

"That doesn't narrow it down much. What is this patron's name?"

She shook her head. "I've never seen him before. I'm sorry that I can't offer much in the way of details. He had a Southern accent, if that helps."

"You're doing fine. Did you see anyone leaving as you drove into the condo complex tonight?"

"No. But as soon as I pulled up here, I saw that her door was partially open. I only went a few steps inside before I called you."

He'd seen her footprints in the snow. Unfortunately, the footprints of the intruder had been covered by fresh snow. Someone who knew Mia's hours at the bar and knew she wouldn't be coming home until the bar closed? But she left early. So where was she?

Hud wrote down Lily's cell phone number and closed his notebook as another patrol rig drove up. "I'll call if I have any more questions."

"I don't know Mia well, but I'm worried about her. This is the second night she's left in the middle of her shift without telling anyone. Before that she was our most reliable employee."

He nodded. If it wasn't for the ransacked condo, he would have just figured the woman had met some man and fallen hard. People in love often became less reliable employees.

Hud assured Lily he'd let her know when he heard something. But he could tell nothing he might say would relieve her worry. After seeing the inside of the condo, he shared her concern.

WITH HER SHIFT finally over, Teresa Evans opened the back door of the bar and looked out at the falling snow. She had mixed feelings about seeing her boyfriend after the fight they'd had earlier before she'd left for work.

But she didn't have to worry about it. The main parking lot was empty. No Ethan sitting out here in his old pickup, the engine running, the wipers trying to keep up with the falling snow. No Ethan at all.

The only vehicles were Reggie's SUV and Ace's old Jeep. Both were covered in snow.

"Do you need a ride?" Reggie asked behind her, making her jump. The other server stopped to frown at her. "Are you all right?"

"I'm fine," she said a little too sharply.

Reggie raised an eyebrow.

"Didn't Lily say Mia left with someone else earlier?" Teresa asked. "Her car's gone."

Reggie glanced to the spot where Mia had parked earlier. Teresa followed her gaze. There was a rectangular spot in the snow where the car had been.

"I guess she must have come back for it," Reggie said with a shrug. "I hope she wasn't as drunk as that customer thought she was. Bad night to be driving as it is."

"Yeah," Teresa agreed. "Or to be working."

Reggie took hold of her arm and gently squeezed

it through Teresa's coat. "Hey, accidents happen. Ace knows that."

It took her a moment to realize that Reggie was referring to the tray of glasses she'd dropped earlier in the evening when she was clearing one of the tables. "Clumsy," she said to cover the truth. "I think I'm coming down with something."

"Is everything okay with Ethan?" Reggie asked, lowering her voice, as they stood under the shelter of the small landing just outside the bar. Reggie didn't look at her when she asked it. Instead, she pretended more interest in digging her keys out of her purse.

Teresa stared through the falling snow, trying to conjure Ethan and his old pickup. "We're good." That wasn't exactly true, but it was too cold to get into it out here in the wee hours of the morning. "I appreciate you asking, though."

"Hey, we're friends. You sure you don't want a ride?" Reggie said, looking around as she found her keys in the bottom of her shoulder bag. "I don't see Ethan."

"He'll be along soon. He probably just fell asleep. I'll give him a call. If worse comes to worst, I'll walk. It's not that far."

Reggie looked skeptical. "You'd be soaked to the skin if you walked in this." But she let it drop, no doubt sensing that whatever was going on with Teresa, it wasn't something she wanted to talk about. "Well, then, I'll see you tomorrow. I just hope it won't be as crazy as it was tonight." With that, Reggie stepped off the covered landing and headed for her car.

Teresa found herself wondering when Mia had come back for her vehicle as she watched Reggie clean the snow from her car and finally drive away. She couldn't shake the memory of what Mia had said to her earlier.

Several cars went by, disappearing quickly into the falling snow. Still no sign of Ethan. Reaching into her pocket, she told herself he had probably fallen asleep and forgotten to set the alarm. Her pocket was empty. She tried the other one. Empty. With a groan, she remembered leaving her cell phone on the breakfast bar earlier. She'd been in such a rush to get out of the apartment and away from Ethan, she'd forgotten it.

Ethan wasn't coming. Had she really expected him to come after the fight they'd had? She considered going back inside the bar to wait, but she didn't want Ace to know Ethan had stood her up. As soon as Reggie's taillights disappeared in the snowstorm, Teresa started the walk home.

The fight earlier had been another of those stupid ones.

"I need to know you want to marry me and have this baby," he'd said while she was getting ready for work.

"Stop pressuring me." Ever since she'd told him she was pregnant, he'd been so protective that sometimes she couldn't breathe. He was determined they had to get married and settle down. His idea of settling down was moving closer to his parents, who lived down in Billings.

"I don't think your new friend Mia is good for you. I saw her talking to some guy the other day. I've seen him before. He's bad news."

Teresa stifled a groan.

"I don't want you getting involved in some drug deal, or worse."

She had turned to face him, unable to hide her growing impatience. Ethan had been like this ever since he'd gone to the law enforcement academy and was now working for the Montana Highway Patrol.

"I'm sure Mia isn't involved in any kind of drug deal."

"Your friend might not realize what she's getting herself into with a man like that."

It made her angry to hear him talk this way. "Mia's a big girl," she'd snapped. "She can take care of herself." When Ethan looked skeptical, she'd added, "Mia carries a gun." Instantly, she'd wished she hadn't added that part.

"She *what?*" he'd demanded.

"It's just a small one. She wears it strapped on her ankle."

Ethan had sworn and begun to pace. "You're hanging out with a woman who carries a concealed weapon? Does she even have a permit to carry it?"

"Damn it, Ethan. Stop acting like a narc."

He had stopped dead in his tracks. *"What?"*

"It's just that you used to be fun. Now you're such a…"

He had waited for her to finish.

"Cop."

Without another word, he'd grabbed his coat and left.

Still, she couldn't imagine him not picking her up. He was too concerned about her and the baby. Something must have come up with his job, she thought now as she walked through the deep snow toward the apartment they shared.

Ethan had been her high school sweetheart. She smiled to herself now as she thought of how they'd been back then. He had been adventurous, up for anything. His friends said he was crazy fun.

But a couple of years ago, he'd almost gotten into some serious trouble with some ex-friends of his. The incident had apparently scared him straight. He was no longer crazy fun. Far from it.

Teresa wasn't sure she wanted to be married to a cop. She wasn't sure she wanted to be married to Ethan. She wasn't even sure she wanted to be pregnant.

Shoving those thoughts away, she found herself worrying about Mia as she ducked her head against the thick falling snow. Tonight she'd seen Mia get into some kind of argument with a man who'd come into the bar alone. The conversation had looked personal—and definitely heated. At one point the man had grabbed Mia's arm. In the skirmish, the man ended up spilling his drink on her.

Teresa had quickly stepped in.

"Back off. I have it under control," Mia had snapped, wiping at her alcohol-soaked jeans.

Teresa might have argued differently, but the man had raised his head and looked right at her before getting up and leaving.

Mia had apologized a while later when they'd both gone up to the bar to get their drink orders. "I just didn't want you getting involved." Mia's gaze had met hers, worry in her eyes. "I might have already involved you too much. I'm sorry."

She'd been startled by her words. Even more startled when Mia had gone to the room where they kept their coats. Teresa saw Mia take something out of Teresa's ski jacket pocket and stuff it into her jeans pocket.

Teresa had confronted her, only to have Mia pull away. She'd stood helplessly as Mia grabbed her tray of drinks and headed off through the crowd toward one of the large tables at the back of the bar.

Not long after that Mia had seemed unsteady on her feet.

As Teresa had gone back over to the empty table where the man had been sitting, to clear his table, she spotted the hypodermic needle lying under his chair. Her heart had begun to pound. Was Ethan right? Was the argument over drugs?

It still gave her chills to remember the look on the man's face when he'd glanced up at her. Not long after that, she'd seen Mia stagger into some man before leaving through the back door. Mia had definitely appeared drugged. Had she left with the man?

She felt a chill now as she slogged through the deep snow, glad she wasn't that far from home. She'd left behind the cluster of buildings that made up the center of Meadow Village. Now there was nothing but snowy darkness. Pines, their branches heavy with snow, stood like sentinels at the edge of the mountain to her right. To her left, the golf course was an empty field of deep snow.

The storm hadn't let up for hours. She kept her head down against the falling snow, but it still clung to her face and eyelashes. With each step, she regretted not going back into the bar and calling Ethan. Sometimes she was her own worst enemy.

At the sound of a car approaching, she moved to the edge of the road. Probably Ethan, she thought. Was it possible he'd simply fallen asleep and on awakening, realized he hadn't picked her up?

She felt headlights wash over her. Chilled to the bone, she could feel the deep wet snow soaking into her jeans up to her knees. She was angry with him, but right now she didn't feel like fighting. Worse, she didn't want her own foolish stubbornness to make her end up walking the rest of the way home just to spite Ethan or try to make him feel guilty.

Once they got back to the apartment, she would take a nice hot shower. Maybe have a beer with him. Or a soda, she thought, remembering that she was pregnant. She might even be up for making love. Anything to take the edge off and forget for just a while that her life was a mess and had been as far back as she could remember.

Teresa shielded her eyes from the blizzard and the bright headlights as the vehicle caught up to her. A thought struck her in that instant. The engine sound was wrong. She knew it wasn't Ethan in his old pickup even before she saw the large black SUV slow to a stop next to her.

It was one of those expensive big rigs like ones she saw all over Big Sky. The windows were dark as well as the paint. She was trying to see inside, to see if she knew the driver, when the back door was suddenly flung open.

The man who jumped out was large and bundled up in a bulky coat. Her heart was already racing by the time he grabbed her. She tried to scream, but he clamped a gloved hand over her mouth and dragged her toward the large SUV. She fought, but he was too strong for her. Still, she got in a few good kicks and punches before he forced a smelly cloth over her mouth and nose, and everything went black.

Chapter Three

Hud got the call just after daylight the next morning. He'd been up all night with the break-in. He needed sleep and food badly, and was on his way home, hoping for both when the call came in.

"My fiancée didn't come home last night."

"Who am I speaking with?" he asked. The man sounded more than a little upset.

"Ethan Cross."

Hud knew Ethan, knew his record. A wild, good-looking kid who'd gotten into trouble a lot before going to the academy and becoming a highway patrol officer.

"Your fiancée is Teresa Evans?" he asked to clarify. Ethan had been with Teresa since high school. That was the nice thing about a small community. Hud knew the players, at least the local ones.

"She works at the Canyon. I was supposed to pick her up after closing, but I got called out on an accident down by Fir Ridge. With the roads like they were, I didn't get back in time. When I realized she wasn't home, I went looking for her. This isn't like her."

Hud took a guess. "Did the two of you have a fight earlier yesterday?" It was an old story, one he'd heard many times.

"Not really a fight exactly. Still, she wouldn't not come home."

"She probably just stayed at a friend's place to let things cool down. Have you checked with any of her friends?"

"There's only one she's been tight with recently. I tried Mia's number, but she doesn't answer."

"Mia Duncan?" Hud asked, and felt his pulse quicken when Ethan said yes. "Have you tried Teresa's cell phone?"

"She forgot to take it when she left for work. I found it when I called her number looking for her."

"Let's give her a few hours and see if she doesn't turn up," Hud said, hoping he didn't have two missing women, since Mia Duncan hadn't turned up yet, either.

TAG COULDN'T BELIEVE how much he'd missed this. As he trod through the knee-high snow on the mountain the next morning swinging the ax, he breathed in the frosty air and the sweet fresh smell of pine.

"How about that one?" Dana called from below him on the mountainside. They had climbed up the mountain behind his cousin's ranch house Christmas tree hunting. Now she motioned at one to his far right.

He waded through the new-fallen snow to check the tree, shook off the branches, then called back, "Too flat on the back. I'm going up higher on the mountain."

"There's an old logging road up there," she called from down below. "I'll meet you where it comes out. If you find a tree, give a holler. Meanwhile, I'll keep looking down here." She sounded as if she was enjoying this as much as he was, but then Dana had always loved the great outdoors.

He felt a chill as he remembered what had happened

to her and her family last spring. Some crazy woman had pretended to be a long-lost cousin, and having designs on Hud, had tried to kill Dana, her children and her best friend, Hilde. Fortunately Deputy Colt Dawson had found out the woman's true identity and arrived in time to save them all.

Tag couldn't imagine something so horrifying, but if anything, his cousin Dana was resilient and Camilla Northland was in prison, where hopefully she would remain the rest of her life.

The new snow higher up the mountain was as light as down feathers and floated around him as he climbed. He had to stop a couple of times to catch his breath because of the altitude. "You're not in Texas anymore," he said, laughing.

The land flattened out some once he was near the top, and he knew he'd hit the old logging road. As he started down it, he kept looking for the perfect tree. Dana's husband, Marshal Hud Savage, had warned him not to let Dana come back with one of her "orphan" trees. Hud hadn't been able to come along with them. He was working on a burglary case involving a condo break-in and a possible missing person.

"She'll find a tree that she knows no one will ever cut because it's so pitiful and she'll want to give it a Christmas," Hud warned him. "Don't let her. You should see some of the trees that woman has brought home."

Tag told himself he would be happy with whatever tree they found as long as it was evergreen. But he knew he was looking for something special. He hadn't had a real Christmas tree in years. Along with getting one for Dana's living room, he planned to pick up a small one for his father's cabin. He knew Harlan probably didn't decorate for Christmas, but he'd have to put up with it this year since his son was determined to spend Christmas with him.

Dana had said she would lend them some ornaments and the kids would make some, as well. Tag couldn't wait, he thought, as he looked around for a large pretty tree for Dana and a smaller version for him and his father.

He hadn't gone far down the logging road when he picked up a snowmobile track coming in from what appeared to be another old logging road. Dana had told him that they often had trouble in the winter with snowmobilers on the property because of the catacomb of logging roads that ran for miles.

He remembered hearing one late last night, now that he thought about it. A lot of people got around that way in the wintertime. For all he knew, his father had been out and about after the bar closed. To visit his girlfriend? The thought made him smile.

"I found a tree!" Dana called from somewhere below him on the mountain. He couldn't see her through the thick, snow-filled pines.

"An orphan tree?" he called back, and heard her laugh. "Hud will have my head," he mumbled to himself as he started to drop off the side of the mountain, heading in the direction he'd heard Dana laugh.

He'd only taken a couple of steps when the sun caught on an object off to his right. Tag saw what looked like a branch sticking up out of the snow. Only there was something very odd about the branch. It was blue.

As he stepped closer, his heart leapt to his throat. It wasn't a branch.

A hand, frosty in the morning sun, stuck up out of the deep snow.

MARSHAL HUD SAVAGE arrived by snowmobile thirty minutes after he'd gotten the call from his wife. He found Dana and Tag standing half a dozen yards away from the body. It was the second time in the past six years that remains had been found on the ranch. Hud could see that Dana was upset and worried.

"It's going to be all right," he told her. "Go on down to the house and wait for the coroner. He'll need directions up here."

As soon as she left, he stooped down and brushed the snow off the victim's face. Behind him, Tag let out a startled sound, making him turn.

"You know her?" he asked.

Tag nodded, but he seemed to need a minute to find his voice. "She works at the Canyon," he said finally. "I think her name is Mia. I ran into her at the bar last night. Or more correctly, she ran into me. Was she... *murdered?*"

"Looks like she was strangled with the scarf around her neck," Hud said. He could see where the scarf had cut into her throat. "But we'll know more once the coroner and the lab does the autopsy."

"I thought it might have been an accident," Tag said.

Hud studied him. He seemed awfully shaken for a man who'd only just run into the woman the night before. "So, what exactly happened last night at the bar?"

He listened while Tag recounted the woman stumbling into him, apparently quite drunk, and how he'd gone out the back door after her to make sure she was all right. "I saw her getting into a pickup with a man."

"And you think her name was Mia?" Hud asked. Could this be the missing Mia Duncan? He had a bad feeling it was.

Tag told him that all he knew was what another

server at the Canyon had told him. "She had apparently left in the middle of her shift."

"Do you know the name of the other server you talked to?"

"Lily. At least that's what the bartender called her."

Hud nodded. "Tell me about the man the victim left with behind the bar."

"Cowboy hat, pickup. It was snowing so hard I can't even swear what color the truck was. Dark blue or brown, maybe even black. That's about it. I only got a glimpse of the man through the snow," Tag said.

"But he got a good look at you?"

He saw that the question took Tag by surprise. "Yeah, I guess he did."

"I might need a statement from you later," Hud said. "If you think of anything else..."

"I'll let you know," Tag said as the coroner and another deputy arrived by snowmobile. The coroner's had a sled behind his snowmobile.

"Dana will have a pot of coffee on when you reach the house," Hud told him. He'd seen Tag's rented SUV parked in front of the ranch house.

Tag nodded and turned to leave.

Hud watched him go, worrying. Dana had just been disappointed by one "cousin." He didn't want her disappointed again if he could help it. But he couldn't shake the feeling that Tanner "Tag" Cardwell knew a lot more about the victim than he'd admitted.

He reminded himself that his instincts were off. He was probably just looking for guilt where there wasn't any.

TAG WAS GLAD he didn't have to talk to anyone on the walk down the mountain. His head was spinning.

He'd been shocked when he'd recognized the dead woman—even more shocked when he'd seen what she was wearing. A leather jacket like the one he'd seen lying over the arm of his father's couch just yesterday.

Since discovering the body, he'd kept telling himself it couldn't be the same woman. Just as his father couldn't be involved in this.

That was why he hadn't mentioned the jacket to the marshal, he told himself. He couldn't be sure it was the same one. But both his father and the woman had been at the bar last night. Tag knew how some women were about cowboy guitar players—even old ones.

A chill had settled in his bones by the time he reached the ranch house. He liked the idea of a hot cup of coffee, but he didn't want to talk to anyone—especially his cousin—about what he'd seen on the mountain.

As he climbed into his rented SUV, he told himself that the woman's death had nothing to do with his father. And yet Tag couldn't wait to reach the cabin. Harlan Cardwell had some explaining to do.

LILY TRIED NOT to roll her eyes at her brother. *"Ace."*

"Don't 'Ace' me. Lily, it's time you got back on the horse. So to speak."

She really didn't want to talk about this and now regretted stopping by her brother's tiny apartment over the bar this early in the morning. She'd come to talk about Mia Duncan—not her ex-fiancé, Gerald Humphrey.

"What chaps my behind is that Gerald was the wrong man for you in the first place," Ace said as he refilled her coffee cup. "That man would have bored you to death in no time."

She thought about how much she and Gerald had

in common. Of course Ace thought him boring. Ace had never understood what she and Gerald had shared.

"But to pull what he did," Ace continued. "If he hadn't skipped the country when he did, I would have tracked him down and—"

"I really don't want to have this discussion," she said, picking up her mug and moving over to the window. The world was covered in cold white drifts this morning. The sun had come out, turning the fresh snow to a blinding carpet of diamonds.

"Sis, I love you and I hate to see you like this."

Lily spun back around, almost spilling her coffee. She couldn't help being annoyed with the older brother she'd idolized all her life. But this was a subject they had never agreed on.

"You hate to see me like *this?*" she demanded. "Ace, I'm *happy.* I have a great life, a rewarding career. I'm… content."

He mugged a face. "Sis, you live like a nun except for the few times a year that I drag you out to help me with the bar."

"We really should not have this conversation," she warned him, wondering now if he had actually needed her help at the bar or if his asking her to work the holidays with him was part of some scheme to find her a man. If it was the latter… She said as much. "Ace, so help me—"

He held up his hands in surrender. "You know how much I need your help. And I didn't mean to set you off this morning."

But he had. "You should be more concerned about your *other* employees. If you had seen Mia's condo…"

"I *am* concerned. I put in a call to the marshal's office first thing this morning, but no one has called me back yet. I called the condo number Mia gave me, but not surprisingly, there was no answer there. I figure once she discovered the break-in, she probably stayed with a friend last night."

Lily wasn't so sure about that since she didn't think Mia had made any friends in the weeks she'd been working at the Canyon. The only person Mia had spoken to at the bar was Teresa. Which had seemed odd because of the age difference.

Mia was in her late thirties, while Teresa was barely twenty-one. Neither was outgoing, so that could be why they'd become somewhat friends, at least from Lily's observation.

So this morning, she'd placed a call to Teresa's cell, only to reach her boyfriend, Ethan. "Mia isn't the only one who's missing this morning," she told her brother. "That's why I came by so early. Teresa didn't come home last night."

Ace seemed only a little surprised, but then he'd been running a bar longer than Lily had been helping out. "Maybe Mia and Teresa are together. I'm sure they'll turn up. Teresa and Ethan probably had a fight. I noticed she was acting oddly last night." He frowned. "But then again, so was Mia, now that I think about it. I saw her get into it with one of the customers. Teresa came to her rescue, but Mia handled it fine."

"Why didn't you tell me about that last night?" Lily demanded.

"Because it blew over quickly. You and Reggie didn't even notice."

"Who was the customer?"

Ace shrugged. "Some guy. I didn't recognize him. Lily, people act up in bars. It happens. A good server knows how to handle it. Mia was great. I'm telling you,

I wouldn't be surprised if they both show up for work tonight."

Lily hoped he was right. "Did you ask Mia why she left early night before last?"

"She apologized, said she'd suddenly gotten a migraine and hadn't been able to get my attention, but since it hadn't been that busy..."

Lily nodded. Had Mia been drinking the night before last as well as last night? If so, Lily really hadn't seen that coming.

But what did she really know about the woman? Other servers she'd worked with often talked about their lives—in detail—while they were setting up before opening and cleaning up after closing. She'd learned more than she'd ever wanted to know about them.

Mia, though, was another story. She seldom offered anything about herself other than where she was from—Billings, Montana, the largest city in the state and a good three hours away. It wasn't unusual for people from Billings to have condos at Big Sky. Mia's parents owned a condo in one of the pricier developments, which made Lily suspect that the woman didn't really need this job.

"What do you know about Mia?" Lily asked her brother now.

He shrugged. "Not much. She never had much to say, especially about herself. I could check her application, but you know there isn't a lot on them."

"But there would be a number to call in case of emergency, right?"

"I think that is more than a little premature," her brother said. "Anyway, if the marshal thought that was necessary, he would have contacted me for the number, right?"

"Maybe. Unless they have some rule about not looking for a missing adult for twenty-four hours. Still, I'd like to see her job application."

Ace got to his feet. "I've got to open the bar soon anyway. Come on."

In the Canyon office, her brother pulled out Mia Duncan's application from the file cabinet and handed it to her.

He was right. There was little on the form other than name, address, social security number, local phone number and an emergency contact number. Most of his employees were temporary hires, usually college students attending Montana State University forty miles down the highway to the north, and only stayed a few weeks at most. Big Sky had a fairly transient population that came and went by the season.

So Lily wasn't surprised that the number Mia had put down on her application was a local number, probably her parents' condo here at Big Sky.

"No cell phone number," she said. "That's odd since I've seen Mia using a cell phone on at least one of her breaks behind the bar."

Lily didn't recognize the prefix on the emergency number Mia had put down. She picked up the phone and dialed it, ignoring her brother shaking his head in disapproval. The number rang three times before a voice came on the line to say the phone had been disconnected.

"What?" Ace asked as she hung up.

"The number's been disconnected. I'll call the condo association." A few moments later she hung up, now more upset and worried than before. "That condo doesn't belong to her parents. It belongs to a retired FBI agent who recently died. The condo association didn't even know Mia was staying there."

At a loud knock at the bar's front door, they both started. Lily glanced out the office window and felt her heart drop at the sight of the marshal's pickup.

Chapter Four

As Tag pulled up in front of his father's cabin, he saw that Harlan's SUV was gone. He hadn't seen much of his father since he'd arrived and wasn't all that surprised to find the cabin empty. Harlan had been in bed this morning when Tag had left to go Christmas tree hunting. He had the feeling that his father didn't spend much time here.

Tag felt too antsy to sit around and wait. He needed Harlan to put his mind at ease. That leather jacket the dead woman was wearing was a dead ringer for the one he'd seen on the arm of Harlan's couch.

Fortunately, he had a pretty good idea where to find his father. If Harlan Cardwell was anything, he was predictable. At least Tag had always thought that was true. Now, thinking about the murdered woman, he wasn't so sure.

Just as he'd suspected, though, he found his father at the Corral Bar down the canyon. Harlan was sitting on a bar stool next to his brother, Angus. A song about men, their dogs and their women was playing on the jukebox.

The sight of the two Cardwell men sitting there brought back memories of when Tag was a boy. Some men felt more at home in a bar than in their own house.

Harlan Cardwell was one of them. His brother, Angus, was another.

Tag studied the two of them for a moment. It hit him that he didn't know his father and might never get to know him. Harlan definitely hadn't made an attempt over the years. Tag couldn't see that changing on this visit—even if his father had nothing to do with the dead woman.

"Hey, Tag," Uncle Angus said, spotting him just inside the doorway. He slid off his bar stool to shake Tag's hand. "You sure grew up."

Tag had to laugh, since he'd been twelve when he'd left the canyon, the eldest of his brothers. Now he stood six-two, broad across the shoulders and slim at the hips—much as his father had been in his early thirties.

After his mother had packed up her five boys and said goodbye to their father and the canyon for good, they'd seen Harlan occasionally for very short visits when their mother had insisted he fly down to Texas for one event in his boys' lives or another.

"I hope you stopped by to have a drink with us," Tag's uncle said.

Tag glanced at the clock behind the bar, shocked it was almost noon. The two older men looked pretty chipper considering they'd closed down the Canyon Bar last night. They'd both been too handsome in their youths for their own good. Since then they'd aged surprisingly well. He could see where a younger woman might be attracted to his father.

Harlan had never remarried. Nor had his brother. Tag had thought that neither of them probably even dated. He'd always believed that both men were happiest either on a stage with guitars in their hands or on a bar stool side by side in some canyon bar.

But he could be wrong about that. He could be wrong about a lot of things.

"I'm not sure Tag drinks," his father said to Angus, and glanced toward the front door as if expecting someone.

Angus laughed. "He's a Cardwell. He *has* to drink," he said, and motioned to the bartender.

"I'll have a beer," Tag said, standing next to his uncle. "Whatever is on tap will be fine."

Angus slapped him on the back and laughed. "This is my nephew," he told the bartender. "Set him up."

Several patrons down the bar were talking about the declining elk herds and blaming the reintroduction of wolves. Tag half expected the talk at the bar would be about the young cocktail waitress's death, but apparently Hud had been able to keep a lid on it for the time being.

Tag realized he couldn't put this off any longer. "Could we step outside?" he asked his father. "I need to talk to you in private for a moment."

"It's cold outside," Harlan said, frowning as he glanced toward the front door of the bar again. Snow had been plowed into a wall of white at the edge of the parking area. Ice crystals floated in the cold late-morning air. "If this can't wait, we could step into the back room, I guess."

"Fine." Tag could tell his father was reluctant to leave the bar. He seemed to be watching the front door. Who was he expecting? The woman who'd been in his cabin yesterday?

"So, what's up?" his father asked the moment Tag closed the door behind them.

"I need to ask you something. Who was at your cabin yesterday when I showed up unexpectedly?" Tag asked.

"I told you there wasn't—"

"I saw her leather jacket on the couch."

Harlan met his gaze. "My personal life isn't—"

"A woman wearing a jacket exactly like that one was just found murdered on the Cardwell Ranch."

Shock registered in his father's face—but only for an instant.

That instant was long enough, though, that Tag's stomach had time to fall. "I know you couldn't have had anything to do with her murder—"

"Of course not," Harlan snapped. "I don't even know the woman."

Tag stared at his father. "How could you know that, since I haven't told you her name?"

"Because the woman who owns the leather jacket you saw at my cabin came by right after you left this morning. She is alive and well."

Tag let out a relieved sigh. "Good. I just had to check before I said anything to the marshal."

"Well, I'm glad of that."

"I had to ask because this woman is the same one who stumbled into me last night at the Canyon—the same bar where you and Uncle Angus were playing. After seeing that leather jacket at your cabin…well, you can see why I jumped to conclusions."

"I suppose so," his father said, frowning. "Let's have that beer now. We'll be lucky if your uncle hasn't drank them."

"The woman worked at the Canyon Bar," Tag said, wondering why his father hadn't asked. Big Sky was a small community—at least off-season. Wouldn't he have been curious as to who'd been murdered? "She was working last night while you were playing in the band.

A tall blonde woman? I'm sure you must have noticed her. Her name was Mia."

Harlan looked irritated. "I told you—"

"Right. You don't know her." He opened the door and followed his father back to the bar. Angus was talking to the bartender. Their beers hadn't been touched.

The last thing Tag wanted right now was alcohol. His stomach felt queasy, but he knew he couldn't leave without drinking at least some of it. He didn't look at his father as he took a gulp of his beer. He couldn't look at him. His father's reaction had rocked him to his core. A young woman was murdered last night, her body dumped from a snowmobile on an old logging road on the Cardwell Ranch. He kept seeing his father's first reaction—that instant when he couldn't hide his shock and pretend disinterest.

"You two doing all right?" Angus asked, glancing first at Tag, then at Harlan. Neither of them had spoken since they'd returned to the bar. Tag saw a look pass between the brothers. Angus reached for his beer and took a long drink.

Tag picked up his, taking a couple more gulps as he watched his father and uncle out of the corner of his eye. Some kind of message had passed between them. Neither looked happy.

"I'm sorry but I need to get going," he said, checking his watch. "I'm meeting someone." He'd never been good at lying, but when he looked up he saw that neither his father nor his uncle was paying any attention. Nor did they try to detain him. If anything, they seemed relieved that he was leaving.

Biting down on his fear that his father had just lied to him, he reached for his wallet.

"Put that away," his uncle said. "Your money is no good here."

"Thanks." He looked past Angus at his father. "I guess I'll see you later?"

"I'm sure you will," Harlan said.

"Dana's having us all out Christmas Eve," Tag said. "You're planning to be there, aren't you?"

"I wouldn't miss it for anything," his father said. He hadn't looked toward the door even once since they'd returned from the back room.

Tag felt his chest tighten as he left the bar. Once out in his rented SUV, he debated what to do. All his instincts told him to go to the marshal. But what if he was wrong? What if his father was telling the truth? He couldn't chance alienating his father further if he was wrong.

On a hunch, he pulled around the building out of sight and waited. Just as he suspected, his father and uncle came out of the bar not five minutes later. They said something to each other as they parted, both looking unhappy, then headed for their respective rigs before heading down the canyon toward Big Sky.

Tag let them both get ahead of him before he pulled out and followed. He doubted his father would recognize the rented SUV he was driving. It looked like a lot of other SUVs, so nondescript it didn't stand out in the least. He stayed back anyway, just far enough he could keep them in sight.

His uncle turned off on the road to his cabin on the river, but Harlan kept going. Tag planned to follow his father all the way to Big Sky but was surprised when Harlan turned into the Cardwell Ranch instead. Tag hung back until his father's SUV dropped over a rise; then he, too, turned into the ranch. Within sight of the old two-story farmhouse, Tag pulled over in a stand of pines.

Through the snow-laden pine boughs, he could see his father and the marshal standing outside by Hud's patrol car. They appeared to be arguing. At one point, he saw Hud point back up into the mountains—in the direction where Tag had found the dead woman's body. Then he saw his father pull out an envelope and hand it to the marshal. Hud looked angry and resisted taking it for a moment, but then quickly stuffed it under his jacket, looking around as if worried they had been seen.

Tag couldn't breathe. He told himself he couldn't have seen what he thought he had. His imagination was running wild. Had that been some kind of payoff?

A few minutes later, his father climbed back into his SUV and headed out of the ranch.

Tag hurriedly turned around and left, his mind racing. What had that been about? There was no doubt in his mind it had something to do with the dead woman his father had denied knowing.

DANA STARED AT the Christmas tree, fighting tears.

"It's not *that* ugly," her sister, Stacy, said from the couch.

Last night, Dana, her husband and her two oldest children had decorated it. It hadn't taken long, since the poor tree had very few limbs. Hud had just stared at it and sighed. Mary, five, and Hank, six, had declared it beautiful.

Never a crier except when she was pregnant and her hormones were raging, Dana burst into tears. Her sister got up, put an arm around her and walked her over to the couch to sit down next to her.

"Is it postpartum depression?" Stacy asked.

She shook her head. "It's Hud. I'm afraid for him."

"You knew he was a marshal when you married him," her sister pointed out, looking confused.

"He's talking about quitting."

Stacy blinked in surprise. "He loves being a marshal."

"*Loved.* After what happened here on the ranch last spring, he doesn't think he has what it takes anymore."

"That's ridiculous." A woman pretending to be their cousin had turned out to be a psychopathic con artist. "Camilla fooled us all."

Dana sniffed. "Not Hilde." Her sister handed her a tissue. Hilde had tried to warn her, but she'd thought her best friend was just being jealous and hadn't taken her worries seriously. Not taking Hilde's warnings seriously had almost gotten them killed.

"Hilde's forgiven you, right?" Stacy asked as Dana wiped her eyes and blew her nose.

"Kind of. I mean, she says she has. But, Stacy, I took some stranger's word over my best friend's, who is also my business partner and godmother to one of my children!"

"You and Hud both need to let this go. Camilla is locked up in the women's state prison in Billings, right? With six counts of attempted murder, she won't get out until she's ninety."

"What if she pretends to be reformed and gets out on good behavior? Or worse, escapes? We're only a few hours away."

"You can't really think she's going to escape."

"If anyone can, it's her. Within a week, I'll bet she was eating her meals with the warden. You know how she is."

"Dana, you're making her into the bogeyman. She's just a sick woman with a lot of scars."

Dana looked at Stacy. Her older sister had her own scars from bad marriages, worse relationships and some really horrible choices she'd made. But since she'd had her daughter, Ella, Stacy had truly changed.

"I'm so glad you're in my life again," Dana said to her sister, and hugged Stacy hard.

"Me, too." Stacy frowned. "You have to let what happened go."

Dana nodded, but she knew that was easier said than done. "I have nightmares about her. I think Hud does, too. I can't shake the feeling that Camilla isn't out of our lives."

CAMILLA NORTHLAND WAS surprised how easy it was for her to adapt to prison. She spent her days working out in the prison weight room, and after a month of hitting it hard, figured she was in the best shape of her life.

She'd tuned in to how things went in prison right away. It reminded her of high school. That was why she picked the biggest, meanest woman she could find, went up to her and punched her in the face. She'd lost the fight since the woman was too big and strong for her.

But ultimately she'd won the war. Other prisoners gave her a wide berth. Stories began to circulate about her, some of them actually true. She'd heard whispers that everyone thought she was half-crazy.

Only half?

Like the other inmates, she already had a nickname, Spark. Camilla could only assume it was because of the arson conviction that had been tacked on to her attempted murder convictions.

She'd skipped a long trial, confessed and pleaded

guilty, speeding up the process that would ultimately land her in prison anyway. It wasn't as though any judge in his right mind was going to allow her bail. Nor did she want the publicity of a trial that she feared, once it went nationwide, would bring her other misdeeds to light.

The local papers had run stories about the fire and Dana and her babies and best friend barely escaping. Dana and Hilde had become heroes.

It was enough to make Camilla puke.

So now she was Spark. Over the years she'd gone by so many different names that she was fine with Spark. She liked to think that whoever had given her the new moniker had realized she was always just a spark away from blowing sky-high.

She knew that if she was going to survive, let alone thrive here, she had to be in the right group. That, too, was so much like high school, it made her laugh.

The group she wanted to run with had to be not just the most fearsome but also the ones who ran this prison. She might be locked up, but she wasn't done with Hud Savage and his precious family. Not by a long shot.

Being behind bars would make it harder, though, she had to admit. But she knew there were ways to get what she wanted. What she wanted was vengeance.

So the moment she heard about fellow prisoner Edna Mable Jones, or Grams as she was fondly called, Camilla knew she would have it.

TAG HADN'T REALIZED where he was going until he saw the sign over the front door. The Canyon. As he pulled up in front of the bar, the door swung open and the barmaid he'd met the night before stepped out and headed for an SUV parked nearby. He figured that by now Hud would have talked to her and anyone else at the bar who'd known the victim.

Earlier, he'd told himself there was nothing he could do but wait for the marshal to catch the killer. That was before he'd talked to his father—and witnessed the meeting between Hud and Harlan at Cardwell Ranch. As much as he didn't want to believe his father was involved, he knew in his heart that Harlan was up to his neck in this. He was more shocked that it appeared the marshal was involved, as well.

As he watched the brunette head for her SUV, he realized he'd come here because he'd hoped Lily would be able to help him. She had worked with the dead woman. She also might know something about Harlan since apparently the Canyon Cowboys had played at the bar on more than one occasion.

She had started to climb into her vehicle, but when she saw him, she stopped. Frowning, she slammed the door and marched over to Tag's rental SUV.

"You," she said as he put down his side window. "I just told the marshal about you and how you were the last one to see Mia."

He laughed, clearly surprising her. "Other than the killer. Also, the marshal already knows about me. Hud Savage is my cousin-in-law. I'm the one who found her body."

Lily pulled back, startled. *"You?"*

Tag hadn't heard the bartender from last night come out of the bar until he spoke. "Lily, you're starting to sound like an owl," he said as he joined them.

"This is the man I told you about," she said to the bartender. "The one who said Mia was drunk." She narrowed her eyes when she looked at Tag again, accusation in her tone and every muscle of her nicely rounded body. "He *claims* he's related to the marshal."

The bartender shook his head at Lily and reached past her to extend his hand. "James McCabe, but everyone around here knows me as Ace. You must be one of Harlan's sons, right?"

"Tag Cardwell."

"Cardwell?" Lily said in surprise.

"This is my sister, Lily, but I guess you two have met." Ace seemed amused.

Then his sister said, "He found Mia."

Ace nodded somberly. "We're in shock. In fact, I just put a note on the door that we're going to be closed tonight. We didn't know Mia that well, but the least we can do is close for the night in her memory." He glanced at his watch. "I told the marshal I would stop by his office. I better get going." He squeezed his sister's shoulder and said, "Nice to meet you," to Tag before he walked over to an old Jeep and climbed in.

Neither Tag nor Lily spoke until her brother had driven away.

"Sorry about—"

Tag waved her apology away. "You don't know me from Adam. I would have been disappointed if you hadn't suspected me."

She narrowed her eyes at him again as she realized he was flirting with her. "Have you remembered any more about the man Mia left with last night?" she asked, all business.

He shook his head. "I wish I'd gotten a better look at him or paid more attention to the truck he was driving." But it had been snowing hard and he'd had no reason to pay that much attention.

"I can't believe anyone would murder her."

He nodded, thinking what a shock murder was in a place like Big Sky. Crime was so low people felt safe here. When he was young, he and his brothers were allowed to wander all over this country. Looking back, he knew there'd been a fair share of close calls while climbing rocks, swimming in the river, skiing and sledding off the side of mountains. But they'd never known the kind of danger the dead woman had run across.

"You said you didn't think she had a boyfriend, right? Did you ever see her talking with someone in the bar she might have had an interest in?" *Like a member of the band,* but he didn't say that.

"No one she seemed interested in. She just did her job. I never even saw her flirting with anyone. So maybe she did have a boyfriend. She didn't talk about her personal life." Lily sighed and started to walk to her vehicle again.

"Lily?" He liked the name and it seemed to fit her.

She turned to look at him over her shoulder, leery again.

"If you ever want to talk, or maybe…" He dug in his coat pocket, thinking he might have one of his business cards. When he felt something odd shaped, cold and hard, he frowned and drew it out. "What the…?"

Lily stepped back to his open window. "What's wrong?"

"This," he said, holding up the object he'd found. "I don't know what it is."

"It's a computer thumb drive," she said, then eyed him as if she thought he was messing with her.

"I know that," he said. "The question is, what is it doing in my coat pocket? I have no idea how it got there."

"When was the last time you checked your pockets?" she asked.

He shrugged. "I bought this ski jacket before I flew out here. Yesterday was the first time I've worn it."

She frowned. "Are you saying it wasn't in your pocket when you left Texas?"

"I don't know. I don't think so. All I can tell you is that it isn't mine." He tried to remember where his ski jacket had been. Last night at the cabin, his father had taken his coat and hung it up. Was it possible he'd put the thumb drive in the pocket? Why would he do that?

With a start, Tag remembered the dead cocktail waitress stumbling into him, grabbing his coat and holding on to him as he tried to help her get her feet under her. A chill ran the length of his spine as he remembered her words.

"You look like him."

Was it possible she meant Harlan?

Before he could shove the thought away, Lily said, "Is there any chance Mia put it in your pocket last night?"

Chapter Five

"I think we'd better see what's on that thumb drive," Lily said. "There's a computer in the bar office." With that she turned and headed for the front door. She heard Tag Cardwell come up behind her as she inserted her key into the lock.

"Why would she put this in my pocket?"

Lily shook her head. She had no idea. Just as she had no idea why Mia had left early two nights in a row or why Tag had thought Mia was falling-down drunk. She said as much as she opened the door to the bar, locking it behind them, before leading him to the office.

"Isn't it possible she was pretending to be drunk?" Lily asked, although that seemed even more far-fetched.

"She wasn't pretending," Tag said.

"Then she got drunk awfully fast after I talked to her." Stepping behind the desk, she held out her hand for the thumb drive.

"She smelled boozy, but it could have been drugs."

Lily shook her head. "Not Mia." But even as she said it, she realized again how little she really knew about the woman.

"You know, I was just thinking," he said as he handed over the thumb drive with obvious reluctance. "It's possible one of my brothers put it in my pocket at the airport as I was leaving. We're in business together, so it could be tax information they wanted me to look at. My brother and my nephew saw me off at the airport. In fact, my brother held my coat while I was looking for my ticket."

She could tell he wanted the thumb drive to turn out to be something simple and innocent. No one wanted to think they had any kind of connection to a young woman's murder. She figured he was probably right. The other was too much like a spy movie.

As she considered Tag, she had to admit he would make a great spy. He looked like the kind of man who could save the damsel in distress. He definitely was sure of himself. But a spy with a Stetson and a Texas accent? It had more appeal than she wanted to admit, and she quickly shook the image off.

Lately her mind had been wandering into the strangest places. She knew what her brother would have to say about it. He was determined she find another man after what she liked to think of as "the Gerald Era" with its straight-out-of-a-country-and-western-song bad ending.

She pushed in the thumb drive, and Tag came around the end of the desk to stand next to her. He smelled like winter, a blend of cold and pine. She ignored the masculine scent just below the surface as she ignored the way her nerve endings jumped with him standing so close. Maybe her brother was right and it was time to get back on that horse that had thrown her.

It was definitely time to quit the cowboy clichés.

The icon came up on the page. She hesitated only a moment before she clicked on it. A series of random letters appeared.

GUHA BKOPAR
CAKNCA IKKNA

BNWJG IKKJAU
HSQ SWUJA
YHAPA NWJZ
NWU AIANU

LWQH XNKSJ
IEW ZQJYWJ
YWH BNWJGHEJ
HWNO HWJZANO
DWNHWJ YWNZSAHH
DQZ OWRWCA

"It's just gibberish," Tag said with a relieved laugh. "It looks like some kid was playing on a computer."

Lily nodded, feeling disappointed. "It does look that way," she agreed. She checked, but this page was the only thing on the thumb drive.

She'd wanted answers so desperately about Mia that she'd latched on to the thumb drive, determined she could solve the mystery. It was the way she approached life, her brother would have told her. Full steam ahead—as long as it was logical. The thumb drive hadn't been the answer, nor had she jumped to the logical conclusion. It wasn't like her.

Tag stepped away, shaking his head. "Maybe it was something my nephew put in my pocket. Ford's five and is always playing on the computer. He was at the airport with his dad the day I flew out."

"You're suggesting your five-year-old nephew put this on a thumb drive for you?" she asked skeptically.

"It's probably his idea of a goodbye letter. My brother would have put it on the thumb drive for him. Jackson is a single parent," he said as if that explained it enough for him.

Lily wasn't as convinced. Admittedly, she'd been so sure Mia had put it in his coat pocket last night that she hated to give up the possibility. How nice it would have been if whatever was on the thumb drive would provide a clue to the woman's murder. Unfortunately the world seldom worked the way she thought it should.

"I was wondering," Tag said. "Since the bar won't be open tonight..."

His words didn't register until much later. Lily was busy staring at the letters on the screen trying to make them into more than they no doubt were.

The fact that the letters were all capitalized substantiated Tag's theory that they were probably done by a child who had just happened to hit Caps Lock before he started typing.

What interested her was that the lines were so short—none more than fourteen letters. The columns were also short, one on top of the other, broken halfway down by an empty line, then an equal number of lines below that. Six each. Awfully neat for a child, she thought, but then it could have been random—just like the letters.

She mentioned this to Tag without looking away from the screen.

"You *counted* them?" He laughed, then sobered when she sent him a withering look. "Sorry, it just seems odd to me that you'd count them."

Lily tried not to let his comment annoy her. "I'm a mathematician. I tend to count things."

His dark eyes widened. "A *mathematician?*"

She could tell he was fighting a grin, hoping she was joking. "I teach math at Montana State University," she said simply. Lily had seen too many men's eyes glaze over when she'd tried to explain her love of mathematics or how important it was for solving economic, scientific, engineering and business problems. Few people realized they used math in so many ways in their daily lives. Nor did they care, for that matter.

"Oh," was all he said. Much better than the men who said, "So you're smart." After that, they quit calling.

"Would you mind if I kept this for now?" she asked, pointing at the thumb drive.

Tag shrugged. "It's all yours. I'll check with my brother, but I'm betting my nephew Ford is behind this." Clearly, he was no longer worried about it. "I could call you later and let you know."

Lily realized that earlier he'd been about to ask her something about tonight. Had he been about to ask her on a date? She hadn't dated since Gerald. The thought of going out with this cowboy—

"I'll need your number," he said.

"So you can let me know what your brother says about the thumb drive. Right."

"Right," he said, looking amused at how flustered she had become.

She scribbled her number on one of the Canyon Bar business cards and handed it to him. Then she saved the page to the computer, emailed herself a copy, ejected the thumb drive and stood holding it.

"You sure you don't mind me keeping this for now?"

He grinned. "No problem. If it is a letter from my nephew, well, I think I got the gist of it," he said with a laugh.

And if it wasn't? She pocketed the thumb drive before walking him to the door. Ace had made a sign he'd posted, saying because of a death, the bar would be closed for the day. It was taped to the door as she let Tag out.

He seemed to hesitate before heading to his SUV. “I’m sorry about Mia.”

“Thank you. Let me know what your brother says about the thumb drive.”

Tag nodded and looked as if he had more he wanted to say, but after a moment, he touched his cowboy hat and left.

TAG HAD ALMOST asked Lily McCabe out. Mentally he kicked himself as he climbed behind the wheel of the SUV. Lily had lost a woman she’d worked with. She probably wasn’t interested in going out with the man who’d found the victim’s body. Not tonight anyway.

There’d be another chance before he left, he mused. He just hoped she didn’t think the reason he hadn’t pursued it was that she taught math. Wouldn’t she have to have a PhD to teach math at a university? He let out a low whistle that came out frosty white in the winter air. Beautiful *and* smart. Everything about Lily McCabe intrigued him.

The temperature was dropping fast, but he hadn’t noticed until he sat down on the pickup seat. It was as cold as a block of ice, hard as one, too.

He got the engine going. The heater was blowing freezing-cold air. He turned it off until the engine warmed up, rubbing his hands together. Even with gloves on, his fingers ached. He really should have gone with the more expensive rental—the one with the heated seats. But he was a Texas boy who’d forgotten how cold it got up here in Montana.

When he reached his father’s cabin, he saw that Harlan hadn’t returned. He couldn’t imagine where he might have gone, so he went inside to wait. Lily McCabe had taken his thoughts off his father and his growing suspicions. But now, standing in his father's empty cabin, they were back with a vengeance.

He desperately wanted to believe that Hud would find the killer and clear all this up. Unfortunately, he kept picturing his father handing the marshal the thick envelope. What the hell was going on?

At the window, he caught a glimpse of Lone Mountain looming against the cold blue sky and thought about going skiing. But he felt too antsy. Maybe his father had gone over to Uncle Angus's.

As he started to leave the cabin, he remembered his promise to call his brother. He dialed Jackson's number and was relieved when he answered on the third ring.

"How's Montana?" his brother asked.

Tag thought it telling that Jackson hadn't asked how their father was first. "It's beautiful. Cold and snowy. I'm thinking about heading up to the ski hill." Not quite true, but it sounded good.

Jackson laughed. "Glad I'm in sunny, warm Texas, then."

"As the youngest, you probably don't have the great memories I do of the canyon. But this place grows on you. Summers here are better than any place on earth."

"How's Harlan?" Jackson and their brothers had quit calling him Dad a long time ago.

Tag wasn't sure how to answer that. "I went down to this local bar last night and listened to him and Uncle Angus play in their band. He really is a damned good guitar player. Mom might have been right about him having a chance at the big time."

"Yeah, right," Jackson said, clearly losing interest in this part of the conversation. His brother had thought he was a fool to want to spend Christmas with their father—let alone surprise him.

"You know how he is," Jackson had said. "I just hate to see you get hurt."

"I'm not expecting anything," Tag had said, but he could tell his brother didn't believe him. As the eldest, he had the most memories. He'd missed his father.

He realized that he'd had more expectations than he had wanted to admit. He'd wanted Harlan to be glad to see him. He'd also wanted Harlan to act like a caring father. So far he was batting zero.

"I need to ask you a question," Tag said. "When you and Ford saw me off at the airport, did Ford put a thumb drive in my pocket?"

"You mean one of those computer flash drives?"

Tag felt his heart drop. "I thought maybe he'd written me a goodbye letter on the computer and you saved it to one since I found one in my pocket."

"You do know that Ford is five and doesn't know how to write goodbye letters, right?"

"Yeah, but what's on the thumb drive looks like a kid typed it, pretending he was writing a goodbye letter."

"Sorry, I had nothing to do with it, but I'll ask Ford if he knows anything about it." He left the phone, returning a few moments later. "Nope. Ford's innocent. At least this time," he added with a laugh. "So, when are you coming back?"

"I'm not sure." Earlier he'd told his uncle he was leaving right after Christmas. That was before he'd officially met Lily McCabe. "Probably after New Year's."

"Hope you solve the mystery of the thumb drive," Jackson said with a laugh.

"I'm sure it's nothing." He thought of Mia and his father. He hoped to hell it was nothing.

LILY PUT THE thumb drive into her laptop the moment she got to her house. The house was small by Big Sky standards—only three bedrooms, three baths, a restaurant-quality kitchen, a large formal dining room and an open living room with a high-beamed ceiling.

The structure sat back into the trees against the mountainside and had a large deck at the front with a nice porch area next to the driveway and garage. She'd chosen simple furnishings, a leather couch in butterscotch, her mother's old wooden rocker, a couple of club chairs with antique quilts thrown over them.

The dining room table was large, the chairs comfortable. It was right off the kitchen and living room. That was where she kept her computer because she liked the view. She was high enough on the mountain that she could look out through the large windows at the front of the house and see one of the many ski hills and the mountains beyond. It felt as if she could see forever.

The moment she inserted the flash drive, the letters came up again on the screen. It looked like a foreign language, one with a lot of hard vowels.

She knew she didn't want the letters to be random and that she was going to be disappointed if Tag was right and they were just gibberish typed in by a child.

But as she pulled up a chair, she thought about Mia. What if she was the one who'd put this thumb drive in Tag's jacket pocket—just as her imaginative mind had suggested? He'd said that Mia could barely stand up she was so drunk. Or drugged. What if she'd needed to get rid of the thumb drive?

Her heart began to beat a little faster as she thought of Mia's condo. Was the thumb drive what the person had been looking for? She knew she was letting her imagination run wild and it wasn't like her.

Her earlier thoughts of Tag Cardwell as a cowboy spy was to blame, she told herself. And yet this could be the stuff of secret-agent novels. A spy who's been compromised and has to ditch the goods, an encrypted message and a mathematician who gets involved in solving the mystery.

And gets herself killed, she thought with wry humor.

But she couldn't help studying the letters. She knew a little about codes because they involved math and because she'd played around with them as a girl, sending "secret" coded messages to her friends about the boys she liked. Her friends struggled with the deciphering and tired of them quickly.

It had been years, but she remembered some of the basics. She began to play with the letters, noticing there were eighteen *W*s and sixteen *A*s.

The most common letters in the English language were *E, T* and *A*. So if these were English words, then *W* and *A* were probably one of those more frequently used letters. Though by the position of the *A* letters, they represented something other than *A,* she thought.

Her cell phone rang, making her jump. She was surprised to hear Tag's voice.

"I talked to my brother. He says the thumb drive didn't come from Ford."

"Really?" She was already pretty sure of that anyway, but she did like the sound of his voice. He had a wonderful Texas accent.

"I'm sure there's another explanation," he said.

She was, too.

"I'd better go. Just wanted to let you know." He seemed to hesitate.

She felt her heart beat kick up even against her will.

"Okay," he said.

"Thanks for letting me know. Maybe I'll talk to you later."

"Yeah."

She hung up, a little disappointed he hadn't asked her out—if that was what he'd been about to do earlier—but now all the more determined as she studied the letters again. Codes often involved simple addition or subtraction. She should be able to break this one by trial and error, but it would take time.

If it really was a code. She was glad she hadn't mentioned her suspicions to Tag, though. He thought she was geeky enough as it was.

TAG SWUNG BY his uncle's cabin. Who better to get the truth from than Harlan's brother? Tag had seen the look pass between them. He had a feeling there were few secrets between the two of them. If his father had a girlfriend, Angus would know.

But when he knocked at the door, there was no answer. He glanced in the curtainless window. The cabin was small, just three rooms, so he could see the bed. Clothes were thrown across it, the closet door open as if he'd packed in a hurry.

At the bar earlier, Angus hadn't mentioned going anywhere, especially this close to Christmas. Tag thought about the way the two of them had acted as they were leaving the bar. All his suspicions began to mushroom.

He checked the makeshift garage and found Angus's rig gone. Maybe he'd gone over to his daughter's. Tag drove on down the canyon to the Cardwell Ranch. This time Marshal Hud Savage was nowhere to be seen.

"I went by your dad's cabin," he said after Dana answered the door and ushered him into the kitchen, where she was baking cookies. The babies were napping, she said, and the two older kids, Mary and Hank, were with their aunt Stacy.

"It looks as if Angus is going out of town. I thought you might—"

"He's been called away on business," Dana said. "He wasn't sure when he'd get back, but he promised he would try his best to be here Christmas Eve."

"He got called away on business?" Tag couldn't help his skepticism or the suspicion in his tone. He couldn't imagine what business his uncle might have other than buying new guitar strings. "Just days before Christmas? What kind of business?"

She shot him a questioning look. "He's never said. Why?"

Tag let out a surprised sound. "So this isn't unusual?" Dana shook her head. "And you've never asked him?" He hadn't meant for his tone to sound so accusatory, but he couldn't help it. How could she not know what her father did for this so-called business?

"In case you haven't noticed, our fathers do their own thing. I'm not sure exactly what they do, but occasionally it takes them out of the canyon for a few days, usually on the spur of the moment."

This news came as a complete surprise. "Harlan does this, too? I didn't think either of them ever left. So they're *both* involved in this *business?*"

She gave him an impatient look, then shrugged.

"Aren't you suspicious?"

She chuckled. "*Suspicious?* Dad could have a whole other family somewhere. Maybe more than one. But if that's the case, he seems happy, so more power to him."

Tag couldn't believe her attitude. "Has either of them ever had girlfriends locally?"

She thought for a moment. "Not really. Maybe a long time ago. Like I said, they seem happy just doing their thing, whatever that is." She pulled a pan of cookies from the oven and deftly began sliding them onto a rack to cool.

As she did, she said, "Angus and I aren't that close. I'm busy with the kids and the ranch and Hud, and Dad's a loner, except for his brother...."

"I always thought that if I lived here, Harlan and I would be closer," Tag said as he took a seat at the table and watched her. He couldn't help feeling disappointed. He'd really thought this trip would bring him closer to his father. If anything, it seemed to be pushing them even further apart. "What is it about those two that they aren't good with their own kids?"

Dana sighed. "Or with their wives. They just aren't family men and never have been. But don't let that spoil your Christmas here," she said, and handed him a warm cookie. "We're going to have a wonderful time whether they make it Christmas Eve or not."

"Yes, we are," Tag said, sounding more upbeat than he felt. Right now, he felt as if the Grinch had already stolen Christmas.

After he left the ranch, he drove around aimlessly, hoping he might see his father or uncle coming out of one of the local businesses. Finally, he stopped for something to eat, but barely tasted the food in front of him.

When he came back out, he was surprised it was already getting dark. The sun had disappeared behind Lone Mountain several hours ago, and the deep, narrow canyon was shrouded in shadows. He'd forgotten how quickly it got dark this far north in the winter.

As he drove up to his father's cabin, he was relieved

to see Harlan's SUV parked out front. He'd half expected that, like Angus, Harlan had taken off for parts unknown on some "business" trip.

Wading through the snow and growing darkness toward the cabin, he was determined to get the truth out of his father. No more lies. Either that or he would have to go to the marshal with what he knew. Nix that. He'd have to take his suspicions to the cops in Bozeman, since he wasn't sure he could trust Hud. Admittedly, he didn't know much about Mia's death—or about his father's possible involvement. Just a gut feeling—and a leather jacket.

Deep shadows hunkered around the edge of the cabin as Tag started up the steps. He'd shoveled the steps and walk early this morning before he'd left to go Christmas tree hunting. That now seemed like a lifetime ago.

There had been some snow flurries during the day close to the mountains. The snow had covered the shoveled walk. Tag slowed as he noticed the footprints in the scant snowfall.

His father had had company. Several different boot prints had left tracks up the walk. One had to be his father's, but there were at least two others. His brother? But who else? He'd gotten the feeling his father had few visitors. Then again, he hadn't thought his father had female visitors and he'd been wrong about that.

Only one light shone inside the house. It poured out to splash across the crystal-white snow at the edge of the porch.

He slowed, listening for the sound of voices, hearing nothing. From the tracks in the snow, it appeared whoever had stopped by had left.

He thought of Dana now. Unlike her, he had to know what was going on with his father. He wasn't buying that they had "business" out of town occasionally. Monkey business, maybe.

As he opened the door and looked in, all the air rushed from his lungs. The cabin had been ransacked. He stared, too shocked to move for a moment. Who would have done something like this, and why?

He thought of the thick envelope that his father had given the marshal. Was that payoff money to keep a lid on what his father and uncle were involved in? The envelope had been thick. Where would his father get that kind of money? Not from playing his guitar at a bar on weekends.

Drugs? It was the first thing that came to mind. Were his father and uncle in the drug business?

At the sound of a groan, he rushed in through the debris to find his father lying on the floor behind the couch. Tag was shocked to see how badly Harlan had been beaten.

He hurriedly pulled out his cell phone and dialed 911.

Chapter Six

Hate is a strange but powerful emotion. Camilla went to bed with it each night; it warmed her like wrapping her fingers around a hot mug of coffee. It was her only comfort, locked away in this world of all-women criminals. The place didn't feel much like a prison, though, since it was right in the middle of the city of Billings.

Only when she heard the clang of steel doors did it hit home. She was never leaving here. At least not for a very long time.

Of course the nightmares had gotten worse—just as the doctor had said they would. She'd known they would since they'd been coming more often—even before she'd been caught and locked up. She'd wake up screaming. Not that screaming in the middle of the night was unusual here.

The nightmare was the same one that had haunted her since she was a girl. She was in a coffin. It was pitch-black. There was no air. She was trapped and, even though she'd screamed herself hoarse, no one had come to save her.

The doctor she'd seen a few years ago hadn't been encouraging, far from it. "Do night terrors run in your family?" he'd asked, studying her over the top of his glasses.

"I don't know. I never asked."

"How old did you say you were?"

She'd been in her late twenties at the time.

He'd frowned. "What about sleepwalking?"

"Sometimes I wake up in a strange place and I don't know how I've gotten there." But that could have described her whole life.

He'd nodded, his frown deepening as he'd tossed her file on his desk. "I'm going to give you a referral to a neurologist."

"You're saying there's something wrong with me?"

"Just a precaution. Sleepwalking and night terrors at your age are fairly uncommon and could be the result of a neurological disorder."

She'd laughed after she left his office. "He thinks I'm crazy." She'd been amused at the time. Back then she hadn't been sleepwalking or having the nightmare all that often.

Unfortunately that was no longer the case. Not that she worried about it all that much. So what if she got worse? It wasn't as though she was going anywhere, and everyone here already thought she was half-crazy.

So, Spark. How would you say you're dealing with prison life?

In her mind's eye, she smiled at her pretend interviewer. "I exercise, watch my diet and, oh, yes, I have Hate. It keeps me going. Hate and The Promise of Retribution, they're my cell mates."

Tell inquiring minds. Who's at the top of your hate list and why?

"It's embarrassing actually." Camilla thought about the first time she'd laid eyes on Marshal Hud Savage. The cowboy had come riding up on his horse. "Do you believe in love at first sight?" she asked her fictional interviewer. "Then I have a story for you."

"YOUR FATHER SAYS he didn't get a good look at the intruders," Marshal Hud Savage told Tag later that night at the hospital.

"How is that possible? They beat him up. He had to have *seen* them."

"What makes you think it was more than one man?" Hud asked.

"The tracks in the snow. There were three different boot prints. I'm assuming one pair was Harlan's."

Hud nodded. He seemed distracted.

Tag felt that same sick feeling he'd had earlier today when he witnessed his father with the marshal. "Harlan didn't mention anything when the two of you talked just after noon today?"

Hud frowned. "Why would Harlan—"

"You didn't see my father earlier today? I thought he said he was stopping by your place to talk to you."

The marshal's eyes narrowed before he slowly shook his head. "Harlan told you that? Maybe he changed his mind."

Hud had just lied to his face. "I must have misunderstood him." Tag felt sick to his stomach. What the hell was going on? "I hope you're planning to find who did this to him and why."

"I know my job," Hud snapped. "Look," he said, softening his tone. The marshal appeared tired, exhausted actually, as if he hadn't had much rest for quite a while. "When your father is conscious, maybe he'll remember more about his attackers."

It angered him that Hud was trying to placate him. "*If* he comes to." Harlan had fallen into a coma shortly after the EMTs had arrived to take him to the hospital. What if he didn't make it?

"Harlan's going to be all right," Hud said. "He's a tough old bird."

Tag hoped Hud was right about that. His cell phone rang. He checked it, surprised to see that the call was from Lily McCabe.

"Excuse me," he said, and stepped away to answer it. "Hey."

"I think it's in code." Lily sounded excited.

"Code?"

"The letters on that thumb drive, I think they're two lists of names."

"Names?" A call came over the hospital intercom for Dr. Allen to come to the nurses' station on the fourth floor, stat.

"I'm sorry. Did I catch you in the middle of something?"

"I'm at the hospital. Someone ransacked my father's cabin and beat him up."

"Is he all right?" She sounded as shocked as he felt right now.

"The doctor thinks he's going to recover. He's unconscious. The marshal is here now." He looked down the hall and saw that Hud was also on his cell phone. Tag wondered who was on the other end of the line. Uncle Angus?

"Did he tell you that Mia Duncan's condo was also ransacked?"

It took Tag a moment to realize she was referring to the marshal—not Harlan or Angus. "No, he didn't mention that." Another reason not to trust Hud—as if he needed more.

"That's odd. First Mia's condo is ransacked and she's

murdered, then your father's cabin and he gets beaten up. This is Montana. Things like that just don't happen."

Apparently they did. "That *is* odd," he said. First Mia's, now his father's place? Had Harlan come home and surprised his intruders? Or had they torn up the place *after* they tried to kill him?

"I'm sure there's no connection."

"Yeah." He didn't want to see a connection to his father and the murdered woman, but the coincidences just kept stacking up. "So you say those letters are actually names?" He knew he sounded skeptical.

"I have only started decoding them, but yes, they appear to be names. I can't really explain it over the phone. But I thought you'd want to know right away."

He glanced down the hall. Hud was still on his cell phone, his back turned to Tag. What if Mia had put that computer thumb drive in his pocket last night?

"I want to see what you've found." More than she could know.

"You're welcome to come up to my place when you're ready to leave the hospital."

"Give me your address. I'll come over as soon as I can, if that's all right."

She rattled off an address on Sky-High Road up on the mountain. "It's at the end of the road."

As he disconnected, he saw the doctor coming down the hall. "Harlan is conscious," he said to the marshal, then looked in Tag's direction. "He'd like to see his son."

Hud started to say something, but the doctor cut him off. "He said he'll talk to you after he talks to his son."

Tag walked down the hall and pushed open the door into his father's hospital room. Harlan looked as if he'd been hit by a bus, but he was sitting up a little and his gaze was intent as he watched Tag enter.

"You gave me a scare," Tag said as he stopped at the end of his father's bed.

"Sorry about that." Harlan's voice was hoarse. He was clearly in pain, but he was doing his best to hide it. "The marshal will catch the little hoodlums. How times have changed. They're targeting old people now for our prescription drugs." He chuckled even though it clearly hurt him to do so.

"Whoever beat you up, they weren't after your arthritis medicine," Tag said evenly. He couldn't believe how angry he was at his father for continuing to lie to him. "What were they really looking for, *Dad?*"

His father's expression hardened. "Stay out of this, son. That's why I wanted to see you. I want—"

"That woman who was at your cabin was Mia Duncan, wasn't it?"

Harlan sighed. "I told you. I don't know anyone by that name."

Tag shook his head and tried to still his growing anger. "You just keep lying to me. What business is Uncle Angus away on?"

"Why are you asking me that?"

"Because the two of you are inseparable. You can finish each other's sentences. You have to know where he's gone and why."

"I guess what I should have asked is why is it any of your business?" Harlan said, an edge to his voice.

Tag pulled off his Stetson and raked a hand through his hair as he tried to control his temper. "I know something's going on with the two of you, and it has to do with that woman who was murdered. Angus owns a snowmobile and he knows those old logging roads behind the ranch. You own snowmobiles yourself. I would imagine the two of you have been all over that country behind the ranch. Is it drugs? Is that the business you're in that gets your cabin torn up and you beat up and in the hospital?"

His father let out a sigh. "Do you realize what you're saying?"

"You lied to me. At the bar, I saw you watching the door. You were expecting Mia. You were shocked when I told you she was dead. That's why you didn't ask who was killed. Because you *knew*."

"This conversation is over." He reached for the buzzer to call the nurse.

Tag stepped to the side of the bed and caught his father's arm to stop him. "Tell me it isn't true. Tell me I've got it all wrong." He hated the pleading he heard in his voice.

His father met his gaze. "You have it all wrong."

"Then you don't mind if I keep digging into her death."

"Leave the investigating to the people who are trained for it. Please, son. I don't want to see you get hurt."

His father had already hurt him by not being in his life. But did he really believe Harlan Cardwell was… what? A drug dealer? Worse, a killer?

He met his father's steely gaze. "Then tell the truth."

"Stay out of this, Tag. It isn't what you think."

"I hope you're right—given what I'm thinking."

Harlan closed his eyes. "Tag, I need you to go back to Texas." When he opened them again, Tag saw a deep sadness there. "This isn't a good time for a visit. Please. Go home. Don't wait until after Christmas. If you don't—"

The door opened and the doctor came into the room. Harlan looked away.

"If I don't leave… What are you trying to tell me?" Tag demanded of his father. "That if I continue digging in your life I'll end up like that woman you don't know?"

"I'm sorry," the doctor said. "Did I interrupt something?"

"No. My son was just leaving," Harlan said. "Please don't tell your mother about this. I'll call you in a few days in Texas."

"Don't bother. I'll see you before then," Tag said, and left.

"YOU HAVE TO tell him the truth," Hud said after the doctor had left.

Harlan looked up at him from the hospital bed. "You know I can't do that." He motioned to the pitcher of water on the bedside table, and the marshal poured him a glass.

"He's your *son,*" Hud persisted. "He isn't going to stop. That damned stubbornness seems to run in your family."

Harlan took a drink of water and handed back the empty glass. "I need you to persuade him to go back to Texas."

"I wouldn't count on that happening. He seems to know that you stopped by the ranch earlier today."

"How would he know that?" Harlan shifted in the bed and grimaced in pain.

Hud shook his head. "He knows and he's suspicious as hell of both of us."

"Have you heard anything from Angus?"

"Nothing yet."

"I tried to warn Mia…." Harlan looked away.

"She knew what she was getting into."

"I warned her what could happen if she got too close to the truth." Harlan turned back to him. "You didn't find anything?"

"Nothing. If she had it, then whoever killed her took it. Tag said she was drunk when he saw her at the bar."

"She had to be pretending to be drunk, maybe so she could leave early and not be stopped. Or maybe they got to her somehow." Harlan gently touched his bruised and swelling jaw. "We still don't know who was waiting for her outside the bar?"

"All Tag could tell us was that it appeared to be a dark-colored pickup and the driver was wearing a cowboy hat. I could take him in to look at mug shots."

Harlan quickly shook his head, then groaned in regret for doing it. "I need my son kept out of this. Do whatever you have to to make that happen."

"I can't very well arrest him without a reason to charge him."

Harlan closed his eyes. "You'll think of something. He seems hell-bent on finding out the truth. You know what's at stake. Stop him."

IT BEGAN TO snow as Tag left the hospital. He felt shaken as he slid behind the wheel of his rented SUV. What were his father and the marshal involved in? A cover-up regarding Mia Duncan's murder? Lily had said that Mia's condo had been ransacked. Clearly, whoever was behind this was looking for something.

He feared he knew what. Worse, that Lily had it.

As he watched large snowflakes drift down through the lights of the parking lot, Tag suddenly realized how late it was. But he couldn't stand the thought that Lily was in danger if that thumb drive was what the killers were looking for.

He started the SUV, still debating what to do because of the late hour and the snowstorm. Was it possible that Lily was right and Mia had put the thumb drive in his pocket? Why would she do that? Why give it to a complete stranger? Unless she knew she had to get rid of it quick?

With a start, he was reminded again of what she'd said.

"You look like him."

Had she known he was Harlan's son?

Tag shook his head. She'd been drunk or high on drugs. She hadn't known what she was saying. He thought of his father. He couldn't believe Harlan and Angus were drug dealers. And yet he didn't really know them. He especially didn't know his father, and the way things were going, he doubted he ever would.

His heart began to beat a little faster as he threw the SUV into Drive. Lily had the computer flash drive. If there was even a chance she was in danger… He drove by his father's cabin and got a pistol from Harlan's gun cabinet. He told himself he was just being paranoid.

As he headed toward Big Sky, he drove as fast as he could. He couldn't help being worried about Lily up in the mountains all by herself. He tried to assure himself that she was safe. No one knew she had the thumb drive.

His mind kept going back to last night in the bar and Mia, though. He remembered the way she'd clutched his jacket. She *could* have put the thumb drive in his pocket. Now she was dead. His father was in the hospital. And the killers were looking for something. It was too much of a coincidence that he'd found the thumb drive in his pocket. And now Lily thought she'd discovered the information on the computer USB was two lists of names in some kind of code?

Ahead, the road to the summit was a series of switchbacks that climbed from the river bottom to nearly the top of twelve-thousand-foot Lone Mountain. The snow fell harder the higher he drove. He had to slow down because of the limited visibility.

His mind was still whirling as he passed Big Sky Resort and left behind any signs of life. Up here, there was nothing but snowy darkness. He still couldn't get his mind around what was happening. His father was involved in whatever was going on, and so was the marshal, and he was betting his uncle Angus was, as well.

Harlan had said it was a bad time for a visit. No kidding. He was determined that Tag return to Texas. Hell, Harlan had almost threatened him, insinuating that if he stayed, it could be dangerous. Would be dangerous.

Heart racing, he reached into his pocket for his cell phone to call Lily. He had to make sure she was all right and to let her know he was almost to her house.

But as he started to place the call, he glanced in his rearview mirror, feeling a little paranoid. *You're not paranoid if someone is really after you,* he thought as he noticed a set of headlights behind him.

He watched them growing closer. The driver behind him was going too fast for the conditions and gaining on him too quickly. Tag looked around for a place to pull over, but there was only a solid snowplowed wall on one side of the road and a drop-off on the other.

Giving the SUV more gas, he sped up as he came out of a curve. Ahead was another curve. He could feel the glare of the headlights on his back, glancing off the rearview mirror and his side mirrors. The vehicle was almost directly behind him.

Tag told himself that the driver must be drunk or not paying attention or blinded by the falling snow. Unless the person behind the wheel was hoping to make him crash.

He tried to shake off even the thought. He wasn't that far from the road up to Lily's house. Suddenly the headlights behind him went out.

Glancing in his mirror again, he was shocked to find the vehicle gone. Had the driver run off the road? Or had he turned off? There had been a turnoff back there....

Ahead, Tag saw the sign. As he turned, he looked back down the main road. No sign of the other vehicle. Breathing a sigh of relief, he drove on up the narrow, snowy road. Wind whipped snow all around the SUV. He had his windshield wipers on high and they still couldn't keep up with the snow.

The road narrowed and rose. He knew he had to be getting close. He thought he caught the golden glow of lights in a house just up the mountain. His fear for Lily amplified at the thought of her alone in such an isolated place.

A dark-colored vehicle came out of the snowstorm on a road to his right. He swerved to miss it and felt the wheels drop over the side of the mountain, the SUV rolling onto its side. His head slammed into the side window. He felt blood run into his eye as the SUV rolled once more before crashing into a tree.

Chapter Seven

The snowstorm blew in with a fury. Inside the house, Lily could hear the flakes hitting the window. It sounded like the glass was being sandblasted.

She shivered and checked her watch as she went to put more logs on the fire. Tag said he would come as soon as he could. She told herself he'd probably been held up by the storm. She just hoped he would be able to get up the road.

Her house sat by itself on the side of the mountain, far from any others. The road often blew in with snow before the plows made their rounds. Since she didn't usually go to work at her brother's bar until the afternoon, it hadn't ever been a problem.

But tonight, she was anxious to show Tag what she'd come up with so far and she worried since there had already been some good-size drifts across the road when she'd looked out earlier.

She'd worked trying to decode the random letters until her head ached. What if she was wrong? What if this was nothing? But she was convinced that there were two lists of names. She'd gotten at least a start on the code, making her more assured that she was on the right track.

A loud noise from outside made her jump. She

stopped stoking the fire to listen for a moment and heard it again. Her pulse spiked before she could determine the sound.

She couldn't help being jumpy. Wasn't it enough that a woman she worked with had been murdered last night and another one was missing? But Lily didn't kid herself. Her nerves were more because of Tag and the thought of the two of them alone in her house.

Another noise, this one a loud thud. She peered out at the porch swing an instant before the wind blew it back into the side of the house again with a loud thump. The shadows had deepened on the porch, running a dark gray before turning black under the pines. The porch light illuminated only a small golden disk of light against the falling snow.

Hugging herself, she assured herself that there was nothing to be afraid of up here. She'd always felt safe. The porch swing thumped against the side of the house, followed by a loud thud closer to her front door. Probably that potted pine she had by the door. She started to turn back to her work when something caught her eye. Fresh footprints in the snow on the steps up to the porch.

A gust of wind blew snow against the glass. For a moment, it stuck, obstructing her view. Tag? Could he have come to the door and she hadn't heard him?

The knock at the door made her jump. She chastised herself as she hurried to the front door, thankful she'd been right and thankful, too, for Tag's company. Even for a short period of time tonight, she would be glad to have him around. Mia's murder must have her more shaken than she'd let herself admit.

As she turned the knob, the wind caught the door and wrenched it from her hand. It blew back on a gale, banging against the wall.

Blinded by the cold bite of the snow and wind, she blinked. Then blinked again in astonishment.

"Gerald?"

LILY HADN'T SEEN Gerald since the day before their wedding that had never happened because he hadn't shown up.

She stared at him now. Nothing could have surprised her more than to find him standing there, caked in snow and huddled into himself to block the wind.

"Would you mind if I came in?" he asked pointedly. "It's freezing out here."

She nodded, still too stunned to speak, and stepped back to let him enter, closing the door swiftly after him.

He brushed snow from his blond hair and slipped out of his wool dress coat, holding it at arm's length to keep the snow off him. He wore dark trousers, dress shoes and a white shirt, including a tie. The knot was a little crooked, which surprised her. Gerald valued preciseness in all things.

As he looked up at her, his blue eyes seemed to soften. She was struck by the memory of the two of them. Just last summer they'd been planning a life together. She remembered the smell of his aftershave, the feel of his fingers on her skin, the taste of his mouth when he kissed her. Like the wind outside, the force of his betrayal scattered those once pleasant memories, leaving her bereft.

She saw with a start that he was still holding his coat out as if waiting for her to take it. She finally found her voice. "Gerald, what are you doing here?"

The one thing she'd told herself she'd loved about this man was that he never wavered. Gerald exuded confidence. While she often felt swept along in his wake, she'd been happy to be part of his life even if it meant accepting that he knew best and always would.

"I had to see you," he said. He seemed to study her for a moment before he added, "I figured you'd be here. You look…tired."

She bristled at his words. Leave it to Gerald to speak the cold truth. He'd never been good at tempering his observations. "It's been a rough day. One of our servers was murdered."

"*Your* servers? You mean your brother's. You *are* still at the university, aren't you?"

"Yes." It annoyed her that he'd never understood why she spent the past few Christmas and New Year's holidays up here at Big Sky helping her brother. He'd always insinuated that Ace was using her and that serving cocktails was beneath her.

Gerald must have seen that he'd irritated her because he softened his tone and asked, "How *is* James?"

"Fine." There was no reason to pretend any further that Gerald cared about her brother. He had always refused to call him anything but James, saying that Ace was something you might call a dog.

"You said you had to see me," she reminded him.

He was still holding his coat away from him as he looked behind her into the living room. "Is there any chance we could sit down and discuss this like rational evolved human beings?" There was an edge to his words as if he'd expected her to be more gracious.

She thought how he hadn't shown up at the wedding. The pain and hurt had dulled over the past six months, but there was still that breath-stealing reminder when she thought of her humiliation.

She'd hadn't been heartbroken—not the way she would have been had she and Gerald shared a more passionate relationship.

"We're cerebral," Gerald used to say. "It's a higher level of intimacy than simple passion. Who else could appreciate you the way I do?"

"And who else could love such a math nerd," his sister had said, "but another math nerd?" That, too, Lily had believed was true. So what if they didn't have a passionate relationship? They had math.

She thought of Tag and his comment, *"You counted them?"* He'd thought she was joking. Probably hoped she was joking.

But Gerald had embarrassed and hurt her and left her feeling as if no one would want her if he didn't. Now, though, he was back. What did that mean?

"Yes, please sit down." She took his coat and hung it up, feeling conflicted. She wanted to throw him out and yet she wanted, needed, to hear what he had to say.

Leaning toward throwing him out, she reminded herself that Gerald had understood her in a way no other man had and he had come all this way to talk to her. And while they hadn't been the perfect couple in some aspects, they had a lot in common, since Gerald had been the head of the math department. That was until he took a job in California without telling her.

"Can I get you something to drink? I have a wine you might like," she said, using the manners boarding schools had instilled in her.

He shook his head as he tested the couch with his hand, then sat down. She'd forgotten he did that. He tested things, weighing them as to how worthy they were, she'd always thought. For a long while, she'd thought that was why he hadn't shown up at the wedding. She just hadn't met his high level of quality.

"Please sit," he said, looking up at her still looming over him. "You're giving me a crick in my neck."

She sat across from him and immediately wished she'd gotten herself a glass of wine. Also, her instant response to his command annoyed her. She almost got back up just to show him he couldn't come into her house and start telling her what to do after what he'd done to her.

"I'm sorry," he said, stilling her in her chair.

Those were two words she'd never heard from him before. She waited for more.

"I can't explain my actions."

And still she waited.

"I deeply regret what I did." Gerald had always been a man of few words as if they cost him each time he spoke and he refused to waste a single one.

A gust of wind rattled the window behind her, making her turn. All she could see was blowing snow and darkness beyond the arc of the porch light.

"Are you expecting someone?" Gerald demanded, clearly annoyed that her attention had wavered.

She thought of Tag. He apparently wasn't coming. "No. No one." Lily had barely gotten the words out of her mouth when there was pounding at the door. She jumped up in surprise. So did Gerald.

"I thought you weren't expecting anyone," he said suspiciously.

She said nothing as she hurried to the front door. As she opened it, a gust of wind and snow whipped in, but she hardly noticed.

"What happened to you?" she cried when she saw Tag standing there, his face covered in blood.

"SOMEONE RAN ME off the road," Tag said as she ushered him into the house. "Do you still have the—" The words *thumb drive* died on his lips as he saw the man standing behind her.

"We need to get you to the hospital," she cried.

"No," he said, his gaze still on the man standing in Lily's living room. "I'll be all right."

"Then at least let me clean up that cut over your eye. I'll get the first-aid kit." As she hurried past the man toward the back of the house, she said over her shoulder, "This is Gerald." Lily disappeared into a back room, leaving Tag alone with the man.

A brittle silence fell between them until the man said, "I don't believe I caught your name, but you're bleeding on her floor."

"Here," Lily said, hurrying back into the room with the first-aid kit, a washcloth and a towel. She shot Gerald a warning look as she passed him. "His name is Tag. Tag Cardwell."

"Tag?" The man said it and grimaced. "Charming."

Lily seemed to ignore him. "Sit down here and let me see about that cut. Are you hurt anywhere else?"

Tag grimaced as he lowered himself into the chair she pulled out. "Just beat up and bruised. My ribs hurt, but they don't feel broken. Everything else seems to be working since I was able to walk the rest of the way up here." He grimaced again as the washcloth touched the cut on his temple.

"Sorry," she said, and reached into her pocket. "Here, take two of these. The prescription is a recent one of mine from a sprained ankle I had." She jumped up to hurry to the kitchen for a glass of water.

He took the pills and the glass of water she handed him. He tossed the pills into his mouth and downed them with the water. His gaze met hers as he handed back the empty glass. "Thanks."

"What is this about you being run off the road?" Lily asked.

Now that he was here, Tag was questioning what exactly *had* happened. He'd been so anxious to get to Lily and make sure she was safe… "Just some driver who wasn't used to Montana weather." At least he hoped that was all it had been. The driver had kept going, though, hadn't even stopped to see if he was all right. But if he really was drunk, then he wouldn't want to be involved.

Gerald cleared his throat. "I should probably go since you're obviously busy," he said as he walked over to the table. His fingers ran along the top of the open laptop computer sitting there.

"Please don't touch that," Lily said, and got up to go to the table. She closed the computer and pulled out the thumb drive, dropping it into her sweater pocket before returning to Tag. Picking up the washcloth, she began to bathe his face.

"I can do that," Tag said, and took the cloth from her, smiling at her tenderness. He wiped away the dried and frozen blood he could feel on his face before she took the washcloth back and dabbed at a couple of places he'd apparently missed.

"It seems I'm not the only one anxious to talk to you tonight, although I didn't make as dramatic an entrance as your…friend," Gerald said, plainly irritated. Tag wondered what he had interrupted.

"If you're staying in the area, Gerald, perhaps we could talk tomorrow," she said without looking at the man as she gently dabbed at the area around Tag's cut before reaching for the antiseptic.

"What choice do I have if I hope to get this settled?" Gerald snapped.

"I thought it *was* settled," she said, anger sparking just under the surface. Tag liked the heat he saw in her eyes and thought about the first night they'd met. A woman with attitude, his favorite kind, he thought as he felt the pain pills start to work.

"This is definitely not what I'd hoped for," Gerald said with a sigh. "I will call you tomorrow if you think you can make time for me."

"Fine."

Tag wondered what was unsettled between them, but was smart enough not to ask. Yep, the pills were definitely working. They were strong, which was fine with him. He hurt all over and was thankful when the pain began to numb.

"I'm sorry if I interrupted something," Tag said as the door shut behind Gerald. "It sounded as if he really wanted to talk to you tonight. I didn't mean to run off your boyfriend." Yep, the pills were working. He felt drunk with them. Whatever they were, they were *very* strong.

"He isn't my boyfriend," she said as she put a bandage on over his cut. "He's my former fiancé."

"You were going to marry that jackass?" The words slipped out before he could stop them. "Sorry."

"I'm afraid you witnessed Gerald at his worst," she said as she finished bandaging his wound.

Tag was trying to imagine Gerald at his best. "So, why didn't you marry him?"

"There," she said, and closed the first-aid kit. "He stood me up at the wedding."

"The bastard. If I'd have known that, I would have slugged him for you."

She met his gaze and began to laugh. "That's what my brother always threatened to do."

"Why didn't he?"

"Gerald left town. This is the first time I've seen him since the day before the wedding."

"And you didn't hit him the moment you saw him?"

She shook her head. "I'm a perfectly reasonable woman. I don't hit people."

"I would have hit him."

She rose to put away the first-aid kit, but stopped. "Are you all right?"

He realized he'd been staring at her, wondering how some goofy older guy like Gerald had gotten a beautiful young woman like Lily to even look twice at him. "Fine. What were those pills anyway?"

"I think I'd better drive you to the hospital or at least down to the clinic. Just let me put this away—"

He caught her arm. "I'd rather hear about this code you told me about."

"I think it's a list of names. I'm still decoding them. If Gerald hadn't shown up when he did…" She glanced toward the door and he saw pain in her expression.

The man had hurt her. Tag really wished he'd slugged him. Was it possible he'd been driving the car that had run him off the road? "He didn't give you any indication why he came up here tonight?"

She shook her head.

"Because I interrupted the two of you. I'm sorry."

"Don't be. I'm not sure there is anything he could say under the circumstances." Her smile was filled with sadness.

"Look, he's bound to have realized what a fool he was. He probably came here tonight to beg you to take him back. Maybe you should call him and—"

"Six months ago, he left me at a church filled with our relatives and friends on our wedding day. Apparently he didn't have anything to say that day. I'm sure whatever he plans to say now can wait a day."

If Tag had been up to it, he would have gone after Gerald and kicked his sorry butt. He couldn't believe it had taken the man six months to come back. "I'm sorry he hurt you like that," he said, taking her free hand. She didn't pull away. "Are you sure you want to take him back? You deserve a lot better." He caressed the back of her hand with his thumb pad. Her skin was so warm and smooth.

His gaze went to her mouth. It was a Cupid's bow, as kissable as any mouth he'd ever seen. "Lily—"

"I really should drive you down to the clinic to make sure you don't have any internal injuries," she said.

"You're not driving anywhere in this storm. I hope Gerald is staying on the mountain and not planning to drive all the way to Meadow Village tonight." Lily said nothing. Nor did she draw her hand back. "I'm afraid we're snowed in," he said, lulled by the pain pills she'd given him and this woman.

"I should show you the code I worked out so far on the data from the thumb drive," she said, and started to pull away, but he drew her back. "Or should we call the marshal first? You really should report the accident."

"Do you still love him?" Tag asked as he got to his feet and, taking the first-aid kit, put it aside. He felt a little woozy.

"Gerald?" she asked. "I don't know. You should sit back down. You're hurt."

"Tell me you haven't been waiting around for the past six months for him to come back." He saw the answer in her eyes and swore.

"Tag." His name on her lips was his undoing. Outside, the storm raged. Inside, he threw caution to the wind as he drew Lily to him.

Chapter Eight

Tag woke naked and smiling. Without opening his eyes, he felt across the bed for Lily, remembering last night and their lovemaking. Finding the bed empty and cold, he opened one eye. No Lily.

He couldn't help being disappointed. Last night had been amazing. He hadn't expected that kind of passion in her, he thought as he touched his shoulder and felt scratches. He chuckled to himself. She'd been wild, surprising herself as well as him, he thought. But there had also been tenderness. Lily McCabe was all woman, as sexy as any he'd ever known.

"Lily?" No answer. His heart kicked up a beat. She wouldn't have tried to leave this morning on her own? Or worse.

Swinging his legs over the side of the bed, he was reminded of the wreck and the aching parts of his body. He managed to pull on his jeans before hurrying barefoot out to the kitchen. He was met with the welcoming scent of coffee and the sight of Lily standing silhouetted against the bright clear morning.

"Hey," he said, relief in his voice. He'd planned to come up behind her, wrap his arms around her and kiss her on her neck, then do his best to persuade her to come back to bed with him.

But she turned too quickly, separating them with more than the cup of coffee in her hand. He stopped short and felt his heart drop. This was not the wild woman he remembered from bed last night. Her expression warned him to keep his distance.

He blinked, confused. Last night had happened, right? He thought of their lovemaking. Was it possible he'd only dreamed making crazy, passionate love with this woman last night?

Lily's demeanor told him it had only been a figment of his drug-induced imagination and if he wasn't careful, he would make a fool out of himself. It wouldn't be the first time. Or the last, he thought. He had to know.

"Uh, did something happen between us last night?"

"Happen?" She took a sip of her coffee, watching him over the rim of her cup. Her hair was still damp from her shower, smelling of jasmine—just as it had last night in his arms. But she was looking at him as if he was crazy.

He remembered how strong the pain pills had been. Sure, he'd felt groggy, but— "I woke up naked this morning and I thought I remembered you and me…" The look she gave him stopped him from being more specific.

"Do I seem like the kind of woman who would fall into bed with a man I hardly know?"

He studied her, considering her words. She wore a turtleneck sweater and jeans. Buttoned up, that was how he would have described her. Nothing like the woman last night.

"No, you don't. But last night—" Last night he remembered finding a side of Lily that was as unexpected as the way she was acting this morning. "Sorry. It's just that I…" He shook his head and warned himself not to get in any deeper.

"I think you really should see what I found on the thumb drive," she said, all business, as she moved to the table where she'd left her laptop and the papers she'd been working on.

He was suddenly more aware of the fact that his body hurt all over and his head felt as if it was filled with lint. He stood looking after her, unable to accept that last night had been nothing more than a dream. He remembered every kiss, every touch. Desire stirred in him.

"Tag?" Lily glanced back at him, her gaze taking in his bare chest. "Perhaps you'd like to get dressed first."

"Yeah." He touched his scratched shoulder. Was it possible he'd gotten that in the accident? He met her gaze and for just a moment—

She quickly looked away, busying herself with the calculations she'd made. "We can discuss this when you come back. I'll pour you a cup of coffee. How do you take it?"

"Black and strong." He realized he needed his wits about him. Not only for whatever was going on with his father and this thumb drive, but with this woman.

LILY WATCHED TAG walk to the bedroom and closed her eyes as she fought the images. She couldn't believe what had happened last night. That hadn't been her, she told herself just as she'd told Tag.

All morning, she'd fretted about what they would say to each other once he woke up. She'd never been like that in her life.

But when she'd realized that he hadn't remembered…

"You took the coward's way out," she whispered to herself, and felt her face heat with embarrassment. Better than the desire that had burned through her veins at the sight of him this morning dressed only in jeans.

She was just glad he didn't remember. What had possessed her to fall into the cowboy's arms last night? Lily didn't delude herself. Seeing Gerald again had thrown her into a tailspin. She'd felt all the hurt and betrayal and a part of her had wanted to forget—and possibly even the score.

Lily laid her head on her arms on the table. She knew it had been a lot more than just escape or getting even with Gerald. She'd *wanted* Tag. Wanted him in a way she hadn't even been able to imagine. He was everything Gerald wasn't. She'd known instinctively that their lovemaking would be nothing like what she'd known with her former fiancé.

"Boy howdy," she said, repeating an expression she'd picked up from Tag. As she heard Tag come out of the bedroom, she lifted her head and pushed away those embarrassing thoughts. She hated lying to him. Fortunately Tag had remembered just enough with the pills she'd given him to think he'd dreamed their wanton night of passion. Best leave it that way since it was never happening again.

The thought gave her a dull ache at her center.

What made her angry with herself aside from lying to Tag was that she felt as if she'd cheated on Gerald. She knew that made no sense. She owed him nothing—less than nothing. But she also knew that he wouldn't have come all the way from California and driven up to her house in a blizzard last night if he wasn't planning on asking her to take him back.

She told herself that she and Gerald belonged together. They were perfect for each other. Both math nerds, they had their careers in common. Last night had just been one of those crazy things that never happened to a woman like her.

Lily convinced herself that she would put it behind her. Gerald was her future. She would forgive him and they would get married—just as it was meant to be.

She quickly straightened as Tag came into the room. But she kept her eyes on the computer screen even though she'd memorized the letters there since she'd looked at them so many times. Remembering she'd said she would pour Tag a cup of coffee, she jumped up and bumped into the edge of the table.

Her coffee sloshed over onto some of the papers. She lunged for them and, off balance, stumbled into Tag—the very last thing she wanted to do.

"EASY," TAG SAID as he caught her.

"I was going to get your coffee," Lily said, more nervous than he'd ever seen her.

"I can get my own coffee. Are you all right?" Holding her like this, he could feel her soft, full curves. He recognized every one of them, he thought with a start. His imagination was great, but not this good. Something had happened last night. But why would she lie?

Because you let her think you couldn't remember, you damned fool.

She pulled away as if realizing he was remembering last night. Or was he still deluding himself? She turned her back to him as she poured his coffee. He could see that her hands were shaking.

Tag wanted to call her on her lie, but when she turned back to him, he saw the glow in her cheeks. Could she be embarrassed about last night? She'd definitely let her hair down, so to speak. How innocent *was* this woman? Surely there were other men besides dull Gerald.

"Thank you," he said as he took the coffee cup she offered him. Lily was clearly rattled. Maybe she regretted last night and really was embarrassed.

What was it she had said? "Do I seem like the kind of woman who would fall into bed with a man I hardly know?"

"So, what's this about a code?" he asked, and took a sip of his coffee. He saw Lily's instant relief as she hurriedly sat back down at the computer. He could see where she had been writing a series of numbers and letters on scratch paper.

"After I came back here, I began to play with the letters. I know they appear to be random, but I don't think they are," she said, eyes bright. She clearly loved this stuff. "They appear to be part of a code. Julius Caesar invented one like it nearly two thousand years ago. He was invading countries to increase the size of the Roman Empire and he needed a way to communicate his battle plans with his generals without the enemy finding out by intercepting his messages."

"How do you know all this?" Tag asked, even more intrigued by this woman.

"It's math. Simple addition or subtraction, actually. Caesar, instead of writing the letter *A,* would write the letter that comes three places further in the alphabet, the letter *D.* When he got to the end of the alphabet, he would go right back to the beginning so instead of an *X,* he would write an *A.* You get the idea."

He did, but he wondered how the devil she'd figured that out and said as much.

"The more I studied the letters, the more they didn't appear random at all. The spaces made me think they were a list of names."

"Written in code?"

She nodded, her eyes bright. She was in her element. He wondered if he would ever see all the different sides of Lily McCabe. "A version of Caesar shift."

"And you can read what it says?"

"Not completely yet. It's a case of trial and error with only twenty-five different possible shifts before you can see a pattern. Caesar shifted the alphabet forward three spaces. This code is tougher, but in the end it will come down to simple mathematics."

He couldn't help smiling at her passion. He had a flash of her in his arms, naked, her skin silken and scented with jasmine, her mouth wet as she dropped it to his. Tag shook himself, the image so real he almost kissed her.

She didn't seem to notice. She was studying the letters on the page and her scribbles again. "Though I would have thought someone who didn't want the code deciphered would have used symbols instead of letters," she said, bending over one of the papers. "That way there could be four-hundred-billion possible combinations instead of only twenty-five. Not that it couldn't be broken by frequency analysis, though. Mary, Queen of Scots, used symbols for her code when plotting against Elizabeth the First. It got her beheaded."

Lily stopped talking and looked up at him, her gaze locking with his. "Your eyes haven't glazed over," she said, sounding surprised.

"This is fascinating. I'm amazed. How did you figure it out?"

"I'm using the frequency analysis method. Since *E, T* and *A* are the most frequently used letters in the English alphabet and there are eighteen *W*s and sixteen *A*s…The *A*s are not really *A*s, you understand. Once you have the most-used letters, it is just a matter of figuring out the rest of them."

He watched her bite her lower lip in thought.

"I can't help thinking whoever made up the code is a novice at this," she said. "They probably went online, typed in codes and thought 'here's one.' The problem is they must have written this in a hurry because they made mistakes, which is making it harder for me to decode."

Nothing about what she was doing looked simple to him. Just staring at the letters made his headache worse.

"I should be able to break it soon," she assured him.

"Lily, I have a bad feeling that the reason Mia's condo was ransacked and my father's, too, was that they were looking for this thumb drive."

"Then you should take it to the marshal," she said, handing it to him. "I have a copy of the letters on my computer, so I can keep working on the code."

He nodded, although he had no intention of taking it to the marshal. Not until he knew which side of the fence Hud Savage was on.

"Until we know what's really on this," he said, "I wouldn't mention it to anyone, all right?"

She nodded.

"I need to get to the hospital and see my father, but I don't like leaving you here snowed in alone."

She waved him off. "The plows should be along in the next hour or so if you want to take my SUV."

He wasn't about to leave her here without a vehicle even if he thought he could bust through the drifts. "Are those your brother's cross-country skis and boots by the door? If you don't mind me borrowing them, I'll ski down to the road and hitch a ride. My brothers and I used to do that all the time when we were kids."

"If you're sure...." She turned back to the papers on the table. "I'll keep working on the code and let you know when I get it finished."

She sounded as if she would be glad when he left her at it. He was reminded that she also had plans to talk to her former fiancé today. He felt a hard knot form in his stomach. Jealousy? Hell, yes.

Except he had nothing to be jealous about, right? Last night hadn't happened. At least that was the way Lily wanted it. He fought the urge to touch her hair, remembering the feel of it between his fingers.

"I want you to have this." He held out the pistol he'd taken from his father's. "I need to know that you are safe."

She shook her head and pulled back. "I don't like guns."

"All you have to do is point it and shoot."

Lily held up both hands. "I don't want it. I could never..." She shook her head again.

"Just in case," Tag said as he laid it on the table, telling himself that if someone broke into her house and tried to hurt her, she would get over her fear of guns quickly. At least he hoped that was true.

LILY STOOD AT the window, watching Tag cross-country ski down the snowed-in road until he disappeared from sight. He glided through the new snow with no wasted movement. She could practically see the muscles rippling in his arms and back.

At the memory of the feel of those muscles, she shivered and stepped away from the window, cradling her mug of hot coffee to chase away the chill. Why had she lied to him about last night?

It wasn't a lie. She wasn't the kind of woman to

fall into a stranger's arms. Nor did she recognize that woman who'd made such passionate love to Tag last night.

What had she been thinking? She was still shaken. True, she'd been thrown completely off balance by finding Gerald at her door.

In her heart of hearts, she'd dreamed of him coming back, begging her to forgive him. She'd just expected it to happen a lot sooner. That *was* what he wanted to talk to her about, wasn't it? He wanted her back. He'd realized what a colossal mistake he'd made. That was what it had to be. Gerald was safe, and right now she wanted safe, didn't she?

What would have happened if Tag hadn't shown up when he had? Would she have let Gerald stay? Would they have made love as they'd done in the past? Or would they have had a wild, passionate night as she had with Tag?

Wasn't that what she'd always wanted?

As hard as she tried, she couldn't imagine Gerald ever being like that.

But their relationship was built on intellect and a shared passion for math, she reminded herself.

She closed her eyes, images of her lovemaking with Tag making her go weak in the knees. She quickly opened her eyes. She'd never get the code finished if she kept letting her mind stray.

And yet as she headed for the computer again, she couldn't deny the ache low in her belly. She wanted Tag again.

That was why she had to see Gerald. She needed to put an end to these thoughts. All last night had been was one wild fling before she took Gerald back.

And if Tag had remembered last night?

Lily sighed and glanced toward the open bedroom door and the rumpled sheets. The two of them would be in that bed right now.

She blew out a sigh that lifted her drying bangs from her forehead. Her skin felt oversensitive as if Tag's touch was branded on it. She hugged herself for a moment, remembering how wonderful he'd been. She worried though that he was in trouble because of the thumb drive.

Determined to figure out the code, she had started back toward the table and her laptop when she saw the gun. Stepping to it, she gingerly picked it up with two fingers, then wasn't sure what to do with it.

One of the drawers in the kitchen was still open from where she'd gotten a clean dish towel out this morning. She walked over to it and dropped the gun into the drawer and closed it. She wouldn't need it. Even if she did, she knew she could never fire it.

She had started back to work on the code when the phone rang not ten minutes later. The sound irritably jerked her out of her calculations. She saw it was Gerald and almost didn't answer.

ONCE TAG REACHED the main road, he easily caught a ride to his father's cabin. The day was bright, sunny and beautiful, so there was a lot of traffic coming and going on the road to the ski hills.

At his father's cabin, he called the rental company about the wrecked SUV. The cabin was still a mess, but the crime-scene tape had been removed. He changed clothes and headed for the two-car log garage next to the cabin, anxious to get to the hospital and see his father.

But when the garage door moaned open, he saw something that stopped him dead. His father's SUV was gone. With a start, he remembered that the SUV had been parked outside yesterday when he'd found his father had been attacked.

He tried to tell himself that a friend must have borrowed it as he climbed into Harlan's old pickup. The key was in the ignition. Harlan always left his keys in his rigs as if daring someone to steal them. Maybe that was what had happened, although he feared there was an even simpler explanation.

When he reached the hospital and walked into his father's room, Tag wasn't surprised to find the bed empty.

"Are you looking for Mr. Cardwell?" a nurse asked as he let the door close with a curse.

"Yes. Has he been moved to another room?" He knew he was only deluding himself.

"I'm sorry, but he checked himself out."

"Against doctor's orders, right?"

The nurse smiled and nodded. "He is a very stubborn man."

"Isn't he?" Stubborn and hiding something. Tag hated to think what.

There were only two other places he could think of to look for his father. He tried his cousin Dana's first.

Tag found her and her two oldest kids putting the finishing touches on the worst-looking Christmas tree he'd ever seen.

"Do. Not. Say. A. Word," she warned him, and grinned. "This tree needed a Christmas."

"It needs limbs and needles," Tag said. "Jingle Bells" played on the radio in the kitchen, and he thought he smelled ginger cookies baking. For a moment, he wanted to help string the paper garland the children had made and curl up in front of the fire. This was the

Christmas he'd envisioned. Not one involving lies and murder.

"It's one of Mama's orphan trees," six-year-old Hank said. "It made Daddy laugh."

"But it made Mama cry," the younger Mary said.

"Tears of joy," Dana hurriedly added, and smoothed a hand over Mary's dark hair so like her mother's. "Want to join in the fun?"

"Thanks, but I need to find my father. You haven't seen him, by any chance, have you?"

Dana shook her head. "I did hear that he checked himself out of the hospital. I'm sure he's fine."

Tag wasn't so sure about that. "You haven't heard from Angus, have you?"

"Grandpa is away on business," Hank said, making his mother smile.

"I thought I'd check his favorite bar…." He could see that Dana wasn't going to be of any help. Because she didn't understand her father any better than he did his, she'd taken a "whatever" attitude. He wished he could.

ACE LOOKED UP when Lily walked into the bar. "What's wrong?"

Where did she begin? "Someone ran Tag off the road last night on the way to my place. He could have been killed. He played it down, but I think it has something to do with the thumb drive he found."

"Tag?" Her brother grinned. "On the way to your place? I thought there was a rosy glow to your cheeks."

If he only knew. "That's all you got out of what I just told you?" She shook her head. "Gerald showed up at my place last night."

That got his attention and wiped away Ace's cat-who-ate-the-canary grin—just as she knew it would. "What did that bastard want?"

"I'm pretty sure he wants me back."

"What?" Ace demanded. "I hope you told him where he could stick—"

"Tag interrupted whatever Gerald was going to say. I'm on my way to meet Gerald now."

"You're actually thinking of going back to him."

Her brother had a way of seeing through her that annoyed Lily to no end. "Gerald and I have—"

"So help me, if you take that lily-livered son of a b—"

"It's my life, Ace."

He shook his head. "Exactly. You want to spend it with a stiff shirt like Gerald? Or a man like Tag Cardwell?"

She wanted to point out that neither Tag nor any other man like him had asked, but changed the subject. "Did you hear what I said about someone running Tag off the road last night?"

Ace nodded. "Does he think it was an accident?"

"He pretended it was."

Her brother rubbed his jaw. "Teresa hasn't turned up yet, and with Mia murdered… I just don't understand it. This is usually such a safe place."

She glanced at her watch.

"Don't do it, Lily."

She looked at her brother, confused for a moment.

"I know you. You're going to end up feeling guilty for not taking him back—after *he* deserted you on your wedding day." He shook his head again. "Why aren't you mad? You should be spitting nails. He doesn't deserve you."

She nodded, thinking Tag had pretty much said the

same thing. "I have to go. Are you opening the bar tonight?"

"Got to. If Teresa isn't back, I'm going to need you to work."

"Don't worry. I'll be here."

"Lily?"

She had started to leave, but now she turned back to look at her brother. Even frowning, he was drop-dead gorgeous. Why hadn't some woman snatched him up? Or was he like her? Always playing it safe, afraid to really let go and fall for someone who made him see fireworks on a freezing winter night just before Christmas.

Ace shook head as if changing his mind about whatever he had been going to say. "Just be careful, okay?"

She had to smile. Too bad he hadn't been around last night to warn her. It was a little too late now. "Always levelheaded. That's me. And, Ace, don't mention the thumb drive to anyone, okay?"

Chapter Nine

It had been weeks in this prison and Camilla was growing all the more impatient. She was wondering what she was going to have to do to make Edna's acquaintance, when one of the woman's minions brought her a note.

She had to think outside the box to decipher the misspelled words, but then again not everyone in prison had a master's degree. Hers was in psychology. Basically, a con man's dream curriculum. No wonder she was so good at reading people.

Except for Hud Savage. You certainly read him wrong, didn't you, Miss Smarty-Pants?

Her mother's voice. She ground her teeth. That "misstep" had cost her dearly. Which was why retribution had such a nice ring to it. *You know retribution, don't you, Mother?*

The note from Edna wasn't a request, but a command appearance, making her think about telling the inmate standing in front of her what she could do with her missive. The woman, a skinny former addict with a tattoo of a rattlesnake around her right wrist, was known as Snakebite. The nickname probably had more to do with her disposition, though, than the tattoo.

Feeling in a generous mood and needing to get her plan moving, she merely smiled and said, "Okay."

"Now, bitch."

Camilla considered kicking the woman's butt, convinced she could take her.

Snakebite had the good sense to take a step back as Camilla got to her feet.

Edna was waiting for them in the craft area of the prison. A kind-looking woman with a huge bosom and small delicate hands, she looked as if she should be in a kitchen baking chocolate-chip cookies for her grandkids. Which could explain her nickname, Grams.

"I heard you've been asking around about me," Grams said, and motioned to the chair across the small table from her. Snakebite took a position next to the wall along with another of Edna's "girls," a large woman called Moose.

"I heard you were the kind of woman who got things done."

Grams lifted an eyebrow.

Camilla leaned in closer. "I didn't get a chance to tidy up before I got sent here."

Grams smiled. "So you're a neat freak?"

She laughed and leaned back. "I guess I am."

"It isn't cheap cleaning up messes."

Camilla smiled. She had money stashed around the country under a dozen different names and she had ways to get to it. "I didn't think it would be."

"How do I know I can trust you?" Grams asked.

"The same way I know I can trust you. Otherwise how would either of us be able to sleep at night?"

The older woman laughed again and slid a pen and paper across the table.

Camilla wrote "Marshal Hud Savage" on the slip of paper and slid it back across along with the pen.

Grams raised a brow again.

"Is there a problem?" Camilla asked.

"Not a problem exactly. I'm just curious. Is this personal or business?"

"I wouldn't think you would care. It's personal," Camilla said, remembering the way Hud had rebuked her. "It's *very* personal."

Grams shrugged and tucked the piece of paper into her bra. "I'll get back to you."

"How long before it's done?"

"Patience," she said as she pushed herself to her feet. "Time is relative in here. But I think you'll be pleased." With that, Grams padded off, her "girls" behind her.

Camilla picked up a lump of clay from a tub left on the table and began twisting it in her hands. First Hud. Then she would take care of the rest of his precious family. As Grams said, she had nothing but time.

WHEN GERALD OPENED his motel room door, Lily took a step back.

"Don't look so surprised to see me," he said irritably. "You act as if you expected me to leave town before you arrived."

When he'd called, he'd sounded…odd. Hurt, no doubt because she hadn't fallen into his arms instantly. Hadn't forgiven him without hesitation. That she'd been more concerned with Tag than him last night.

"Truthfully, Gerald, I don't know what to expect from you," she said as he moved aside so she could step in out of the cold. She took in the room. Gerald had always been excessively neat. The bed was made, his suitcase perfectly packed and open on the luggage rack by the wall.

"I told you I needed to talk to you," he said behind her, a slight whine in his voice.

She turned to look at him. "But you didn't say why."

"I didn't get a chance before your…friend showed up. Lily, I hate to see you get involved with someone like him."

"I beg your pardon?"

"That cowboy. What could you possibly have in common with him?"

If he only knew. "That's none of your business."

Gerald let out a snort. "You can't be falling for a man like that."

She started to deny that she was falling for Tag but stopped herself. "I can fall for anyone I want to."

"Lily," he said impatiently.

"Gerald," she said, matching his tone.

His eyes narrowed.

"Gerald, just tell me what it is you want."

He let out a long sigh. "I had hoped we could sit down and discuss this reasonably like intelligent adults, but if you insist…" He met her gaze. "I shouldn't have done what I did."

"No, you shouldn't have. Is that all?"

"No," he snapped. "I told you about my little sister who lives in California."

Lily frowned. "She works for a bank."

"An investment company," he said, and looked away. "She got into some trouble. I had to…help her." His gaze met hers. "I didn't want to hurt you, but I really had no choice. She's my little sister. That's why I took the job in California, why I've done everything that I have."

"You had a choice, Gerald. You could have told me about your sister, you could have told me you didn't want to get married *before* the wedding. Don't tell me you didn't have a choice."

"You are making this very difficult, Lily."

"Oh, I'm sorry, Gerald." He usually didn't get sarcasm, but she had laid it on so thick, even he got it.

He had the decency to look chastised. "I'm sure it was also difficult for you."

"Difficult, Gerald? You mean when I had to explain to our friends and family why you left me standing at the altar when I didn't have the *slightest* idea?" she demanded, surprised at her anger. Even more surprised that she was letting it out. Gerald had always felt such a show of emotions distasteful at best. In her, he'd seen any emotional display as a sign of immaturity. Since he was eleven years her senior, she'd locked up all her emotions so as not to seem childish.

But now she thought of Tag and her brother, both filled with righteous indignation over what Gerald had done to her and demanding to know why she wasn't furious. Because she had every right. Just as she had every right to let her anger come out now.

"I apologized for that," Gerald said evenly.

"Six months later," she pointed out. "Not that I have any more idea now than I did then why you would do such a rude, disrespectful, embarrassing, ob—"

"I couldn't go through with it right then. My sister needed me and I…I panicked, all right?"

She raised a brow. "*You* panicked?"

"You have to know how hard this is to admit. I found myself in a position where I had to make a decision…. I should have told you."

"You think?" Speaking of childish.

He narrowed his eyes as he studied her. "I knew you'd be upset, but I had hoped you wouldn't be bitter."

She almost laughed.

"You seem so…different."

She *did* laugh. "You know, Gerald, being stood up at the altar changes a person."

He seemed not to know what to say.

Lily hadn't thought she'd changed from the woman who'd agreed to marry the head of the math department at the university, but she realized she had. She was stronger, just as her brother had said. She'd gotten over the initial pain and realized that she'd survived one of the most awful things that could happen to a woman.

Last night when she'd seen Gerald, all those old initial feelings had come back in a rush. Followed quickly by the hurt and betrayal.

Since then, she'd let herself admit that she *was* angry. No, she was furious with him and all the more furious with herself because she'd actually thought about taking him back. She'd actually wanted that ordered life he'd promised.

But standing here with him now, she knew that her night with Tag had changed all that. She'd never loved Gerald the way a woman should love a man she was about to marry. Tag had shown her what she'd been missing. Passion. And now that she'd experienced it, she could never go back to that lukewarm idea of love she'd shared with Gerald.

Nor had Gerald loved her enough to be honest with her. Plus, as Tag had said, Gerald was a coward for not facing her on their wedding day.

"Was there something else?" she asked her former fiancé, feeling the weight of the past lift from her shoulders.

Gerald looked confused. He'd obviously come to her thinking all he had to do was tell her he was sorry and that he wanted her back. He seemed more than a little astonished that that hadn't been the case.

"I guess there is nothing else to say. I made the decision to help my sister. If it matters, you're making that decision easier."

"I'm all about making your life easier, Gerald," she said.

"I didn't mean to make you angry again," he added quickly. "You know I tend to speak sometimes without considering how it affects others."

She started for the door.

"I couldn't help noticing when I was at your house that you were working on something," he said. "Is it something I can help you with?"

Lily turned to look at him. "That's nice of you, but—"

"I would like to help you. I'd feel better about the way I'm leaving things between us," he said.

She felt herself weaken. She'd been interrupted so much she hadn't been able to work on decoding the data she'd taken off the thumb drive. If Tag was right and this information was important in Mia's murder case… "I *could* use your help."

He looked pleased as well as curious as she dug in her bag and pulled out the papers she'd been working on. She set them on the desk, spreading them out as she explained what she'd come up with so far.

"It would be easier if I had the original," he said, glancing at the papers.

"I don't have it with me."

He nodded, pulled up a chair and, taking one of his pens from his pocket protector, began to check her work—just as he had done when he was her teacher.

Lily watched him. She'd known how easily he could

be distracted with a puzzle involving math. The mathematician in her still loved that about him.

"Interesting," he said as he bent over the letters.

GUHA BKOPAR
CAKNCA IKKNA
BNWJG IKKJAU
HSQ SWUJA
YHAPA NWJZ
NWU AIANU

LWQH XNKSJ
IEW ZQJYWJ
YWH BNWJGHEJ
HWNO HWJZANO
DWNHWJ YWNZSAHH
DQZ OWRWCA

She'd decoded enough to see a pattern, but it hadn't held up either because whoever had come up with the code had been in a hurry and made mistakes or because they'd gotten confused and sloppy.

As she watched Gerald work, she saw that she'd been right. There were two lists of names. It amazed her how quickly he filled in the names. She had to give him credit. Gerald really was a master at this sort of thing.

"You were on the right track," he said. "Just off a little." Within minutes, he'd come up with two lists of names. "Is this all?" he asked, sounding disappointed as he handed the sheets to her and rose from the chair. "You're sure there was nothing more on the original data?" He obviously would have much preferred some cryptic message. She would have, as well.

She glanced at the names, one of them taking her breath away.

Gerald didn't seem to notice as he walked over and closed his suitcase with a finality that rang through the room. But when he turned toward her again, he said, "You and I are good together, Lily. You need me, now maybe more than you realize. I should leave you my cell phone number in case you change your—"

"I won't change my mind, Gerald," she said as she shoved the papers into her shoulder bag with trembling fingers.

"I see." He had pulled out his business card as if about to write his new cell phone number on it, but now he stuck it back into his pocket. "I hope you don't live to regret this, Lily. Clearly your behavior has taken a dangerous trajectory—if that cowboy is any indication."

She smiled. She'd never been one to hold grudges, always quick to forgive and forget. But she took some satisfaction in realizing that Gerald was jealous. If he only knew.... "Goodbye, Gerald."

He started to reach for her as if to kiss her cheek as he used to do when they parted, but she stepped back and walked out the door, leaving him standing there.

She had a death grip on her shoulder bag and the papers inside, and couldn't wait to show Tag. As she walked out, she heard Gerald's cell phone ring.

"Yes, I talked to her," he said into the phone. "No, she won't listen to reason."

Gerald had apparently involved one of his sisters, Lily thought as she rushed to her vehicle. *No, she won't listen to reason?* She gritted her teeth, never more glad that she hadn't weakened and gone back to the man.

She was so deep in her thoughts that she didn't even notice the large black SUV parked next to her on the driver's side. Nor did she hear the back door of the SUV open or the man jump out directly behind her.

Lily didn't even have time to scream as something wet and awful smelling was clamped over her mouth and she was dragged into the black pit of darkness in the back of the massive SUV.

Chapter Ten

Hud got the call on his way from the hospital. He'd gone by to see Harlan Cardwell only to find that the man had left without anyone having seen him leave.

The marshal listened to the news on the other end of the line with the same sinking feeling he'd had earlier. Another young woman's body had been found.

"I'll be right there," he said, hung up and turned on his flashing lights and siren. If he could have gotten his hands on Harlan Cardwell right now…

Last night at the hospital he'd demanded to know more than the information he'd been given yesterday at the ranch.

"We think it's possible Mia passed information to someone when she knew she was in trouble," Harlan told him. "She and Teresa Evans were apparently friends. Teresa would be the most likely person to give the data to if she was in trouble, which could explain Teresa's disappearance."

Hud had shaken his head in frustration.

"I wish I had an answer for you. They tried to kill me earlier. If Tag hadn't come along when he did …"

"Aren't you getting too old for this?"

Harlan had chuckled even though it must have hurt him. "I only got involved again because of Mia." His voice broke. He cleared his throat. "I just talked to the coroner a few minutes before you came in. Mia had been drugged. We can only assume one of the patrons at the bar stuck her. She must have realized it too late to get the item to me. I'm sure she did everything she could to finish her mission."

"If Mia gave whatever this information is to Teresa Evans, then they have it."

Harlan shook his head. "Apparently Teresa didn't have it. They're still looking for it. At least that's what I'm hearing."

"How many more are they going to kill to get it?" Hud had demanded, and seen the answer in Harlan's eyes.

So the call that a young woman had been found on the ice at the edge of the Gallatin River hadn't come as a surprise—just another blow. Hud felt helpless for the second time in his life. The other time, just months ago, was when he realized a psychopath had his wife and children.

TAG GLANCED AT his watch and then tried Lily's cell phone again. It went straight to voice mail just as it had done the three times he'd tried before. He didn't leave a message.

He'd been trying since he'd gotten her cryptic message.

"Tag, the list is decoded. There's a name on here... you need to see. Call me. It's urgent."

When Lily had mentioned that she thought the thumb drive had two lists of names on it, he'd thought of his father. Was his father's name on it?

Tag thought of the ransacked cabin. His hand went to his pocket. He closed his fingers over the small computer flash drive. He'd thought taking it would protect Lily. But now she'd decoded it and had found a name. A name that had put her in danger?

Earlier he'd driven down to the Corral Bar, but the bartender said he hadn't seen Angus or Harlan since yesterday. He didn't seem that surprised, which Tag took to mean both men disappeared occasionally.

It baffled him as he drove back toward Big Sky.

Like a lot of Montana winter days, this one was blinding with brilliance. The sun hung in a cloudless robin's-egg-blue sky and now shone on the fresh-fallen snow, turning it into a carpet of prisms.

As he pulled up in front of the Canyon Bar and climbed out, he sucked in a lungful of the freezing air. Nearby pines scented the frosty breeze. He didn't see Lily's car, but he figured her brother would have heard from her by now. The fresh snow creaked beneath his boot soles as he crossed to the bar.

The front door was open even though the bar wasn't scheduled to open for another hour. As the door closed on the bright winter day behind him, Tag stopped just inside to let his eyes adjust to the semidarkness.

"We don't open for another..." Ace's words died off as he looked up from behind the bar. "Tag, come on in. I forgot to relock the door after Lily left."

"So you've seen her today?" Tag asked as he walked over to the bar.

Ace's expression changed into one of mild amusement. "She looked better than I'd seen her looking in a long time."

"Then she told you about Gerald."

"Gerald didn't put those roses in her cheeks," he said with a laugh. "What can I get you to drink?"

"Nothing, but thanks. I was looking for Lily."

"Like I said, she was by earlier. Gerald called her. She went to see him." Ace stopped in midmotion, a bar glass half-washed in his hand. "You met Gerald, right?"

"Last night."

"Then you know he's all wrong for her."

Tag didn't feel he could weigh in on that.

"I hate it, but she went to hear him out," Ace said with a disgusted shake of his head. "I was hoping we'd seen the last of him. I'm afraid she'll go back to him. Maybe already has."

That would explain why Lily wasn't answering her phone. "Maybe I will have that drink, after all," Tag said, and took a stool. "Just a draft beer."

Ace laughed and reached for a clean glass as the bar door opened again and a large silhouette filled it.

HUD PARKED AT the edge of the fishing access road a few hundred yards from the river and walked. His head ached, his stomach felt oily. It took all his mental strength not to stop and throw up in the fresh snow at the edge of the road.

He could see the flashing lights ahead. The coroner had been called. Second time in two days. Another dead young woman.

The body lay on the edge of the thick aquamarine-blue ice in a bed of snow. At first glance it appeared the woman had lain down in the snow to make a snow angel. Her arms were spread wide, facedown, legs also splayed. He'd guess she'd been thrown there and that was how she'd landed. Which meant she'd been dead before she hit because she hadn't made a snow angel. She hadn't moved.

"What do we have?" Hud asked the coroner after giving a nod to his new deputy, a man by the name of Jake Thorton. He'd come highly recommended but hadn't been tested yet. Nor had Hud made a point of getting to know the man. Jake seemed to keep to himself, which was just fine with his boss.

"Looks like strangulation," the coroner said. "Maybe that combined with hypothermia. Won't know until the autopsy. But she didn't die here."

Hud nodded. "Do we have an ID?"

"Found her purse in the snow over there," Deputy Thorton said. "Her name, according to her Montana driver's license and photo, is Teresa Marie Evans, the missing woman last seen at the Canyon Bar."

Teresa had a winter scarf tied too tightly around her neck—just like Mia. "Tire tracks?" Hud asked Jake.

"The road hadn't been plowed. Didn't look as if any vehicles had been down it. But there were tracks. I saw that she was dropped by snowmobile," he said. "I took photos."

Hud nodded at the young handsome deputy, thankful he was on the case since his own mind was whirling. All his self-doubts seemed to surface in light of another death. Dropped by snowmobile just like the last one.

"I'll let you handle this, notify the family, do what has to be done," he told Jake, and looked at his watch. Police officer Paul Brown's funeral was in two hours. Hud wasn't sure how much more death he could take.

AS THE MAN stepped into the Canyon Bar, the door closing behind him, Tag saw that it was Gerald, Lily's former fiancé. Or should he say now current fiancé? Had Lily gone back to him?

He waited almost expectantly for Gerald to approach the bar. The beer he'd downed turned sour in his stomach as he braced himself for the news. Like her brother,

Ace, Tag thought this man was all wrong for the woman he'd made love to last night. He reminded himself that Lily had regretted their lovemaking. Had that alone driven her back into this man's arms?

"Lily left this," Gerald said, and dropped a torn sheet of paper on the bar.

Tag's first thought was that she'd left a note for her brother.

"What am I supposed to do with this?" Ace asked after giving it a cursory glance and tossing it back on the bar.

"I wonder why I wasted my time," Gerald said with a shake of his head, and turned to leave.

Tag shifted on the stool to see what was on the sheet of paper. He recognized Lily's neat script. His pulse took off like a rocket when he saw the familiar array of letters from the thumb drive.

He quickly picked up the partial sheet of paper. It had been torn. Only a few of the original letters from the thumb drive were on the sheet. Next to them were other letters that made...*names.*

He didn't recognize any of them and frowned. Lily had been upset on the phone. *"Tag, the list is decoded. There's a name on here...you need to see. Call me. It's urgent."*

She'd wanted him to see a name, but it wasn't on this portion of the original sheet of paper.

"Wait a minute," he called to Gerald's retreating back. "Where's Lily?"

Gerald stopped, impatience in his stance, and then turned with a sigh. "You're asking *me?*"

"*You're* the one she went to see," Ace interjected.

Lily had solved the code. Whatever name had upset

her wasn't on this sheet. Tag slid off his stool and moved quickly to Gerald. "*Where's* Lily?"

Gerald gave him a smug, satisfied smile. "The last time I saw her she was leaving my motel room."

"Did you see where she went from there?"

He looked angry. "If you must know, I wasn't paying any attention."

Tag turned back to the bar and Ace. "Lily's message earlier said it was urgent I see these names, but I don't recognize any of them. Where are the rest of them?"

"What does it matter?" Gerald asked sarcastically but he stepped back toward the bar.

"Trust me, it might be a matter of life or death."

"Don't tell me she's in trouble because of what is written on that paper," Ace said as he leaned across the bar to take the scrap of paper in Tag's hand.

"Lily was convinced these letters had something to do with Mia Duncan's murder."

Ace let out a curse.

"That list of names?" Gerald asked. "*Murder?* This was exactly what I feared when Lily insisted on working in a...bar."

"Gerald," Ace said in clear warning. "Don't make me come over this counter and punch you." He turned to Tag. "What do we do?"

"If Lily's right, then I know who I need to talk to," Tag said. "If things go badly, though, can I depend on you to bail me out of jail?"

"I'm going with you," Ace said only seconds before a bunch of skiers came through the door and headed for an empty table. "I'll close the bar and—"

"No. Lily might come back here. Or you might be contacted. Anyway, you can't get me out of jail if you're in there with me." Tag scribbled his cell phone number on a bar napkin. "Call me if you hear anything."

Ace nodded as another group of patrons came through the bar door. Reggie showed up then in jeans and the Canyon Bar T-shirt, like the one Lily had been wearing the first night Tag met her. The night he'd also met Mia Duncan.

"I suppose you're both going to just assume I would be of no help?" Gerald asked.

"Call the bar if you hear from Lily," Tag told him, thinking Lily might contact Gerald before either him or her brother. "Ace will pass along the message." He started for the door.

"That scrap of paper in your hand. That has only some of the names on the lists Lily showed me," Gerald said. "I can't imagine how it could matter, but I'm the one who helped her decode them. If you have the thumb drive…"

Tag stopped at the door and turned. His hand went to the thumb drive in his pocket. "How do you know about that?"

Gerald rolled his eyes. "How do you think? Lily asked me to help her finish decoding the names."

So it was like that, Tag thought. Lily wouldn't have told him about the thumb drive or asked him unless she trusted him, unless she had gone back to him.

"Ace, can we borrow your computer?" Tag asked, and led the way to Ace's office.

Gerald sat down behind the desk, then held out his hand. Tag dropped the thumb drive into it and sat as Gerald went to work. It didn't take him long. When he finished, he printed out a sheet with the names on them and handed both it and the thumb drive back to him.

Two lists of names, just as Lily had suspected. The

names began to jump off the page at him. This was why Lily had wanted him to see them.

Mia Duncan's name was high on the list.

Not far under it was the name Harlan Cardwell. Directly under that was Marshal Hud Savage.

KYLE FOSTER
GEORGE MOORE
FRANK MOONEY
LOU WAYNE
CLETE RAND
RAY EMERY

PAUL BROWN
MIA DUNCAN
CAL FRANKLIN
LARS LANDERS
HARLAN CARDWELL
HUD SAVAGE

What the hell is this? He had no idea, but he was all the more worried about Lily. "You're sure you don't know where Lily went after she left your motel room?" he asked Gerald.

"I thought she must have left with you."

"Why would you think that?"

"Because she left her SUV in the parking lot."

"What parking lot?" Tag demanded, feeling his heart slamming against his rib cage. The names on the list. While he had no idea what they meant, he had a terrible feeling that they had gotten Mia Duncan killed, his father beaten to within an inch of his life and both Mia's and his father's homes ransacked. And now Lily appeared to be missing.

"The Happy Trails Motel down the highway," Gerald said.

Tag headed for the door at a run, praying he was wrong and that there was an explanation other than the one that had him terrified.

"I'll drive up to her house and check there," Gerald said to his retreating back. "You better not get her killed, Texas cowboy."

Tag didn't have time to go back and slug the suit or he would have.

The drive to the motel, although only half a mile, seemed to take forever.

He was in sight of it when he heard the news report on the radio. He hadn't even realized the radio was on, droning in the background, until he heard the announcement come on.

"A woman's body has been found along the Gallatin River two miles south of Big Sky. The name of the victim is being withheld pending notification of family. If anyone has any information, please call the marshal's office...."

An eighties song came on the radio.

Not Lily. No, it couldn't be Lily.

Ahead, he saw Lily's SUV parked off by itself. His stomach dropped. As he jumped out, he could see where another vehicle had pulled in next to it. And in the snow that the plow had left, he could see that there'd been a struggle.

Lily's boot-heel prints had made a short trail from her SUV driver's-side door to whatever had been parked next to it.

Chapter Eleven

As Tag drove straight to the marshal's office, he kept remembering the marshal and his father, heads together, arguing about something before his father gave Hud an envelope. Money? A bribe? A payoff?

Whatever it was, it had something to do with Mia Duncan—and if he wasn't wrong, the damned thumb drive in his pocket and the names on it.

He didn't know his cousin Dana's husband. This trip to Montana had been the first time they'd met. Was it possible Hud was crooked?

Tag hoped not for his cousin's sake. But look how she'd turned a blind eye to whatever Harlan and Angus did when they left the canyon. Would she be the same way if her husband were on the take?

All Tag knew was that he didn't trust the marshal. But right now he needed to know who had been found near the river. He glanced at the list again, surprised by the one name that seemed to be missing. Teresa Evans. How did she fit into all this? Or did she? He'd heard that she was missing. Was it her body that was found by the river?

He had to know.

Just as he had to know why both his father's and Hud's names were on the list. He had no idea what to make of that. Or how this list from the thumb drive could have anything to do with what was going on. Why would anyone be ransacking residences at Big Sky, let alone killing people for it?

All he could assume was that the names were important. *Why else had Mia put the thumb drive in his pocket?* he wondered as he stormed into the marshal's department and demanded to see Marshal Hud Savage. How important? He was about to find out since Hud Savage's name was on one of the lists.

"He's gone to a funeral," a pretty, redheaded young woman told him.

That threw him. "Whose funeral?"

"Officer Paul Brown."

The name was like a lightbulb coming on in his face. Paul Brown. He was also on the list.

"I just heard on the radio about a woman's body being found by the river." He held his breath. "Tell me it isn't Lily McCabe."

The woman dispatcher frowned. "Lily? No. But I can't give you—"

Not Lily. He felt his heart rate drop some. Not Lily. Not yet. "Where is the funeral?"

The dispatcher hesitated.

"I wouldn't ask but it's urgent," Tag said. "Another woman has disappeared."

"By now they would be heading for the graveside. Sunset. It's between Bozeman and Belgrade on the old highway. If you hurry—"

But Tag was already out the door.

LILY WOKE TO darkness, dying of thirst. Her mouth felt as if it had been stuffed with cotton balls. She tried to swallow as she sat up and blinked at the blackness around her.

At first she'd thought she was in the bedroom and Tag was beside her. But in a flash, the earlier events came back with the terror of her abduction.

Panic overtook her like a blizzard. Where was she? Her hand touched something cold and she recoiled. As her eyes became more adjusted to the dark, though, she saw that it was only a water bottle.

She snatched it up and drank half of it before a thought surfaced that made her quickly pull it away from her lips.

What if it was drugged? Or poisoned? Or all the water she had for however long she was going to be trapped here?

She didn't kid herself that she could climb off this mattress and walk out of here. The edges of the room began to take shape as her eyes adjusted to the darkness. Knotty-pine walls, dark with age, a linoleum floor. No apparent windows. One door. She could make out a tiny strip of light around its frame.

A basement, she thought, in some older house or cabin. Probably a cabin, which might mean she was still in Big Sky.

She considered yelling for help only an instant before she heard heavy footfalls coming down what sounded like stairs above her.

Lily thought about getting up, hating to be at such a disadvantage on the bed, but when she tried, she found she was too weak to stand. Sliding on the mattress until her back was against the wall, she stared in the direction of the single door in and out of the room. She told herself that the person wasn't coming to kill her or he would have already done that, but she knew killers probably weren't logical.

Whoever was outside the door put down something on the floor. It made a shadow under the door. Then she heard the key being turned in the lock. The door swung open along with blinding light before a large figure filled the doorway.

STANDING AT THE edge of the graveside service, Marshal Hud Savage tightened his grip on his hat held at his side as he saw Tag Cardwell pull up and get out of his father's old pickup.

Hud was in no mood for trouble and yet one look at the young man's face and Hud knew that was what was heading for him. He stepped a few feet back from the others. "Not here," he said under his breath as Tag reached him.

"Here or you come with me now," Tag said quietly under his breath. "Your choice. Unless you want everyone here to know about you."

Hud gave him a sidelong glance. "I could have you arrested—"

"I have what you've all been looking for. Set up a trade for Lily. *Now.*"

That got Hud's attention. He turned and headed toward the old pickup Tag had arrived in. Once there, he turned on the man. "What the hell are you talking about?"

"Lily McCabe. I know you have her and if you hurt her—"

"Tag, I don't know what you're talking about. Is Lily missing?"

"I'm tired of playing games with you and my father and uncle," Tag said, and swore.

Hud listened as Tag told him about seeing the leather jacket on his father's couch, catching his father in a lie, seeing Hud and Harlan the day Mia Duncan's body turned up.

"You've got it all wrong," Hud said when Tag finished.

"Yeah, that's what my father keeps telling me. Where is he, by the way?"

Behind them, Hud heard the graveside funeral procession breaking up. "We can't talk about this here. What was that that part about a thumb drive?"

Tag smiled. "So you did hear me. Make the call. As soon as I see Lily—"

"I can see how you might think I'm involved in all this—"

"We don't have time to—"

"I'm telling you the truth. Show me what you have. Maybe between the two of us we can—"

"So help me, if you have touched a hair on her head—" Tag swore, and grabbed Hud by the throat. A minute later he was being pulled off the marshal by two other law enforcement officers who'd been at the funeral. A minute after that he was in handcuffs in the back of Marshal Hud Savage's patrol SUV on his way to jail.

"YOU'RE BEING CHEATED."

The raspy words entered Camilla's right ear, the hoarse whisper sending a chill down her spine. She was standing in the prison chow line, not that she was hungry. She ate because food kept her strong. If she ever had a chance of getting out of here, one way or the other, she needed to keep up her strength.

"Don't turn around."

She fought the urge.

"She shouldn't be charging you." She could feel the woman's breath on her neck, hot and damp and putrid.

Camilla waited. Prison was teaching her patience and she'd become an astute student since she hadn't killed anyone yet.

"Just nod your head if I'm right." The woman moved closer. Camilla had to steel herself not to shudder. "You're paying Grams for a hit on a cowboy cop, right?"

Just like in high school, rumors ran rampant. This one just happened to be true.

She gave a short nod and could no longer contain the shudder.

The woman behind gave a snort. "His name was already on the list."

Camilla turned in her surprise to find Snakebite behind her. Their eyes met, Snakebite's as hard as obsidian. She turned back around as the line moved and felt sick to her stomach. Not because Grams had planned to charge her *and* someone else for the same hit. But that Marshal Hud Savage was about to be killed and it wouldn't be her doing.

She wanted to howl out her pain and yet she couldn't even step out of line. She shuffled forward, the smell of some awful casserole filling her nostrils and making her even more nauseated.

I have to get out of here.

Not just out of the line, but out of the damned prison.

I have to get out of here.

Camilla hadn't realized she'd said the words aloud. Not until she heard the raspy voice answer.

"I thought you might say that."

MARSHAL HUD SAVAGE pulled off onto a narrow snowy road that ended at the river's edge.

"You should take off my handcuffs," Tag said from the back of the patrol SUV. "Might look more believable that I made a run for it when you kill me."

Hud cut the engine and turned to look at him in surprise. "You think I'm going to kill you?" He let out a curse and shook his head. For months he'd been telling himself he'd lost his edge. That he wasn't any good at this anymore. He'd never felt more assured of that than at this moment.

"I'm not a dirty cop," he said, feeling himself hit bottom. "Why would you think—"

Tag snorted. "I saw my father give you an envelope the morning Mia Duncan was found murdered. Tell me that envelope wasn't filled with money."

"It wasn't." He thought of the paperwork Harlan had finally turned over to him. The agency was always holding out on him. With a shock, he had just been told that he had a dead agent on his hands and Harlan had still wanted to keep secrets. They'd argued until Harlan had finally given him some information.

"Look, I don't care, all right?" Tag said. "I just want to find Lily."

"So do I. That's why you have to help me with what you know."

"You expect me to trust you after all the lies you've told me? I know my father was seeing Mia Duncan."

"You have it all wrong."

"So you all keep telling me," Tag snapped.

Hud took off his Stetson and raked a hand through his hair. "I don't know how you managed to get so deep in all this." He met Tag's gaze. "I pleaded with Harlan to tell you the truth, but he didn't want you involved."

With a sigh, he said, "Mia was an agent. Your father was working with her."

"An agent?" Tag let out a laugh. "And my father was working with her? What would Harlan—"

"Harlan and Angus are retired, but they often help when needed."

Tag shook his head in obvious disbelief. "You're telling me my father and uncle are…agents?"

Hud nodded. "They've always worked undercover operations because they had such perfect covers with their band. Apparently Mia was getting close to busting a murder ring."

"Murder ring?" he said, sounding disbelieving.

"We're wasting time. You want to find Lily, you have to tell me about these names you said she had." He could tell that Tag didn't believe him. "You have to trust me if want to find Lily."

"Take off my handcuffs. If I can trust you, then trust me."

He hesitated. Tag was a loose cannon. He'd gotten involved and now Lily McCabe was missing. Hud already had two dead women. He hoped he wasn't making another mistake.

"I know you don't trust me, but I have reason not to trust you, either," Hud said as he got out of the patrol SUV and opened the back door. "You show up just before Mia is killed and we only have your word that she left with some Montana cowboy in a pickup."

"You can't be serious. Take off my handcuffs. I think I have what everyone is looking for."

Hud lifted an eyebrow, then unlocked the cuffs and watched Tag rub his wrists. He'd taken a chance with one of Dana's so-called cousins and almost gotten his family killed. And here he was again, taking another chance, one that could get him killed, as well.

TAG'S HEAD WAS whirling. He still wasn't sure he believed Hud, let alone trusted him. But right now he needed all the help he could get finding Lily.

"I have a partial list of some names that came off a thumb drive that I now believe Mia Duncan put in my coat pocket the night she was murdered." He dug out the scrap of paper with only a few of the names and handed it to the marshal.

Hud stared down at it, his eyes widening.

"You recognize the names?"

"Two of them are men who were recently released from prison," the marshal said as he turned the scrap of paper over, no doubt looking for more names. "One of them is dead. The other one, Ray Emery, is from around here. I don't recognize the others. Where is the rest of this sheet?"

Tag felt his heart hammering in his chest. He hoped he wasn't making a mistake that would get Lily killed—not to mention himself. He reached in his pocket and handed Hud the complete list from the thumb drive that Gerald had provided.

KYLE FOSTER
GEORGE MOORE
FRANK MOONEY
LOU WAYNE
CLETE RAND
RAY EMERY

PAUL BROWN
MIA DUNCAN

CAL FRANKLIN
LARS LANDERS
HARLAN CARDWELL
HUD SAVAGE

He heard the air rush from the marshal's lips and watched him swallow.

"This is the murder list," he said. "You say Mia put this in your coat pocket at the bar that night? Those names." He pointed to the ones on the top. "Those are the killers."

"And the names on the bottom?" Tag asked, his heart in his throat.

"Those are the hits."

"My father's name is on that list."

Hud nodded. "So is mine."

"How many of them are already dead?"

"Two that I know of. Paul and Mia. But Cal and Lars could already be dead by now."

"Then my father might be next." He met the marshal's gaze and let out a curse as he had a terrible thought. "You don't think they took Lily, not for the list, but..."

"As bait to flush out your father. Harlan said if you hadn't come by his cabin when you did, he would be dead. They wanted the thumb drive, but they didn't want him dead until they had the list that incriminated every prisoner who'd been released."

"I don't get why it's so important."

"In order to get released prisoners to kill for them, they had to promise their anonymity. If word got out that the feds had gotten hold of one of the lists..."

All Tag could think about was the fact that his father's name was on the list and the ones above might already be dead.

"Where is Harlan now?" When Hud hesitated, Tag said, "It's too late to hold out on me now."

"I honestly don't know. Apparently Mia had been working with a prison snitch. She'd heard that several prisons had started a type of co-op. For a fee, you can have someone on the outside killed. A recently released inmate kills someone he doesn't know, has no connection to. In return he gets either money or a favor. The idea is that the former inmate won't get caught because he has no motive."

Tag got it. His heart pounded as he realized why they were so desperate to get the thumb drive. "This list links the hits with the former inmates." This was incriminating stuff that could shut down the murder ring.

"I know Lily knew Mia and was the one who discovered her condo had been ransacked, but why do you think her disappearing has anything to do with the murder list?" Hud asked.

"Lily was with me when I found the thumb drive in my pocket. Once she took a look at what was on it, she determined it was written in some kind of code."

Hud frowned. "How did they know she had the thumb drive—let alone that she'd decoded it?"

Tag felt his heart drop. "I don't know. I thought she and I were the only ones who knew about it."

AS THE MAN entered the room, Lily was blinded by the sudden light for a moment. He carried a tray and she caught the smell of a microwave dinner. Her stomach growled. She was surprised that she was starved. It seemed odd to her to think about food at a time like this.

Her gaze went from the tray to the man. He was big

and bulky with hamlike hands and arms covered with tattoos. Over his head, he wore one of those rubber Halloween masks, this one of an ogre.

She didn't miss the irony as she watched him put down the tray on the end of the mattress. She thought about jumping up and making a break for the door. Or grabbing the tray and attempting to hit him with it.

But even if she hadn't felt so weak from whatever they'd knocked her out with, she knew either attempt at escape would be wasted effort. Better to eat the food he'd brought, get her strength back and bide her time.

He didn't say a word as he turned and walked out of the room. Nor did he appear to be worried about a surprise attack from behind.

She thought she probably should have tried to make conversation with him. Hadn't she heard somewhere that in a situation like this you needed to make yourself as human as possible to your abductor?

But Lily was smart enough to know that this wasn't a garden-variety abduction. The fact that they hadn't killed her outright probably meant they were holding her hostage.

Just as she surmised that this had to have something to do with the thumb drive and Mia's murder—as she and Tag had guessed.

The thought of Tag brought tears to her eyes. Why hadn't she admitted that they'd made love? They would have been in her bedroom at the house in each other's arms—instead of her being here.

She'd let fear keep her from him. But she'd never seen herself the way she was with Tag last night. Nor had she ever felt as close to another human being. She ached for Tag Cardwell, and that scared her, too, because she feared Gerald was right and Tag was all wrong for her. A mathematician and a Texas cowboy? Their lives were miles apart in more than distance.

And yet she couldn't get him out of her racing heart. She tried not to let herself think about what would happen if these men didn't get what they wanted as she dragged the tray over to her and dug into the food. It was as wonderful as it was awful. She thought of Gerald and his contempt for any food that wasn't four-star-restaurant quality.

She actually smiled at the absurdity of it all since she practically licked the cardboard container clean. The food made her feel a little stronger. But what boosted her more than anything was the knowledge that Tag would be looking for her.

Lily hugged herself, thinking about last night and their lovemaking. He was the kind of man who would ride in on a big white horse and save her. A sob escaped her lips. What if he hadn't gotten her message? Or worse, what if these men had already found Tag and taken care of him?

She assured herself that the cowboy wouldn't let her die without a fight.

Chapter Twelve

Everything could be bought for a price. Camilla had learned that at an early age. That price though was often very high—and too often wasn't monetary. So she'd spent her life paying dearly.

Because of that, it didn't come as a surprise that what she now wanted would be very costly. Snakebite had slipped back into the lunch line, returning with a hoarsely whispered cryptic message. "The laundry room. Right after dinner."

Camilla ate as if it were her last meal. It just might be, she thought as she studied the solemn faces around the table. Something was up. She could feel it on the electrified air. Even the guards seemed to sense it. Out of the corner of her eye, she saw them moving restlessly around the perimeter.

The walk down to the laundry room seemed interminable. But her resolve kept her moving. Whatever Snakebite had planned, it would be worth it if she could get the retribution she so desperately needed.

The laundry was busy with worker bees. Most of them didn't look up. Only two guards kept watch. Camilla felt the hair stand up on the back of her neck as first one of the guards stepped out and then the other.

She had one of those panicky moments, pure stomach-dropping, adrenaline-surging, breath-stopping moments before two of the women who'd been folding sheets turned and came toward her.

The first blow knocked the air out of her and smashed her teeth into her lips. The second blow cracked a rib. She tasted blood and began to fight back with everything she had.

Had she been set up from the beginning? Or was this part of the plan?

Right now it didn't matter. She was fighting for her life.

THE SOUND OF a cell phone ringing took both Tag and Hud by surprise. As Tag dug his cell phone out of his pocket and started to answer it, the marshal laid a hand on his arm.

"They could be calling to trade Lily for the thumb drive," Hud said. "Agree to meet them."

The phone rang again. "Hello?"

"It's Ace." Even over the roar of the bar crowd in the background outside his office, Tag could hear fear in Lily's brother's voice. "I just got a call demanding the thumb drive or they are going to kill Lily."

"What did you tell them?"

"To call you."

"Good." He disconnected and looked at the marshal, knowing he'd been listening in. "I'm going to give them the thumb drive."

"You have it on you? Let's take it to the office and make a copy," Hud said as he got out and motioned for Tag to get in the front seat of the patrol SUV. "I need to try to reach your father and let him know what's happening. For all we know, Harlan has already rescued Lily."

Tag wasn't going to hold his breath on that one. He still couldn't get his head around his father and uncle being agents, even retired ones. His mother had to have known. Was that another reason she'd left Harlan and Montana—or the real one?

As he climbed into the front of the patrol SUV and Hud started the engine, he touched the thumb drive in his pocket and prayed. Whoever had Lily had to believe that no one had been able to break the code. Otherwise, the thumb drive was useless to them and they would have no reason to keep Lily alive.

LILY DIDN'T FEEL so shaky after she ate. She still had a horrible taste in her mouth from whatever had been on the cloth the man had forced over her mouth. And, of course, there was the fear.

She did her best to hold it down, tempering it with the knowledge that someone would be looking for her. Not Gerald. By now he would have flown back home. She realized she probably would never see him again.

Her lack of regret made her feel a little sad. She'd almost married the man, would have if he had shown up that day. Gerald didn't know it but he'd saved them both from a horrible mistake, she thought as she got up from the mattress. Her eyes had adjusted to the dim light enough that she wasn't afraid to move around. She started on the wall next to the mattress on the floor and, moving like a blind woman, felt her way around the room.

She wasn't sure exactly what she hoped to find. Another door other than the one she'd heard the man lock behind him? A window? Anything that would give her a chance of escaping?

The room was larger than she'd thought, cleared of

any furniture. The knotty-pine walls made her think it was someone's cabin that was seldom used and that she was in the old, musty basement.

Lily tried to picture where it might be, but she had no idea how long the men had driven to get her here. Nor did she know what time of day it was. Or even what day since she didn't know how long she'd been out. She still felt groggy as she slid her fingers along the wall and took tentative steps.

She no longer wore a watch. She depended on her cell phone for the time. Her phone was in her purse, wherever that was now.

"Ouch." Her fingers connected with a wooden frame. A door frame? No, she realized as she felt around it. A window. She felt cloth and jerked. Dark fabric tore away from a basement window, bringing with it a choking amount of dust. She'd been right. This basement hadn't been used for some time.

With the window uncovered, Lily had hoped for more light. But unfortunately the snow had covered the dirty glass. Still, it was a little brighter inside the room without the dark curtain.

One look at the size of the window and she saw that it wasn't an avenue of escape. She was slim, but not slim enough to get out the window even if snow hadn't been banked up against it.

Taking advantage of the dim light, she quickly moved around the rest of the room, discovering another window and tearing off the cloth that had been tacked up over it. Less snow was banked against this one so it let in a little more light.

She could see the entire room. Definitely a basement. Musty and old and unused. Whose? Did the men who'd brought her here even know? It could be some cabin that no one used anymore.

When she reached the door, she tried the knob but of course found it locked. As she moved back to the bed, she felt her fear increase. She couldn't see how she could possibly escape this room unless she could outsmart her captors.

She had just sat down on the mattress to consider how she might do that when she remembered the sound of the man unlocking the door. No dead bolt. He'd used a key and it had made an odd sound. She stared at the door. It was very old, the wood a dark patina, so old it had a skeleton key.

Quickly she moved to the door and bent down to peer into the keyhole. There were two things about skeleton keys that gave her hope. One was that they fit in a rather loose-locking mechanism. Two was that they were often left in the other side of the door.

She could see the end of the key and the light around where it didn't quite fill the keyhole. At the sound of heavy footfalls, she scrambled toward the bed, stumbling over something. Her purse?

Grabbing it, she quickly searched for her cell phone. Gone, of course.

Hearing someone approaching, she sat down on the mattress and tucked the purse behind her to wait, her mind alive with an idea.

AT THE MARSHAL'S office, Hud copied the thumb drive onto his computer, then made a copy for Tag. "I'm going to have to keep the original."

Tag insisted on checking to make sure it had copied the information before he agreed. Then Hud told him to wait just outside his door while he made a couple of calls.

He'd started to protest, but the marshal cut him off. "Don't make me lock you up, okay? I'm going to try to reach your father. If you get the call, don't answer it until you let me know."

Tag nodded. He had little choice since all he could do was wait for Lily's abductors to call. Looking for her would be like looking for a needle in a haystack. There were too many places they could have taken her.

All he could think about was that two women had been killed and the killers had Lily. He could feel the clock ticking. He clutched the thumb drive in his pocket and prayed that they wouldn't find out that Lily had decoded what was on it.

He was too nervous to sit still. Getting up, he walked down the short hall until he was just outside the marshal's office. He could see Hud on the phone, his back to him. The door was partially open and as he moved toward it, he heard what Hud was saying.

Tag stopped, frozen in place as he listened.

"Ray Emery, huh? Okay, give me the directions to his ex's house." He repeated them as he wrote them down.

Tag recalled the name Ray Emery had been on the murder list as one of the former inmates. Ray apparently had an ex-wife who lived just outside Big Sky.

Whoever was on the other end of the line must have given him an order because Hud said, "I don't like locking him up, even for his own good…I know. I can't do anything until he gets the call…Don't worry, I won't let him play hero, but I'm doing it my way now…Yeah? So arrest me. This is your mess, Harlan. Your name is on that list next, and mine's after that…Yeah, I'll do that."

Tag had heard enough. His father wanted Hud to lock him up in jail. Once the call came in…

When the marshal hung up, he quickly placed another call. This one to the Bozeman office requesting assistance. He would need two deputies to escort someone to the airport and make sure he made the flight.

Tag didn't have to guess who that would be. He eased down the hall and let himself out the back door. Fortunately someone from the funeral had seen that Harlan's old pickup was returned to Big Sky.

Tag had seen it parked out in back of the marshal's office when they'd driven up. The keys weren't in the ignition or even on the floorboard. But Tag knew where his father kept a spare one. Their mother had learned the trick from Harlan, apparently while the two were married.

He opened the small lid over the gas cap and felt around, smiling as his fingers closed around the key.

Within minutes, he was driving out of Big Sky, headed for Ray Emery's ex-wife's house down the canyon.

WILMA EMERY LIVED in an old cabin off the road in an isolated area on the river. The cabin was pre–Big Sky and the resort, when a lot of people had summer places that were rustic, basic and far from pretentious. This was one of them.

The cabin backed up to the river and was hidden from the road by trees. Tag parked in a wide plowed spot nearby, got out and walked over to look at the river. The land was much higher here than the water.

There was a narrow trail that wound down to the water, one no doubt used by fishermen in the summer.

Now it was snow-packed, but there were tracks where some hard-core fisherman had gone down recently and fished in an open area before the surface had frozen over again.

Tag took the trail, half sliding in the snow because the embankment was a steep wall of rock and snow. He landed feetfirst on a large snowcapped rock at the river's edge.

He felt thankful he hadn't ended up breaking through the ice at the edge. As he glanced to the south where the water curved away, he couldn't see Wilma's cabin. But he knew about where it should be. He made his way across the icy round granite boulders, headed in that direction.

As he reached a point where he guessed the cabin should be just up the steep embankment, he spotted another narrow winding path upward.

The path was full of snow, almost indistinguishable. He kept thinking of Lily, his heart quickening, his stomach dropping. He had to find her. Those words were like a mantra in his ears as he scaled the embankment, slowing toward the top. He'd gotten her into this. He had to get her out.

The cabin was completely surrounded by trees. He stopped behind one large pine, its boughs low and thick, concealing him from view of the windows he'd glimpsed on this side of the cabin.

He listened, not sure what he hoped to hear. Lily screaming? That thought sent ice down his spine. As he moved toward the cabin, he thought of Lily naked in his arms last night. The woman had gotten under his skin as no woman ever had before. He would find her. He just prayed it would be soon enough.

Why hadn't the kidnappers called?

HUD HAD BEEN wondering if he was doing the right thing about Tag Cardwell as he came out from making the calls. "I still couldn't reach your father..." The rest of the lie died on his lips.

Tag was gone.

Hud swore as he hurried out to the dispatcher. "What happened to my prisoner?"

Annie looked up in surprise. "Your prisoner? It wasn't like he was handcuffed or booked..."

Hud didn't wait for the rest. He knew Annie was right. He'd screwed up. Tag had to have known he was going to be either detained in jail or shipped out of state on some other type of security warrant.

He couldn't worry about Tag now. He had to find Lily McCabe before he got the call that another woman had been murdered. He felt a sudden surge of that old feeling of wanting to put the bad guys away, that whole incredibly dangerous and yet amazing need to fight for good over evil, with the belief that he was born to do this.

He'd thought he'd lost it. He'd thought he'd needed to turn in his star because he wasn't up to doing this anymore. It made him furious with himself that he'd had these months of self-doubt. He would go down fighting because in his heart this was who he was. He couldn't escape this any more than he could escape whatever had led him down this path to begin with.

Ray Emery's ex lived down the canyon in a cabin on the river. He was betting she knew where her ex-con husband was. Emery's name was on the list.

Hud's cell phone vibrated. He checked the number. Harlan. Hud hesitated only a moment before he answered the call. "I don't know where your son is," he said into the phone. "He's like his old man. Stubborn and determined."

Harlan swore.

"I'm on my way to see Ray Emery's ex now," Hud said.

"If you see Tag again, lock him up."

"Don't worry, I will." He hung up and just hoped Tag Cardwell didn't get himself killed. Assaulting an officer would hold Tag for maybe a few hours, but as determined as Harlan's son was to find Lily, Hud knew he'd be out as soon as he could call a lawyer.

But hopefully all of this would be over by then.

LILY PICKED UP HER PURSE.

Moments ago the man in the mask had come down and taken her tray and brought her another bottle of water. Again, neither of them had spoken. She'd waited until he was gone before she moved to the window with the most light.

She'd just assumed the men who took her would have taken her purse. Digging through it, she saw that other than her cell phone, nothing seemed to be missing—not even the papers Gerald had decoded the names onto.

Her heart began to pound hard. Surely they would have searched her purse for the computer flash drive. They must have ignored the papers with the names. She noticed in the dim light that Gerald had scratched out some of the letters she'd had down, replacing them with others.

She frowned. That was odd. He'd changed all the names but a couple of them. If she'd had the code wrong, wouldn't those have had to be changed, as well?

TAG HAD JUST reached the corner of the cabin when he picked up the sound of an approaching vehicle. Through the trees he watched the marshal's car pull up out front. He waited until he heard Hud pound at the front door before he edged to the back of the cabin.

Through the dust-coated window he could make out what used to be an old screened-in porch that had been entirely closed in.

He moved to the door and tried it. The knob turned, and the door groaned as he pulled it just open enough to slip in.

The back porch smelled musty. He moved to the rear door, settled his hand on the knob and prayed it, too, would be unlocked. That was what was amazing about most rural places in Montana. People didn't feel the need to lock their doors.

The door opened and he felt his heart soar. The hinges creaked softly as he slipped through. He could hear voices. Hud's deep voice. A woman's higher shrill one.

Tag found himself standing in a short hallway. He moved quickly to the first closed door, opened it. Junk room. Second door, bedroom. Third door, bathroom.

By then he could see the small cluttered living room, off it, a kitchen table and the strong smell of burned coffee.

The marshal and the woman were arguing, the woman's voice rising and falling. He could make out most of what was being said.

"I told you. I don't know where Ray is and I don't care. He won't be coming back here. He knows better than to try."

"I know you're still in contact with him," Hud argued. "You visited him just two weeks ago."

"To make sure he knew he wasn't coming back here," she snapped, voice rising again. "I'm not the criminal here. You don't have the right to come here and threaten me."

"I'm not threatening you, Wilma. Two women have been murdered. Another is missing. If Ray is involved—"

"It's his business, none of mine. That's all I have to say to you."

Tag heard the creak of the old door as she started to close it.

"If you hear from him—" The door closed.

Tag tiptoed quickly back down the hallway. He realized he wouldn't be able to reach the back door, so he slipped into the junk room.

He could hear the woman muttering under her breath and the moan of the wooden floor under her feet. It sounded as if she'd gone into the living room. To watch from the window to make sure Hud was leaving?

Silence, and then the creak and moan of the floor. She was dialing someone on her cell phone. He could hear that distinctive *beep, beep, beep* with each number she touched, then the sound of ringing.

He realized she must be standing just outside his door in the hallway by her bedroom.

"The marshal was just here," she said by way of introduction when the other end answered. Silence, then, "You *know* what I told him. That I didn't know where you were. He knew I'd come to see you just before you got out." Another beat. "No, he left. I need my money. No, I don't want to come up there. You know how I hate that road."

More silence. He heard her grunt a couple of times, then argue that she was coming to get what was hers.

"Fine. I'll wait until dark, and then I'll drive up… Why do you say that?…Stop being so paranoid. So your name is on some list. What does that prove?…Stop yelling at me. You're the one who got us into this." She sighed and he heard the creak and groan of her footfalls as she moved away.

He held his breath, thinking what the marshal had said to him on their way back into town earlier. "You're not trained for this. You have no idea what you're getting yourself into, just how dangerous it is."

Tag had mentally argued that he did know. But at this moment, he had to admit, he was just starting to realize how out of his league he really was.

Chapter Thirteen

Hud had planned to wait around and see if Wilma Emery made a move. He figured if she knew where her husband was, she might go to him. Or at least contact him.

But as he drove away down the road and pulled over, he got a call from his father-in-law.

"I've got some news," Angus said. "Can you meet me at your house?"

Hud figured if Angus talked to Harlan, he knew about the list, knew that his son-in-law's name was on it. "I'll be right there."

He drove home, ready to pack up his family and send them anywhere that might be safe. He wasn't running because he knew there was no place he would ever feel safe. He felt more alive than he had in months.

When he walked into his house, he saw that Angus hadn't said anything to his daughter about what was going on. No doubt he was waiting for Hud to tell her about the murder list and about his name being on it.

"Dad is back from his business trip," Dana said when he came through the door.

"I can see that. Honey, I need to talk to your dad…."

"I should check on the kids," Dana said, getting to her feet.

Hud was surprised she would leave them alone so quickly. It wasn't like her. He saw her send a curious glance toward them as she climbed the stairs, but she said nothing more. Nor did he and Angus until they heard her close the upstairs bedroom door.

He turned on his father-in-law. "If this is about the list—"

Angus was on his feet, finger to his lips, head cocked toward the kitchen.

Hud followed him. "Lily McCabe is missing. Tag has taken off looking for her only God knows where," he whispered once they were in the kitchen. "I'm sure Harlan told you about the list." He pulled the paper from his pocket and shoved it at his father-in-law. "Lily McCabe was decoding it."

He couldn't help being angry because he'd come into this so late. Until Mia Duncan had died, he thought both Angus and Harlan were out of this business. He'd had no idea that they were still involved in these kinds of things. Like Dana, he didn't pay much attention when either came or went. Until now.

"You should have trusted me," he said as he watched Angus take in the names on the paper. He didn't seem surprised—not even that his son-in-law's name was there.

Paul Brown was dead. Hud hadn't wanted to believe these lists even existed. But now he was staring the truth in the face. Worse, he didn't know who would be coming after him.

After a moment, Angus turned on the water, just letting it run into the sink, before he answered. "Where did you get this list?"

Hud told him what Tag had told him.

"Do you have the thumb drive?"

"Yes, but Tag has a copy. He plans to trade it for Lily."

Angus nodded. "This list," he said, wadding up the paper in his hand and tossing it into the garbage, "isn't the right one."

"What?"

"Lily McCabe must have decoded it wrong or Mia passed the wrong one."

Hud raked a hand through his hair. "Then my name isn't on the list?" He saw the answer in his father-in-law's expression and swore under his breath.

"Harlan's in Billings at the women's prison."

Hud felt his stomach roil. "You're telling me Camilla is the one who put the hit out on me?" He knew that shouldn't have come as a surprise, not after what had happened the day Camilla was sentenced.

As she was being taken from the room, she was led past him. She stopped just inches from him.

"I will get you if it's the last thing I do," she whispered through one of her innocent smiles. "You *and* your family." Then she'd laughed as they'd dragged her away. He'd been hearing that laugh in his sleep for months.

Angus met his gaze. "It's more complicated than that."

There was both compassion and fear in the older man's gaze. Hud didn't even need to hear the rest. He knew. He'd known deep in his soul that this wasn't over. That it wouldn't be over until that crazy woman was dead.

"Camilla Northland has been taken to the hospital," Angus said. "She got into an altercation with two other inmates in the laundry room. Harlan hasn't been able to talk to her yet. But with this hit out on you, we need to get Dana and the kids out of here."

TUGGING OFF HIS Stetson, Hud ran a hand through his hair. The sun had set, and deep shadows had filled in under the pines.

"How do you suggest we get your wife and children away from here two days before Christmas?" Angus asked.

He knew his wife. "We have to tell her the truth. She has a right to know. She's strong. She'll—"

"She won't leave you, you should know that."

"Yes, he should know that," Dana said from the kitchen doorway.

DARKNESS CAME ON quickly in the canyon. From a silky gray as the sun passed behind Lone Mountain, the canyon took on a chill even in the summer.

In the winter once the sun was gone, the canyon became an icebox. Even if the snow on the roads had thawed during a warm December day, the melt now froze solid, the roads suddenly becoming ice-skating rinks.

Tag didn't see the dark coming, but he felt it. Wilma Emery had been moving restlessly around the cabin. He thought he heard her packing, the closet door in the bedroom across the hall opening, the *ting* of metal hangers as clothes were pulled off them, then the sound of dresser drawers being opened and closed.

She dragged something heavy from the bedroom and down the hall toward the front door. He knew he would have to move fast once she left. Not the river route he'd taken to get here. He would have to reach his father's pickup quickly if he hoped to tail her. He couldn't lose her.

He heard the front door open, followed by a series of grunts and groans and bumps and scrapes; then the door slammed shut.

Tag counted to five and opened the storeroom door. No sound came from the front of the cabin. Hurriedly he moved to the living room and peeked out of a crack in the curtains.

A solid-looking woman was shoving a huge duffel bag into the back of an older dark-colored large Suburban.

He hurried out through the back, the way he'd come in, and worked his way along the side of the cabin in time to see her go back into the cabin. He knew he was taking a chance, but he rushed down the road toward where he'd left his father's truck.

Behind him he heard the sound of an engine kick over. The dual golden beams of headlights shot across the frozen expanse to his left. He rushed into the pines and hurriedly climbed behind the wheel of the old pickup. As he slid down in the seat, the lights of the Suburban washed through the cab.

He held his breath, listening, half expecting the Suburban to slow, and then stop. There was no doubt in his mind that Wilma Emery was armed and dangerous. Or that he was in over his head.

But she didn't slow, didn't stop and a moment later the cab of the pickup went dark again. He sat up, heart pounding. As the Suburban headed out the narrow snowy unpaved road, he noticed that the right taillight had burned out.

Tag doubted that the woman would check her rearview mirror, but he couldn't take the chance. He waited until Wilma was almost to the highway.

He'd purposely left the key in the ignition, afraid he might lose it on his hike along the river to the cabin.

Now he pressed down on the clutch and brake and turned the key as he watched the Suburban turn onto the highway. The engine groaned but didn't turn over.

"Don't do this," he said to the truck. "Not now." He tried again. The engine groaned. "No!" He could see Wilma getting away. She was headed to meet her husband—and Ray Emery had Lily. He was sure of it.

He prayed that the pickup would start and tried it again. The engine groaned, but sparked and turned over. It was feeble. The cold engine vibrated the whole pickup as it rumbled.

Tag feared it would die and not start again, but when he put it in gear and let his foot off the clutch, it lurched forward out of the pines. He didn't turn on his headlights, following the darker shadows of the ruts through the snow, until he reached the highway.

He'd seen Wilma turn left onto the highway—away from Big Sky. Tag did the same. He couldn't go too fast. The highway was shiny in his headlights when he turned them on and he could feel the tires slipping on the glaze of ice on the pavement.

The highway was a crooked snake that wriggled through the Gallatin Canyon. This far south of Big Sky, there was little traffic. Skiers would have made their way home by now.

By the second bend in the road and no sign of Wilma Emery, he was starting to panic. Had she turned off? He had been watching, but there were few side roads along here.

Another curve and he saw the one red taillight shining in the distance. His pulse began to drop back to normal. *I'm coming, Lily. Hang on.*

LILY PRAYED FOR darkness, hoping that whoever was upstairs would need sleep. She didn't dare try anything as long as they were moving around up there.

Earlier she'd heard a male voice and figured he must be talking on the phone, but she couldn't make out what he was saying. Her stomach churned at the thought of them talking about her. Talking about what to do with her.

She felt confused. She'd thought they wanted the thumb drive. It was the only thing that made sense. But if that were the case, why hadn't they taken the papers from her purse with the names on them?

And if they didn't want the thumb drive, then why were they still keeping her alive? It didn't make any sense.

She moved to the door again and peered through at the tiny spots of light around the key. She was so tempted to try to get out that if it hadn't been for the sound of footfalls upstairs, she would have tried to get the key.

Hurrying back to the mattress, she curled against the cold pine wall and stared at the door, fearing one or both of them would come down at any moment and kill her.

At the sound of a door slamming upstairs, she froze. Had he left? She waited, praying that he'd left her here alone, because from what she could tell, there was only one man upstairs. She'd seen only one man since she'd been grabbed in the parking lot of the motel.

She heard a door open and close again, then the creak of the floorboards over her head, and knew she wasn't alone. She hugged herself and waited for the darkness outside the window to settle in and hopefully lull her abductor to sleep.

"TELL ME," DANA said as she stepped into the kitchen.

Hud saw her grab the edge of the kitchen table as if she knew she was going to need to hang on to something. He looked at his father-in-law, then at his wife. Dana was strong. She'd weathered many storms on this ranch. She'd single-handedly fought her siblings for the land that was her legacy.

"Someone has put a hit out on me," he said simply.

She nodded, glanced toward the kitchen window. A nervous laugh escaped her lips. She quickly quelled it. "Dee. I mean Camilla." Camilla had come to them pretending to be Dee Ann Justice, a long-lost cousin. "She's the one who put the hit on you, isn't she?"

When Hud didn't answer, she glanced at her father.

"We think it's a possibility," Angus said. His cell phone rang. "I have to take this." He stepped out of the room.

"Do you know who?"

"Apparently some inmates have gotten together and started a co-op type of murder list," Hud said, ignoring the disapproving look Angus gave him from just outside the kitchen. "It will probably be an ex-inmate coming for me. That's why you need to take the kids and leave. Go to my father's. I can call Brick—"

Dana shook her head. "We're safer here, especially if Camilla is involved. She knows everything about us, remember? The first place she would look for us would be Brick's—if she didn't have someone lying in wait for us along the way to West Yellowstone."

Angus stepped back into the room. "I'm sorry, but I have to go."

Hud nodded. Dana studied her father, and then quickly moved to plant a kiss on his check.

"Be careful," she whispered.

"Will you two be—"

"We'll manage," Hud snapped, then softened his tone with his father-in-law as he said, "Go. We'll be fine."

"We will be fine," Dana said, and stepped into her husband's arms. Hud held her tight, more afraid than he wanted to admit that they wouldn't be fine. Far from it.

TAG'S PULSE POUNDED in his ears as he stayed back just enough that he would catch sight of the one red taillight every few turns.

At the mouth of the canyon, Wilma slowed, crossed the bridge and turned onto the old river road.

Tag pulled off just before the bridge in a wide spot and waited. He could see her taillight for some distance now. He waited until he couldn't stand it anymore, then crossed the bridge and turned down the narrow old road.

Out of the canyon now, he could see stars in the clear night sky. They glittered from the midnight-blue canopy overhead. As he drove, the moon came up from behind the mountains to the east, a bright white orb that lit the fallen snow.

Ahead, Wilma's taillight blinked as she braked and turned down a road that led toward the river. He lost sight of her in the thick cottonwoods, but he knew she couldn't go far before she ran into the river.

He found a place up the road to pull over, then started to climb out of the pickup. Hud's words came back to him again. He had no idea what he was going to find down that road.

On a hunch, he reached under the pickup's seat. He found an ax handle. All kinds of other junk. No old pistol. He was disappointed in his father. Nor was there a shotgun or even a .22 rifle hanging from the rack behind the seat.

He tried the glove box and was about to give up and see if he could find at least a tire iron, when he noticed something interesting about the passenger-side floorboard.

He lifted a flap in the rubber mat and saw the handle. When he lifted it, he found more than he'd hoped for.

Until that moment, he hadn't really believed his father was an agent of any kind.

But as he pulled out a Glock handgun, then a sawed-off shotgun—both loaded—he became a believer. Sticking the Glock into the back waistband of his jeans, he hoisted the shotgun, grabbed a pocketful of shells and headed down the road.

Chapter Fourteen

There were two things Tag's father had taught his older sons before they left Montana—to swim and to shoot a gun.

"I'm not having one of my boys drowning in the river because he can't swim," Harlan had told their mother. "And they're going to learn to shoot."

"They're too young," she'd cried as he loaded them into the pickup.

They'd learned to swim in a small deep eddy down in the Gallatin on a warm summer day. Not that the water had been warm. Rivers and lakes in most of Montana never warmed up that much.

But each of them had learned. His father's method hadn't been exactly mother approved. He'd tossed them in one at a time. Sink or swim. They'd learned to swim, kicking and screaming.

With shooting that hadn't been the case. They were boys, after all. Harlan had been strict about safety as well as learning how to load, clean and shoot a gun.

Now as Tag approached the 1940s-looking cabin, he snapped off the safety on the shotgun.

The snow crunched under his feet as he walked. He thought about calling the marshal. Not until he knew for certain that Lily was down here. He still wasn't sure he could trust Hud. The man had been ready to put him on a plane.

Without a cloud in the night sky, the temperature had dropped. His breath came out frosty and white. The moon lit the land, making the snow look like white marble. In the cottonwoods, deep shadows filled the road's ruts. It was hard to see where he was walking. A couple of times he slipped in the icy tracks and almost fell but managed to catch himself.

Tag thought of his brothers. They wouldn't believe it if they saw him, armed and tromping through a dark, snowy night to save a woman. He'd had relationships. He'd just never met a woman who he would have been tromping through a dark and snowy night to save.

Worse, he and Lily didn't even have a relationship. Hell, for all he knew she was planning to go back to her former fiancé. Jealousy dug under his skin at the thought.

Either way, he had to find her.

Ahead, he spotted Wilma's SUV parked in front of the cabin, only this one had a basement. One lone light burned in a window close to the ground at the other end of the building. Inside the house proper, lights blazed.

Tag glanced around. There was no other vehicle. That bothered him. Had someone left but was planning to be back at any time? That seemed more likely than that whoever Wilma had talked to was staying here without transportation.

The thought made him nervous. It was that ticking clock he'd been hearing in his ear since he'd realized Lily was missing. But now it seemed to be ticking even faster.

Move.

He did, through the deep snow, toward the corner

of the house that was the darkest. He could smell the river bottom, the scent of decayed leaves that haunted every riverbed.

As he drew nearer to the house, he could hear raised voices, a woman's and a man's. Edging along the side of the house, he got as close to the front window as he could without being seen.

He took a quick peek. Wilma and the man he'd seen help Mia into a pickup that night behind the bar. The two were standing at the edge of the living room arguing. The man had a gun in his hand. He appeared to be threatening Wilma with it.

Tag's cell phone vibrated in his pocket, making him jump.

CAMILLA KNEW IT was just a matter of time before Marshal Hud Savage learned that she had escaped from the hospital.

She would have liked to check into a motel for a few days, get her strength back, heal. But she couldn't chance it. As bad a shape as she was in from her beating, checking into a motel the way she looked would be dangerous. Not only that, but it would give Hud time to get ready for her.

True to her word, Snakebite had seen that everything she needed had been waiting for her on the outside. She had a vehicle, weapons and what tools she might need. She smiled even though it hurt her mouth to do so.

By now the marshal would have heard that she had been taken to the hospital. He was too smart not to know she might be using it to escape. That Hud would be expecting the worst made it all the more delicious. She had to assume the marshal's office would be guarded.

So would the ranch house. Fortunately, Hud was a lawman through and through. His one Achilles' heel was that he couldn't resist anyone in trouble.

She'd gotten word that he would soon be headed for a cabin down the canyon where a woman named Lily McCabe was being held captive. Camilla was in awe of the working prison network. Hud being called away from the house would buy her valuable time to take care of a few things in his absence.

That and the fact that she knew the ranch layout—even in the dead of night—would make her plan work. She didn't need to worry about getting away. The worst they could do to her was lock her up again. She was already looking at life in prison. There was no way Hud would ever have let her get paroled, and now that she'd escaped, even more years would be added on to her sentence.

If only Hud had wanted her, she thought. They could have been happy together. He would have gotten over the loss of Dana and the kids. At least that was what she'd told herself last spring. She'd wanted him. Deserved a man like him. She'd thought her life would have been so different if a good man had come into it sooner.

But he hadn't wanted her. He'd wanted Dana. She made a face at the memory of sweet Dana and her children. They were always baking cookies and making a racket. And Hud... A hard knot formed high in her chest at the memory of how he had rejected her. The one man she would have done anything for, and he'd rejected her.

Camilla pushed those thoughts away as she drove toward the Gallatin Canyon. She had a mission. Hud would soon know she was coming. She smiled. He just wouldn't be expecting what she had planned for him.

Tag's phone vibrated again. He felt his heart quicken as he realized that the man and woman inside the house weren't on a phone.

He edged away from the window and into the nearby pines, answering the phone on its third ring.

"Hello." He waited. He could hear someone breathing on the other end of line. "What?" he demanded.

"Don't be so impatient."

He didn't recognize the voice as he moved so he had a view of the living room—and the two people standing nearby in the kitchen doorway. They were both facing each other, still having a serious talk.

Tag had to assume the person on the phone wasn't inside this building.

Who the devil was this on the phone, then?

"What do you want?" he asked, stepping back into the snowy pines out of sight.

"You know what I want."

"Do I?"

A low chuckle.

"What about what I want?" Tag asked, half afraid of saying Lily's name. What if there were more people looking for the thumb drive than he knew?

"Your girlfriend?"

He breathed a sigh of relief even though Lily was far from his girlfriend. Then he had a thought. "What makes you think she's my girlfriend?"

Another chuckle. "I was giving you the benefit of the doubt after what I saw through her bedroom window last night."

His heart dropped at the realization that the man who'd run him off the road had followed him to Lily's. He hadn't seen anyone, but he'd left tracks in the falling snow. He'd led the man right to Lily.

"I want to know that she's all right," Tag said. "Let me talk to her."

"That isn't an option right now even though I can assure you, she is fine."

"Not good enough." He'd seen enough movies to know he needed to have proof that she was still alive. What he really wanted to know was if the man was in the house—and if not, where was he?

"Give me a little time," the man said on the other end of the line. "Ten minutes. Then I'll call you back. You'd better have what I want." The man disconnected.

Tag could still hear the two in the house arguing. He quickly backtracked down the side of the house and around to the back. He heard nothing at any of the windows, but when he reached the basement one with the lone light, he bent down, dug away some of the snow and peered in.

What he saw made his heart beat faster. A tray with a consumed TV dinner on it, an empty bottle of water and a used napkin.

Lily was here. He knew it.

He moved to one of the dark basement windows. As he cleared away the snow, he saw that the glass opening was small. Too small for a person to climb out.

He bent down and tried to peer in. The glass was filthy. He wiped at it with a handful of snow and heard a sound on the other side. Stepping back out of sight, he watched the window out of the corner of his eye. A hand touched the glass. A small, female hand.

Tag quickly bent down again. The basement room was too dark for him to see more than a shadowy figure at first. Then she put her face nearer to the glass and he saw her. His heart almost burst from his chest.

DANA HAD GONE upstairs to check on the kids when Hud's cell phone rang. He took the call even though he didn't recognize the number.

"I know where Lily McCabe is," the woman's voice on the other end of the line said.

"Who is this?" He recognized the voice. Wilma Emery. But he didn't call her on it, fearing she might hang up.

"Never mind that. They're holding her at a cabin." The woman gave him hurried directions. "You better make it fast or they will kill her like they—" There was what sounded like a struggle, and then the line went dead.

Hud swore as he disconnected and looked up as his wife came down the stairs.

"What is it?" she asked.

"Wilma Emery just called. She sounded scared. She told me where they're holding Lily McCabe. I don't like the way the call ended."

Dana's eyes widened in alarm as her hand went to her mouth. "What if this is only a ruse to get you to..." Tears filled her eyes.

"I can't leave you and the kids."

She made quick swipe at her tears and seemed to pull herself together, the way she always did when the going got tough. "You have to go. The kids and I will be fine."

His cell phone rang again. He swore when he saw it was Tag Cardwell calling. "Where are you?" he demanded as he stepped out of the kitchen and earshot of his wife.

"I've found Lily."

Hud listened as Tag gave him the same directions to the cabin on the river that Wilma had given him.

"I'll be right there. Just wait. Don't do anything, do you hear me?"

Tag didn't answer and Hud realized he'd hung up. With a curse, he looked to his wife.

"Go."

He knew he had no choice. He was still the marshal. "Please, Dana, I need you to leave with the kids. Get packed while I'm gone."

"Camilla's in the hospital. They'd let us know if she wasn't." She stepped to him, drawing him into a tight hug. "You just worry about coming back to us safe and sound."

"Always."

CAMILLA FINISHED TAPING her ribs in the filling station bathroom. The antiseptic smell of the recently cleaned restroom made her hold her breath. Not that breathing was all that easy with her cracked ribs.

How long before the hospital realized she was gone? She smiled since her ruse would have bought her time.

As she let her gaze lift to the metal mirror over the sink, she was startled because she didn't recognize herself. Her face was swollen and bruised in shades of grays and yellows. Her right eye was black and almost swollen shut.

There was still dried blood on the cut on her upper lip. She was missing a front tooth.

Camilla let out a small laugh, which she quickly killed because it hurt her chest.

"How do you think you're going to do anything as messed up as you are?" she asked the woman in the mirror.

The clock was ticking since she knew every cop in

the state would be looking for her soon. She'd split right away from the other inmate she'd escaped with.

There wasn't safety in numbers—not with them looking as bad as they did. She'd held her own in the fight and done as much damage as she could. She also knew she would attract less attention on her own.

Her face would heal. So would her cracked ribs. But she couldn't take the time. She had everything she needed: a vehicle, money, weapons. The problem was everyone would know where she was heading.

"You could get out of the country," she told her reflection. "You don't have to do this."

Her eyes narrowed at the thought. "You could go to some warm tropical place and sip tropical drinks with the locals." She smiled at the thought, but knew that wasn't her M.O.

She couldn't live with herself if she didn't finish this. Hud would be expecting her to come for him—especially after he heard about the prison break.

He would whisk Dana and the kids off somewhere, thinking they would be safe. Hud wouldn't run, she thought with a lopsided smile. He would think he could best her at whatever she had planned for him.

She loved nothing better than a challenge. Even beat up and in pain, she felt up to it. Hud would be off saving some other damsel in distress. It would give her plenty of time to take care of things at the ranch before he returned.

She could hardly contain her excitement at seeing Hud Savage again. *Soon, Hud.*

TAG KNELT DOWN by the window. Lily was trying to tell him something, but he couldn't hear her. He motioned for her to move back. He could still hear Wilma and the man he suspected was her ex-husband, Ray Emery, arguing even more loudly from another part of the cabin.

He hoped they were far enough away and the basement deep enough that they wouldn't hear what he was about to do. Wrapping the butt of the shotgun around the tail end of his coat, he leaned down and smashed the glass. The sound felt like a gunshot, it was so loud to him.

He listened, afraid the others had heard it. But with staggering relief, he heard the two inside the house still arguing.

"Are you all right?" he asked the moment Lily appeared at the small broken window. He could see her, but he ached to take her in his arms. It was the only way he could convince himself that she truly was all right.

She nodded, looking scared but definitely relieved to see him.

"How many people are in the house?"

She shook her head. "Someone left earlier. I've only seen one man, but I heard someone come a little while ago. It sounds like a woman."

So there was just the redheaded man and Wilma.

"I think the one just got out of prison."

He could feel the cold seeping in through the knees of his jeans as he knelt on the ground. Time was passing. The man on the phone said he would call back in ten minutes—and let him talk to Lily. He had to move quickly.

"I know how you feel about guns, but I'm afraid you're going to need this," he said as he pulled the Glock from behind him and handed it to her through the window. "It's ready to go. All you have to do is pull the trigger. Aim for the largest part of the body." He saw her cringe. "You can do this."

She nodded, a determined look settling on her features.

He gave her a smile, then pulled off his glove and reached through the broken window to touch her face with his fingertips. She closed her eyes, leaning into his warm palm. Tears beaded her lashes when he pulled his hand away.

"I'll be down to get you in a few minutes. If anyone else comes through the door, shoot them."

With that, he stood. From inside the house came the loud report of a gunshot followed by a scream and another gunshot. Tag grabbed the shotgun and ran toward the front of the house.

LILY LISTENED. She heard nothing overhead following the two gunshots and the scream. Her heart was beating like a war drum. Tag had come for her. She'd known he would. He was that kind of cowboy. Wasn't that why she'd made love with him last night? She'd known the kind of man he was. Otherwise, she would never have—

Another gunshot and the pounding of footfalls. She held her breath as she looked toward the door, then down at the gun in her hand. Her heart was in her throat now. Was Tag all right? He'd come to save her, but what if—

She couldn't bear to let herself even think it.

She had to get out of here. She couldn't just stand here waiting for that door to open. Dropping the gun onto the mattress, she moved to the door, willing her trembling to stop.

When she'd heard someone at the window, she'd been just about to push the piece of paper she'd written the codes on under the door. In a perfect world, once she pushed the key through from her side, it would fall on the sheet of paper and she would pull it through. Once she had the key, she could open the door.

This wasn't like any mathematical problem she'd ever come across. This was her life. She didn't know why they had kept her alive. But she feared all of that had now changed. They would kill her and Tag if they got the chance.

She'd held her breath, waiting and praying that the next sound she heard was Tag's voice on the other side of the door.

But there had been nothing.

Lily didn't know how long she'd waited. Until she couldn't take it any longer.

Finally she pushed the sheet of paper slowly under the door, her heart in her throat. She half expected the paper to be jerked away, the door to fly open…

But nothing happened.

Now, willing her fingers not to tremble, she used the piece of plastic fork she'd kept to carefully poke gently into the keyhole.

She felt the key move. If she pushed too hard, the key would fall out—away from the door and the paper she'd pushed under the door.

Too slowly and she chanced that someone would come downstairs—someone other than Tag.

She pushed and prayed and a moment later she heard the key fall and land with a *clink*.

Her heart dropped. It sounded as if the key had missed the sheet of paper. Now it would be out of her reach.

She could barely stand even the thought as she knelt down to see where the key had gone. To her shock, she saw it lying half on, half off the paper.

Her fingers were trembling too hard for her to touch the sheet of paper and try to pull it back inside the room.

She took deep breaths. She had one chance. She stilled her trembling as she knelt farther down and at a snail's pace, she began to pull the corner of the paper with the key hanging off it toward her.

The light caught on the key. It flashed, so close now that she could almost feel it in her hand when she opened the door.

A huge foot suddenly stomped down on the key and sheet of paper. She let out a scream before she could catch herself and fell back on her butt.

As the man put the key in the lock and threw open the door, she scuttled backward, unable to get her feet under her quickly enough to stand.

The large man loomed over her, sans his mask. The light caught on the gun in his hand as he raised it, the barrel pointed at her chest.

"You're too smart for your own good," the man said.

The gunshot was deafening in the basement room. Lily didn't realize that she'd closed her eyes until she opened them to find the man still standing over her.

He had an odd expression on his face.

Lily looked down expecting to see blood, expecting to feel life leaking from her. When she saw nothing, she looked back up in time to see him falling toward her.

She rolled away at the last instant. As he fell face-first within inches of her, she saw the hole in the back of his shirt and the blood seeping out.

As a shadow filled the doorway, her gaze swung to it. The next moment she was in Tag's arms and he was holding her. "We have to get out of here," Tag whispered next to her ear, but he moved as if he couldn't bear letting her go.

She nodded against his chest, then drew back to look at the man lying on the basement floor. "Is he…?"

Tag didn't answer. He picked up the Glock from the mattress, took her hand and led her up the stairs. As they neared the top, he motioned for her to stay back.

She caught only a glimpse of a woman's body lying on the floor near the kitchen as Tag hurriedly drew her toward the outside door. "Was that—"

"Ray Emery's wife. The two of them were arguing. He killed her before I came in."

They stepped out into the cold, wintery night. The sky was ebony and adorned with tiny white jewels. A moon washed over the snow, turning it to alabaster. The freezing air stole her breath. That and the sound of a vehicle roaring toward the cabin, the lights bobbing on the rough snow-packed road.

TAG DREW LILY toward a barn on the back of the property. As they slipped into the pitch-black, he held her to him for a moment until his eyes adjusted to the light.

Now if he could just get Lily out of here. He could hear the sound of the vehicle's engine growing louder. Not the marshal. Not the way the rig was roaring down the road without flashing lights or a siren. No, it was probably whoever he'd spoken to earlier on the phone.

His eyes finally adjusted to the darkness. They fell on the large snowmobile at the door. He stepped away from Lily for a moment to feel if the key was in it. It was.

"When I start the snowmobile's engine, open the barn door the rest of the way and hop on," he told Lily as they heard two car doors slam, followed by shouts from the house moments later.

He started the snowmobile and threw it into gear, as

Lily swung the door wide. He pulled her on as he hit the gas and burst out into the freezing night.

The headlight of the snowmobile bobbed as they took off, racing through the deep snow of the field. Tag headed for a stand of pines, knowing that as long as they were in the open field, they were too perfect a target.

A bullet whizzed past.

Lily wrapped her arms around his waist as they sped across the field, the snowmobile busting through drifts and sending up a cloud of fresh snow. The air filled with ice crystals as it blew past. Moonbeams played over the surface of the fresh-fallen snow. The winter night seemed to be holding its breath.

When Tag dared look back, he saw the light of another snowmobile coming after them.

Chapter Fifteen

As Hud raced toward the cabin where Tag had said Lily McCabe was being held, the urgent call came in from Harlan.

"Camilla Northland has escaped from prison."

The words hit like a sledgehammer. He tried to breathe, to keep his heart from banging out of his chest. Ahead, he could see the turnoff into the cabin. All he managed to say was, "How long ago?"

"Four hours ago."

"Four hours! Wasn't there a guard outside her door?"

"She got the jump on him. Unfortunately there was a bus accident and the doctors and nurses were busy…."

Four hours would give Camilla plenty of time to get to where she was headed. For all he knew, Camilla was in Big Sky. Even on the ranch. There was no doubt in his mind that she would be coming after him and his family.

Hud fought to take a breath. Fear paralyzed him for a moment. Fear, and the memory of just how far that crazy psychopath of a woman would go to get what she wanted.

He touched his brakes at the turnoff and swung down the old river road. "How?"

"She'd gotten into an altercation with two other women. They were all taken to the hospital because of their injuries. Two of them escaped. Camilla was one of them."

All these months when Dana had been afraid that Camilla would find a way to come after them again, he'd told her not to worry. That Camilla was never getting out of prison. That she could never get to them again.

"She's on her way to the ranch if she isn't already there," he said, hoping Harlan could tell him otherwise.

Instead, the former agent said, "I just talked to Angus. He's headed back there now. I'm on my way, but I can send a deputy—"

"Does Dana know?"

"Angus hasn't told her yet."

"Tell him to call and tell her. I'll be there as soon as I can." He hung up. It took everything in him not to turn around and race toward the ranch. But Tag Cardwell and Lily McCabe were in the cabin ahead. He couldn't let them die even to save his own family.

Ahead he saw two snowmobiles racing toward him.

CAMILLA MOVED THROUGH the dark toward the house. Her ribs hurt. She stopped and had to shift the gun stuck in her waistband. The snow was deeper than she'd thought it would be and had worn her out quickly. Either that or she was in worse shape from the fight than she thought.

In the distance she could see the lights on at the ranch house. Had Dana heard yet that her "cousin" was on the way? Had Hud?

She'd checked before she began her hike. The marshal was still involved in the showdown by the river. Subterfuge at its best.

Camilla pushed on through the fallen snow until she reached the backside of the house. When she'd stayed here last April, she'd come and gone in the middle of the night several times. She'd learned the darkest parts of the yard and the best way to enter so as not to be seen.

Nearing the house, she slowed to catch her breath. Hud's patrol rig wasn't parked out front. She had to believe her information was correct and Hud was still involved down the canyon.

She tried the door. Locked. She smiled, realizing she would have been disappointed if Dana had left the door open for her.

She glanced at her watch. Dana was a creature of habit. She would be upstairs putting the kids to bed right now.

It took only a few moments to pick the lock and, easing the door open, slip inside.

THE WHINE OF the snowmobile behind them grew louder. Tag ventured a look back. He'd gotten Lily into this. He had to get her out. Another bullet zinged past, this one so close it took his breath away. The pines were ahead. Just a little farther and they would be in the trees.

He didn't see the dip in the snow until it was too late. The snowmobile roared down into it, but the skis caught in the deep snow and then hit the ground underneath.

Tag flung the two of them to the side as the snowmobile nose-dived. He rolled. He felt Lily slam into him as they hit the ground and were instantly covered with snow.

He came up only to be blinded by the lights of the other snowmobile. The light suddenly shut off as the sound of the snowmobile motor died and a large dark figure loomed over them.

Tag pulled her closer so his body shielded hers. He could see the shotgun lying just feet away. The snowmobile, its engine still running, its lights dim, buried in the deep snow, idled just feet away.

The moonlight caught the glint of metal as the man pulled a gun from his coat. "The two of you have caused nothing but problems," he said between gritted teeth. "All you had to do was give us the damned flash drive." He aimed the gun at Tag's chest. "Hand it over now or I'll take it off your body. Which is it going to be?"

Tag dug in his pocket and pulled out the computer thumb drive. He tossed it to the man, knowing the man would miss it. The small device fell into the deep snow, making the man swear.

Behind Tag, he felt Lily loosen her hold on him, felt her take the pistol from his pocket. She raised the gun. He could feel her trembling, the hand holding the gun shaking. The killer saw it, too. She couldn't pull the trigger.

Tag lunged for the shotgun lying next to the snowmobile in the snow. The sound of the gunshot made him flinch. He heard Lily cry out. For a moment, he thought she'd pulled the trigger. But the shot had come from farther away.

The man standing over them appeared surprised as he looked down at his chest. The gun in his hand wavered, then fell from his fingers into the deep snow. The second shot dropped the man.

Marshal Hud Savage waded toward them through the snow. Behind Tag, Lily was crying and saying, "I just couldn't pull the trigger. I just couldn't."

Tag took her in his arms, assuring her that it didn't matter, but he could tell that it did matter much more than it should have to her.

AS CAMILLA CAME around the corner from the kitchen, Dana came face-to-face with the woman she'd thought was her cousin only months before.

"Dee—" She caught herself. "I'm sorry, it's Camilla, isn't it?"

"Actually I go by Spark now." She smiled but didn't raise the gun she clutched at her side.

"Cute," Dana said, still surprised how much the two of them resembled each other even though they shared no blood. It had made it so easy for Camilla to pretend to be her cousin. Dana hated how vulnerable she'd been just months ago.

"What now?" Camilla asked, still smiling.

"I guess that's up to you. I always wondered what I would do if I ever saw you again."

"Really?" Her gaze went to the shotgun in Dana's hands, the barrel aimed at her heart. "And now here we are. You know, we would have made great cousins. We're so much alike."

"We're nothing alike," Dana snapped.

Camilla's smile wasn't quite as self-assured as it had been. "Are you sure about that?" She looked past Dana. "I thought you would be putting your children to bed." She cocked her head. "I don't hear the patter of their little feet."

"They aren't here. They're with Hilde."

"Hilde, your good and loyal friend," Camilla scoffed.

"You tried to destroy that friendship, but you failed."

"I'm surprised your *good* friend would leave you, knowing what you were up to."

"I talked her into taking the children so I could get packed to leave since you'd put a hit out on my husband."

Camilla raised an eyebrow. "I don't see you packing."

"No, I've just been waiting for you. You wouldn't just want Hud. You'd come after me and my children again. I decided to get it over with."

"You were that sure I'd come here?"

Dana smiled. "I knew you couldn't let anyone else do your dirty work. You enjoy it too much."

"You might have more backbone than I thought." She glanced toward the front window. "Or you're expecting your husband to come save you."

Dana laughed softly. "You think I'm weak, certainly no match for you, since you were able to fool me so easily, isn't that right?"

Camilla didn't bother to answer, the truth in her smirk. "I bet that shotgun isn't even loaded."

Dana laughed. "Wanna bet?"

"Have you ever killed anyone?" Camilla sighed. "It's not easy. You'll have to live with what you've done."

Dana laughed again. "How would you know anything about living with what you've done? You have no conscience."

"You're wrong. I never wanted to do the things I've done. If I could do it over—"

"That won't work with me anymore," Dana interrupted. "I know you. I can see into the darkness where your soul should be."

Camilla smiled and took a step toward Dana.

"I wouldn't do that if I were you."

"You don't have what it takes. I can see it in your eyes. I'm betting I can raise my gun and fire before you have the guts to pull that trigger."

"That will be the bet of a dead woman."

Camilla stopped moving. Her fingers holding the pistol at her side twitched. "I'm beginning to see what Hud sees in you. Where is he, by the way?"

"Right behind you," Dana said.

"You expect me to fall for that? I turn around and

you jump me?" Camilla shook her head. "What we have here is a standoff. I shoot you. You shoot me."

"Except I have a shotgun which means after I shoot you, you won't be going back to prison so you can escape again and hurt someone else. Nor will I live in fear anymore. This ends here."

HUD HEARD THE shots as he raced toward the front door of his ranch house. He burst in, gun in hand, to find his wife on the floor in a pool of blood. A few feet away, Camilla Northland was struggling to get to her feet. Her left side was a mass of torn bloody fabric. But one look at her and he knew she would survive this—just as she had survived everything else in her life.

The marshal stepped to her quickly and smashed his boot heel into the hand holding the pistol. She didn't even make a sound as he kicked the gun out of the way and rushed to his wife.

"Call 911," he yelled as Tag Cardwell appeared in the open doorway. Hud had told Tag and Lily to stay in the patrol vehicle. He wasn't surprised that Tag hadn't.

"Dana," Hud cried. "Dana, can you hear me?" Leaning down, he placed his head to her chest and with a groan of relief, felt it rise and fall. She was still alive.

Tag was on the phone with the 911 operator. In the distance, Hud could hear the sound of sirens. He saw the crease along his wife's skull where the bullet had grazed her. She was losing blood fast. He quickly yanked off his jacket and shirt and pressed the shirt to her wound as a shadow fell over him.

"Look out!" Tag cried.

As Hud spun around, he instinctively picked up the shotgun lying beside his wife. Camilla loomed over him, a knife raised high. But it was the expression on her face that froze his breath in his throat. She was smiling broadly, her eyes as bright as the moonlight on the snow outside.

She drove down with the blade, aiming for his heart. He rocked back, raised the barrel and fired. As he rolled to the side at the last minute, the knife plunged past him so close he thought he'd felt the whisper of the blade, which stuck in the floor as Camilla fell on top of him. With disgust, he shoved her body aside.

Outside the ambulance's lights flashed as it swung into the yard and two EMTs jumped and ran toward the open door.

"Dana," Hud whispered next to her ear. "Don't leave me. Please don't leave me."

Chapter Sixteen

While Hud went to the hospital with his wife, a deputy marshal by the name of Jake Thorton took Tag's and Lily's statements. By now it was almost daylight.

Tag felt numb. Tomorrow was Christmas Eve. So much had happened that he couldn't imagine celebrating the holiday now. Camilla Northland was dead. His cousin Dana was in the hospital in a coma. Both Angus and Harlan were tying up the loose ends of the murder list case.

"I almost got you killed," Lily had said on the way to the marshal's office. She looked and sounded exhausted. There was a haunted look in her eyes that Tag had desperately wanted to exorcise, but nothing he'd said or done had.

"No," he said, and touched her arm. She flinched and tears welled up in her eyes.

"I couldn't pull the trigger. I just…couldn't."

"It's all right. We're all right. It's over."

She shook her head. "It was all so…senseless."

He knew that she came from an ordered life, one where things always added up and made sense. One and one were always two. She was shaken and remorseful and he would have done anything to change that. But just the sight of him was a reminder that she'd failed herself, and no matter what he said…

He recounted everything that had happened for the second time to the deputy marshal, and then signed the paper that was put in front of him. Lily was being questioned in a separate room. He could see her through the window. She was crying.

His heart ached and he wanted desperately to go to her. But when she happened to look up, her gaze met his and she quickly looked away.

As he left the room, he saw that Ace was waiting for his sister.

"You saved her," Ace said, and shook Tag's hand.

"It wasn't like that."

"Yeah, it was. You found her and got her out of there."

"I almost got her killed because of a stupid flash drive with useless names on it." Lily was right. It had all been for nothing. "Take good care of her."

"Where are you going?"

"Back to Texas. I'm the last person your sister wants to see right now."

Ace looked sad about that. Not half as sad as Tag. He told himself it would never have worked out anyway. He lived in Texas. She lived in Montana. Even if she wasn't going back to her ex… And yet he kept thinking of her hand against that dirty pane of glass and her face in the faint moonlight.

The ache was like a hard knot inside him. He and Lily had never stood a chance. That was all it had been. A chance encounter doomed from the start. So why did it feel as if he was losing something he would yearn for for the rest of his life?

As he looked out into the faint light of daybreak, he

heard Christmas music playing somewhere in the distance. Colorful lights glittered across the village of Big Sky. He hoped he could get the first flight out. He'd had all he could take of Christmas in Montana.

"YOU'VE BEEN THROUGH a lot," Ace told Lily on the way back to his place. The sun was just starting to come up; the sky behind the mountains to the east was silvery with sunrise.

The day was cold and frosty, a misty fog hanging low in the snowcapped pines. Lily watched the landscape slide past and hugged herself even though it was warm in her brother's Jeep.

"I always thought I could take care of myself." She felt her brother glance over at her. "I've never thought of myself as helpless or weak."

"You are neither. I'm not sure I could have pulled that trigger, either."

She shot him a disappointed look. "We both know better than that."

"Come on, Lily. It's over. Cut yourself some slack. You were abducted. You could have been killed. You survived."

She nodded and looked out at the passing wild country. She'd survived but at what cost?

Ace reached over and squeezed her arm. "I'm so sorry. If I hadn't hired Mia in the first place—"

"You sound like Tag. He blames himself for finding the thumb drive when I was there. It's nobody's fault. It's just that it was all for nothing. The names were of no use. Everyone was killing each other for *nothing.* The list was of no use because half the names were wrong on it, I heard at the marshal's office. Apparently, Mia either messed up or they were onto her and gave her a fraudulent one."

Ace drove in silence the rest of the way to his apartment over the bar.

"I'm going to my own house," she said when she looked up and saw that her SUV was parked in the lot behind the bar.

He started to argue, but she cut him off. "All the bad guys are locked up. It's over. I want to go home. Need to go home."

"I don't like the idea of you being alone," her brother said.

She smiled at him. "I need to be alone. I'll drive down tomorrow. We can talk then. Right now—"

"I know, you just need to be alone," he finished for her, and smiled. "You've always been like that. I need people when I'm upset. You need solitude."

"Thank you for understanding."

"The marshal had your car picked up at Gerald's motel and brought here," he said. "Gerald stopped by earlier to say he was flying back to California. Does that mean you didn't take him back? You aren't reconsidering, are you?"

"Would that be so bad?" She held up a hand as her brother started to tell her again what he thought of Gerald. He didn't understand. Gerald offered her a quiet, safe life. Right now that sounded like just what she needed. She opened the passenger-side door of the Jeep and climbed out. "Tomorrow. We'll talk about it tomorrow."

With that she walked to her SUV, beeped open the driver's-side door and climbed in. She needed familiar right now, her own things around her. She turned the key in the ignition. The engine roared to life.

Her brother stood at the front door of the bar, waving as she left. She could tell he didn't like letting her go—letting her even consider going back to Gerald.

The past twenty-four hours were like a bad dream. Gerald showing up, making love with Tag, being kidnapped and held hostage and then Tag's rescue and, ultimately, her own part in it.

She could still remember the feel of the gun in her hand, the weight of it, the touch of the trigger. She'd let herself down. Let Tag down and almost gotten them both killed.

Her phone rang. She glanced at the caller ID. Tag. She couldn't bear to pick up. He would be flying home to his life in Texas. She'd heard him telling the deputy marshal of his plans.

"I need to go back to Houston," he'd said in response to the marshal's question about where he could be reached. "My brothers and I own a barbecue business."

"You're not staying for Christmas?"

Tag had glanced in her direction, and then said, "No, I don't think so."

He'd come over to her then and tried to talk to her, but she'd already put that cold, unemotional wall back up—the one Gerald had always admired about her. She could tell that Tag had been hurt and confused. He'd wanted to help her through this.

She shook her head at the thought as she pulled into her drive. There were tracks in the snow. But she didn't think too much about them. Everyone had been looking for her. Someone must have checked her house after the snow quit falling.

Lily pressed the garage-door opener and watched the door slowly rise in the cold mountain air before she pulled in. She'd just cut the engine, the door dropping behind her, and gotten out when she realized she wasn't alone.

As Tag was getting ready to leave the marshal's office, his father walked in. Tag wasn't up to seeing anyone right now, still stung from the rebuke Lily had given him. She'd acted the same way the morning after their lovemaking. In those moments earlier, she'd made it clear that there was nothing between the two of them.

So it wasn't surprising that he felt a lethal mixture of emotions at just the sight of Harlan Cardwell right then.

"Well, if it isn't my father the agent."

"Retired CIA agent," Harlan said.

"Whatever." He started to walk past him, but his father caught his arm. "We need to talk."

"Really? I flew all the way up here hoping that you might have five minutes for me. *Now* you want to talk? Let me guess. You want to talk about this case—not about you and me. You really don't know how to be a father, do you?"

"No, I don't," Harlan said. "I still need to talk to you."

Tag shook his head. He couldn't help the well of anger that boiled up in his belly. When he'd flown up here for Christmas, he'd told himself he'd had no expectations. That had been a lie. He'd come hoping to find the father he'd never had.

"Why don't we step into Hud's office?" his father said.

"Are you ordering me?"

"I'm asking."

They stood with their gazes locked for a few moments, before Tag relented and stepped into the office.

"Okay, let's get this debriefing over with," he said as Harlan closed the door behind them and motioned his son into one of the two chairs in front of Hud's desk.

"I'm sorry," his father said as he sat down. "You're right. I know nothing about being a father."

"And you never tried to learn."

"I did at first, but I let my job get in the way. It seemed more important."

Tag saw how hard that was for Harlan to admit. "It still is."

Harlan shook his head. "I only got involved because I used to work with Mia's father. I've known her since she was a baby. I could see that she was in over her head and yet..." He raked a hand through his hair. Tag noticed the streaks of gray he hadn't before. He saw the lines around his father's eyes. Saw how much he'd aged as if it had all been in the past twenty-four hours.

He'd seen his father as a guitar-playing, beer-drinking good ol' boy who just wanted to have fun. Now he saw the man behind that facade.

"Stay for Christmas," Harlan said.

"Was the computer thumb drive really worthless?" Tag asked. "Or is that just another lie?"

His father looked sad and disappointed for a moment that Tag had turned their conversation back to business, but finally said, "The original drive was corrupted."

Tag frowned. "Corrupted? Well, at least you have the list that Lily provided you."

"The names Lily McCabe decoded were incorrect. Useless, since there was no way to match up those ex-cons with the deaths of the law officers on the list."

Tag let out a curse. "Lily was so sure—"

"Some of them were right. I don't know why she

wasn't able to get the rest of them. But whatever the reason, it probably saved her life," Harlan said.

Tag felt his heart bump in his chest. He and Lily had tried so hard, but ultimately, they'd both failed. "So now what?"

"I'm retired again. That's why I'd like you to stay for Christmas."

A cheer came up from another part of the office. The dispatcher gave a thumbs-up and mouthed that Dana was going to make it.

"I'll think about it," Tag said, and rose to his feet. His father did the same and held out his hand. Tag shook it, feeling his father's strength in that big hand. "Did Mother know?"

Harlan nodded. "She couldn't live with never being sure if I was going to make it home for dinner."

Tag nodded.

"I hope you stay for Christmas, but I'll understand if you don't."

At the cabin, he packed up his things, realizing he couldn't leave without seeing Lily one more time and saying goodbye. He swung by the bar to find it closed. After a few minutes of pounding on the door, Ace appeared.

"Is Lily here?"

"She was determined to go to her place. I tried to talk her into staying with me, but my sister is one stubborn woman."

Tag smiled. "Determined and strong."

"Well, she's not feeling all that strong right now. She feels she let herself down and almost got you killed. I'm not sure she can ever forgive herself."

"It wasn't like that."

"Tell her that."

"I've tried."

Ace glanced toward the old pickup Tag was driving. "You're leaving."

"I am, but I don't want to go without seeing her again."

"She says she needs to be alone. Sorry."

"Okay." Tag turned to leave.

"I suppose you won't be back."

"Not likely," he said as he walked to his father's pickup and climbed in. The sun had come up behind the mountains and now washed the countryside with cold winter sunlight.

As he drove out of Big Sky, Tag found himself mentally kicking himself. If he hadn't gone to the bar that night and Mia hadn't stumbled into him… If he hadn't found that stupid thumb drive in his coat pocket and let Lily see it. If…

His heart began to pound as he remembered something. He turned around to head back toward Lone Mountain and called his father. "About those names. You said the thumb drive was corrupted and so was the copy Hud made, right? Lily told me that she had decoded some of them, but hadn't had a chance to finish. It was her former fiancé who gave us the list." Tag swore. "I let him use the original flash drive."

Harlan instantly was on alert. "What's his name?"

"Gerald Humphrey."

"What do you know about him?"

"Nothing. Nothing except that it took him six months to show up after he'd stood Lily up at the altar. He supposedly already left on a flight from Bozeman to Los Angeles, California, today."

He heard his father clicking on a computer keyboard. "I'm showing that he was on the flight."

"Is there any way to verify that?" Tag turned onto Lone Mountain Road and headed toward Lily's while he waited.

"I can try to contact the airport."

"But why would Gerald corrupt the thumb drive or give Lily the wrong names?" He could hear his father clacking away at the computer keyboard.

"He recently left his job in Montana to take a lesser one in California at a small private school," Harlan said. "Wait a minute. Next of kin. Gerald Humphrey has a younger sister who was recently sentenced for embezzlement. She got fifteen years and is serving time in a prison in California near the private school where he is now teaching."

Tag's mind raced. Was it possible Gerald was up to his neck in this? He hadn't come back to sweet-talk Lily into taking him back. He'd come back because Mia worked at the Canyon Bar—and she had managed to get the list. Tag cringed. He'd given the thumb drive to Gerald to decode and now it was corrupted.

"Lily mentioned something about Gerald taking a job in California," Tag said to his father. "This co-op killing group isn't just in Montana, is it? It's nationwide?"

"Tag—"

He floored the old pickup as he headed for Lily, praying he wasn't too late.

LILY FROZE AT the sight of a large dark figure standing in the doorway to the house. Her breath rushed from her as her heart took off on a downhill run.

"Lily, I knew you'd come alone."

"Gerald?" He moved then into the dim light so she could see his face. The familiarity of it let her suck in a

couple of calming breaths before she asked, "What are you doing here? I thought you flew back to California."

"I couldn't leave just yet," he said. "Are you going to just stand in the garage all day or come inside?"

She bristled at his tone, but quickly quelled her irritation. There was a reason Gerald treated her like a child. Around him she felt like one.

He was still blocking the door as she approached, but he moved aside at the last minute to let her into her own house. She glanced around. Everything looked just as it had yesterday before she'd left to meet him. Yesterday she'd been so sure of herself. So sure she wanted something different. *Someone* more exciting.

"I'm glad you didn't leave," she said as she took off her coat.

"Really?" Gerald took the coat and hung it up.

She noticed his was also on the coatrack by the front door—in the same place it had been just two nights before. He'd certainly made himself at home, she thought, noticing that he had a small fire going in her fireplace. She'd picked up the hint of smoke as she'd come in, but hadn't registered why until this moment.

Lily resisted the part of her that resented Gerald thinking he could just come in and do as he pleased in her house.

"How did you get into the house?" she asked suddenly, and glanced toward the front door, recalling locking it before she left.

"Through the garage. You do realize I am smarter than your garage-door opener, don't you?"

She studied him, faintly aware that he seemed different. That alone threw her since Gerald had always been so solidly...Gerald.

"I've never questioned how smart you are."

"Really?" he said as he moved around the dining room table, his thick fingers dragging along the smooth edge of the wood.

She saw him slow as he reached her computer and realized that all the paperwork she'd left on the table was gone. She shot a look toward the fire. One of the papers hadn't completely burned.

Her heart began to pound so hard she thought for sure he would hear it. She glanced toward the computer screen but couldn't read what was on it.

"I'm surprised that you never asked me why I decided to move to a small private school in California," Gerald said, drawing her attention back to him.

"I didn't really get a chance to ask before..." She let the rest of what she would have said yesterday die in her throat. She wasn't up to a fight with Gerald. His standing her up at the wedding no longer mattered. It seemed a lot more than six months ago.

"Yes, the wedding," he said, and stopped moving to look at her.

"I don't want to argue about—"

"I didn't come here to try to change your mind."

That surprised her. "Then I guess I don't understand."

"Don't you? I would have thought you of all people would have put it together by now. You were my best student. You disappoint me, Lily."

She frowned. "I don't know what you're talking about."

"The code."

With a sigh, her body heavy with exhaustion, weary from the events of the past twenty-four hours, she said, "None of that matters. The names were wrong anyway. I almost died for nothing. I almost got Tag—" She stopped herself.

"*Tag.* What kind of name is that anyway? Like Ace? Another name you might call your dog?"

Lily studied Gerald then, feeling the weight of the world settling on her shoulders, and said, "I'm sorry if I hurt you, Gerald. Is that what you need me to say? Is that what you're doing here? Because I just don't know what you want from me."

He took a step toward her. "There was a time you would have known." He shook his head as he stopped within inches of her and reached out to touch her cheek with his fingers.

She closed her eyes, trying not to think of Tag's touch, of Tag's embrace, of Tag.

"But that time has long passed."

She opened her eyes, hearing the thinly veiled anger in his voice. "That's why you missed your flight? You just wanted to tell me you don't love me anymore?" A stab of anger made her heart beat a little faster. "Fine. Give it your best shot. I've disappointed you. I'm not good enough for you. Whatever it is, let's hear it. Then leave." She had started to step past him when he grabbed her arm.

"You can't possibly think that I have gone to all this trouble just to have the last word. Don't you know me any better than that?" he demanded. "Are you so besotted with that cowboy that he's turned your brain to mush?"

She tried to jerk free of his hold, but he only tightened it. "So this is about jealousy? You didn't want me but you don't want anyone else to have me, either?"

"So he has had you." He swore, something she'd

never heard him do before. He'd always said that cursing was a lazy, uneducated waste of the vernacular.

She shot him a withering look.

"Stupid cow," Gerald snapped. "Didn't you even question once why your code and mine were so different?"

Lily blinked, thrown off for a moment from the lightning-fast change of topic. "You said mine was off—"

"And you believed me." He laughed. "I guess I will always be the teacher and you will always be the pupil."

She stared at him as if seeing a stranger. She had wondered why she'd gotten some of the names right and yet others Gerald had said were wrong. If her original decoding had been accurate, then…

"I just assumed you were right and I was wrong," she said more to herself than to him. She saw how foolish that had been, not only with the code but also with her entire relationship with this man.

"Come on, my little pupil. *Think.* Don't you remember me telling you about my younger sister who lives in California?" His fingers clutching her arm tightened painfully.

"You're hurting me, Gerald."

"I told you how proud I was of her, that she was even smarter than me," he said as if he hadn't heard her or was ignoring her. "Well, guess what? All that money she was making hand over fist? It was one big lie. Embezzlement. She used that magnificent brain of hers to steal, and worse, she got caught!"

"I don't understand what that—"

"They sent her to prison! *Prison!* They put her with common thieves and killers. My precious baby sister."

His throat worked, his last words coming out in a croak. Tears welled up in his eyes.

Her mind tried to make sense of what he was saying, but she was so emotionally and physically wrung out… She jerked free of his hold and took a step back, banging into the edge of the kitchen counter.

Looming over her, he glared at her as if she were the one who'd sent his sister to prison. "Do you know anything about prison, Lily? No, of course you wouldn't know what a woman like my sister has to do to survive there."

Lily felt a chill run the length of her spine. The murder list. Her mind leapt from that thought to the most obvious one. "You didn't come here after six months to try to get me back."

Gerald gave a laugh, but it came out sounding like a sob. *"Finally."* He met her gaze, his challenging. "I did what I had to do to keep my sister safe. Just as I am going to do what I have to now."

Lily gripped the kitchen counter behind her. She was so exhausted she was having trouble understanding what he was talking about. "Gerald, it doesn't matter anymore. They say the thumb drive was corrupted—"

"I destroyed the information on the thumb drive when your boyfriend let me use it to decode the names," he said with his usual arrogance. "The information is worthless. I also destroyed the paper copies you left at the motel. The one you left was worthless. The original is gone."

Her gaze went to her computer and he laughed.

"While I was waiting for you, I put a virus in your computer that by now has destroyed everything—including the hard drive. I figured you might have used your brother's computer at some point, so when I used it to give your boyfriend the names, I also made sure a virus will destroy all his data."

He was enjoying showing how superior he was to her and the rest of the world. She'd seen that trait in him but never quite like this. What scared her was the feeling that he'd come here to do more than gloat.

A bubble of fear rose in her throat until she thought she would choke on it. "So you took care of everything."

"Not quite," he said as he closed the narrow space between them. "There is only one more copy I need to destroy." He tapped her temple. "I used to be so jealous of the way you could remember the most random things. You could remember entire lists of numbers and letters." He smiled and nodded. "You do remember the original thumb drive lists, don't you? I knew it. You've never been able to hide anything from me."

Chapter Seventeen

Tag left the truck at the bottom of the last hill and ran the rest of the way up the road to Lily's house. He'd brought one of the guns from his father's hidden stash, but he was praying he wasn't going to have to use it.

Maybe Gerald really had gotten on the flight to California. Maybe the fact that he had a sister in prison had nothing to do with anything that had been going on.

Tag knew he was clutching at straws. There were two many coincidences. Gerald was up to his eyeballs in this. Worse, Tag had handed over the thumb drive to him. He'd trusted Gerald because he'd been so desperate to find Lily and get her out of this mess. He'd only gotten her in deeper.

Unfortunately there would be no way to prove Gerald had corrupted the thumb drive. Even the fact that he'd given the feds the wrong names could be swept under the rug as a simple mistake.

So why would Gerald do anything stupid right now when he could walk away free?

Because Lily still had a copy of the information on her computer, Tag thought with a sinking heart.

As he neared the house, he prayed he would find Lily alone, Gerald long gone.

But when he climbed up onto the deck and moved to

the front window, he saw Lily and Gerald in the kitchen. He didn't need to hear what they were saying to each other. He could tell by their body language and their expressions that they were arguing.

His stomach roiled at the sight. Lily was backed up against the kitchen counter. Gerald was looming over her.

Tag tried the door, not surprised to find it locked. He was afraid to knock. He needed the element of surprise, and even with it he feared what would happen next.

He picked up a large flowerpot from the deck and, stepping back, hurled it through the window. Glass rained down in a shower onto the deck as the huge window shattered.

Pulling his gun, Tag quickly jumped through the opening into Lily's living room.

Gerald had turned in surprise at the sound of the breaking glass. His eyes widened at the gun in Tag's hands.

"Get away from him!" Tag yelled as he strode toward them, the gun aimed at Gerald's chest.

Lily seemed nailed to the floor. Her eyes widened in alarm, her mouth opened as if to scream, but nothing came out.

In that instant, Gerald took advantage of her inability to move and grabbed her, locking his arm around her throat as he backed the two of them against the kitchen counter.

"That's far enough," Gerald said as Tag advanced. "Come any closer and I'll break her neck."

Tag stopped at the edge of the dining room. Out of the corner of his eye, he saw Lily's laptop still open on the table, but the papers she'd been doing her decoding on were gone and there was the faint smell of smoke from the fireplace in the room.

"Drop your gun. Slowly," Gerald ordered.

Tag could see the painful hold Gerald had on Lily and knew he couldn't get a shot off without risking her life. Gerald was using her like a shield. Tag slowly lowered his gun, but didn't drop it.

"What's going on, Gerald?" he asked as he carefully bent down and placed his weapon on the floor, never taking his eyes off Lily's.

"Now kick the gun over here."

Tag did as he was told. The gun skittered across the floor. Gerald slowly reached down, dragging Lily with him, and picked up the gun with his free hand, never releasing his hold on her.

"You really should have gone back to Texas and left Lily alone."

LILY HAD FELT too tired to fight Gerald earlier. Now things had changed. She found a reserved strength she hadn't known she possessed. Gerald had the gun pointed at Tag. For the second time in two days, she was faced with a life-or-death situation after more than thirty-two years of an ordered, overly structured life. The only time she'd felt she wasn't in control was when she came up here to the Canyon to work for her brother.

Until this.

"Let him go," Lily said hoarsely from the choke hold on her throat. "This is between you and me."

Gerald's laugh held no humor. "That might have been the case yesterday when I pleaded with you to come back to me. Maybe we could have worked something out then…."

"You sold out your own fiancée," Tag said as he took

a step toward the dining room, forcing Gerald to turn a little in order to keep her in front of him.

"Ex-fiancée," Gerald snapped, and motioned the gun at him. "Didn't she mention that to you? I'm surprised. I thought the two of you…"

"That's what I planned to tell you," Lily said. She shifted so she was closer to the kitchen counter. Her hand snaked behind her as she sought out the drawer where she'd dropped the gun earlier. "I was hoping it wasn't too late for us, Gerald. I wanted the life you offered where I knew who I was." There was a ring of truth to her words since that was exactly what she'd been thinking on her way home.

Tag's gaze widened a little, his expression saddening.

"It's not too late, Gerald," she continued as she eased the drawer open. "As you said, there's no proof you've done anything wrong. You've destroyed everything, all that you need to worry about anyway. If you kill this man, then that all changes."

She eased the drawer open, feeling Gerald loosen the hold on her a little. Her fingers curled around the handle of the gun.

"You had second thoughts?" Gerald said quietly next to her ear.

She nodded. His hold loosened even a little more. She could breathe, and for a moment that was all she did. Then she slowly lifted out the gun, holding it at her side out of his range of sight. "I was going to come back to you."

As if he felt the truth in her words, his surprise moved through his body. He seemed to slump against her.

"I don't understand," he whispered.

Tag was looking at her as if he didn't understand, either.

"I wanted safe," she said.

"Safe?" Gerald repeated, and let out a hoarse laugh, the irony not lost on him.

Tag's gaze went to her side. He gave a small shake of his head at the sight of the gun clutched in her hand.

"Nothing has changed," Gerald said, his tone almost pleading. "We can get past this. Our lives can be exactly like we planned. Even better after this."

Lily had to bite her tongue. Did he really think they could pick up where they'd left off? All forgiven and forgotten?

He was crazier than she'd thought.

In the distance, she heard sirens and realized how badly this could go if she didn't move quickly. "Tag, you should go," she said.

Gerald shook his head and tightened his hold on her. "Lily. We can't let him just walk away. Not now."

"We have to, Gerald. It's the only way."

But even as she said it, she felt Gerald tense the arm holding the gun. He leveled it at Tag's heart. "I'm sorry, Lily, but I think it's too late for us."

TAG KNEW WHEN he came through the door that Gerald was dangerous. The man had come too far and knew there was no turning back. Gerald Humphrey had crossed a line that a man like him couldn't come back from.

For just an instant, Tag felt sorry for him. He could understand wanting to protect someone you loved.

He looked down the barrel of the gun Gerald had pointed at him, saw the man steady it and knew all the talking was done.

At the same time, Tag saw Lily make the decision.

"No!" he yelled as he dived to the side. The first gunshot was followed only an instant later by a second.

The scream that filled the air made the hair rise on the back of his neck. He hit the floor and rolled, coming up to find Gerald Humphrey on the floor holding the thigh of his right leg and writhing in pain.

Lily stood over him, the gun still in her hand, her face as white as the snow outside. Gerald had gotten off one shot before dropping his weapon and grabbing his wounded leg.

Tag quickly stepped to him to kick his gun away before reaching to take the pistol from Lily. She had a death grip on the gun. He eased it from her fingers.

She gave him a barely perceptible nod.

He smiled as he cupped a hand behind her neck and drew her to him, wrapping her in his arms. She hugged him tightly as he breathed the words into the soft, sweet scent of her hair. "You saved my life."

On the floor, Gerald began to curse. "Are the two of you just going to let me lie here and bleed to death? Call a doctor!"

In the distance, Tag could hear the sirens. He pulled out his cell phone, hit 911 and asked for an ambulance as flashing lights flickered across the fallen snow outside the window. Tag watched his father and Deputy Marshal Jake Thorton come racing up to the house, weapons drawn, and pulled Lily closer.

Chapter Eighteen

Christmas Eve it began to snow and became one of those winter nights when the flakes are as large as goose feathers. They drifted down in a wall of white so thick they obliterated everything out the window at Cardwell Ranch.

"Merry Christmas," Tag said as he came up behind Lily.

She leaned back into him and watched the falling snow to the sound of Christmas music and children's laughter. In the kitchen, Stacy and the kids were finishing up baking gingerbread men. Dana had been relegated to sitting at the kitchen table and helping ice the cookies. The smell of ginger wafted through the old ranch house, mingling with the even sweeter scent of evergreen.

Lily could hear her brother in the kitchen. He'd volunteered to help with the cookie decorating, as well. She'd never seen Ace with kids before. He was a natural.

"I always dreamed of a Christmas like this," Lily said, turning in Tag's arms to look up into his face. "I would come home from boarding school to find the house was already decorated by some designer my mother had hired. We always had a white-flocked tree with different-colored lights on it depending on what was in that year. Everything was very…tasteful."

"Compared to an amazing tree like this one?" Tag joked, nodding toward Dana's "orphan" tree.

Lily laughed. The tree wasn't what most would consider a Christmas tree, but she loved that it was decorated with ornaments the children had made. Her mother would never have allowed a tree like that in her house.

How different her life and Ace's would have been if her mother had adopted an orphan tree and let her children decorate it. Would Lily have ever agreed to marry a man like Gerald Humphrey?

She thought of Gerald. He'd confessed to everything but refused to name names to protect himself in prison—as well as his sister. Lily had been able to supply the letters from the original thumb drive from memory. After they were decoded, the FBI had the names and was now rounding up the former inmates who had done the killings. For the time being at least, the co-op murder group had been shut down.

"That is the most beautiful Christmas tree I have ever seen," she said, feeling tears sting her eyes as she turned to look at him. They'd been through so much together in such a short time and yet she felt as if she had always known him.

Tag cocked an eyebrow at her, then smiled and pulled her in for a kiss.

"You're only supposed to kiss under the misseytoe," said a small voice behind them. Lily turned to find Dana's daughter, Mary, pointing at the mistletoe hanging near the door. "That's where Mommy and Daddy kiss."

Mary's older brother, Hank, came into the room in

time to make a grimacing face. "They are always kissing. Gross."

Tag and Lily laughed. A moment later Ace came into the room carrying a tray of gingerbread men. The twins, Angus and Brick, now fourteen months old and their cousin, Ella, now almost two, came toddling into the room following the cookies. They had icing smeared across their faces. They were followed by their aunt Stacy with a washcloth.

"I decorated those," Ace said with obvious pride as he pointed to the perfectly decorated cookies.

"I did those," Mary said, pointing to some cookies that were unrecognizable under all the different colors of icing.

"I can't tell the difference." Lily grinned at her brother.

Hud and Dana joined them, Dana in the wheelchair her husband had insisted she stay in until she was stronger. She was plenty strong, Lily thought. She recalled her own moments over the past few days when she'd been stronger than she'd ever believed she could be. So much had changed, she thought, glancing over at Tag. Or maybe she'd just changed. She would never admit it to her brother, but she had been afraid to live life. She'd thought she'd wanted safe and sedate, just as she and Ace had been raised.

But Tag had changed all that. No matter what happened in the future, she knew she could never go back to being the woman who'd been willing to settle for what Gerald Humphrey had offered her.

At the sound of sleigh bells, everyone in the room went quiet. Christmas music played faintly from the kitchen as heavy boots stomped across the porch. An instant later the door flew open and a Santa Claus suspiciously resembling Tag's father filled the doorway.

Mary and Hank let out cheers and ran to him. Santa was followed into the house by Angus dragging a huge bag loaded with gifts. Tag looked at Lily and saw the delight in her face. He wished he could see that look on her face always.

Jordan and his very pregnant wife, Deputy Marshal Liza Cardwell, arrived moments later with presents. Not long after that, Dana's brother, Clay, landed by helicopter out by the barn in a shower of snow. He came in signing Christmas carols and got them all singing around the fireplace and the orphan tree.

As Tag felt Harlan's aka Santa's arm drop over his shoulders, a lump formed in his throat. He'd wanted a Montana Christmas, and he couldn't have asked for a more perfect one than this.

He wished this night would never end, he thought as he watched his family opening presents around the tree. But the holidays were almost over and Texas and the rest of his family and their business loomed large on the horizon.

LILY WOKE JUST as the sun was peeking over the mountains. She hadn't wanted to open her eyes. Lying under the down comforter, she was warm and cozy, still feeling the effects of her lovemaking with Tag not that many hours ago.

It had been the best Christmas Eve of her life and she thought it funny she could think that, given that she'd almost been killed in the days before. Last night, Tag had been so gentle. She shivered at the thought. He'd brought her back to her house after midnight, swept her up into his arms and carried her to the bed.

He'd kissed her so gently, so sweetly. She'd thought she'd only imagined the passion from their first love-making. But then the kisses had become more amorous. She'd felt heat race through her veins, making her skin sensitive to the touch. He'd peeled away her clothing, kissing each patch of skin he revealed, finding places on her body to caress as if memorizing every inch of her.

She'd reciprocated, loving the feel of his skin and the way he shuddered with delight as she moved over him. They kissed and touched until, both naked and barely able to contain themselves, they'd finally coupled. Locked in each other's arms, they'd let their passion run wild like the storm outside.

Just the thought of their lovemaking made Lily reach over to the other side of her bed, expecting to find Tag's warm body. Earlier they'd been spooned together.

Her eyes flew open. The bed was empty. Loss raced through her on the heels of fear. Would Tag just leave? Last night he'd said he didn't know how he would be able to tell her goodbye when the holidays were over. Had he gone back to Texas?

Grabbing her silk robe, she moved toward the living room, terrified she would find a scribbled note and Tag Cardwell gone.

But as she rounded the corner, she did a double take. With everything that had been going on, she hadn't had time to do the little decorating she normally did for Christmas.

That was why she was shocked to see a large beautiful Christmas tree standing in the front window. It shone with an array of colored lights and ornaments. Tag stood in front of it wearing nothing but a pair of jeans.

She looked at him in surprise.

He grinned. "You like it? I got Hank and Mary to

make ornaments for it, and my father gave me some of the ones from when I was a child."

Tears welled up in her eyes. "I *love* it."

"I wanted you to have that old-fashioned Christmas you always dreamed of—not just the one at Cardwell Ranch."

She rushed to him and threw her arms around his neck. "Oh, Tag."

He held her to him, the lights of the tree flickering in the early-morning light. "I can't leave you, Lily. And I can't ask you to quit your job to move to Texas," he said finally, holding her at arm's length.

She tried to swallow past the lump in her throat.

TAG LOOKED INTO Lily's beautiful face and felt so much love for her that it nearly knocked him to his knees.

"There is only one thing I can do," he said. "It was actually my father's idea."

Last night, Harlan had stopped him as Tag and Lily were leaving Cardwell Ranch. "Are you really headed back to Texas?"

"Christmas is over," Tag had said as Lily walked on out to her SUV they had arrived in. "I have a business to run with my brothers."

"I just wish we'd had some time to get to know each other better."

Tag had laughed at that. "Oh, I think we got to know each other quite well."

"I'm serious. I wish you would stay longer. You know Big Sky could really use a good Texas barbecue joint."

"Your father gave you the idea?" Lily said now.

He nodded, smiling. "He thinks I should open a Texas Boys Barbecue joint in Big Sky. What do you think?"

She laughed and leaned up to kiss him. "That is the best Christmas present I could have asked for."

"Really?" he asked with a grin. "Then I guess I'll have to take this back." He drew a small dark velvet box out of his pocket. "I was going to wait until later under the Christmas tree, but I can't wait another moment."

Her heart began to pound.

"I know it probably seems fast—"

She shook her head and he laughed.

"Yeah, that's kind of the way I feel," he said, and he opened the box. The winter light caught the diamond, sending a prism of brilliant light ricocheting around the room.

"I love you, Lily McCabe. Marry me someday? Someday soon?"

Lily laughed and nodded through her tears as he slipped the ring on her finger.

* * * * *

"You're so damned beautiful."

Holt drew back a step. "We shouldn't do this."

"I disagree," Cecelia insisted.

Of course she would. But it was a mistake, more on her part than his.

"I don't want to be gentle with you." He wanted to scare her, wanted to back her off. But it wasn't fear he saw in her eyes, it was…anticipation.

"So don't be gentle." She tugged at his tie and slid it out of his collar.

"Cecelia." It was the only coherent word he could get past his lips.

"I'm right here."

Her fingernails scraped lightly across his chest.

"I'm not that white knight you're looking for," he said with an ache that almost undid him.

"I don't care."

WOULD-BE CHRISTMAS WEDDING

BY

DEBRA WEBB

First published in Great Britain 2013
by Mills & Boon, an imprint of Harlequin (UK) Limited,
Eton House, 18-24 Paradise Road, Richmond, Surrey TW9 1SR

ISBN: 978 0 263 90380 5

46-1113

Harlequin (UK) policy is to use papers that are natural, renewable and recyclable products and made from wood grown in sustainable forests. The logging and manufacturing processes conform to the legal environmental regulations of the country of origin.

Printed and bound in Spain
by Blackprint CPI, Barcelona

Debra Webb wrote her first story at age nine and her first romance at thirteen. It wasn't until she spent three years working for the military behind the Iron Curtain and within the confining political walls of Berlin, Germany, that she realized her true calling. A five-year stint with NASA on the space-shuttle program reinforced her love of the endless possibilities within her grasp as a storyteller. A collision course between suspense and romance was set. Debra has been writing romance, suspense and action-packed romance thrillers since. Visit her at www.debrawebb.com or write to her at PO Box 4889, Huntsville, AL 35815, USA.

Debra Webb wrote her first story at age nine and her first romance at thirteen. It wasn't until she spent three years working for the military behind the Iron Curtain and within the communist police state of Berlin, Germany, that she realised her true calling. A five-year stint with NASA on the space shuttle program reinforced her love of the endless possibilities within her grasp as a storyteller. A collision course between suspense and romance was set. Debra has been writing romance, suspense and action-packed romance thrillers since. Visit her at www.debrawebb.com or write to her at PO Box 4889, Huntsville, AL 35815, USA.

Chapter One

The National Mall, Washington, D.C.
Thursday, December 18, 11:45 a.m.

So this is how it feels to be a traitor.

Emmett Holt exited the metro at the Mall. Of all his less-than-admirable traits and accomplishments, this one had brought him to an all-new low.

There was no going back from this, no explanation or excuse he could offer for the damaging evidence he was about to hand over. While it was only a flash drive, it felt like a fifty-pound weight-lifting plate from the gym. He knew Director Thomas Casey had someone tailing him and he knew better than to waste time trying to make that identification.

If this sting backfired, if either Thomas Casey or his nemesis, Bernard Isely, got impatient, Holt—standing between them—would get cut down in the crossfire. Not exactly the way he'd seen himself going out of this business, much less this world.

Handing over the reports from the Germany mission when Casey had killed Isely's father was a stop-gap measure. Isely wanted both the intel on the old mission and the vial of the deadly virus Mission Recovery had seized two months ago.

It didn't take a genius to know Isely wanted a whole hell of a lot more than that. The man had one goal: to exact revenge and destroy Director Casey.

Holt was running out of excuses to keep both men at bay. And timing was everything.

He walked with purpose toward the National Air and Space Museum gift shop, just another man picking up another gift amid the throng of tourists. The weather was clear and the wind cold, but winter hadn't turned truly bitter yet and people were still wishing for an idyllic white Christmas.

Holt could only wish he would still be alive come Christmas.

He stopped where the text message had told him to stop, feeling like a damned puppet on a string. Even knowing at the beginning that it would come down to this didn't make it easier to stomach the reality of doing so. He was used to giving orders, not taking them.

Handing over this tiny piece of technology and the huge intelligence it stored marked the beginning of the end.

It might have been a few years since his last field op, but the skills didn't go away. They were far too deeply engrained. He checked his phone, made the drop and didn't die or get arrested as he walked back to the metro station.

"Did my warning help?"

Holt didn't miss a step as Isely joined him on the escalator. "Sure."

After receiving a picture of Director Casey's sister, Cecelia Manning, and the single warning of "Beware," Holt had dug into the woman's recent history to see what threat or purpose she might pose for Isely. Or for him.

He'd learned all kinds of details he didn't want to know, from her favorite perfume to her tight circle of wealthy friends who toddled about doing charitable works.

Then he'd found the big splashy occasion he knew Isely had been looking for: the charity gala the widow had organized to benefit cancer research in memory of her late husband. The event offered the perfect opportunity.

"And?" Isely prompted.

Holt wasn't inclined to answer truthfully. He'd exhausted himself planting bugs in the woman's house, a GPS tracker on her car, opening a profile that matched hers on an online dating site and monitoring her general safety while maintaining his own responsibilities at Mission Recovery.

"And her family will join her at tomorrow's event," Holt replied, giving the man what he wanted.

"You will take the appropriate action?"

Holt nodded, letting his hand shake just a touch. He didn't want to oversell it, but a traitor would have reservations and a few jangling nerves at this point. He had a wild hope that a specialist would come charging in—now—before this got messy.

"I will send the address when it is time."

Holt nodded again as the train came into the station.

"Don't worry, my friend." Isely's hand landed heavy on Holt's shoulder. "You have a new team now. You are not alone."

Friend?

Isely couldn't know it, but that was Holt's worst fear.

Chapter Two

Alexandria, Virginia, 2:15 p.m.

"I know you're disappointed, Mom."

Cecelia Manning filled two mugs of coffee and handed one to her daughter, Casey. She watched Casey add a scant teaspoon of sugar and a hefty dollop of milk.

When the risk of milk ending up on her counter was minimized, she said, "My application was accepted."

"What?" Casey's mouth dropped open in shock. "You can't be serious."

"I am completely serious," Cecelia replied. She decided hiding the pain her daughter's reaction had caused was best for now. Neither her daughter nor her brother approved of her desire to go into fieldwork for the CIA, but Cecelia had had more than she could take of the boredom and routine of pushing paper around the agency office.

Her husband had worked in the CIA for the entirety of their married life, until he'd passed away just over a year ago.

Her brother was the director of an elite team of covert agents known only as "Specialists." Her daughter had gone into CIA fieldwork, as well. Yet they all expected her to… what? Continue in her predictable, safe role, making Sunday dinners and birthday cakes and learning to knit while she waited for Casey and her new husband, Levi, to provide the grandchildren she wanted to spoil.

She sipped her coffee and saved the scream of frustration for when she was alone again.

"Mom, you can't."

"Can't?"

Casey's eyes flared as she obviously caught the warning Cecelia had packed into that one word.

"I didn't mean *can't* like that."

Cecelia sipped her coffee, waiting. More than a little curious how her daughter intended to wrench her foot out of her mouth.

"It's just..." She shrugged. "You're my mom."

Cecelia traced the handle of her bright stoneware cup.

"Fieldwork is crazy," she added.

Holding her daughter's gaze, she waited for an intelligent argument to arise. Not that she'd let anything deter her from her plans. Since her husband's passing, she'd merely gone through the motions of day-to-day life and now she was ready for something new. She *needed* something new... Like a life where she felt needed and...wanted.

She'd survived the shock and grief of losing the man she'd loved and expected to grow old with. She'd learned to cope with a quiet house and the sympathetic looks of her friends and neighbors.

Her work had been an anchor, steadying her as she moved from one stage to the next. Now it felt like a stone dragging her to the bottom of the Potomac when she thought of sitting behind a desk for the rest of her working days.

With William buried and their daughter a happy newlywed, Cecelia's life, unexpectedly, was her own, and she was determined to see just what she could do with it.

"Mom? You're not even listening."

"No," Cecelia admitted. "I'm not. Whether you approve or not, I'm making this move."

"Mom."

"Casey." She mimicked her daughter's exasperated tone. "I appreciate your concern, but I didn't leap into this blindly. This decision isn't a whim or even a midlife crisis." She saw Casey blush and knew her daughter had indeed suggested those unflattering theories. She and her uncle, Cecelia's brother, had discussed this move at length. "The agency wouldn't have accepted my request if I didn't have the physical or mental fortitude to succeed."

She held up a finger. "If you dare mention the Equal Opportunity Act, I'll throttle you. Don't think I haven't learned a thing or two about minimizing risk already. I am not as naive or helpless as you seem to think."

Casey held up her hands in surrender. "You're a self-defense ninja."

"Don't you forget it, either." Cecelia smiled. "I know enough about the process to know my two closest relatives did not recommend me."

"That's not true."

Cecelia let the fib go unchallenged. Her family wanted the best for her, but they just had a different idea of what that looked like. "And don't worry. You've been through the training yourself. It's not like they're dumping me out on the street first thing Monday morning."

Casey sighed. "Wouldn't it just be easier to take some vacation and travel? Field operations isn't a game, Mom."

Her daughter's complete lack of confidence cut deep, but she supposed it was to be expected. When you walked one path for the duration of a relationship, changing directions was bound to stir things up.

Maybe there had been enough talk of change for the moment. "How is Levi?"

"He's fine. His plane gets in around eight."

"And being married is wonderful?"

"Yeah," Casey admitted with a secret little smile. One Cecelia remembered wearing long ago when she was that age. "You're sure you're okay with us spending Christmas with Levi's mom in Florida?"

"Of course. You're now part of his family, too. Don't worry about me. I have plans of my own."

"You do?"

"Sure. I bought a ticket for—"

The doorbell rang and Casey shot her a curious look. Cecelia only smiled as she set her coffee aside. "I have friends. We even do stuff," she added with a wink. "It's probably about tomorrow night."

Before she reached the front door, it opened and her brother, Thomas Casey, walked inside. The tension was a palpable force rolling off him and bouncing around the narrow foyer.

Worst-case scenarios bounded through her head before she regained control. She'd learned early in her role as a wife and mother that a cool head was the best asset she could bring to any situation.

"What is it?" She said a quick prayer that it wasn't his new wife, but her mind absolutely blanked when he laid his hands gently on her shoulders.

The doctor who'd explained William's terminal diagnosis had done that, wearing a similar grim expression and looking at her with an emotion caught somewhere between sympathy and pity.

She shrugged out from under her brother's touch and shook off the uncomfortable memory. Whatever had brought Thomas rushing into her home, she instinctively understood she wasn't going to enjoy the news.

"Casey's here," she said, stepping out of his reach. "Come on back to the kitchen and have some coffee."

"We need to talk."

She swallowed the bitter words dancing on the tip of her tongue. Why did her family have so little faith in her abilities? "Not if you're here about my move to ops next month."

"That got approved?"

She rolled her eyes. No amount of good manners could have stopped the exasperated reflex. Temper wasn't something she frequently indulged in, but right now she was ready to do the one thing she'd never done in her life: kick her family out of her home.

Casey brightened considerably when she spotted her uncle. After a warm hug, they stood side by side and faced Cecelia.

"Go ahead and say whatever you need to say." Let them try to deter her. Teaming up against her would get them nowhere. She was making the move to ops, regardless. She'd already made arrangements for a house sitter while she was training.

"Why don't you take a seat, Casey?" Thomas nudged her to the stool at the counter beside Cecelia. "You may as well know the truth of what we're up against."

"I beg your pardon?" Cecelia stared at her brother as a fresh wave of concern rolled over her. "What truth?"

"You have to go into protective custody. Today. Right now, Lia."

A chill raised the hairs at the back of her neck. Her brother didn't shorten her name unless he was seriously distressed.

"I'll go pack a bag for you, Mom." Casey hopped off the counter stool, but Cecelia stayed her with a look.

"Why do I need protective custody?"

Thomas slumped forward, leaning his forearms on the counter and lowering his voice. "The analysts picked up some chatter about you."

"Me?"

"You're in danger. A pawn in a bigger game," Thomas growled. "It's my fault." He pushed back from the counter and paced away, then swiveled back. "One of my enemies plans to kidnap you. At least that's the rumor making the rounds."

"Oh, that's going too far, Thomas. We both know none of your enemies could possibly know about me." Her brother was the director of Mission Recovery, a covert team so dark, not even the president was routinely briefed on their operations. When Thomas or his Specialists were in the field, their cover stories were solid, with no links to their real lives. The only way an enemy could know about his connection to her… Oh, dear God.

"He has a mole inside my team. The kidnapper is likely to be one of my own Specialists."

That was all Casey needed to hear. She slipped by Cecelia and rushed up the stairs.

"That's impossible. It doesn't make sense. Your team is devoted to you and their work. You handpicked each one of them."

Thomas grimaced and scrubbed a hand across his short hair. "Well, I clearly made a mistake somewhere."

"Who?" Stunned, she took a moment to wrap her head around such a ridiculous idea. No one betrayed Thomas Casey. "Who on your team would dare to cross you?"

"It doesn't matter. I'm setting up an op to take him down."

Cecelia relaxed a fraction. "Then there's no reason for me to run and hide."

Thomas glared at her. Having grown up with him, she didn't find the expression so intimidating.

"Lia, this mole is devious. He's been operating right under my nose for months now. When we make the arrest, it's going to stick, but he's going to fight back. Locking down the evidence for this kind of thing takes time. I'm not going to allow you to get caught in the middle."

"Allow?" She laughed. "I'm a grown woman."

"I know that." He clasped her hands in his. "You're one of the strongest people I know."

"So we agree." She met the determination in his blue gaze with an equal measure of her own. "I'll be careful, keep your number on speed dial, but I'm not going into hiding, Thomas. Not under any circumstances. It's my turn to challenge myself."

Besides, even if she wasn't making this career change, she just didn't think she could manage that kind of drastic shift in her plans. Not in the middle of this holiday season.

Last year's holidays had been marred by her husband's death. She'd still been receiving sympathy cards amid the annual Christmas letters and greetings. The abundance of charitable donations made in his name had been kind and wonderful expressions from caring friends.

And nearly unbearable as she wrote out each and every thank-you note. She felt awful and it was as if every bright moment last year was eclipsed by the darkness of her loss. It had been sheer determination and more than a little detachment that had got her through.

Promise me you'll live your life. It was the last coherent conversation she'd had with her husband before the aggressive brain tumor had made her a widow.

She'd been trying to honor that request, and she had no intention of letting a rogue agent and a vague threat get in the way. She was living her life.

"You can't be that selfish," Thomas barked. "Or that foolish."

She reeled back as if he'd struck her.

"I'm sorry. Sorry," he repeated, holding his hands up. "But don't you see if you're out there—" he flung a hand wide "—you become leverage they can use against me to get what they want?"

"For how long?"

"Pardon?"

"How long would you keep me in protective custody? Where would I be? What excuse would I give to the people who are counting on me this weekend?"

Thomas blinked rapidly and frowned as if he were trying to catch up. "I don't know. A couple of weeks, maybe longer."

That would never work. Cecelia shook her head adamantly. "This is the wrong time, Thomas. I realize you didn't plan this, but you know I have commitments."

"The charities and parties can manage without you."

"But I don't want them to. And I won't let a vague 'maybe longer' interfere with my plans." That was exactly what she was trying to change in her life. The idea everyone else seemed to have that nothing she did mattered enough that it couldn't be cast aside at the drop of a hat.

"Cecelia, please cooperate. The man pulling the strings on this won't hesitate to hurt you. He turned one of my own people against me. He nearly killed me a few times over between the airport and Casey's wedding."

"And yet you made it." She patted his cheek. He really didn't need to go so far in his effort to talk her out of this move. "I'll make it, too—if this threat to me even proves more than a rumor."

"I had years of field experience and another trained agent at my side," Thomas protested.

"I'm not hiding."

"Mom," Casey hesitated in the kitchen doorway, a big suitcase behind her. "You might put your friends in danger."

"That's hitting below the belt and it won't work." Cecelia set her hands on her hips. "Your father didn't marry a bubble brain, no matter how the two of you believe otherwise."

"You're twisting things up," Casey said. "This has nothing to do with your career change."

"Maybe it should." The words were out before she'd really thought it through, but she warmed to the idea immediately. "I'm taking leave through the holiday until I report for ops training. Why not use me to trap the traitor on your team?"

"How can you help if you're a victim?" her brother demanded.

"If they make the attempt, you can close in and you'll have your rogue agent. If—big if—I get kidnapped, you'll have someone on the inside."

Thomas shook his head. "No way. I won't risk your life that way. Even if we wired you, this guy would either find it or jam the signal, rendering the exercise pointless."

Cecelia held her ground, undeterred. "You can get creative and use me as an asset, or stop wasting your breath. Even if you put me in a safe house, I wouldn't stay there." Not this year. She had plans, a ticket to the Caymans and maybe even a new friend who might be encouraged to join her on a holiday getaway. But she wasn't sharing that. As unsettled as these two were about her career change, she didn't want to see how they would come unglued over her personal secret.

"If you were asset material, I'd have recruited you already."

Casey gasped, but Cecelia gave her brother her most serene smile. "When is this kidnapping supposed to happen?"

"I don't have a hard date. The analysts are working on it."

"I see."

"Who is the mole?" Casey wanted to know.

"I've narrowed it down to two people."

Cecelia arched an eyebrow. He'd already avoided this question once.

"Has to be either my deputy director or his assistant. They're the only ones who have the access to the information we've discovered that has been leaked to my enemy."

"And your gut says who?" Cecelia pressed.

Thomas sighed, rubbed his temples. "My money's on Deputy Director Holt. He's the only one who would know where to start looking. I just don't think his assistant could manage this alone. As much as I hate to admit it, it has to be Holt."

Cecelia rode out the jolt of surprise, hoping the two people staring at her didn't notice. She thought about it for a minute or two as Thomas went on about how he was still having trouble accepting the man would turn like this. Cecelia sipped her coffee, found it had gone cold. She dumped it out and poured a fresh cup.

Okay, reality check. What were the odds that two men named Holt would come to her attention within weeks of each other, one working for her brother and another through the online dating site?

Didn't take a master spy to figure that out. Slim to none, she figured.

Might as well put it on the table. "Emmett Holt?" she asked.

"Yes." Thomas scowled. "How do you know his name?"

"A man by that name was a last-minute donor to tomorrow's gala fundraiser," she hedged. And he'd been flirting with her online for the past few weeks. Those emails and text messages had been fun and full of life, but those feelings were fading quickly with Thomas's bleak news.

She'd learned long ago that coincidences usually weren't a matter of chance. She wouldn't put it past her brother to encourage a member of his team to make a dating connection and set her up like this, just to keep an eye on her. And he'd be feeling pretty guilty if the man he assigned to such a task was working against him.

But Thomas didn't look the least bit guilty, only stunned.

She moistened her lips and asked the question. "You didn't know he contacted me?" If this wasn't Thomas's idea, she wasn't about to clarify the precise manner of contact had been a dating service. They'd balked enough at her career plans.

She held her breath, a big part of her hoping there really were two Emmett Holts.

"How does this guy spell his name?"

She glanced to her daughter. "Casey, bring me my purse, please."

"It's right here." Casey already had it balanced on the top of the suitcase.

"Aren't you efficient?" Cecelia pulled out her tablet and brought up the details about the charity gala she'd organized for the pediatric children's oncology unit in memory of William. "There." She highlighted the line on the screen that showed donor names, addresses and emails, and then turned it so her brother and daughter could see it. "I was told he called the office yesterday morning, asked how close we were to the goal and then donated the balance."

"Holt?" Thomas gaped at her.

"So it is the same man?"

Her brother nodded then growled. "Looks that way. Think about it, Lia, why pick your cause?"

"Generosity? Maybe he needed a tax write-off. That happens this time of year." She could tell her brother didn't put much stock in either possibility. Yesterday she'd thought it was the gesture of a wealthy man more than a little smitten with the gala's organizer. Now… Well, now he had more than a few questions to answer.

Just her luck. The first guy who managed to stir any feelings in her and he had an ulterior motive.

"This would put him right next to you tomorrow night."

"You're being melodramatic." Truth was she had asked for tomorrow's seating chart to be adjusted when she learned he would attend. She'd had every intention of getting "next to him" and thanking him personally during their first real date, scheduled for this evening. She wasn't about to mention those plans in front of her brother and daughter.

"He might not even show up." She wouldn't think twice about having him tossed out if he didn't clear up a few things tonight.

"Oh, he'll show." There was a calculating gleam in Thomas's eyes. "And he'll find a way to kidnap you. It's the perfect venue and it would be a terrible embarrassment to me if I'm not there to protect you."

"That's absurd. Tomorrow's venue is perfect for raising money for the charity. Besides, I'll be surrounded by the trained agents and retired spies who make up our extended family all night long."

"Then it's a scouting mission," Thomas argued. "I'm telling you, Holt doesn't do anything on a whim. Every mishap of the past two months points directly to his office. This is the beginning of the grand finale. I can feel it, Lia."

Casey gave a thoughtful hum. "Wouldn't a guy who's made it to the second in command at Mission Recovery be more careful than that? Sounds a little half-baked to me."

Cecelia could have hugged her daughter. She thought the same thing, but knew Thomas wouldn't have entertained the suggestion if she'd offered it. It wasn't that she blamed him—he only wanted to protect her—but she was weary of being overshadowed and underestimated.

As the wife of a CIA operative, she'd learned to support and assist her husband in the real world, she had her own security clearance and even though she'd spent her career to date in the completely safe admin side of the agency, she knew how to think through a problem like an operative.

Her daughter's and her brother's consistent underrating of her was her own fault, she supposed. She'd let it happen by design and circumstance. They were used to her in a certain role: sister, mother, head chef, cheerleader and most recently caregiver and occasional confidant. Change was difficult, and she hadn't discussed her plans with them; she'd just put in the request to move to ops.

She'd told herself it was to see how she fared on her own merits, but it was just as much about delaying their inevitable resistance.

"Relax, Thomas. I'm safe and I'm perfectly capable of staying that way." She infused confidence into her voice. "You'll both be at the event tomorrow and we'll be surrounded by a room full of people. Go vet the hotel security staff if it makes you feel better." She wrote down the contact name from her notes. "Your Mr. Holt can scout all he wants, but we all know he won't be able to lift a finger against me. At least not and get away with it."

Thomas took the note and stalked out of the house without another word.

Cecelia turned to Casey. "Well, since you've got everything packed, I might as well go check in at the hotel and make Thomas happy."

"I can move there with you. Keep you company."

Cecelia bit back the frustrated reply as she loaded the used coffee mugs into the dishwasher. "You stay here like we planned and enjoy some quiet with your new husband when he arrives." She'd have to put this place up for sale one day, but it didn't have to be today. The place was just too large for her to keep up on her own. Especially if she was away a lot.

"We came to see you, Mom."

"And I appreciate it, sweetheart. We both know your uncle's already assigned a detail to hover over my shoulder." She flicked a hand in the direction of the street. "I know for a fact the Millers haven't had a week's worth of plumbing trouble and yet the van is still out there."

Casey walked toward the front window to look. "He just wants to keep you safe," she said with a soft laugh.

"I know that. It's only a ten-minute drive to the Plaza." She was already mentally adjusting her plans to give her date a chance to explain himself before Thomas barged in and wrecked it.

Was she that desperate? Maybe.

Whatever Emmett's reasons for reaching out to her through the online dating site and making the donation, she felt there was potential for a *real* connection between them. What she didn't feel was that he posed any threat to her.

Thomas would call that naive. Casey would call it wishful thinking.

She called it intuition, and she'd learned to trust her instincts long ago.

Cecelia was going on that date.

Chapter Three

Mission Recovery Training Center, 3:24 p.m.

Emmett Holt braced his elbows on his knees and caught his breath while he unwound the hand wraps protecting his knuckles from the heavy bag. The sweat dripped from his brow, trickled down his arms. Most days a hard workout cleared his head, but he'd been balanced on the edge for too long.

He recognized the signs, knew the inherent danger, but there was no going back.

Not now. He glanced up at the news ticker scrolling across the bottom of the television screen. No inexplicable illness outbreaks. No one closing in on him here at the gym with weapons drawn and handcuffs ready.

Every hour that passed without incident only amped up his tension.

This game had very real, life-altering consequences. Life ending was more accurate. For the inevitable innocent victims, as well as Isely and his team of instigators who'd launched this frustrating drama.

He crossed the gym and locked his ankles into the inversion table, then eased back. For a long moment, he just let himself hang there, upside down, daring anyone to take a shot.

Neither side would make a move here, not in public. It was the shadows he had to worry about. And those were all around him…every move he made.

Hands fisted, he crossed them over his chest and started the first set of fifty crunches.

He focused on the count, only letting his mind wander once he was relaxed and stretching out the burn.

Isely still had the one thing Holt needed to secure: the last vial of a deadly new virus. And Holt had more of what Isely wanted: damaging information on Director Thomas Casey.

Years ago, Casey had gone undercover in Germany, disrupting an exchange that would have set the Isely crime family at the pinnacle of the black-market weapons business forever.

It was one of those rare, landscape-changing deals, and Mission Recovery had successfully stopped it.

That's what they did, the whole reason the team existed. God, he was going to miss having that kind of clear purpose in his life.

Holt did a slow-burn second set, then paused to think some more.

He glanced around the gym, and though there were only a few other Specialists around, he felt like they were watching him too closely and with too much wariness lurking behind those neutral expressions. Did they expect him to just lose it with a violent outburst or remorseful confession? Which one of them had been on his tail when he made the drop for Isely?

Months ago he'd have chalked up the wide berth they gave him to being the deputy director. He wasn't popular with the team. That hadn't bothered him much before. His management style was simply different from Casey's, more aloof.

It wasn't his job to make friends.

But since he'd chosen to take this mission on his own, with no one else read into the situation, he felt the unavoidable onset of mild paranoia. Holt told himself to relax. Even if Casey had started to piece it together, he wouldn't have shared such a damning theory with the entire team.

Not yet, anyway.

Holt took a deep breath, reminding himself he'd been trained to succeed at all costs. It shouldn't be such a surprise that his current efforts made him a potential target. That's how he'd planned it.

He came back to an upright position slowly to avoid the disorienting head rush, then unlocked the ankle bar and moved to an empty weight bench to work on his back.

Everyone thought he was just a suit, sitting in the successor's chair. Days like this were a clear reminder to the team that his strengths went well beyond pushing paper and signing off on personnel evaluations.

"Sir?"

He recognized his assistant's voice, as well as her polished black pumps when Nadine stopped in front of him.

He sat upright and pushed a towel across his face. "What is it?"

"Two of the messages you've been expecting."

Holt tossed the towel over his shoulder and accepted the cell phone she handed him. One number was blocked, but the terse text message left no doubt the sender was Isely.

The clock is ticking.

Holt scrolled, switched to the voice mail message with a shake of his head. The world was full of ticking clocks.

The silky feminine voice, definitely a product of a private school, drifted into his ear and eased the tension in his shoulders. "Thank you for the substantial donation, Emmett. We've reserved a seat for you at tomorrow's event. We're thrilled that you'll be able to join us so we can personally express our appreciation for your generosity."

Cecelia. It was exactly the opening Isely had ordered him to create. He smiled, unable to temper his enthusiasm for their date tonight. He struggled to keep it in the appropriate perspective. She was part of the job, but he'd discovered a few layers under the polish that tweaked his curiosity.

After all, despite popular opinion, he was human.

Holt handed the phone back to Nadine. "Thank you."

She nodded. "Yes, sir."

"Do you have plans tonight?"

"No, sir."

He studied her, but couldn't be sure if she was lying. It didn't matter. They both knew she'd cancel her plans if necessary to fulfill his request. "I could use your help in Alexandria."

"Black tie?"

"No." So she'd seen his reservations for the weekend. The reservation he wanted her to see anyway. "A few hours of recon." Isely's impatience made him nervous. He wanted someone out there he knew he could count on. "I'll get you the details."

With a polite nod, Nadine left him to finish his workout.

He powered through the strength routine, Isely's ticking clock in the back of his mind as he hit the treadmill.

Specialist Blue Callahan, well, Drake now that she was married, stepped onto the machine next to him. Like the others, she'd been handpicked for her post within Mission Recovery and she'd met the man who'd become her husband on an assignment. She had, in fact, been backed up on that mission by none other than the one and only Lucas Camp.

There was no love lost between Holt and Lucas. The older man had a method and when Holt replaced him here at Mission Recovery, he'd developed his own methods. Holt had reason to believe that despite his retirement, Lucas had been poking around in Holt's professional life. Probably his personal life, too. It was never a good thing to have a man like Camp second-guessing decisions.

Lucas Camp was a master in the business of spying. But he was out to pasture now and he needed to get right with his place in the world of spooks.

Keeping his face in neutral, Holt's mind spun through the potential pitfalls and traps Blue's appearance might present to his timeline.

"Deputy Director," she said, acknowledging him with an easy smile. "Working hard?"

"Always." He increased the programmed interval workout to the next level. "Big plans for the holidays?" It seemed the question on everyone's lips this month.

"Not particularly. A party or two, then Noah and I are headed back to the island for a quiet celebration. You have plans?"

"About the same as last year." That was one detail the team knew for certain about him—he had no family and no inclination to create one.

The glance she slid him held a bit of concern. "If you're ever in the mood for a warm, quiet beach, you're welcome to stay in our guesthouse."

He nodded, unable to come up with a verbal response. Not because of the effort to maintain his pace on the treadmill but because she'd shocked him. No one on the team—other than Thomas Casey—had ever aimed a social invitation in his direction.

Blue looked for all the world like she meant it, but he knew her impeccable field skills and had to consider this approach might be a trap. "I'll let you know," he replied.

He got through the rest of his cardio without incident and headed toward the locker room to clean up. Half an hour later, as he walked upstairs in the direction of the solitude of his office, he had to forcibly turn his thoughts away from the likelihood that this might be his last hour in this building.

As Holt entered the suite of offices that included his, Specialist Jason Grant was waiting for him, kicked back with a magazine in one of Nadine's reception chairs. So much for solitude.

"Grant."

"Sir," he said, setting aside the magazine and getting to his feet. "Do you have a minute?"

Holt looked him up and down, recognized the relaxed demeanor of a man fresh from vacation—this time on a honeymoon. Grant was slated to replace him as deputy director when Holt advanced to the director's post. Assuming of course Holt didn't die or wind up in prison in the next week or so. "Marriage suits you."

"Thanks." Jason rocked back on his heels, pushed his hands into his pockets.

"Come on in." Holt left the door open as he entered his office, counting on Jason's choice to close it or leave it open to give him a clue about what might be on the younger man's mind.

The door closed with a soft click.

Holt took his seat, relieved there wasn't a weapon in his back or a bullet in his brain just yet. He needed just enough lead time to get through the next forty-eight hours. Then he'd happily take whatever discipline Mission Recovery wanted to mete out.

He unbuttoned his suit coat and settled into his chair. Jason mirrored his movements, taking the chair across the wide desk.

"What can I do for you, Grant?"

"Just a quick follow up on the Las Vegas operation."

Anticipation pricked Holt. "That case is closed."

"I realize I failed you—"

"Relax." Holt tapped a pencil against the arm of his chair. "My evaluation doesn't read that way. As far as Mission Recovery is concerned, you did a fine job out there."

"But—"

"A piece of advice?"

Jason nodded.

"Let it go. There's nothing to clarify, nothing to be concerned about beyond the holidays and your next mission."

"Which is?"

Holt forced his lips into a smile. "To enjoy the holidays with your new wife."

But Jason's eyebrows were drawn together. "Permission to speak freely?"

Holt dipped his chin. "Of course." One day, if he didn't get caught in his own trap, they would need to be completely candid with one another as director and deputy director.

"I don't think I believe you."

Holt didn't move a muscle as more of that anticipation leeched into his veins.

"I've gone over it every way possible, sir," he added with more sarcasm than respect. "That whole business in Vegas felt like a setup."

"You have good instincts," Holt admitted. "And I agree with your assessment. If you're implying I had anything to do with it, I'd ask you to give that a great deal more thought before you say something you'll regret."

Jason's gaze narrowed, but he kept his mouth shut. Kudos to the young man. He was going to make a top-notch deputy director.

"I have nothing but respect for you and your talents." Might as well add a compliment to the ugly truth, Holt thought. He hesitated, could practically hear the figurative ice cracking under his feet as he prepared to share details better kept under wraps. "Ours is a world of secrets, as you know. We have a mole in Mission Recovery. You can only imagine the distress and effort we've put into making a solid identification, but the director and I are working to resolve the problem."

"How can I help?"

"You know Director Casey has a history with Isely. See what your Interpol connections can give us on his operations over there."

"Anything in particular?"

Holt gave in and sighed. Another lie was hardly going to matter at this point. "I want to pin down the biologist who manufactured this virus Isely has been trying to unload."

"You think Isely means to manufacture more?"

"It would be one hell of a residual income. Just see what you can turn up." Holt could only hope the diversion would keep Jason distracted until this God-forsaken mission was over.

When Jason left, Holt addressed the blinking icon that indicated he had another message on his cell. Blocked number.

They know. I have adjusted the timeline accordingly.

No! Holt's temper nearly boiled over. If Isely used someone else to kidnap Cecelia Manning, Holt would be forced to expose himself to one side or the other before he had the evidence in hand to clear his name and maintain Mission Recovery's anonymity.

It was impossible. No one here could possibly know. Not yet. Of course Director Casey would have suspicions. He was supposed to have suspicions. Holt had been feeding Isely information very few people could access. But he'd put the breadcrumbs in the system, left enough room for doubt so he could finish the task the right way without jeopardizing too much or laying Mission Recovery bare for the government vultures and rabid media to pick over.

Isely didn't have the franchise on making adjustments. Holt knew how to scramble, scrap and fight dirty when it was necessary. A few years behind a desk didn't change the core of a man.

For nearly a year now, he'd let Isely see what he wanted to see, a disgruntled, ambitious second-in-command who resented Casey almost as much as Isely himself. It had been the performance of his life and he wasn't about to abandon it now when he could almost see the end of these dark days.

Adjustment negates impact, he replied via text on the disposable and untraceable burner phone Isely had provided. Deep down, Holt knew Isely preferred the showy, public embarrassment that kidnapping Cecelia from the gala would provide.

Long minutes passed and Holt mentally composed and deleted at least ten incriminating text messages. If he sent any of them, if he left the director no room for doubt, it would make it damn near impossible to nail Isely before the bastard slipped away to run his operation from a non-extradition country.

Holt had put himself in so many different shoes and looked at this from everyone's perspective he'd almost lost sight of his own agenda. Protecting Thomas Casey was top priority and preventing the exposure of Mission Recovery was essential. He cringed to think of the careers ruined and lives irreparably disrupted if the worst happened.

Finally, the cell chirped with another text message. Proceed as planned.

He'd been close enough to Isely these past months that he knew his enemy believed this news would bring him relief. He'd portrayed himself to Isely as a man who needed the stability of guidance and a set schedule. But that was the act. Holt knew better than to trust Isely to keep the leash on whoever had been chosen to take over should Holt get caught or falter.

Isely had resources and he used them well. Holt was plan A. There would be a plan B eager to step up and prove their worth in order to gain promotion and prestige within Isely's operation.

Well, there was one sure way to keep Cecelia safe until Holt could move in on schedule. Holt crossed to his office safe, pulled out an alternate ID and a stack of cash and prepared for his date with the director's sister.

It was laughable. The stuff of comic tragedies. He was about to prevent a kidnapping by becoming a proper gentleman.

Chapter Four

Old Town Alexandria, 7:12 p.m.

Cecelia turned up the collar on her wool coat for the short walk to meet her friends at their favorite wine bar in Old Town. It was the place they'd brainstormed tomorrow's gala and it was fitting to celebrate their success with a toast there tonight. The temperature was dropping but the moon was bright overhead, and the crisp winter air cleared her head. She breathed deeply now, knowing in a few days' time she'd be breathing warm, humid air in the Caymans.

It was no surprise the dark sedan had followed her from the house to the Plaza hotel. When she thought about it, she realized one like it had either been parked at the corner of her block or shadowing her for the past couple of days. She walked on, resisting the urge to tell the driver to go back and report that Director Casey's sister could take care of herself. She should give Thomas some credit. Clearly he suspected she'd balk at protective custody, and he'd brought the safety measures to her.

She was nearly to the bar when two men approached her. They wore U.S. Navy-issue wool peacoats over jeans and heavy boots, but that was where the resemblance ended. The hair broke regulation, as did the beards. Her first thought was they were longshoremen on leave, but Old Town Alexandria wasn't exactly a shipping hub.

"Ma'am?" They stopped just in front of her. "Excuse me. Do you know the area?" the taller man asked with a faint trace of a French accent.

Thomas's warning blasted through her and she told herself it was far too early in her budding ops career for paranoia. Her hands fisted around the car key in her pocket. There was security nearby in the dark sedan, and by now Casey and her new husband were probably watching from a rooftop, and Cecelia was close enough to the bar that she could call for help if necessary.

"Yes," she replied with a nod, determined to keep an open mind. "What are you trying to find?"

"Do you know the restaurant owned by the retired hockey player?"

She relaxed, releasing her grip on her key. They were French Canadian hockey fans. "Of course." She gave them directions and wished them a good evening as she entered the wine bar.

Looking around, she realized she was the first to arrive, so she claimed a high-top table near the front window of the swanky little bar and waited for her friends. While she was thrilled with their progress and the news that they'd hit the pre-event fundraising goal, with every passing hour she was losing enthusiasm for the event itself.

Her daughter and brother would attend with their new spouses, and she'd be the lonely, courageous widow.

She rubbed at the fading indentation on her ring finger where her wedding band used to sit. Even after William's death, she'd worn it, not quite ready to part with it.

After Casey's wedding in October, she'd had it cleaned and stored it in the safe at the house. Her friends had been supportive and so far her family hadn't noticed. Or maybe they just hadn't known what to say. They'd probably been too distracted with news of her career change to notice a change in her jewelry.

Now here she was, intent on meeting a man who could be an enemy of her brother…of her. She was prepared. Cecelia might not carry a handgun in her bag, but she always carried her trusty Taser. She was far from an expert with handguns, but she'd taken the necessary classes for using the Taser.

"Cecelia?"

She swiveled toward the deep voice she recognized from a few phone calls. The polite smile she always wore in public slipped a little when she met the intense, gray-blue gaze of the man who'd approached her table.

Danger was her first thought, with *delicious* chasing right behind it. His picture on the dating profile hadn't been doctored. And it hadn't done him justice. Those eyes, so cool and clear, were framed by the stark contrast of slashing dark eyebrows, thick dark hair and chiseled features.

His mouth tilted up at one corner. "Emmett Holt." He extended a hand. "I hope I didn't startle you."

"Not at all, Mr. Holt." She struggled to remember to breathe. To remember her brother suspected him of a terrible betrayal. Instead, all his wit and charm in their previous online conversations danced through her mind. "A pleasure," she managed. *Please let him be one of the good guys.* It would be so unfair to wind up with a shark on her first dive back into the dating pool.

The upturned corner widened into a full-blown smile and his eyes crinkled a bit at the corners. She barely stifled an admiring sigh. "Forgive me," she said, searching for her composure. "Did I get the time wrong?"

According to her calendar, they were meeting at eight,

after her toast with her friends. She had the sudden, bizarre urge to keep him all to herself. Dating was going to be enough of a shock, but dating a man who looked like this? Tomorrow night would be soon enough to show him off. She felt flushed in a way she'd almost forgotten about.

"Not at all. I got to town early. Planned to have a drink to settle my nerves before you arrived." He leaned closer. "Dare I hope you're here for the same reason?"

She shook her head, feeling a goofy grin fighting for control of her face. "I'm meeting friends. A last-minute review for tomorrow's event."

"Ah." He looked around. "Smart planning."

"I tend to do that."

That half smile was back. "Just as you stated in your profile." He winked. "I'll just wait over there at the bar until it's my turn."

The way he said that launched a swarm of butterflies in her belly.

"Wait. Your generosity..." She trailed off, searching for words as a surge of unexpected emotion swamped her. "Well, we thank you."

"It's a good cause," he replied. "I'll be waiting at the bar."

She watched him walk away—drinking in the way his trousers fit his backside, like a woman too long stranded in the desert. Abruptly she realized he might catch her foolish behavior in the reflection of the mirror behind the bar.

She specifically made the effort not to check if he'd caught her staring, instead turning her gaze back toward the door. Her willpower was rewarded as her friends came in together in a rush of cold air and happy voices. They raised a glass to success, double-checked every last-minute detail, right down to their personal shoe selections, and then parted company until tomorrow.

Half an hour had never seemed to drag more. Which was a terrible thing to be thinking. These were friends she had enjoyed for years. Friends who'd carried her through all stages of motherhood, a few lonely anniversaries and eventually her husband's diagnosis and decline.

Cecelia pushed all of that to the back of her mind. That was the past. Her future was waiting for her on the other side of the holiday season. And oh, my, her present was right there watching her from the end of the bar. With her purse and wool coat over her arm, she squeezed through the growing crowd to join Emmett Holt.

"Hi." Reminding herself she couldn't be certain about his motives and discovering her intuition was blurred by her shocking attraction to him, she didn't know how else to start. "Sorry to have kept you waiting."

"Not a problem," he said, offering her his seat. "I enjoyed the view. Would you like another glass of wine?"

"Just water, please." She didn't think alcohol would help her manage her fascination and she needed to focus if she was going to get some straight answers out of him.

He signaled the bartender, and she had a tall glass of water with a wedge of lemon within seconds. The bartender leaned close. "How are things going, Cecelia?"

"Great. Thanks, Ted."

Ted glanced at Emmett and then back to her. "Do you and the ladies have everything all set for tomorrow night?"

"Definitely."

"Glad to hear it." He moved on down the bar to serve the next customer.

"A friend of yours?"

She glanced at Emmett while she sipped her water, letting the cool liquid soothe her dry throat. He looked a little perturbed with the bartender's familiarity. Was he jealous, or did he see a potential interference with his kidnapping plan? Her intuition couldn't pin it down. Granted, she hadn't tried dating since her husband died and she didn't know if this was business or pleasure yet—only that part of her was seriously hoping for the latter.

"My friends and I meet here almost every week," she explained. "You work in DC. Surely this isn't your first trip to Alexandria."

"No, it isn't."

Well, that was less than enlightening. She tried a different tack. "Is there a particular area or way you'd like us to use your donation?"

He smiled, slowly, and though it was hard to tell in this light she thought maybe he blushed a bit. "No. You're free to use the money how you see fit."

"Okay." She watched him carefully, searching out any clues to his intention with her. But watching him carefully meant taking in the details. He oozed confidence and he obviously worked out. He was trim without being skinny and if his forearms were any indication, his biceps and shoulders would be beautifully sculpted.

He angled his body, effectively sheltering her from the crowded room and making this public encounter suddenly feel a lot more private.

Her heart rate fluttered, but with awareness rather than a more appropriate concern. He was close enough she recognized the citrus and cedar notes of his cologne. Her husband had preferred—she cut off the thought. That was *then.* This moment, this evening, was all that mattered right now.

Live your life.

But something else about Emmett reminded her of her husband and her brother. She'd been around the type long enough she would have picked up on it even without Thomas's warning this afternoon. Emmett gave the appearance of being focused on her, but he was surreptitiously inventorying their surroundings and the people coming and going around them.

She'd caught her daughter doing the same thing more than once since Casey started working in ops. Situational awareness was a skill taught to field agents in the CIA as well as any other number of agencies. If she'd asked him, she knew he could give her an accurate description of everyone in the room and the best way out if any trouble cropped up.

He was definitely one of her brother's Specialists, and the last shred of hope she'd clung to that their meeting online had been a coincidence dwindled to zero. She needed a plan, needed to get to the bottom of his motives before she wound up used—or worse.

The man might have a generous streak, but it didn't require an active intuition to see there was more under the charming surface. "It was a pleasure to meet you, but maybe this isn't the best night for dinner. Let's talk more tomorrow at the gala." She slid off the stool just as someone behind him shifted, and she found herself pressed tight against his warm, hard body.

Speaking of situational awareness… She looked up at him, captivated by the cool gaze that only increased her body temperature.

"Why don't we go somewhere less crowded?"

Yes! "I'm not sure that's such a good idea." She inched away from him, fighting the overwhelming urge to get closer. "As generous as you are, we're scarcely more than strangers."

"I made a reservation for us at that steak house down the street."

The crowd shifted again, and this time he braced to

keep from bumping into her. She was outrageously disappointed.

"Come on." He smiled and her heart jolted. "Let's share an appetizer and then you can decide if dinner is an option."

She felt herself nodding an agreement before she could voice a reasonable excuse.

He took her coat from her grasp and held it for her, straightening the collar and smoothing his hands over her shoulders. He retrieved his coat—a supple leather bomber-style jacket—from the hook just under the bar top.

He gestured for her to go first, and when she checked the reflection, she saw his eyes weren't on her, but the crowd around them. Something wasn't quite right. Was he protecting her or preparing to snatch her away?

Oh, she had to get her brother's voice out of her head so she could find her own way through this situation. She pushed through the door to the street and turned to just ask him outright, but another of his smiles completely derailed her train of thought.

"Is it always so crowded in there? It's a wine bar."

His beleaguered expression earned her sympathy. Apparently the profile notation that said he didn't like crowds was truthful. Giving him the benefit of the doubt, she said, "It's a popular wine bar. And every place is busier since we're closing in on Christmas." She gestured to indicate the white lights and holiday color dressing up the Old Town district of Alexandria.

"Fair point," he agreed, falling into step beside her.

"Was the holiday spirit what moved you to make that donation?"

His lips twitched and he ducked his head to avoid a low-hanging strand of white lights. "In part. I'm not typically one for the holiday spirit. Mostly it was you. After we met online, I poked around and found that video your organization posted. Who could resist?"

Plenty of people in this economy, she'd discovered. "What is it that you do, Mr. Holt?"

"You call me Emmett online," he reminded her.

His low voice sent a ripple of anticipation across her skin. "Emmett," she repeated, like a besotted schoolgirl.

"I'm in private security."

She turned her gaze toward the street, hiding her unjustified disappointment. Even if their online flirtation was genuine, she knew he wouldn't have told her what he really did and who he really worked for. It would have been a breach of security at this stage. Even as the director's sister, she wouldn't know Mission Recovery existed if she hadn't been married to a man like William. She told herself it was too soon to have any opinion on situations that fell into the delicate area of security clearances.

Still, she needed to know if he was here as friend or foe. "Ah, that explains it."

"Explains what?"

She shrugged. "The way you scout a room and keep track of people. Don't worry. It's not obvious to most women."

He gave her an arch look.

"I have relatives who are also in security-related jobs. Par for the course this close to DC," she added, wishing he'd take the bait and elaborate. Wishing she had the courage to demand clarification. It felt so uneven to be this attracted to a virtual stranger without any idea if his responses were sincere. It was an odd sensation to realize someday in the field someone would look at her and wonder the same thing.

"It's a habit we all develop, I suppose."

"A matter of survival," she agreed. "Or so they tell

me." Come January she'd be getting the training first-hand. No more inferring from the vague references her family made. It was an exciting thought, and she grinned with anticipation.

"Now, that's quite a look, Mrs. Manning."

"Cecelia," she corrected. "I'm changing jobs after the holidays and whenever I think about it, I get excited."

"What type of change?" He pulled open the door of the restaurant and she stepped into the dim alcove.

"Just something more active." If he could hedge, so could she. It was good practice, anyway. "My company had openings in another department. All the recent charity endeavors made me realize I'm ready to get out from behind a desk."

He gave his name to the hostess and they were seated immediately. "What have you been doing?" he asked when they were settled in a cozy corner booth.

"I focus on basic administration for the human resources department. It's utterly boring, sifting through the same documents day in and day out. The job served its purpose while our daughter was growing up, but I'm ready to branch out now."

"You seem eager to try something new."

"Precisely." A man as perceptive as Emmett had probably already noticed that her hormones were willing to start that something new with him at the first opportunity.

The waiter came by with water and offered the evening's specials. They ordered drinks and the sampler of appetizers and Cecelia returned to her task of trying to unravel Emmett's motives.

"How long will you be in town?"

"Probably just through the weekend."

"Probably?" she echoed. Where had her conversational

skills gone? He'd been trained to divert the curiosity she was so clearly showing, but she could do better.

"I'm really just here for you. For the gala," he added as though it was an afterthought. "Haven't had much cause to pull out the penguin suit lately, figured I should enjoy it. After that, it's back to work."

"In DC?"

"Same as everyone else in this area," he said with that half smile that made her want to sigh.

She agreed with a nod. "You won't take time off for the holidays?" Before her brother's announcement this afternoon, she'd been determined to boldly invite him to join her on a beach in the Caymans in a few days' time.

"Someone has to keep the office running. All the other guys have family." He shrugged. "I volunteer to stick around on holidays and put out the occasional fire so they don't have to."

"That's thoughtful of you."

One shoulder hitched in a casual shrug. "When you have kids, you should be there for them."

"That was my philosophy."

But now it was her turn to do something solely for herself… The problem was, this part may have been a mistake.

Chapter Five

Holt gave her credit for a gentle interrogation style, but he recognized the effort for what it was. It might only be first-date protocol, but maybe Isely had been right and Casey had started moving to intercept him already.

How to ask her what she knew without blowing it all to hell? That was the real question.

He started to ask then paused when the phone Isely had given him shivered in his pocket. It would likely be the address where he was supposed to stash Cecelia tomorrow night. He'd spotted a couple of Isely's men in the area already and the idea made him wary about being tailed.

"Excuse me one second."

He checked the phone and his stomach clutched when he read the terse message and recognized the address of a local warehouse. His worst fear confirmed. Isely's men had informed their boss that Holt and Cecelia were together and Isely wanted her tonight. *Damn it.* Holt needed to slow things down or his whole counter-operation would crash and burn. Isely might get a measure of revenge moving in on Cecelia tonight, but he wouldn't get the full effect Holt had promised when they'd been planning and negotiating terms.

"Problem?"

"No, not at all." He smiled and put the phone away. "Just a work thing."

"I understand. It happens."

She looked more disappointed than understanding. Her late husband had probably ruined many personal evenings with sensitive work distractions. Holt had the strange urge to show her a different side of men in security-related careers.

Not smart.

He turned the phone off and showed her the black screen before tucking it into his coat pocket. "There. I'm off the clock. Meant to do that earlier, but I needed the navigation app." Her smile was worth the lie. Worth all of the lies he'd been telling lately.

The appetizer sampler arrived and for a few minutes they just indulged in the cheese and cured meat selection. He couldn't remember the last time he'd felt this comfortable, this normal with a woman. Especially a woman who was a target.

Her manners were perfect society matron, but her little hum of appreciation as her lips closed over her fork had him thinking of other things. Things he had no business thinking about with a woman like Cecelia Manning.

She was a gorgeous, walking temptation with her feminine curves, long golden hair and wide blue eyes. He knew from her profile and additional background searches she kept herself fit with tennis and yoga. Yoga meant flexibility.

A few images from the Kama Sutra zipped through his mind like a slideshow and he nearly choked on the cracker in his mouth. Giving in to lust wouldn't do either of them any good. If he lived through the next forty-eight hours, he might ask her for a do-over and take her on a real date that didn't involve looming thugs happy to do the bidding of a famous crime boss.

Of course, dating her for real meant Director Casey would definitely kill him. The entire concept was irrelevant. His career allowed no time for the sort of commitment a woman like her would require.

He caught her checking her watch. "Am I boring you already?"

"No, not at all." Her smile was apologetic. "Just a mother's habit. My daughter's new husband is flying in tonight. I'm expecting her to call or text and let me know he arrived."

"They came to support you for tomorrow's gala?"

"And an early Christmas weekend, just the three of us." She sipped her wine. "They'll spend the real holiday with his mother in Florida. None of them are much for cold weather."

"What about you?"

"It doesn't bother me much. Winter's part of life." Her eyes went wide and she laughed. "I sound like some cheesy book on the self-help clearance rack."

"No apology necessary. Without winter we don't appreciate spring and summer. But a snowblower makes life easier."

"Very true."

"Is it a challenge?"

"What do you mean?"

"Watching your married daughter so recently after losing your husband?" He cursed himself. Hadn't meant to say that. Bringing up an ex was bad enough on a first date, but dredging up her dead husband, a man whom she'd loved deeply by all accounts? He was starting to understand why he didn't bother with dating. He sucked at it. "You really don't have to answer that."

"It's okay." She rested her fork against the small plate. "Losing William was the worst thing I've had to deal with." She took a deep breath and let it out slowly, worrying her lower lip with her teeth. "Well, you have some idea."

"Pardon?"

"You said you saw the video."

"Right. I did. Go on."

"Losing a spouse isn't an easy road, and getting past it doesn't seem to be something most people understand. This might sound harsh, but I can honestly say I'm comfortable with where I am now and who I want to become."

He couldn't reply. The emotions swirling in her eyes and that quick, nervous nip and release of her lower lip told him more than she wanted to reveal, he was sure. But her voice had been steady. She really was ready to move on with her life.

It made him feel even more like an ass for deceiving her.

The online dating thing had been the perfect ploy. The donation only added to the good-guy points he'd been racking up. By tomorrow, when she knew who he really was and why he'd approached her, she'd probably never forgive him.

Over the rim of her wineglass, she studied him, her expression contemplative.

To keep from squirming, he chose a successful field-tested tactic and went on the offensive. "Like what you see?"

"I think you know I do."

He leaned forward. "Want to do anything about it?"

"I believe I do." She leaned forward, as well. "Let's start with dinner."

They laughed, but there was no mistaking the building sexual tension between them. The conversation continued as if they were old friends rather than potential new adversaries, until the meal was delivered by the manager, who took the opportunity to greet Cecelia and chat briefly about tomorrow's event.

When they had the table to themselves again, Holt glanced up from the task of slicing his steak. "Does everyone in town know you?"

"Only the people who've helped with the fundraisers. The manager here donated a romantic dinner package to the silent auction."

Holt took a bite and nearly sighed with pleasure. "I may have to make a bid," he said. "This is worth a second trip."

She grinned. "Good plan."

Things were going so well Holt almost let down his guard and enjoyed himself. What he'd started as basic recon after that nasty warning message from Isely had turned to a genuine long-distance attraction. He'd been captivated by the depth of personality she expressed in their emails and brief phone calls. She was much more than a beautiful widow with a caring nature balanced by brains and a clever wit.

In person, all of that was magnified. He was more than a little startled by how much he liked her. Typically, he didn't like getting to know people—so few were reliable and everyone wanted something—but Cecelia Manning was the exception that made him want to bend his rules about relationships.

Except this *wasn't* a relationship. He had to remember this was the most critical mission of his life. If he botched this, her hurt feelings would be the least of his problems. His boss would lose his sister and their covert team of Specialists would be exposed.

Holt had enough experience to know you didn't reach the goal by dwelling on all the things that could go wrong.

There were already so many things wrong with this situation, starting with his general trepidation about ruining tomorrow's event, even by necessity. Yet dwelling on what could go right filled his head with thoughts of a more personal nature. If he'd suspected this kind of complication, he never would have opened an online dating account with which to lure her.

"I apologize," she said suddenly.

He questioned her with raised eyebrow.

"I've been rambling. I know you donated to the charity, but that doesn't mean you want to know about the minutiae involved behind the scenes. It's just filled all of my waking hours these last weeks."

"I enjoy listening to you." It might be the truest thing he'd said all night. Her smooth voice was like cool water after a long run on a hot summer day. It just rolled over him, easing the tension he'd been hauling around since his first contact with Isely.

"Uh-huh." She rolled her full lips between her teeth as if she was trying not to laugh. "You glazed over for a minute."

"If I glazed over, it was because I was thinking about things I shouldn't be thinking about."

"Work?"

"No." He loaded the word with enough meaning to imply he'd been thinking something much more personal and immediate. Intimate. And while it wasn't another outright lie, he needed to avoid all of the above. If he kept her out of Isely's clutches, she would never need to know the difference.

He reached across the table for her hand, then hesitated just before he touched her, giving her a chance to retreat. She didn't. Her gaze on his, she turned her hand over and used her thumb to trace the long scar that curved down the length of his index finger.

It was all he could do not to flinch from the gentle contact.

"Tell me about yourself."

"Not much to tell." He was a spy who didn't exist, a man who wouldn't exist if he didn't find a way to rein in Isely once and for all. He looked away, took in the perimeter of the room once more. "It was all in my profile. I'm not the sort to hold back."

She tipped her head to the side and traced that scar again. He wanted to tremble.

"I don't remember anything in your profile about this."

With her touching it, he was having trouble remembering the incident himself. The scar was a souvenir from a mission in Dubai. It had required minor surgery and months of rehabilitation for the nerves to recover and settle back to normal. If she kept caressing that thin white line, the nerves might never settle again.

"I slammed it in a car door and wound up needing minor surgery. Interesting process, really." He tilted his hand to look at it himself, but didn't withdraw from her touch.

"The recovery?"

"No. The surgery."

Her pale eyebrows arched and her whole body went still. He found himself fascinated by the reaction, wondering how she might react in other situations. "You watched them operate?"

"Sure," he said with a shrug. "They gave me a nerve block." Since he'd gone into the mission alone, he hadn't had anyone around to watch his back. General anesthesia would have left him too vulnerable.

"That's..."

Vulgar, sick, disgusting. He was ready for all of those words and worse.

"Amazing," she said, stroking her thumb across the ridge of his knuckles.

When had such a basic touch turned so damn hot? "Pardon me?"

"You heard me. Very few people have that kind of curiosity. Or courage."

"I don't know about courage." If he'd been wearing a tie, he would've tugged at it. Her eyes held something he'd rarely seen aimed his way—admiration. It left him speechless. He pulled his hand away. "Maybe I'm just an incurable insomniac."

She laughed, and he almost laughed with her, except one of Isely's crew chose that moment to lumber into the restaurant bar. The dark-haired man, whom Holt knew as Cal, took up residence on a bar stool where he could clearly observe Cecelia.

Isely's teams were nothing if not well trained. They were always in pairs, which meant at least one more man was waiting outside or in the kitchen, ready to take Cecelia off Holt's hands. Tonight was the wrong time to kidnap her, but Isely seemed determined to do so. What had accelerated his timetable?

Turning off the phone had clearly been a mistake. He should have anticipated the active response. Men like Isely, who were used to having every order obeyed out of blind fear if not devotion to the cause, didn't take it well when they were ignored.

"Dessert?"

"Not for me," she replied. "But I'll have a cup of coffee if you want to give the chocolate torte a try. It's marvelous."

He could tell she wanted to check her watch or her

phone for word from her daughter. “I probably shouldn’t keep you out so late,” he said. “Your family is in town and tomorrow’s a big day for you.”

“Our walk-through this morning went well. Everything is in place and tomorrow is just a matter of the finishing touches.” As if to emphasize the word, she touched him again. “I’m glad you’ll be there.”

“Me, too.”

He hoped they would both be there. If Isely succeeded tonight, Holt’s survival would be in the hands of the director. He didn’t maintain much hope that that particular source of judgment would end in his favor.

“Let’s take pity on the waiter and get out of here.” He signaled for the check while she polished off the last bit of wine in her glass.

Times like this reminded him a lack of family was a good thing. Enduring a few lonely holidays was no real hardship if it meant there was no one to get hurt on his behalf. He knew these threats against Cecelia were harder on the director than any of the missions he sent Specialists out to salvage.

Business was one thing. Specialists were trained and willingly stepped into dangerous situations. But knowing an old mission and a current teammate had breached security to put a target on his sister’s back? That would have any decent man twisted up and ready to shoot first and ask questions later.

It was one reason Director Casey’s recent marriage baffled Holt. The man’s personal philosophy of remaining a loner had been a solid foundation he’d adopted long before joining Mission Recovery. Covert operations just didn’t mix well with family dinners, piano recitals and summer vacations. Even dating was a serious minefield when it got tangled up with the job.

"You look troubled," she said, pulling her hair from under the collar of her coat.

"Then it's my turn to beg forgiveness." He raised her hand to his lips and winked as he pressed a light kiss to her knuckles before she could put on her gloves. "Can I walk you back to your car?"

"You could walk me back to the hotel. I'm staying there through the weekend."

"You don't look all that happy about it."

"It was a last-minute decision. We moved gifts and a few other things in today to make tomorrow easier."

There was more to it. His instincts warned he needed to know. "But?"

She opened her mouth to answer, but her phone interrupted them this time. Her smile when she checked the message led him to believe all was well with her daughter. Then it faded and she paled.

"Is something wrong?"

"Nothing serious."

He wasn't convinced, but he wasn't sure how hard to push. They were supposed to be new friends. "If there's something I can do, say the word."

"Thanks, but I'm sure it's just a mix-up." She shook her head, her blond hair swinging, but the smile on her lips didn't reach those stunning blue eyes. She tucked the phone into her pocket rather than her purse this time. "I'll just be glad when it all comes together tomorrow night."

"I'm sure everyone will have a great time."

She raised her crossed fingers. "And drink enough champagne to write big checks."

He laughed with her. "I left my checkbook at home."

She grinned up at him. "You've done enough already. My family and a few close friends bought tickets. It will be nice to see them."

Holt almost tripped. *Close friends?* Who could she mean? It would be bad enough kidnapping her out from under the combined noses of her brother and daughter.

"You aren't very convincing," he said, taking her hand in his as they walked along. It felt too right, too real. This was more than he'd bargained for and he was so much less than she deserved.

"Doesn't matter. I've chattered about myself enough for one night."

"Come on. I'm intrigued." He *needed* to know so he could be prepared. "Maybe we should make a plan so I can be a diversion." He wiggled his eyebrows.

"It's not a big deal." She gave his hand a squeeze. "They mean well and I know they love me. But no one seems very enthused about me getting on with my life."

"Because you're bringing a date to a charity event?"

"No." Her lips twisted in a wry grin. "Because they don't know I'm dating anyone seriously." Her eyes met his. "Tomorrow could get interesting."

He was sure of it. He'd carefully navigated the dating world so no woman would think to classify him as a serious prospect. He was the man women instinctively knew as the fun-while-it-lasted sort. It counted as a success that his efforts to woo Cecelia were convincing, but it unnerved him, as well.

He didn't want her to get hurt—by him or the ugly necessities of the op he was working out. Usually the mission was all that mattered to him. A hell of a time for *this* to happen.

Keeping an eye out for Isely's muscle, he felt the cold, calculating gazes of a surveillance team as they walked down King Street. His instincts were prickling, raising the hair at the back of his neck. Isely was obviously determined to take Cecelia as soon as possible.

Holt wondered at the rushed timeline and knew he'd have to get to a computer soon and see what he could dig up. Maybe Jason Grant's inquiries had set off some kind of alert on Isely's end of this dreadful business. The way things were going, it wouldn't surprise him to have inadvertently sabotaged himself.

In the reflection of a shop window, Holt recognized the man following them as one of Isely's personal bodyguards. The dark sedan that rolled by with government plates was probably a protection detail for Cecelia, courtesy of Director Casey. Just up the block, Holt spotted two more of Isely's men approaching.

Rock, meet hard place.

The dark wool jackets over jeans and heavy boots made as much of a statement to an informed operative as a uniform with flashing name tags.

Holt knew Isely typically valued subtlety and he felt the unfamiliar twist of worry at this abrupt change in the man's method and instruction to his crew. Some new development had to be creating this urgency.

The man had been groomed to lead one of the primary black-market operations in Europe. Vengeance had its place, but even Bernard Isely had to know it paid to keep a cool head no matter the circumstances.

Swing music poured from speakers above a little club two doors down the street. He squeezed Cecelia's hand. "Want to dance?"

"Here?"

"Here could work." He did a quick twirl of their hands that brought her right up against him. She let out a soft gasp that lit a fire in his blood. The move put a sparkle in those big blue eyes and had the added benefit of suggesting both teams should take a step back. He brushed his cheek with hers to murmur in her ear, "But I was thinking in there would be better."

"Hmm. I could be persuaded."

"Good to know." Now they just had to cross the short distance without Isely's men doing anything stupid.

It was too much to hope for.

Isely employed them primarily for their willingness to follow orders without questions. If he'd hoped for the same blind cooperation from Holt, he was about to be disappointed. The bigger guy in the faded navy peacoat shouldered him—hard—as they passed. The contact was enough to jostle him against Cecelia and he had to reach out to keep her from bouncing into another couple on the street.

The guy had good hands, but Holt knew the burner phone had been lifted and replaced with a new one. What new intel had bothered Isely enough to take that kind of precaution?

Holt didn't have more time to think about it. The shorter man had grabbed Cecelia's purse and was tugging both the purse and the woman toward the narrow side street that cut through to the next block.

"Let go!" Holt shouted. He didn't care which one of them complied, but he sure as hell didn't want to get into a fight right here in the middle of King Street.

He heard the squeal of tires and imagined the director's surveillance team would be on them any moment. Cecelia shouted for the police and Holt noticed more than one onlooker pulling out a phone. To help or simply upload a mugging to the internet didn't really matter. He wasn't about to let this become a public spectacle.

He threw his body weight into the struggle and drove both Cecelia and the would-be thief into the narrow side street and out of view.

The tall thug closed in behind him.

"Give us the woman," he growled, shoving Holt forward into Cecelia.

Accelerated timetable or not, Holt refused to hand over Cecelia to this pair. They were too rough around the edges and they looked too hungry. Had Isely put a bounty on her head? Spinning around, he raised his fist and drove a right hook into the tall man's ear.

The man staggered to the side, landing hard against the brick of the nearest building. The guy hadn't expected Holt to resist. Gave him a few seconds to rescue Cecelia.

But she was holding her own. He watched, stunned, as she used her strong grip on her purse straps to jerk her assailant closer and down, while she drove her knee up into his groin.

"Good girl," he said, coming to her side. He urged her toward the other end of the alley. If the squealing tires had been a team watching Cecelia, they weren't rushing in to help. He made a note to analyze it later. Right now they needed to escape. On the next street they could catch a cab and be safely out of reach in less than twenty minutes.

But the sound of glass breaking brought Holt back around.

The taller man wasn't giving up.

"Hand her over." He waved the bottle and charged, the sharp green edge coming closer, closer, until at the last moment, Holt blocked and turned. Determined, the taller man lurched back to his feet, advancing more cautiously this time.

Holt circled, keeping his face to the bottle-wielding thug and trying to get a line of sight on the other man. The shorter of their assailants squared up, flashing a knife.

Damn it. "Call nine-one-one," he barked at Cecelia. Drawing his weapon would blow his cover with her.

As Cecelia made the call, Holt evaluated each man, looking for a weakness he could exploit quickly so they could get out of here before agents, authorities or helpful citizens decided to intervene.

The man with the knife was weaker, but wary. Holt feinted left, and the knife flashed wide of his hip. Holt kicked out and caught the man's knee, and the knife skidded away as the thug crumpled. Cecelia snatched up the weapon.

"Keep that one down," he told her. Neither he nor Cecelia would be here to give a report, but these two deserved a night in jail.

He heard shouts on the street and a siren in the distance. Time was running out for them to get away cleanly. Cecelia was too well known in the area and the last complication he needed was local law enforcement.

The man swung wild, panicking with Holt's resistance and the warning that cops were on the way, and the jagged green edge caught at Holt's coat, dragging at the sleeve. Following the motion, he used the taller man's momentum to carry his fist into the hard steel of the trash bin.

The man howled with pain, but Holt used a quick series of uppercuts into his gut, robbing him of air and instantly silencing him. While he clutched his stomach, gasping for air, Holt drove another roundhouse into his jaw. The attacker slumped to the pavement, unconscious.

Holt turned back to find Cecelia pressing a Taser to the other assailant's thigh. The lady was more prepared than he'd suspected. "Nice job. Let's go."

"But the police—"

"Can take care of it."

Sirens wailed closer and he caught the flash of lights. Just what he *didn't* need tonight: the fastest response time of Alexandria's finest. The longer he could prevent Cecelia from learning his real identity and purpose here, the better.

"Let's go. Your charity doesn't need this kind of bad publicity."

She gave him a strange look but she cooperated, rushing through the narrow lane to join the foot traffic on the next street.

They walked briskly for another block before he flagged a cab and opened the door for her to slide in ahead of him. "Your place or mine?"

When she didn't immediately respond, he opened his mouth, ready to offer the address for the Plaza, but she surprised him.

"Yours."

He struggled not to fidget or show his surprise over her choice as he gave the address for the marina where he kept his boat moored.

What in bloody hell did he do now?

Chapter Six

Mission Recovery Offices, 10:21 p.m.

Thomas jerked to attention when the phone rang in the outer office. He'd sent his assistant home hours ago, instead calling on Holt's assistant, Nadine, to fill in.

"The surveillance team on the line for you, sir," Nadine said.

She'd resisted and tried to make excuses for not staying, but he'd given her an ultimatum: cooperate or resign. Her decision confirmed Nadine wasn't the mole and she'd answered all of his questions about what Holt had been asking her to do.

Unfortunately for Thomas, she didn't know too much. Holt wasn't careless and he didn't rely on Nadine for all of his scheduling. Based on the information she did have, Thomas sent another Specialist to cover the few hours of reconnaissance Holt had asked Nadine to handle. The appointed observation target had been Cecelia's house.

Thomas picked up the phone when the call transferred. "Report."

"We've lost her, Director."

Thomas picked up the painted plaster paperweight on his desk and nearly heaved it at the door before remembering it was a long-ago handmade gift from his niece.

"What happened?"

"You know her GPS isn't working on her cell?"

"No surprise," he barked. "How the hell did you lose her in the first place?"

"Everything was fine. We picked her up when she left the Plaza. She met her friends on schedule, but she stayed after they left the bar."

"And?"

"She eventually left the bar with Deputy Director Holt."

Thomas fisted his hand around the phone. "Where did they go?"

He rubbed his forehead with his free hand, unsure what he wanted to hear. He had a hard time believing Holt would hurt Cecelia on a professional level, and yet Holt wasn't the dating type. At least he'd never dated someone like Cecelia before.

Not to mention that damned chatter about her being the target of a kidnapping attempt.

Damn it!

"They went to dinner at Ray's."

Thomas struggled to calm himself. "Best steaks in Old Town."

"Yes, sir. We uploaded pictures of two men loitering near the restaurant."

"I saw those." He'd been waiting over an hour for the facial recognition software to spit out something useful.

"One of them went inside about a half hour before Mrs. Manning and Holt came out."

"No one got any audio on the dinner?"

"Impossible, sir, unless we'd joined them at the table."

"Understood." Some logistics couldn't be out-maneuvered, especially on short notice. "Do we have anything?"

The Specialist on the other end of the line hesitated. "Not much. We have prints and faces on the two men who tried to steal your sister's purse as she walked back to her hotel."

"She was mugged?"

"No, sir. The assailants were subdued."

"Was she hurt? What about Holt?"

"I don't have a clear answer yet. As I said, we've lost her trail. By the time we hit the scene, the potential victims were gone and the assailants unconscious."

"You left them for the local police to deal with."

"Yes, sir. Seemed like the best option."

Thomas agreed. "So the man hired to kidnap my sister might have just accomplished the job?" It didn't help matters any that Holt had been highly trained in evasion techniques and could effectively disappear without a trace in less than an hour.

After Nadine had spilled her sketchy information, Thomas had gone through Holt's office with a critical eye. An extra identity remained in Holt's office safe, but Thomas knew there should have been at least one more, and the cash earmarked for emergencies was gone.

He wasn't prone to displays of temper, but he was about to lose it this time. This was his sister they'd lost. Every scattered bit of information he had said she was likely in the clutches of a traitor. A traitor with skills and a past no brother wanted to think about.

"Do we have anything close to a lead?"

"No, sir. We're about to run down cab companies. It's the fastest way they could clear the area."

"Or the bus or—"

"No, we've hacked those cameras. She hasn't boarded any of the shuttles or the metro."

It could be worse. That was the prime source of his problem, knowing exactly how much worse it could be. The betrayal cut deep. He had handpicked Emmett Holt to replace Lucas when he retired. How the hell could he have been so wrong about a guy with a pristine record?

He let the two agents he'd put on her go do their jobs. Nadine was monitoring the police scanner in the area, but he also tasked an analyst downstairs with the same job to make sure she didn't miss or withhold anything he needed to know.

His cell phone chimed with a new text message. He grabbed it, ready to chew Lia out for turning off her GPS and dodging the protective tail, only to see Casey's number on the display.

He dialed her number when he saw the message: Call when you can.

"Hello," he said warmly, trying not to let on that her mother was missing. "Did Levi's flight get in on time?"

"Yeah. We're great. Mom moved over to the hotel tonight."

"I know."

"Thought you might. Does the team in the van have any crime-scene equipment?"

"What van?"

"Mom says there's been a van parked in front of the Millers' place for days. She assumed they were here on your orders."

"It wasn't me." Damn it. What exactly had Holt put into motion?

"Levi and I can check it out."

She sounded too ready for action. "Wait. Just leave it alone. I'll have someone deal with the van. Why didn't you call the police if you need a crime tech?"

"Because we're not sure we have a crime."

"Explain."

Casey took a big breath that rushed across the line. "We

found a bug in the kitchen, then searched the house and found two more. The office and the bedroom."

Thomas cringed at the implications of those positions. Cecelia didn't work with sensitive information in her current position at the CIA, but that would change if she made the switch to ops.

"Go on."

"It's just a hunch, but I think someone's been here. Obviously to plant the bugs, but I mean tonight, when I went to the airport to pick up Levi."

If someone had been in the house, why hadn't the Specialist he'd assigned reported anything? His first instinct was to get over there and take a look personally. He used his computer to message Nadine, asking her to get a status report.

"I'm probably overreacting. It's not like I can point to any one thing and say it's out of place, but I just feel like a few things have been searched. I sent Mom a text, but she hasn't replied yet."

His jaw clenched. Being kidnapped had a tendency to interfere with messaging capabilities. "Did you check the safe?"

"Yes. It's fine. I'm thinking we got home before they found it."

"Was anything missing or..." He didn't know quite how to finish the question. Security clearances for the job were one thing, but no matter how much field experience an agent had, investigating family was different.

"Everything looked the same to me. Well, almost the same."

Thomas thought he recognized the problem. "Was her wedding ring in there?"

"Yeah," Casey replied softly.

He had noticed Cecelia wasn't wearing the ring. Obviously Casey hadn't. That was going to be hard for her even though she would want her mother to be happy and to move one with her life. "You okay?"

"Sure." She sniffled. "It's just weird she's moving on."

"Only she can know when it's time."

"Oh, please. Don't try and go all wise on me. I know it bugs you, too."

"A little," he admitted. William had been like a brother, but he was gone now. Cecelia deserved to live the rest of her life. Just not like this.

Mostly because it was Holt. That wasn't entirely true. Up until a few weeks ago, Holt had his utmost respect. Now, as Thomas peeled back the layers on cases going back to June, he was starting to get a picture of a very different man. A man who was in bed with a very dangerous enemy.

Isely had every reason to hate Thomas, and it appeared he had bottomless resources to fund the revenge he'd promised years ago. The financial picture was still coming in, but it was clear Isely's deals since taking over the family business had been savvy, private and lucrative.

"Your mom's smart. She'll find her way. The best thing we can do is keep supporting her." He hoped he hadn't already let her down.

"Right. You've got her covered tonight?"

"Sure thing," he lied. How in the hell was he going to fix this?

"I'm meeting her late tomorrow morning. We have a mini spa thing at the Plaza."

"Sounds good. Can Levi stay at the house? Keep it covered in case whoever planted those bugs comes back?"

"We already decided that was best."

"Great minds," Thomas said. "Enjoy the rest of your evening."

"We will. See you tomorrow night, Uncle Thomas."

"Can't wait."

Thomas stared at the phone when the call ended. He should get out to Alexandria, but something—that gut instinct he'd learned to trust—told him to wait.

Instead, he called in a favor with the local police. They could check on any cars that didn't belong in Cecelia's neighborhood. Then he picked up his cell phone and called his wife to give her an update on the degrading situation.

Hearing her voice would be the only thing good about this night.

Chapter Seven

The marina? It was just one more question on the list spinning through Cecelia's mind, none of which she wanted him to answer here in the cab.

She didn't need the echoes of her brother's warning to reach the obvious conclusion that Emmett Holt wasn't some average guy with a private security firm, as he'd posted in his online profile. The surprise attack and resulting tension between them made it clear they both knew there was more going on here.

"Are you hurt?"

He didn't reply, just sat beside her, his body rigid, his hands on his knees. His eyes, she knew, were scouring the street, looking for any sign they were being followed.

Adjusting her purse, she reached over and laced her fingers through his. He startled, then stared. First at their joined hands, then slowly he lifted his glacier gaze to meet hers.

"I'm a good listener," she said, low enough that the cab driver wouldn't overhear. She told herself that this was part of what a good field agent would do…but she wasn't entirely sure that was the motive for her actions.

She prayed she wasn't being a fool.

Still, of all the things she might have told him, that one point seemed the most relevant. It didn't make sense. He'd obviously lied to her about a few things, but something about the man beside her—the frown twisting his face, the tension in his body—made her say that first.

She had the odd feeling he was in over his head. As a deputy director of an elite covert team, it didn't seem entirely reasonable. Her brother's team of Specialists was well trained to salvage ops that slid sideways and out of reach. Their success rate was ridiculously high because Thomas wouldn't tolerate anything less. What could possibly worry a man with that kind of experience and expertise?

The potential answers didn't offer any sort of comfort. Just the opposite.

Remembering how one attacker had demanded *her,* she shivered. Her apparent savior shifted, tucking her under the shelter of his arm. She should tell him those same men had asked her for directions just a few hours ago, should tell him she knew who he was. She should tell him about the message Casey had sent a few minutes ago.

But she couldn't bring herself to say any of those things in the cab. "Thank you," she said, as the post-adrenaline tremors set in.

He rubbed her shoulder and pressed a kiss to her hair. It wasn't the kind of gesture she expected from a worldly operative or a man supposedly betraying his team and country. There was an inherent kindness behind the comfort he offered her.

"You did well," he said.

Not from her perspective. "You did all the hard work." She traced the rip in his jacket sleeve. "It's ruined."

"It's replaceable."

"We should have a real conversation."

"Probably," he said, twisting a bit to peer out the back window.

"Will we?"

He didn't reply, just squeezed her shoulder once more.

Her tremors eased up as the cab driver turned into the marina entrance. The landscaping on either side of the drive was draped with colorful holiday lights, but it didn't do anything to lift her mood.

A loud party overflowed the marina building and she did a mental rundown of the local calendar, trying to figure out if she'd know anyone attending, but she couldn't recall who had rented the space for tonight.

Would she call out for help anyway? Or just keep going with the flow and hoping this man was the hero she wanted him to be?

Maybe her daughter and brother were right. Maybe she didn't have the right stuff for this kind of work.

"Looks like quite a bash going down," the cab driver observed as Emmett paid the fare.

"Sailors always know how to party," he agreed. "Thanks for the lift."

Instead of leading her around toward the water, he guided her straight toward the raucous party. "We're not dressed for this kind of event," she protested.

He looked her up and down and the resulting shiver had nothing to do with fear or adrenaline. Only anticipation. "Not every party is a gala." The wind caught her hair, but he smoothed it back behind her ear. "You look very good to me."

And he looked pretty damned gorgeous, even after the fight in a grimy alley. At this point she wanted answers. He had a point, though. The safety of a friendly crowd held a good deal of appeal just now. "We need to talk."

"We will. I promise." His mouth thinned to a grim line. "As soon as we're safe." He urged her closer to the front doors.

"What's going on? What did those men want?" Besides her.

"We'll figure that out," he promised, "as soon as we know we're not being followed anymore."

Since those two men had been stalking her before the encounter in the alley, she couldn't actually blame him for what happened. Truth was, he had saved her from God only knew what sort of fate. For now, she had no choice but to trust him.

"I thought you gave this address because you had a boat here," she murmured as they checked their coats and prepared to join the revelers inside.

"Even if I do have a boat here, I'm not going to lead whoever followed us right to it."

Spy 101, she mused as she looked over his shoulder. "I don't see anyone."

"Doesn't mean they aren't out there."

Now, that sounded ominous. And more than a little paranoid. But she could tell he was sincerely concerned about the likelihood of more trouble. And he was highly trained. Like Thomas.

"Then we should go to the police."

"Not yet."

She refused to take another step. "Why not?"

"Trust me. I'll explain later." He took her elbow and urged her forward again. "Come on, it's time to blend in and get festive."

She pushed a hand through her hair and tugged at her sweater. From the guests they'd passed already, she knew it wasn't black tie, but she got the impression it was a private company event. "You're serious about crashing."

"As a heart attack." He held up the tag from the coat check and gave her a look she knew was meant to put an end to her balking. "Just to buy some time."

The man looked around the room as if the crowd had taken over his home uninvited. "We won't blend in at all if you keep doing that," she warned.

"Doing what?"

"Scowling. It's not *festive*." She circled a finger at his face. "We're crashing a party and you look like you're on the way to your execution. Try a smile." She gave him an example.

His first attempt—a grimace—actually scared her a little. She glanced over his shoulder at the door. "Relax. They were just a couple of muggers," she said, though neither of them believed it. "We weren't followed."

So far. She mentally crossed her fingers as she drew him deeper into the anonymity of the party and joined the line waiting for service at the bar.

"Not smart," he grumbled at her ear.

"Look around." Everyone carried some sort of drink. "This was your idea. You want to blend," she said with a wink. She swayed provocatively to the music pounding through the room. "And those thugs interrupted us before we got to dance."

She hoped a drink and a dance would be enough to stop the ruination of what had started as a perfectly lovely evening. Keeping it simple, she ordered a beer for each of them and then led him to a spot just off the dance floor. If this was really some sort of operation that involved her, this was the perfect time to prove she had what it took for fieldwork.

She clinked her beer bottle to his. "Happy holidays."

"Cheers." He tipped the bottle back, but kept his eyes on hers.

In the improved light of the party, she could see the red abrasions on his knuckles. They'd likely be dark bruises by morning. "Do you want ice for that?" She wondered how he'd managed not to break any bones.

"I'm good." He rubbed the cold bottle across the marred skin while he studied the crowd.

"Yes, you were." She stepped a bit closer. "Thank you, by the way."

"You said that already." He frowned at her, but she decided it was because she wasn't what he expected. Well, that made them even. "You certainly adapt quickly."

"I've—"

"Mrs. Manning?"

"The woman knows everyone in town," he grumbled.

Cecelia found herself in the exuberant, slightly tipsy embrace of a young woman who'd gone to school with Casey.

"Merry Christmas, Heather." Too late, Cecelia remembered the invitation she'd declined. Heather's father was a broker and their girls had been on the varsity field hockey team in high school. William had made a few investments with him, but they weren't particularly close friends.

"I didn't know Daddy invited you. Oh, my gosh!" She stepped back, eyed Cecelia up and down. "You look amazing!"

"You're too kind."

"Daddy is going to go nuts." Heather leaned close, but didn't lower her voice. "He's always had a thing for you." She put her hand over her lips. "Oops."

Cecelia cringed at the dark expression clouding Emmett's eyes. "Heather, let me introduce you to my *date,* Mr. Holt."

He did a fine job pretending to enjoy the introduction, but Cecelia knew better. His gaze was cataloging faces and he was looking for ways to make a hasty exit.

"Anyway, I'm so glad you came," Heather effused.

The music changed to a Latin beat and Emmett captured her hand. “Let’s dance,” he said, pushing their beer bottles toward Heather. She barely had time to wave a farewell to the younger woman as Emmett tugged her into the crowd of dancers.

His hands molded to her hips; his touch burned with a hot purpose through the fabric of her slacks as he started to lead. She grinned and rested her hands lightly on his shoulders for balance. Already she realized this wasn’t a ballroom rendition of the salsa he had in mind, but something much more intense. Sexy.

Something much more fun.

Thank heaven the party guests were drinking heavily enough that they wouldn’t remember Mrs. Manning crashing the party and grinding it out with a stranger in public.

She couldn’t help it. Blaming the adrenaline or just her eagerness to reclaim her life, she tossed her head back and laughed at the absurdity of it all. She had to play the part, didn’t she? Wasn’t this exactly what spies did in the field?

When she met his gaze again, his half smile was full of a different kind of heat. A heat that made her want to take chances and explore their options, no matter who he was or how many interruptions they had to endure.

For the past three weeks, he’d been charming her with clever, interesting emails and photographs of architecture and sailing—his two passions outside work, according to his profile. That had been enough to captivate her even before she’d realized his profile picture had been current—and incredibly accurate.

The man was a walking—dancing—invitation to sin. Right now she should be insisting on finding a quiet corner and getting some real answers, but she couldn’t pull her head out of the sexy spell he was weaving around her.

The logical part of her brain knew he was doing it on

purpose. An applied technique for either protection or distraction, she wasn't sure. Wasn't even sure she wanted the answer just yet. Instead of being terrified by the near miss in the alley, she felt exhilarated. There was an energy Emmett drew out of her that she hadn't felt in far too long.

More than surviving, more than managing life, she realized she was really living again—for the moment.

The revelation would have made her stumble, but Emmett was there. His hands guided her, brushed her body as they swiveled and rocked in time with the fast pulse of the music.

He used his eyes to tell her they'd been followed, and turning her, she spotted a pair of burly men hovering at the sliding door that opened onto the wide deck. They must have come around from the dockside rather than the front door as she and Emmett had done. With their well-worn coats and rough clothing, they didn't blend in with anyone other than the two men who'd attacked them in the alley.

She did a slow turn to face him again, then leaned in close on the next forward step. "Plan?"

"I'm thinking."

Step, sway, forward, back. Cecelia laid her palms on his. "We can't let them start a fight here. People will get hurt."

"I know," he growled.

"They said they wanted me."

"Yes."

"Want to hand me over?"

"No. Unless you know something I don't."

She shook her head. "Kiss me."

"What?"

Her idea was flimsy at best, but it was all they had. The bad guys wanted her. She could be bait, especially with Emmett ready to assist her.

Her heart stumbled at the thoughts. Was she really ready to do this? Play bait…and kiss this man?

"Kiss me when the dance ends. Make a scene out of it." The dance carried them apart for a moment, then back again. "I'll go to the restroom. If they follow, we can subdue them there and leave through the back door."

He didn't look happy about it. Apparently, no one wanted to credit her with any skills beyond marriage, motherhood and pushing paper. It wasn't her first brush with disbelief, but there would be plenty of time to deal with her bruised pride later.

Besides, she had a lifetime of hearing William, Thomas and more recently, Casey, talk about how to execute a proper egress in the most unusual of circumstances.

The music soared as the song ended and Emmett put a flourish on the last move, dipping her back over his arm and bringing her back up so fast in the next beat that her head spun. Then his mouth captured hers.

His fingers speared into her hair, his palm hot, firm and somehow gentle where he cradled her head. She gripped his shoulders for balance, digging into his firm muscles when he shifted, taking the kiss deeper. His thigh wedged between hers, his other hand splayed across her back.

Her breath stalled in her lungs, but she didn't care. She'd told him to make a scene and he was doing a fine job of it. His tongue stroked boldly against hers, making dark, silky promises her body wanted him to keep.

The cheers and catcalls brought her back to reality with a shock. He released her so suddenly she swayed. She touched her lips, staring at him a long moment before remembering she was supposed to make a break for the restrooms.

He drew her body close to his and she had the wild hope he would kiss her again.

“Go,” he whispered against her cheek as the next song started.

Cecelia went. Like the hounds of hell were on her heels. Within seconds she heard heavy footfalls behind her as she rounded the corner. On a prayer the restroom might be empty, she pushed through the door into the ladies’ room and spun a quick circle in search of anything she could use as a weapon. She should have gone back into that alley for her Taser. She’d dropped it after putting that creep down. She’d never had to use it before.

If she couldn’t Taser a guy without being shaken, how was she ever going to fire a weapon?

“Focus, Cecelia,” she muttered. She needed a weapon. Nothing presented itself, and she knew her best bet was to barricade herself in one of the stalls and wait for Emmett.

She scrambled into a stall, set the latch and climbed onto the closed toilet seat. As the two men barreled in, Cecelia peered through the crack in the stall door and nearly groaned when a young woman stepped out of the stall closest to the door. *Heather.*

“Uh, wrong door, guys.”

“Where is Mrs. Manning?”

These two knew her name? Any lingering notion she’d harbored that the attack after dinner had been a random mugging or a case of mistaking her for another woman fled. Not that she’d really believed it, even at the time.

“Not in here. You guys are at the wrong party,” Heather added, trying to get around the men to the sink. “Get out.”

One of the men caught Heather’s arm hard enough to make her cry out.

“Show yourself, Manning.”

Dear Lord. Cecelia couldn’t let them hurt the younger woman. “Let her go,” she said, stepping out of the last stall.

“Come with us. Now,” the other man ordered.

"As soon as you let her go," Cecelia repeated with far more calm than she felt.

The man holding Heather pulled a gun and pressed it to Heather's side. The girl paled. "We all go together."

"Not acceptable." Cecelia inched closer to the next stall, judging the reach of the second man. *Come on, Emmett.* None of the self-defense moves she knew were applicable from this distance. She had to find a way to get Heather away from that gun.

"Last warning," Cecelia promised. "Let. Her. Go." She took a step closer with each word and on the last she let the second man catch her arm. She resisted and then suddenly gave in when he pulled harder. The result brought her careening into his chest and the momentum carried them both into his partner.

The four of them landed in a heap against the wall with Cecelia on top. The gun, thank God, had fallen closest to her. She stomped and punched on every sensitive area possible as she scrambled to her feet.

"Run, Heather!"

Heather obeyed, bolting through the open doorway as Emmett rushed in and Cecelia grabbed the gun.

"Can I just shoot them?" Maybe the weapon part wouldn't be as difficult as she'd thought. What kind of lowlifes would use a young woman as leverage?

"Works for me."

Both men started to protest. Cecelia glanced at Emmett and her heart skipped when he smiled at her.

"Do me a favor and just kneecap them," he suggested.

She adjusted her aim and the men shouted again until Emmett silenced each with precisely placed pressure on the carotid artery.

"We should get you out of here."

"Will you tell me what the hell is going on?" she demanded.

"Just as soon as I figure it out," he said, handing her coat to her.

Emmett searched the unconscious pair for identification while she shrugged into her coat. He examined their phones and wallets as she dropped the small revolver into her purse. If she hadn't been watching him closely, she would have missed the quick move when he put a phone from his jacket into the pocket of one of the men.

With more questions begging to be asked, she followed him out of the restroom, down the corridor and out the back door of the building. If Heather had rushed out to call the police, it hadn't stopped the partying.

If someone had asked her, Cecelia wouldn't have been able to logically justify her decision to stick with Emmett as he led her away and toward the water. The sounds of the party faded, replaced by the soothing lap of water against the moorings and their soft, rapid steps on the planks of the gangway.

Darkness enveloped them beneath the low glow of the sparsely placed lamps marking the intersections of the gangway with the narrow floating docks that stretched out toward the water.

Emmett took her hand, steadying her as they turned down the last dock. Boats rocked gently in the slips on either side. If he had been sent to kidnap her, she was making it easy for him. But she couldn't make herself believe that was his goal.

He'd had ample opportunity and offers to let others do it for him. No, there was more going on here, and as soon as she knew they were safe, she was going to demand answers.

He stopped abruptly and pressed a finger to her lips. "You have the gun?"

She nodded.

"Good." He withdrew his finger. "Sit here and use it if you have to."

"Where are you going?"

"Just wait here while I make sure it's clear."

"I could run," she pointed out.

That stopped him. He turned back slowly. "Do you want to?"

The edge in his voice—sharper than that broken bottle—was enough to make her grateful she couldn't see what was surely a cold expression marring his handsome face.

"No." Not yet, she amended silently. She could only assume the men who had attacked them were working for Thomas's enemy. That was the only explanation that made sense.

But that only proved her brother's point that his enemy couldn't have found *her* without access to highly classified files. Files that technically didn't exist. Files a deputy director could access easily.

"Let's go."

She jumped and nearly dropped the revolver she'd balanced on her knee. He'd returned in complete silence; the dock hadn't even shifted. "How'd you do that?"

"Practice." His hand cupped her elbow. "Three steps down," he advised when he paused again at a slip.

She couldn't see much beyond the general shape of the boat and she took the steps slowly in the dark. The boat rocked slightly beneath her feet with her third step.

"Left," he said, guiding her with his strong hands.

Looking that way, she saw a sliver of light seeping through a thin crack of a hatch near the boat's bow. She felt him next to her, a bundle of tension and heat, his intriguing scent mingling with the water and night.

"Just follow me. You're safe. You have my word."

His voice, his touch, both made her *feel* safe. But was she?

With one hand on the gun in her pocket, she followed him farther into the dark, wondering what the hell she'd gotten herself into. In reality, she didn't have a choice here. What she had was an opportunity. An opportunity to help her brother and the CIA take down a traitor.

And maybe to prove she wasn't a total fool.

She prayed she wasn't a total fool.

Chapter Eight

After securing the door, Holt watched Cecelia turn a slow circle, taking in the quarters of his modest cruiser, and waited for the disappointment. He should have known she'd be too polite to let it show.

"It's gorgeous," she said, sounding breathless.

"Thanks," he muttered. He didn't believe her. His boat wasn't gorgeous, it was simple. Sure, he'd chosen the finest materials when he'd done the necessary upgrades, but the streamlined design made the most of space best described as cramped. It hadn't bothered him before because he hadn't planned to ever share these quarters with anyone. Seeing her here had him questioning his solitary plans, which was a completely random and impossible line of thinking.

She was the director's sister and a potential victim he was trying to protect by pretending to date her. Key word: *pretending.* He had to keep that in mind.

"Were you sailing on this when you took those pictures down along the Florida Keys?" She moved about the space, touching his things. His body reacted as if she were touching him.

"That's where I picked her up," he said. It surprised him how much pleasure he got from her enthusiasm for the boat and the pictures he'd taken. Sailing wasn't in her online profile and his searches hadn't revealed any recent love of the sea, but by now he should expect the unexpected where Cecelia Manning was concerned.

Holt rarely encountered anyone who surprised him as much as this beautiful woman. She was nervous about being here alone with him. But she'd come willingly. That said, she still clutched the weapon in her pocket.

"You can let go of the gun. I'm not stealing you away." Not tonight, anyway. Based on Isely's behavior, it looked like tomorrow was still task one on the agenda.

She visibly attempted to relax, withdrawing her hand from her pocket but leaving the weapon there in case she needed it. As if she knew what the move did to him, she ran her newly freed hand along the polished teak of the cabinetry.

Holt had to look away. His imagination painted a vivid picture of her hands running over his skin with the same blatant appreciation.

Wasn't going to happen. Not once she knew the truth. Hell, she probably already knew more than she should. Focus, man. He needed a change of clothes. To get the grime of thugs off him.

"It's so warm."

He stopped in the process of emptying his pockets onto the narrow table, certain he hadn't heard her correctly. "Pardon me?"

"The cabin," she said. "I would have expected it to be cold down here."

Ah, that made more sense and was a complete departure from where his thoughts had traveled. "Yeah. That's part of the design." He opened the laptop he kept on board and inserted a flash drive. "I'll get you back to your hotel just as soon as I check out a few things." Primarily that it would be safe to take her there. Highly unlikely, but he had an obligation to check.

"No rush. It's nice to just breathe for a moment."

"You should call your brother and let him know you're safe."

Holt didn't like the look she sent his way but he ignored it, putting his energy into gaining some insight about Isely's inexplicable escalation. If she hadn't known who he was before, she'd certainly already figured out plenty about him.

"So you do know who I am. Who I'm related to."

"I know you're Cecelia Manning. Recently widowed, philanthropist and your slice backhand is the best shot of your tennis game. You enjoy time with friends, your weekly yoga class and prefer pinot noir to merlot."

"The wine thing wasn't on my profile."

Time to face the music. There was no more time for games. "No, I learned that by perusing your wine rack."

"You've been in my *house?*"

The astonishment on her face sucker punched him. He gritted his teeth for a second then said the rest. "Easier to plant the bugs that way."

"You bugged my house." She swore softly, but with enough heat that he knew her cooperation was over.

He'd just have to deal with that. Better to clear the air here and now so they could be on the same page moving forward. She might hate him for his tactics, but he couldn't leave her alone now. Not with Isely's erratic behavior. Holt opened his mouth, but her clear, regal voice filled the galley instead.

"Thomas did put you up to this. I'm going to kill him with my bare hands," she finished with a low growl. "He's getting better at lying to me. There was a time when he would never have been able to pull something like this over on me."

Her statement about Casey gave him pause. "No. Wait. You can tell when he's lying?" It was something Holt still hadn't mastered and a skill that would be useful beyond measure. Assuming he managed to keep his job.

"Apparently not anymore," she glared at him, then she bit her lip and her eyes shimmered with unshed tears.

"Don't do that." He could not deal with a weepy woman tonight. Not any time.

Less than half an hour ago, she'd danced like they'd never been jumped in the alley. Her eyes had been clear when she'd agreed to kneecap the assailants at the party if necessary. Why would learning their connection had been a setup distress her so?

"Don't worry. I won't crumple." She gazed upward and blinked rapidly. "I'm just angry."

An unexpected emotion nudged him. Guilt. "You're wrong. Sort of. Thomas had nothing to do with this. Unless you told him, he doesn't know about us."

"Us?" She gave a short, brittle laugh.

"Us." He forgot the mission and the phones and reached across the small cabin for her, realizing he'd lose her cooperation completely if he didn't handle this right. Her cooperation was critical in these next hours, even if Thomas didn't understand that yet. If she broke down in a panic or flew off in a rage, Isely would have her—and use her against the two most knowledgeable agents in Mission Recovery.

She shrugged him off, but there was nowhere for her to go. He wrapped his arms around her waist, holding her close until she stopped struggling. "Just let me explain."

"You lied to me. All these weeks." Tears threatened again, but she prevailed. "I'm an idiot."

"No, you're not. I lie to everyone. It's part of the job, and I'm very good at my job."

She blew out a sharp breath that shifted her bangs out of her eyes. "I know. I know."

"From what I hear, you'll be joining the ranks of people like me next month."

She rolled her eyes. "Of course a man in your position could find that out."

"Are you excited about the move to ops?"

She scowled up at him, clearly unwilling to change the subject. Wisps of her hair were tangled at the corner of her long lashes and he cautiously moved them to the side.

At least the tears were gone and she looked like her composed self again. And mad as hell.

"Thomas said someone wants to kidnap me."

Holt nodded. "That he was right about that should be obvious after two attacks in as many hours."

"He mentioned your name."

Holt stiffened. "Good."

Those lake-blue eyes of hers went wide. "Good?"

"That's what I need him to believe." He took in the clenched teeth. "His warning is why you thought about ditching me at the bar." That last part was a guess, but coming to that conclusion was fairly easy.

She sniffed, clearly annoyed he'd deduced correctly. "And just what am I supposed to believe, Mr. Holt?"

There was an easy answer, but he couldn't get the words past his lips. Lips that wanted to taste hers again and show her the honest, brutal need for her beating like a drum inside him.

To preserve his sanity, he released her and took a step back. To seal the deal on her continued cooperation he said what he needed to say. "When I learned you might be a target, I used the online profile to get closer. Thomas doesn't know anything about my approach, and I'm sure he'd be furious to know how much I've come to care for you."

She scoffed, turning her back on him and tracing the wave design carved into the cabinet door. "He said I was a pawn."

"To his enemy, you are."

"But not to you."

He should clarify, admit the confusion twisting inside his gut where she was concerned, but they were short on time. On some level what he said wasn't a lie. But this was new territory for him, these emotions unfamiliar. This was no time to be confused. He slid onto the bench at the table and set out the phones he'd taken from Isely's men.

Rather than dwell on the confusion, he focused on the facts. "The team Thomas assigned to follow you is in a world of hurt about now. Please send him a text that you're okay and safely in your room."

"I should." She pulled out her phone, tapping it against her open palm. "No matter what I tell him, he'll only follow the GPS signal here."

"You disabled that before you left the hotel to meet me."

She gave him a startled look, but didn't deny it. "For the date that wasn't," she groused.

"I think it would've been a great night if we'd been left alone."

"Maybe," she allowed.

"Why'd you do it?"

"The GPS or the date?"

"The GPS." Though he'd be lying to himself if he didn't admit he would very much like it if she answered both questions.

She shrugged. "Thomas likes a challenge. I assume he recruits like-minded people."

Holt laughed at her accurate assumption. "Here I

thought it was because you were ashamed to be seen with me."

She leaned back against the woodwork she'd admired and did something with her phone before dumping it back in her purse. She drummed her fingers lightly as she watched him.

He didn't care for the close study, but he managed to ignore it.

"I was never ashamed to meet you. Not even after Thomas warned me off. I was curious. Excited," she admitted. "And not at all ready to share you with my overprotective family or nosy friends. I was determined to prove that Thomas was wrong about you. I'm reassessing that conclusion just now."

"Are you always so candid?" He started downloading the text messages and recent locations logged by the system since the phones were activated.

"No."

He counted himself fortunate in that much, at least. "How did you plan to explain my appearance tomorrow night?"

"Vaguely."

She was smiling, he could hear it in her voice. It worried him. Not the smile specifically, but recognizing her inflections so well already. Not recognizing, he amended, reacting to. That was the issue here. Recognizing what others were thinking was his job. Reacting this way to anyone was not.

"What are you doing?"

"Reviewing communications," he said. Then an idea occurred to him. Cecelia didn't like her brother and daughter doubting her. "Want to help?"

"Sure."

She slid onto the bench beside him and the hint of vanilla in her perfume tugged at his senses. The scent was one he associated with innocence, but the images she inspired were in no way innocent. Having her join him had been a mistake. A rookie mistake. He hadn't made one of those since he'd actually been a rookie. He handed her a phone and told her to run through the call log and text messages.

"We'll take out the SIM cards and toss the phones on our way to the hotel."

"*Our* way?"

"There's no way I'm letting you out of my sight. They'd have you in less than a minute."

"I'm not that easy."

"No, you're not. But they *are* that good."

"Thomas thinks you're working with them. I get the impression they think you're working with them."

Ah, more of that refreshing frankness. He slid down the bench and away so he could gather the few things he needed. He didn't reply to her fishing comment.

"Oh, I get it. That's what they're supposed to believe."

"You're a quick study. Can you finish this while I pack?"

"If you tell me what I'm looking for."

"You'll know it when you see it. One-word messages. Addresses. There's probably nothing incriminating anyway, but I want to try."

His laptop and tuxedo were already at the room he'd booked under an alias at the Plaza, but he wanted a change of clothes, his camera and the money and gun he knew would trace back to Isely's illegal operation.

"Emmett?"

"Yeah?"

"Who is Irina?"

The name wasn't familiar to him. "Could be a contact."

"Hmm. There's a date listed in the next message." She nudged the phone across the table to show him the text message. "It's this Saturday."

The day after the gala where Isely had ordered him to kidnap her. He thought of the warehouse address he'd received at the restaurant. A warehouse on the water would be the perfect staging area and make it easy for Isely to take Cecelia out of the country.

"What are the other numbers?" she asked.

He looked. "Best guess is latitude and longitude." As specific as an address could be, Holt thought with more than a little frustration for not anticipating an exchange at sea. Without a deeper investigation into the name listed, he couldn't make assumptions.

"But—"

He cut her off. "We can analyze it later." He made sure the information was downloaded, then closed the computer and tucked the SIM cards into his camera bag. "For now we have to get you back to the hotel without being intercepted by your brother or Isely's crew."

"Sounds like fun."

He stared at her, caught the sparkle in her eyes. "You're serious."

She nodded. "I'll think of it as an early training exercise."

"Except this is real and your life is in danger."

"Seems like mine isn't the only one. You appear to have a few enemies of your own."

"A few more now since I didn't hand you over to Isely's men tonight."

"Why does he want me?"

"So he can cause your brother pain." But he was starting to suspect there was more going on in Isely's mind than just his determination to destroy Thomas's family and reputation.

"What did Thomas do?"

"His job."

Holt doused the lights in the cabin, relieved when the darkness seemed to mute Cecelia, as well. She was asking too many questions he wasn't ready to answer.

Tomorrow night, when he was sure the two of them were away cleanly, he'd tell her everything. He was counting on her to understand and be willing to do what was necessary to save her brother and the Mission Recovery team from disaster.

She didn't know it yet, but after witnessing her courage tonight, she'd become the ace up his sleeve. Her initiative gave him hope they both might yet get out of this in one piece.

The boat rocked gently in the slip as they moved up on deck. "We have to get out of here before the local police start searching the docks." Not to mention Isely's goons.

"You're sure the police can't help us?" she asked.

He steadied her as she took the wide step across the dark water to the dock. They moved quietly toward the gangway. "I'm the bad guy, remember? More to the point, people in our line of work are supposed to avoid getting caught."

"We can't just sail away?"

"I wish," he muttered. "Too many people know you around here. They'll send a unit to your house as soon as your friends at the party mention your name."

"Maybe that's a good thing. My daughter sent a text earlier. She thought someone had been in the house while she'd gone to the airport."

"Was anything missing?"

She shook her head. "It's probably nothing, just her uncle's concern for me weighing on her mind. Police involvement will only aggravate Thomas. He's had a team parked on my street, watching the house, for days."

Holt considered telling her the observation team hadn't been sent by Thomas, but it could wait. He was more concerned about the break-in at her house. One more wrinkle in an op he might never iron out the way he wanted to.

She paused just outside the soft glow of the light where the dock met the gangway. "There's no way the police won't be looking for me. Heather witnessed those men attempting to take me. I should just go into the marina and give a statement. I can prove you were there to help me."

"Not a good idea. I wish we could prove you weren't even there."

"Too many camera phones for that to work," she said, sounding weary for the first time.

Holt pulled out the remaining functional burner phone and called the cab company.

"You have the number memorized?"

"I saw it on the dash of the cab on the way here," he said.

"You have a photographic memory?"

He nodded. "The one good discovery from my childhood." Why had he said that? His childhood had no significance here, aside from the street smarts he'd learned that might help them. "I don't think your brother has turned over my name yet. Any friends on the police force?"

"Of course."

"Of course," he echoed. "You have friends everywhere. Call one of them. Give him some line about gala business and offer to give your statement at the hotel." He checked his watch. "In an hour."

"It's a twenty-minute drive."

"Let's hope so."

"What should I say about you?"

"Nothing if you can get away with it. If you have to say something, call me protective detail. That should hold up for a day or two."

"Then what?"

"By then, if this isn't fixed, we'll probably both have bigger problems than leaving things out of a police report."

He handed her the ball cap he'd brought from the boat. "Put your hair up and keep your head down. Button your purse inside your coat." She gave him a questioning glance and he explained, "Changes your shape."

"The cab is meeting us two blocks south of the marina."

"You know, we could just walk back to Old Town."

He stared at her. "It's an option. As is stealing the car Isely's team used to get here."

"Did you take the keys?"

"Yeah." He patted his pocket and withdrew the key, tossing it out into the water. "It would be a mistake. If the police aren't on it, Isely will be tracking it."

Her gaze fell to the slice in his coat. "The cab it is."

Action decided, he guided her away from the water. They walked quickly toward the marina, keeping to the grassy areas cast in shadows, far away from the disrupted party.

"What do I say if someone stops us?"

"Accuse me of kidnapping and plead for help."

"But you—"

"Make a scene," he suggested as she had earlier. "Consider it good practice. This won't be the first tough choice you make in ops," he said. "Ditching me is an easy call. Trust me, I'm used to it."

Chapter Nine

Cecelia knew she would never just ditch him. She might not entirely understand what he was up to, but she didn't believe he was out to hurt her or that he was really working against Thomas. If she'd had any doubts, they had vanished almost completely when he'd risked himself to protect her from those men. She made the call to her friend on the police force.

When she put the phone away, her nerves were evident from her rapid, foggy vapor-cloud breaths in the cold night air. It was obvious enough that Emmett quietly instructed her to cover her mouth and nose with her scarf. It made her feel a bit like a train robber from the Wild West, but it worked. She appreciated the pointer.

She studied the way he moved, his effective blending of confidence and caution, and tried to emulate it as they slipped away from the marina. The flashing lights and distressed voices of partygoers faded behind them as they walked down to meet the cab.

When they were once more in the relative safety of the cab, she pulled down her scarf and grinned up at him. This kind of thing probably wasn't supposed to feel like fun, but it was so much better than sitting at her desk watching her life tick by.

The part of her that rebelled at the thought of ditching

him was positively giddy that it hadn't come to that. She understood the logic of his plan, but it was the flash of grief in his eyes when he'd admitted he was used to it that bothered her. Whoever had left him somewhere in his past had scarred him in the process.

It made her angry on his behalf, made her want to let him know some people could be trusted to do the right thing. That was a concept he should know from working with her brother's covert team, but she knew from William that a sense of isolation was a frequent result of long-term undercover operations.

The man was a loner. Most spies were, for obvious reasons, but she got the sense that he'd been that way long before her brother had recruited him to Mission Recovery.

"How did you land such a great job?"

She knew from the hard line of his mouth and cocked eyebrow he understood exactly what she meant. She could also see he didn't want to tell her.

"Standard first-date question," she teased, catching the smile on the driver's face reflected in the rearview mirror. He wanted her to sell one picture to anyone the cops might find and question, but after he'd saved her—twice—she was determined to sell another version of their story.

He'd behaved admirably all night—the perfect gentleman and valiant defender. However he'd managed to raise Thomas's suspicions, she knew it wasn't as simple as Thomas might believe.

"Fair enough." He rubbed his hands together, blowing on them as if he was chilled. "I'd finished a rather delicate piece of work during an internship in New York City. It caught some attention and a recruiter arrived. It took some convincing, but eventually I made the change."

She knew how to read between the lines, to sort fact from necessary fiction, but usually she had a frame of reference. With Emmett, she only had the online dating profile and the knowledge that he'd been trained to lie, to adapt to the cover story when necessary and make it believable.

One day soon, assuming she survived whatever *this* was, she'd be doing the same thing.

She'd seen many resumes cross her desk at the office, and she understood the natural language that bolstered rather average accomplishments. With Emmett, she sensed the reverse was true. His self-reliance and swagger wasn't all show. It was a direct result of practice becoming a string of successes.

She'd married William so young. It gave her the unique perspective of watching him change through the course of his career, especially in the early years. Those had been some rough days, being a wife and stay-at-home mother while learning how to read a husband who couldn't discuss his day without breaking security protocols.

"A delicate piece of work" could mean anything, which meant New York might be the kernel of truth. Or the whole story might be completely false.

Emmett surprised her by taking her hand in his. "I like my job and I've enjoyed my time with the company. It's been good work."

Said like a man who didn't think he'd be at it much longer. Already he was putting Mission Recovery in the past tense.

Indirectly, her husband and daughter had taught her more than she realized, including the inherent risks of working with an agent with a fatalistic attitude.

She shouldn't be thinking about snooping into his past. As much as she tried, she couldn't even come up with a good reason to do so. The kiss—as stunning as it was—didn't count. Her friends from the grief-counseling group would probably say she was transferring her feelings for William to Emmett. Except she'd never confessed to them she didn't have the capacity for that depth of feeling anymore.

Logically, the feelings she was experiencing tonight were most likely due to her innate need to nurture and fix. And to show her appreciation for his protection, of course.

As the cab pulled up to the hotel, she wondered if her motives really mattered. Her brother said she was a target and Emmett had proved his determination to keep her safe. She had to consider the possibility his effort was a ruse to get her to lower her guard, but she was willing to give him the benefit of the doubt. For tonight, anyway.

"Go on and give your statement," he said, nudging her to the front door. "I'll be upstairs. You know how to find me."

She didn't watch him go, didn't need the distraction of his body right now. She was smart enough to know setups happened, but through her years as a wife and mother she'd learned to trust her intuition.

There was more to Emmett Holt than he showed, and her instincts said if he didn't open up to someone about his real mission, he was headed for a downfall. Cecelia pulled the cap from her head and ran her fingers through her hair as she crossed the lobby to meet the detective leaning against the front desk, a paper cup of coffee from the complimentary service in his hand.

"Thanks for meeting me here," she said. "It's been a busy evening."

Detective Jerry Gadsden had been a friend of their family for years. As she approached, he drew her into a friendly hug. "It's good to see you, though I wish it was purely social. Do you want coffee?"

"No, thank you." She stepped to the open cooler and

plucked a bottle of water from the shelf. Her palms were damp, but her throat was dry. She was about to lie to a friend and essentially file a false report.

"Why aren't you at home?" He gestured for her to take a seat on the small sofa, while he settled in the closest chair.

"The gala is tomorrow." She waved a hand in the direction of the wide staircase curving around the atrium and up toward the second level ballrooms. "It's easier to stage the details from here."

He nodded. "You should have waited for the police at the marina."

"I know." Cecelia hesitated. Not because she didn't know how to answer, but because she felt someone watching her. She didn't dare give in to the urge and reveal Emmett's presence. "I was so scared. Those men just burst into the bathroom." She twisted the cap and took a sip of the water. "Is Heather all right?"

"Heather is the young woman you rescued?"

Cecelia nodded.

"She's shaky, but she'll be fine. Her father said he'd like to thank you."

"I believe he's on the guest list for tomorrow night." Did they think those men had been after Heather? Could she be that lucky?

Detective Gadsden smiled. "You might want to suggest an extra donation for being a hero."

"A hero?" Cecelia laughed that off. "I wouldn't go that far. I only did what any woman would do in my place."

"With great skill, if I might say so."

"You know William insisted on self-defense training for Casey and me."

"Bet you hoped you never had to use it."

She nodded.

"So walk me through what happened."

Cecelia told him the story, minus Emmett's involvement and the previous encounter in the alley.

"Pardon me for saying so, but did you change clothes? Most of the guests at the marina were dressed a bit more for a party than you are now."

She leaned forward, rolled the bottle of water between her palms. "I had a date and we decided to stop by the party on a whim."

"I see."

And she could see the judgment stamped on his face. She wanted to scream but managed a smile, biting back the sharp reminder that it had been over a year since she'd buried her husband. She'd reconciled herself to losing him for more than a year before that. Her counselor had explained that disengaging emotionally was normal under the circumstances. She'd tried to stop it but had failed. William had made her promise she would get on with her life, for heaven's sake.

"How did you meet?"

She sat back, startled by the question. "You can't think my date had anything to do with this?"

"Just gathering information," he said. "We've had an increase in personal thefts. Happens this time of year. And people are more vulnerable to scams during the holidays."

The irony. Emmett was a scammer of an entirely different nature than her friend could comprehend.

"We met online," she said, knowing she had to cooperate. Fighting him would only cast more unwanted suspicion on Emmett. "Three weeks ago."

"Where is he now?" He glanced around the lobby. "I'd like to talk with him."

"You know, I'm not sure." She should have anticipated that question. Her façade was about to crumble. Why did she ever believe she could do this? "I ran out the back and left him there. At the marina. I guess I wasn't such a good date for him. He's probably regretting that expensive dinner he sprang for."

While her friend scrambled to find the proper response, she brushed her bangs off her forehead. "So much for Bachelor Number One." She thought of the kiss, hoping it would make her blush. "I can give you his office number if you'd like to call him tomorrow."

"No home number? No cell?"

She squirmed in her seat. "Guess we hadn't made it to that stage yet. Tonight was our first date in person."

Detective Gadsden picked up on her embarrassment and gave her a sympathetic look. "Dating stinks. When Jen divorced me, it took a while until I felt human again. I know your loss is different, but it will get better."

She appreciated his compassion, and though she should feel bad for misleading him, she didn't. "I'll have to take your word."

"Please do. Now, I still have to give this new friend of yours a call."

"Right." She fished her cell phone out of her purse and read off Emmett's office number.

"Cecelia, do you want me to check him out for you?"

"No. Thank you." She shook her head. "I doubt he'll want to see me again after tonight, anyway."

"If a little random trouble scares him off, he's not good enough for you," Detective Gadsden said.

He had no idea how much she agreed with him. If only she could convince Emmett. "Thanks for the support. Are we done? I'm exhausted."

When he nodded, she stood up, ignoring her wobbling knees. She just wanted to get up to her room before her body collapsed from the post-adrenaline rush.

"You'll be here through the weekend? In case I have other questions," he explained.

"Yes. Tomorrow will go late and it seemed best to crash right here."

"All right." He hugged her again. "Take care of yourself."

"I will."

Detective Gadsden had hardly cleared the lobby before her thoughts turned back to Emmett. She knew he would be close and she made a mental note to ask him where he'd been hiding while she'd talked with the detective. There was no way he'd gone upstairs without her.

He didn't join her in the elevator, and he wasn't waiting in the hallway by her suite door. Worry began to gnaw at her. His absence couldn't be a good thing. She took a step back, ready to go look for him when the door opened.

He filled the doorway with his dark scowl. "What are you waiting for?" He reached out and drew her inside, throwing the deadbolt as soon as the door was closed behind her.

"I thought… Weren't you—"

"I estimated you could make it upstairs on your own."

"Well, of course." She glanced around, noticing a laptop and a garment bag that hadn't been there before she'd left hours ago for the wine bar. His leather jacket was on a hanger in the small closet and he'd stripped off his sweater and rolled back the cuffs of his shirt. She'd never known she could be so attracted to a man's forearms.

She really was in way over her head here. She cleared her throat. "You were serious about sticking *close*."

"Don't worry. I'll bunk on the couch."

"Surely you'd be more comfortable in your own room. I'm safe here." She still had the handgun. A new fear niggled at her. What if the gun had been used to murder someone? She should have mentioned to Gadsden that she'd gotten it from one of those thugs at the marina. Even though that was not quite right, the ones from the alley were likely friends of the two who'd come after her at the marina. But if she'd told him about the gun, he would have wanted to confiscate it. She wasn't ready to turn it over… yet. She might need it.

"And I intend to make sure you stay safe." He used his foot to push the small duffel bag he'd brought from his boat into the space between the chair and sofa. "You told your detective buddy I was protective detail?"

"No. I told him you were my date. A protective detail would have followed me into the lobby." And he knew as well as she did that a protective detail wouldn't have danced with her. Or kissed her senseless.

"A detail might just as easily have kept an eye on you from a distance."

"Which is what you did."

He shrugged.

She changed the subject. "Did you get some ice for your hand?"

"It's fine." He slipped his hands into his pockets. "Get some rest. We can work out a plan for tomorrow in the morning."

She didn't dignify that with a response, too busy studying the contrast his strong, masculine presence made against the filmy tulle of the gift baskets she'd prepared for her planning committee. The entire room was filled to bursting with gala details in a riot of greens, reds and plaids. Folders on the desk were stacked alongside a box of thank-you cards she'd planned to work on after her date. She wasn't up to the task anymore. Two bank boxes of silent auction bid sheets and photos of items too big or too valuable to display were on the counter. Rolls of raffle tickets were stacked next to the boxes. They'd be lucky to find enough space to make coffee in the morning.

The weight of the evening settled heavily onto her. What the hell was she doing? Maybe she'd overestimated her ability. Maybe she was trying to prove something she couldn't manage.

With those daunting thoughts echoing in her head, she fell back on what she knew best. "I should attend to your injuries. Would you like me to brew a cup of coffee?"

"I'm fine, Cecelia. You don't have to be the perfect society hostess here."

If he only knew that she wasn't thinking hostess thoughts at all as she gazed at him. No, her thoughts were sliding down an altogether different path. Maybe she needed the escape. It was the only reasonable explanation for her inability to find her balance in his presence.

When they'd first made plans to meet, she'd indulged in more than a few fantasies of how tonight might go, of what might come next.

She'd never planned to jump straight into bed with him—though he had the body and the face to tempt a saint. But desperate hormones and brotherly warnings aside, she was happy to discover that she had enough self-respect not to be stupid.

She had, however, played out a number of possible good-night scenarios. None of which involved a not-safe-for-work public display of affection on a crowded dance floor. She didn't regret it, other than knowing how much it altered her expectation of any kisses in her future.

Startling and bold as it was, she found herself contemplating how to get him to kiss her again. "Thanks for saving me tonight. I didn't expect the extracurricular, um, fun. I'm glad you were there."

"Just part of the service."

She was immediately irritated by his cavalier attitude until she realized he did it on purpose. He was pushing her away. Unfortunately for him, it only made her more determined to understand why.

"Don't do that," she said, folding her arms over her chest as she faced off with him.

"Do what? We should call it a night. We're both tired."

"Yes, I'm sure we both are. But that's no reason to push away someone who's trying to show a little gratitude."

"You're reading more into this than there is, Cecelia."

"I respectfully disagree." She'd scanned a few of the brief, ambiguous text messages on those phones. As a concerned former wife of an agent and mother of another, she recognized the signs of an agent weary from the task.

"Of course you do." His lip curled in a sneer and he turned his back on her.

If she didn't know better, she'd blame his surly demeanor on the job. But she had experience with others in his field and recognized there was more lurking under the surface.

"Does that loner routine work well for you?"

He spared her an annoyed look as he settled into a chair with his laptop. "Loner would imply that it does."

"I think you're trying to convince yourself you like being alone," she said, falling into the chair next to his. "But the solitude obviously scares you."

"Obviously? What is this, pop-psychology 101?"

Inside, she cringed at the purposely hurtful remark. "Maybe. If you need to talk, I'll listen."

"Talking isn't my preferred form of therapy."

The blatant lust in those enigmatic eyes made her redefine the meaning of attraction. A smart woman would have the sense to run away. She just wanted to get closer.

How those cool eyes of his could give off such intense heat was a mystery she wanted to solve. "That was crass."

"But honest."

He had her there. It might have been the most straightforward answer he'd offered. Except it was another answer designed to give him distance. She ought to just honor the signals and retreat, but something, some intangible factor, kept her butt in the chair.

"Emmett—"

He cut her off with a sharp glance. "Enough. I mean it, Cecelia."

She met his steely gaze with one of her own. "Those text messages you had me skim gave a certain impression."

"That we're up against a serious enemy?"

She nearly did a victory dance at the *we* he probably hadn't meant to use.

"That you've basically been a double agent for some time now."

"Which makes me as untrustworthy as your brother believes."

"Not exactly. I got the impression that you're very good at your work."

He stared at her, but his eyes weren't giving her any clues this time.

"You're good enough to make people believe whatever you want them to believe."

He didn't reply.

"What you need them to believe. You just ignore your own needs in the process."

"I still have some research to do." He dropped his head back and spoke to the ceiling. "What will it take to get you to drop this?"

"One answer. Do you really enjoy photography?"

He rolled his head toward her, his lips parted on an unspoken oath and a "how is that relevant" look in his eyes.

She arched an eyebrow, waiting.

"Yes," he replied quietly. "Now go on and get some rest. You've got a big day tomorrow."

She left him alone to do his research. After going through her nightly rituals, Cecelia slipped between the sheets of the big hotel bed and stared at the ceiling. Her racing thoughts kept circling back to one place: her brother and daughter might be right after all. If her shaking hands were any indication, she wasn't cut out for ops.

She laced her fingers and tried a slow, meditative breath. It didn't help. She was too frustrated with the way she'd barely managed to carry on with a date and keep her senses about her. Granted, the date had been complicated by other issues, but so would her life be if—*when*—she made the career change.

Logically, she knew training would prepare her, give her the tools to carry out fieldwork more effectively. Still, her hands rattled against the cool, smooth sheets.

Her first date since losing her husband and she had nearly got the man killed in an alley brawl because she wouldn't give up her purse. Thomas had been right to doubt her when she'd volunteered to be an asset. She'd only been fooling herself to believe she could do this.

She closed her eyes and saw that broken bottle slice through the air toward Emmett. One false move and he would have been the one needing a paramedic.

She was exaggerating. It was a lesson in perspective. The moment only looked worse to her because she'd been scared. But Emmett had held his own. More than that. He'd been so calm, so professional.

Rolling to her side, she punched and fluffed the pillow. She'd had more training than the average woman, knew better than most people how to protect herself in a physical altercation. William had insisted on teaching her what he thought she needed to know in case she'd ever been targeted by *his* enemies.

Yet, tonight, when it had mattered, she'd pulled out the Taser at the first opportunity. So much for her bold eagerness to jump into fieldwork.

She closed her eyes and tried to see her husband's face, tried to imagine what he would have said or done if he'd been in that alley with her. The image was more difficult to conjure than it should have been.

Instead, Emmett dodging the broken bottle, landing uppercuts and that jaw-cracking hook, those were the images that filled her mind. The more she tried and failed, the worse she felt about the whole evening.

What kind of loving wife gave a man two and a half decades, nursed him through a terminal illness and then blanked him from her mind when the first bit of eye candy showed an interest?

A false interest, she added, factoring in the rest of the details.

She told herself this exercise would be easier if she'd been at home. In the back of her bureau drawer, she kept one of William's favorite T-shirts. All of his other clothes had been donated to charity, but that shirt was her last indulgence, a sachet of memories when she buried her nose deep in search of his scent.

A scent that had faded months ago.

Live your life.

At the time, she'd smiled and promised to do just that, knowing he was already more than halfway gone. She'd been by his side through every terrible stage of his disease, but shutting down her emotions had been the only way to survive the agony of watching his body wage war against the unrelenting cancer.

His doctors and nurses had told her to put him in hospice, but she couldn't justify it. She'd been strong enough to care for him, and her employer had held her job while she'd done what needed to be done.

Though he was too ill to know in his last weeks, she'd honored his last wish. He'd died peacefully in his own home, surrounded by the familiar things they'd collected in the process of building their life as husband and wife.

By the time his body had surrendered, her relief was palpable. She barely had tears left to shed at the memorial as so much of her grieving had been done in those quiet, endless hours alone with him.

Friends and family called her brave. She didn't have the courage to correct them. Didn't have the decency to admit she'd parked her heart back with that last good conversation and simply gone through the motions until his struggle had finally ended.

Tonight had proved she hadn't gained any courage in the year since. She'd let Emmett handle everything while she'd mostly cowered.

William would agree with Casey and Thomas and tell her she had no business in ops. As much as she wanted to reinvent her life, herself, maybe she should stick with the more passive pursuits of charity fundraising and… needlepoint.

She groaned into the pillow. She'd always hated needlepoint.

"Cecelia?"

He was silhouetted in the bedroom doorway, the light from the other room glowing behind him. "I'm fine," she said in a rush. "Didn't mean to wake you."

She was half tempted to send her brother a text and let

him know she'd basically wound up in protective custody after all. Of course, Thomas probably still considered Emmett the enemy.

She couldn't believe she was sharing a room with a man again. In the broadest sense of the word, anyway. Who knew a year could make so much difference? It had been even longer than that since she'd had a healthy partner to share any part of her life with, and she'd learned to rely on herself. The challenges had taught her she enjoyed quiet, setting her own schedule and having no one to answer to.

But that left no one to answer her.

The silhouette shifted. "Need to talk about it?"

"No, thank you," she replied.

"Now who's ignoring their needs?"

"I'm fine," she said firmly.

"You did well tonight."

She didn't have a polite reply for that. It seemed rude to argue with the man who'd saved her from being kidnapped. Twice. The man who refused to leave her alone in the hotel suite she'd booked for the weekend just to simplify logistics for tomorrow's event.

Admin and logistics, those were her strengths, a little voice reminded her. Not ops.

"Do I make you uncomfortable?"

Yes! "No," she said. Both answers were true, but she couldn't possibly explain that to him. She rolled onto her back and sat up, uncaring if her hair was tousled. "Are you uncomfortable here with me?"

There was a long pause before he said, "I'm worried about you."

He didn't strike her as the worrying type. "Why?"

"Anyone would be in shock after what we handled tonight."

"You can rest easy. I'm not in shock."

Racked with guilt about forgetting my husband so easily, yes. Shock, not so much. Between her family and her job—even as an admin for the CIA—she'd heard enough to know what had happened could have been much worse.

The silhouette at the door moved again. *Come closer,* she pleaded silently. *Touch me, talk to me. Help me forget what a horrible person I am.* But using him that way would only compound her mistakes. As much as she wanted a repeat performance of that kiss on the dance floor, she'd had enough guilt for one day.

She'd used those unending hours during the long, lonely months to think about what being a widow meant to her, what her life would look like without a husband to provide and care for. In her mind she'd seen herself growing stronger with her forced independence. Now she wondered what kind of fantasy she'd been spinning.

"All right. I'm a light sleeper if you change your mind."

She was a light sleeper, too. First as a result of motherhood, and more recently from all those nights listening for her husband's final breath. Emotions tangled inside her, threatened to burst from her. "Emmett, wait."

"Yes?"

"Tomorrow." She fisted her fingers in the sheet. "Will you please show me how you got the information off the phones?"

"You want a technology lesson?"

"If you don't mind."

"Sure. Nothing I did tonight is a big secret."

"Can I help you research the Irina name?"

"That's what I've been doing. It's a yacht registered in the Bahamas."

"Oh."

"The text could just as easily reference a new associate. We can dig deeper tomorrow."

She sensed he was holding something back. "Okay. When it's time, will you really let me help?"

"Time?"

"When you're ready to wrap this up, I mean."

"Are you asking to help me plan and execute the take-down?"

She swallowed. "I'm already scheduled to be the bait, aren't I?"

He moved through the darkness of the room toward her. The dim light from the door backlit him, but she couldn't see his face or his eyes. His scent filled her senses and she felt the mattress sag as he sat on the corner of the bed.

"No matter what your brother said, I won't let anyone hurt you. That was never the plan."

"I believe you." She scooted closer to him, to his heat. Maybe she had lost her mind but she just couldn't help herself. "Let me help you. At least show me how not to be a stumbling block and what you're planning."

"You have the gala and your guests to think about."

"Gracious hostess is a role I've mastered. Could do it blindfolded. What you could teach me will help me when I move to ops."

"We don't exactly do things according to CIA protocol, Cecelia."

She wanted to reach for the light so she could gauge his expression but knew it would blow the intimacy of the moment and snap the fragile thread of hope that he might agree. "It would still be an informative exercise."

He huffed a derisive breath. "Too informative is more like it. What I've been doing has been dark since I learned Isely was gunning for Thomas and everything he's built at Mission Recovery."

"Teach me or I won't go quietly when it's time to take me to Isely."

"Blackmail doesn't suit you." The bed shifted as Emmett stood up. "You have no idea what you're asking." His silhouette filled the doorway again. "Get some sleep and we'll discuss it in the morning."

It wasn't the yes she'd hoped for, but it wasn't an outright no. Cecelia pulled the covers close, a smile on her face as she settled her head on the pillow. After a moment, she realized her hands weren't shaking anymore.

Maybe there was hope for her, after all.

Chapter Ten

Plaza Hotel, Alexandria
Friday, December 19, 8:05 a.m.

Holt's phone rang at five minutes past eight o'clock. Nice of the detective to give him time to settle at the desk job indicated by his profile at the online dating site. Why couldn't she have just stuck with the protective custody idea? Her detective pal would have bought that line considering who her husband had been.

The questions were easy enough that he might have handled them in his sleep, which was a good thing considering his mind was otherwise occupied with thoughts of the woman in the bedroom.

She didn't seem to have any idea at the wealth of talent lurking inside her. She'd played the detective brilliantly last night. If he hadn't already known it from watching the interview, the tone of the detective's questions today would have confirmed it.

"I suggest you move on to the next woman on your list," Detective Gadsden said.

Holt was amused by the detective's lack of subtlety. "Do you have a vested interest in Mrs. Manning?" He hoped not. He had enough—more than enough—adversaries to dodge on this op already.

"I've known her a long time. She deserves better than a man who'd leave her stranded."

"Check your notes, detective. She ran out on me." He disconnected the call and pushed the phone onto the clip on his hip.

He returned to his computer and considered checking in with Nadine, or even the director, but changed his mind. Neither of them could tell him what he wanted to know: Why was Isely rushing the plan?

He thought back to the intel on that flash drive. He'd precisely crafted the files he'd given to Isely, embellishing where necessary to blur the truth. It was his fault Isely knew about Cecelia, and whether the director ever believed him or not, he'd guarded her carefully since he'd been forced to reveal the connection.

He'd assumed kidnapping Cecelia was simply one part of Isely's plan for the director's downfall. But the shift, the new desperation, didn't fit and it brought up a host of potential disasters.

There had only been two changes in Cecelia's life since Isely proposed this kidnapping. Her online relationship and her internal career change within the CIA.

Holt didn't like the way it was adding up. According to her, she didn't do anything all that interesting in her little corner of administration. He scrubbed at his face. As much as he dreaded it, he was going to have to interrogate Cecelia about her work.

"Everything okay?" Cecelia asked from the doorway.

"Fine. Just dealt with your detective." He turned to face her and wished he hadn't. She'd emerged from the bedroom with a well-rested glow. Bright green lace peeked out from the white of the fluffy hotel robe she wore. "Coffee's ready."

"Thanks." She crossed the room, wisely giving him a wide berth, and poured herself a cup. "So what's first?"

"Breakfast."

By the time they'd pushed the room-service cart back into the hallway and she'd left to take a shower, the implied intimacy was getting under his skin.

He hadn't lived in such close proximity to a woman since the dorms in college. The scents and sounds and rituals had been intriguing, amusing and thoroughly educational on a less-than-academic level.

After two failed attempts at real relationships, he had given up on the idea of a true and lasting one in favor of hot, brief affairs where both parties knew what they were getting into.

You lied to me. Her words echoed in his mind this morning every time he looked at her. Lying was part of his life, and his secrets had been the breaking point of those early relationships. As a Specialist, the need for deception hadn't changed. Not with this case, and not with her.

He was more than a little surprised Director Casey hadn't kicked down the door yet to protect both his sister and the team he was sure Holt was deceiving. By now the man had to know they were together. Or had been together. Well, not together-together, though that still held serious appeal.

He pushed a hand through his hair and forced himself to stop overthinking the situation with Cecelia.

She was a means to an end. He had measures in place so she'd never really be in jeopardy. Unfortunately, he couldn't explain that to anyone yet. Not even her. Only sincere worry and a convincing effort by Thomas to rescue her would convince Isely of his loyalty.

He heard the hair dryer start up and knew he only had a few minutes more to think up something else to teach her. She'd mastered the phone dumps over the scrambled eggs. He understood what she was really asking and he gave her points for turning what might have been an awkward situation to her favor.

She'd warned him their day would be consistently interrupted with her friends calling and even coming and going from the suite. To prevent questions, they'd moved all of his belongings into the bedroom.

If anyone caught them together before the gala, she promised to refer to him as her security detail. He figured it was too little too late, especially after that kiss on the dance floor last night. No doubt someone at the party had captured the moment with a camera or cell phone. He'd been more than a little surprised the detective hadn't come across it yet.

He was rubbing his lips, remembering the moment, when a soft rap on the door drew his attention. He crossed the room, peered through the peephole and saw two brunettes in the stylish conservative attire that marked all of her friends. He felt underdressed in the faded jeans and black polo shirt he'd pulled on after his shower, but he opened the door anyway.

"Oh." The bright smiles faded as both women gaped at him. "We must, ah…"

"Looking for Cecelia?"

"Yes," they replied in unison, obviously relieved and startled at the same time.

"Names?"

They frowned, but gave him the information. Recognizing the names from the list of expected visitors Cecelia had given him, he stepped back and invited them inside.

"I'm with hotel security," he lied. "I'll let her know you're here."

He walked away before they could ask him why she

needed security in her room, but his excellent hearing caught the murmurs of appreciation and speculation that he was the same guy spotted with Cecelia last night.

Great.

Last night's stunt at the marina had clearly made Cecelia grist for the gossip mill. It was all he could do not to remind these two they were supposed to be her friends.

He kept his mouth shut. If Cecelia moved into ops, she'd have to deal with twisted perceptions as a natural part of getting through the day.

Holt paused at the bathroom door, his train of thought completely derailed at the sight of Cecelia wrapped only a bath towel.

Other women he'd spent time with in close proximity had done their hair last. Not her.

Catching his reflection in the mirror, she turned off the hair dryer. "Problem?"

His temper flared in an automatic defense against the rush of lust coursing through his body. "There's a perfectly good robe right here," he growled, pulling it off the hook and tossing it at her. "You've got company."

She smiled at him, her polite "life is lovely" smile. "I'll be right out."

He turned, uncertain of how to escape. He didn't want to chat with the Junior League twins in the other room and he couldn't stand here staring as Cecelia put on something more appropriate.

He bit back an oath and crossed to the window in the bedroom, positioning himself so she had privacy. Maybe he'd get lucky and a sniper would put him out of his misery.

The suite door opened and closed, the feminine voices rose and fell and then Cecelia returned to the bedroom. He didn't have to look—the light floral scent of her body wash drifted across the room and teased his senses.

"You can turn around. I'm dressed and they're gone."

He turned, but it was a mistake. The cream colored, body-skimming top with spaghetti-thin straps and jeans that molded to her hips and thighs were almost more tempting than the towel had been.

A vivid image of him sliding those straps down and away played out in his head before he yanked his gaze back up to her eyes. "We have work to do."

"I'm ready." She pulled on a thick cardigan sweater and walked back out to the sitting room. He enjoyed the sweet view of her backside, then had to wait a moment until he was sure he had his wayward lust under control.

He couldn't let this attraction interfere with what had to be done here.

As he joined her in the other room she announced, "We have an hour or so before Casey stops by."

"Awesome." He picked up his laptop and set it on the low coffee table in front of the couch. "Isely wanted to kidnap you last night," he began without preamble. "We need to dig in and find out why he changed his schedule."

"Changed?"

"Yeah. The original plan was to take you from the gala tonight. Bigger shock value," he pointed out.

"So should I assume he'll make another attempt?"

"Yes."

"Okay." She picked up her tablet. "What do you want me to do?"

"When they grab you, don't panic."

She tilted her head, laced her fingers and pushed her hands forward like a pianist limbering up before a recital. "Okay. I meant what do you want me to do now? Can I research the location in that text message?"

"Go ahead." Inspiration struck. "See if you can connect the location to the name of the ship."

"If the yacht is the Irina we're after."

"Exactly."

Reluctantly, he sat beside her and started his own search for the possible catalysts that might have Isely looking at Cecelia.

After a few comfortable minutes of silence, she said, "I think we're after the yacht. Those numbers come up as a location in the Atlantic Ocean, not too far off the coast."

Holt mentally cringed. That kind of "address" didn't bode well for Cecelia or Thomas's chances of rescuing her. Isely knew Holt could sail, and an exchange at sea likely meant Isely had found Holt's boat in the marina.

Not good. Even worse was that the location hadn't been sent to Holt, only to one of Isely's most trusted men. Holt started searching slip registrations for rentals matching the original operation timeline.

"Are you hacking into the marina?" Cecelia was looking over his shoulder. "You promised to show me your process."

Not exactly, but there was no use getting into a debate. "If he means to sail into the sunset with you, we need to be prepared."

"Do you like working with my brother?"

The question came out of nowhere. She was constantly surprising him with her accurate assessments, even when her mind seemed to be elsewhere. Director Casey was the kind of boss who had a man's back. It was the one piece of this task that regularly pricked at Holt's conscience. Thomas Casey didn't see eye to eye with Holt, and that was never going to change. This mission would be the final straw for Holt. Win or lose—and Mission Recovery would win—he'd started to realize no one would ever trust him again.

Even if he came away from this clean, without that trust

he could never take over for Director Casey as planned. He'd known this was a career-ending op but hadn't bothered to dwell on it. Had in fact been in active denial about it as recently as yesterday when he'd tasked Grant with finding the biologist.

"Emmett?"

"Your brother is a good man and a good boss. I've got nothing but respect for him."

"You're doing this—and planning to take the fall—to protect him."

He turned on her to let her see the dark edges he hid behind layers of polish and training. "I'm doing this because it needs to be done. Isely has a deadly new bioweapon and he blames your brother for the death of his father and undermining their business reputation. I'm doing what I have to do."

"He certainly seems to be paying plenty of people to come after me."

"That's what bothers me," Holt admitted. "The original plan was simple. Just me, you and a drop-off point."

"Hmm."

He didn't like the sound of that hmm. He tried to ignore it, to finish the trail of breadcrumbs that would help Director Casey save Cecelia in case things went sideways on him tonight.

"What?"

"Nothing. Just wondering what you made him believe about you."

He sighed, closed the top on his computer. "Why do you care?"

"You promised to teach me something. How did you convince him you could be bought?"

"Why do you think it's as simple as money?"

"Because you donated a substantial amount of money

to my charity. I suspect that was because you didn't want any part of the money he had paid you."

He stood up and paced away from her. "Nothing better to dump it into."

"Maybe not, but I think it's more likely you enjoyed putting his blood money to good use."

How in the hell did she see him so clearly? "The donation put me in your circle." He waved his hands to indicate the suite. "What better way to enable Isely's vengeance?"

"Hmm."

"Stop that," he snapped.

"What?" She gave an exaggerated flutter of her eyelashes.

"Isely has to believe you're oblivious." He'd convinced jaded, field-tested operatives on both sides of the law, but he couldn't fool this one woman. "Lives are on the line here, Cecelia."

"I understand." She set aside her tablet and walked straight up to him. "More than you, I think."

Nothing short of a major earthquake could have uprooted him as she wrapped him in a hug. A *hug,* for crying out loud. He didn't know where to put his hands, so he kept them off her.

"Thank you," she said, "for everything you've sacrificed to protect Thomas." Her heart was shining in her eyes as she gazed up at him. "Casey's wedding day would have been ruined without Thomas."

"He got himself out of that. I had nothing to do with it."

With one last squeeze, she stepped back, and her lips curved into a warm, sincere smile. "I don't believe you."

"It's the truth." He rubbed at his mouth, told himself to shut up. "I'm not the white knight from a fairy tale." But she made him want to be, and he hated himself for the failure.

The thought was so foreign, so unprecedented, he actually didn't know what to say next.

She slid into the chair, crossed her legs and drummed her fingers against the upholstery. "Oh, no, you're definitely bad-guy material. At least that's what you want me to believe."

"It's more true than you know."

"If you say so." She shrugged one delicate shoulder and blew him off.

"God, you're stubborn."

"I am. It comes in handy." She reached over and patted the couch. "Now, come on and show me something useful before we get interrupted again. I'm not letting you renege."

"A bad guy would renege," he pointed out.

"I'm sure you're right."

She was going into ops, and from what he'd heard through the bugs he'd planted in her house, no one close to her supported the decision.

Sure, they'd had more years with her, knew her far better than he did. Apparently that blurred their vision, or maybe they just didn't realize how strong she had to be to do what she'd been doing all these years: waiting and praying that a loved one in harm's way would come home safe.

From where he stood, Cecelia Manning was smart, brave and determined. Possibly too determined, he amended as she continued to stare him down. The CIA would be lucky to have her in an operations capacity.

He pulled up one of the fake files he'd given Isely and a picture he'd previously sent to use as an example. Side by side from his laptop to hers, he taught her the basics of how he manipulated the intel. She was a quick study, using the tips he showed her to embed information in photographs, to transfer files away from the home system and to leave breadcrumbs that pointed in another direction.

"Emmett?" She waited for him to glance at her screen. "How does this look?" She tucked her hands under her legs as if she feared he would see them tremble as he reviewed her first effort at concealing information in a digital photo.

He reviewed her coding, then asked her to show him the research she'd found on the Irina. "Thomas is an idiot."

CECELIA'S FINGERS WENT still on the keyboard. As a little sister perpetually in her brother's shadow, it wasn't that she didn't have cause to agree, but she wanted to be sure why this man thought so. "Do I need to defend my brother?"

"I bugged your house, remember? I heard that crack he made about not recruiting you."

"Familiarity breeds contempt," she said lightly. She'd had a lifetime to get used to it. "It would be more accurate to say he's averse to change. I'm the baby sister and I've been a predictable and known quantity in his life since I was born. He can't help wanting to keep me in that box."

"I have a feeling your current situation will blow the lid right off that box," he said.

"Agreed." She switched to another window so he could check that code, as well. "Did I do this one right?"

"Nice work."

She wanted to celebrate but decided to save it for private. "Thanks."

"You'll make a good partner one day."

"Not that you ever use them."

"What do you mean?"

"I was thinking of last night and the possible break-in at my house. You were with me, and you appear to be working this operation alone. Or you were. Who else would have cause to search my home?"

His cool eyes went flat and she knew he shared her concern. "I've wanted to ask you about that and about your work. It's possible Isely thinks you know something or can access something valuable."

"I don't know anything of value to a man like him. Unless he's in the market for a human-resources lackey."

"You're no lackey," he grumbled.

She appreciated the vote of confidence, especially from this unexpected source. "I'll do a little research—"

"No. Leave that to me. I have more free time than you do today."

She glanced at her watch. "Casey and the girls will be here soon. We have appointments with the hotel spa before it's time to dress for the evening."

"Tell me I don't have to go along."

His stricken expression made her laugh. "Relax, no one's going to tie you down and force you to have a mani-pedi."

"I don't want to know what that is."

"Such a bachelor," she teased.

"Always." He packed up his computer. "If you promise not to leave the hotel, there are a few things I should see to in person."

"Isely?"

"Best to keep a volatile client calm."

As if he read her worry before she could say a word, he traced the curve of her shoulder with his fingertip, instantly distracting her. "I'll come back up to dress when you've all cleared out."

"But you will be there tonight?" The thought of never seeing him again slashed through her, made her ache.

He nodded.

"Say the words, Emmett. Tell me you'll be at the gala

as my guest, not just because Isely wants you to be there." She hadn't meant to say that last part, but there it was.

"I'll be there for you."

"Thank you," she whispered, weak with relief.

A new awareness arced between them. For her it came from having an expert field agent take her seriously as much as her growing affection for a man determined to stand apart from the world…and to keep her safe in the process.

He wasn't the only one who knew his way around and through computer systems. At his side, she'd done almost as much digging as learning today, and discovered his past—at least those days before he went behind the technological curtain of Mission Recovery—was full of white-knight behavior.

Since June he'd systematically alienated each of his allies, but thanks to what he'd taught her, she knew he was doing all the wrong things for all the right reasons.

She understood she might very well be interpreting his actions favorably on purpose, but she didn't care. Intuition told her that white knight had been buried deep, for a long time, as a matter of survival.

"Give me your phone."

She found it on the table and handed it to him. He entered something and handed it back. "Keep it on and keep it with you. As long as Casey stays close, he won't make a move. I'm speed-dial one if anything happens. Just call and leave the line open."

"And if you need me?"

His smile sent butterflies winging through her belly. "You'll know."

"Emmett, whatever happens tonight, please know that I trust you."

He stared at her for a long moment. "Sweetheart, you really shouldn't."

Chapter Eleven

She had to admire his timing. Emmett had cleared the suite minutes before Casey had knocked on the door. They caught up on family and simple things, but serious talk had to wait as her friends arrived to help shuttle things downstairs.

They'd just returned from setting up the gift table when the suite phone rang and Cecelia cringed as Casey picked it up. What if it was Emmett? Would her daughter disapprove of her social life as much as she disapproved of her new career goals? Would she call Thomas and give away Emmett's location?

"Sure, she's right here." Casey covered the receiver with her palm. "A detective for you."

"Jerry?"

Casey shook her head as Cecelia took the phone and introduced herself.

"Ah, Mrs. Manning. If you could come down to the hotel café, please. We just need another moment of your time."

"We're terribly busy. I gave my statement to Detective Gadsden last night. Can't this wait until tomorrow?"

"I'm afraid not. We have suspects in holding, but I can't keep them there without cause. I just need you to take a look at a few photos."

"Of course. I'll be right down."

She knew there was more to it. Detective Gadsden should have been asking her these questions. The voice wasn't quite right, either, but she refused to cower again. She'd be safe enough in the café with her daughter beside her.

"I have to go downstairs for a moment and look at a couple of pictures. Apparently they have some suspects in last night's trouble. Will you come with me?"

"Sure, Mom."

Cecelia gave an excuse to the other women who were taking the last load of items out of the suite, then she and Casey headed downstairs.

"It didn't sound like Detective Gadsden," Casey said.

"No, it wasn't. He must have sent a colleague." She punched the button for the lobby level as well as the floor above it. "Can you keep an eye on me—be my backup—and still let me handle whatever this is?"

"Are you expecting trouble?"

"After last night, I wouldn't be surprised by anything." That was an understatement, for sure. "It should be a straightforward process, but if I'm wrong, do the right thing and call your uncle."

"You know I will."

Cecelia's palms were damp as the elevator stopped and the doors opened at the second floor. "I mean it, honey. Don't interfere, just make the call."

Casey didn't look happy about it, but she made the promise as the doors closed between them.

At the café, a man with dark hair brushed back from a face that might have passed for mid-twenties stood up from a nearby table as she paused at the hostess station.

"Mrs. Manning?" He flashed a badge, and then extended his hand. "A pleasure to meet you. I've ordered coffee."

Closer now, she could see he wasn't as young as first glance implied. "Thank you, but I'm terribly short on time."

"A big night ahead of you." He gestured for her to join him at his table.

"Yes." She settled into a chair and waited for him to resume his.

"I've heard about the gala. The pediatric department is fortunate you're on their side."

He was a little too slick for Cecelia's taste, and there was something in his eyes that warned her to tread carefully. Her phone was in her lap, turned on and ready to press the number one.

"It was my husband's idea, and I'm pleased to carry it out." She poured herself a cup of coffee in hopes of appearing far calmer than she was.

He pushed a folder across the table and opened it. Only two pictures were inside, and neither of them bore the slightest resemblance to last night's assailants. She looked from a candid shot of her brother to a similarly candid shot of Emmett. Then she looked back up at the man who was certainly not a detective.

And then she knew. She'd walked right into his trap. "Mr. Isely?"

He nodded. "Forgive the deception."

Emmett would be furious, and she'd never forgive her stupidity if she let herself get taken. She scooted her chair away from the table. "I really must get back to the preparations upstairs."

"But I only need a moment. Which man means more to you, I wonder?"

Terror lit in her body. The air in her lungs turned to stone.

"Do give me an answer. I have a man positioned behind your daughter, ready to put a bullet in her head at my command."

With a steady hand, Cecelia raised her coffee cup to her lips, smiling over the rim. She would not alarm the other patrons or give this monster any reason to hurt her daughter.

"I love my brother."

"Blood over lust, then?"

She waited, her hands calm in her lap as she glanced around. "Where is Mr. Holt?"

"Not to worry, he'll be here to dance with you again tonight. As they say, I'm banking on it."

Who was this man? He dared to make a move like this—in the open? He had to know that her brother as well as Emmett would be watching her. The bastard seemed fearless. *Do this right, Cecelia.* She needed to play the part. Make the right moves. For all their sakes. "Will you be in attendance, as well? I might be able to arrange a seat in exchange for an appropriate donation."

Isely stared at her. "You are remarkable."

"Thank you." She set the cup down, thankfully without cracking the saucer. "If you'll excuse me?"

"Not quite yet. Where is the formula?"

"I have no idea what you're talking about." And that lack of knowledge sent a chill skating down her spine. This man was dangerous in a way she'd never faced before. She'd met all kinds of people through her husband's career and living in this area, and she knew everyone had secrets. But Isely oozed lethal in an entirely different capacity.

"You are a very poor liar," he said. "I advise you to choose discretion over valor here, Mrs. Manning. Unless your skills improve, you will need a great deal of assistance from friends in your new career. We might come to a mutually profitable arrangement if you cooperate now."

"I believe the term is 'asset.' And I will never be one of yours."

"Tell me where I can find the formula or I will take down your brother and expose his crimes for the world to judge."

His threats and arrogance ignited something dark and deadly deep inside her. She felt the shift like an earthquake as her resolve kicked into high gear. She never considered herself capable of blood lust, but she had an overwhelming need to send Mr. Isely straight to hell. The man sold weapons to the highest bidder, invested in research for the sole purpose of profiting from atrocities. He was as low as a life form could be.

"You'll try to do that anyway," she countered.

"Try?" He arched a brow. "No, no. I always succeed in my endeavors. However, one detail from you could prevent much suffering."

"No. I don't quite trust you, sir." She knew he would eventually try to take down Thomas anyway, for the sake of his revenge if he got nothing else from this venture. She had to pause to keep from shouting. Or leaping across the table and attempting to strangle him. Either action would surely be construed as a signal to shoot Casey. "As for Thomas, he can take care of himself."

"I know you need to believe it."

It was too much. He didn't know her, would never know her. The pricey suit and cultured voice were merely a costume to hide his lack of humanity. By design or circumstance, he'd become something absolutely vile. But he would never know her or her brother.

"You know nothing about me or my needs." She was

a moment away from tossing the coffeepot at his head. "I cannot give you what I do not have. I suggest you take your own advice and discreetly crawl back under the rock where you belong."

"Well, well." He sat back in his chair, a reptilian smile sliding across his face. "You are a delightful surprise. I am so honored, Mrs. Manning, to be the first to see this side of you."

"You will not succeed." She leaned forward. "I won't let you."

"Oh, I look forward to our next meeting." He stood. She did the same. "Have a lovely evening."

She had to find Emmett… She blinked, realized she had totally forgotten to hit the speed dial for him.

Too late to worry about that now. She had to find her daughter.

Chapter Twelve

Plaza Hotel, 7:35 p.m.

From across the balcony, Holt watched Cecelia navigate the sparkling rainbow of expensive gowns anchored by tailored and rented tuxedos. Most of the men had worn classic black tie, but a few had chosen more festive touches of holiday color in honor of the season.

Holt wasn't one of them. He'd been honest with her about that. He didn't do holidays, had never had a reason to. In her red tulle ball gown with its jeweled waist she was as untouchable as ever; still, his hands itched to do so.

He only had to keep himself under control for one more night. Then it would be over, one way or another.

With a flute of champagne in his hand, he exchanged pleasantries with people who only assumed they knew him, and wondered if he'd been foolish to attempt this alone. Cecelia had been right about one thing. He was exhausted from maintaining surveillance to assure her safety, searching her history for common ground and keeping up appearances at his real job. It would all be worth it if he could get her out of here alive and stop Isely.

The large crowd, even bigger than he'd expected, shifted and flexed, blocking his view of her again. He hustled up the staircase to take a better position. There was a younger blonde glued to her side. The daughter. At least Cecelia was guarded well. Even without the benefit of the research photos he'd studied, their resemblance was uncanny. And while he hadn't spotted Director Casey specifically, Holt knew he'd have several people in place.

Now he just had to dance between the sharp blades of Isely's revenge and the director's protective nature. Preferably without getting sliced to ribbons in the process.

Since Isely's first warning, Holt had searched through every detail about Cecelia's life. Nothing he'd turned up indicated any reason to worry about her endangering Isely's ultimate revenge plot against Thomas.

Today, as he'd put his escape plan and backup options in place, he dug deeper still and hadn't found the thing that explained Isely's uncharacteristic impatience. He'd searched headlines and found no change in current events. He'd poured through obituary columns and death notices and come up empty.

The widow had no field experience, and though the CIA employed her, it was in a legitimate, low-key administration post. She'd only recently returned to that post after taking four months' leave to care for her husband during his losing battle with brain cancer.

She hadn't been close enough to the agency to even catch a rumor that might assist or harm the German crime lord, and yet Holt couldn't shake the feeling that something was very, very wrong.

What did Isely know about the woman that had him so focused on her?

It remained the unanswered question, so Holt turned his mind to what he did know: Isely. The man was smart. Devious. Determined beyond reason to destroy Thomas Casey. As the sister, Cecelia had obvious value as leverage to cause pain. People were mere tools to a man like him.

Thank God there weren't too many men like Isely in the world. Of course, in Holt's line of work he saw more than his fair share of them.

A man with a booming voice announced the orchestra was ready, and three wide ballroom doors opened on cue.

He watched the crowd flow through them, Cecelia and her daughter standing at the center greeting donors with gracious smiles. Other people important to the charity foundation did the same at the other two doors, but Holt decided he'd wasted enough time.

Setting his champagne aside, he returned to the ballroom level and gave Casey a cursory nod as he greeted Cecelia. Immediately the daughter went on alert, but Cecelia's perfect society smile didn't so much as flicker.

He didn't know whether he should be pleased or insulted.

"So glad you've arrived, Mr. Holt," she said. With a quiet word to her daughter, she slipped her arm through his. "Let me show you to your table."

This was unexpected. "That's really not necessary. I just wanted you to know I was here."

"I knew." Her smile remained, but her blue eyes showed clear relief.

"What happened?" He'd had his phone on all day. His random yet frequent checks of her safety had indicated nothing untoward had occurred. "You didn't call."

"There was no need. This way."

She guided him through the sea of round tables set for ten and he took stock of the setup, comparing the final arrangement to the plans he'd read in her suite last night. At the far end of the room, on the other side of the wide dance floor, the long head table perched on a riser. A podium stood ready at the center of the head table, a small orchestra to one side and what appeared to be a DJ's table on the other.

Two walls of the ballroom were lined with long tables draped in snow-white linen and decorated with Christmas colors. Silent auction items were laid out with suggested starting bids on each paper. Four bar stations were prepped, but currently closed.

His concern grew with every step she took closer to that head table. He'd known his donation would get her attention, but being front and center was more publicity than he wanted. Dining with half of the moneyed elite of Alexandria and Washington, D.C., wasn't his idea of discreet. Would nothing go right in this last stage of his plans?

Alarms went off in his head when a familiar couple entered through a side door. Lucas Camp and his wife, Victoria Colby-Camp, strolled in, Lucas's limp barely evident this evening. They approached the round table closest to the dance floor and were soon joined by Thomas Casey and Cecelia's daughter, along with her husband, Levi.

He'd known about the connection. Cecelia considered Camp a dear friend. The man was Casey's godfather. But of all the friends she might have in attendance, this one man, working with or without Thomas, could ruin everything.

It was increasingly clear Holt was going down in flames tonight. He'd been prepared for that. But he could not let any of them get in the way of his keeping Cecelia safe.

Still, of all the contingency plans he'd made, this was one he hadn't anticipated. He started crafting an excuse to leave, knowing he could duck back in and take her later, but she led him straight up to a place at the end of the head table. Next to a place card with her name.

What the hell?

As the event organizer, shouldn't she be closer to the

podium? Relieved as he was not to be seated with Camp, he had to wonder what game she was playing.

"This isn't necessary."

"Of course it is," she countered. "You singlehandedly lifted us to our pre-event goal and your gift will inspire others in the room to follow your example and give generously."

"I can't."

"You must." She lowered her voice, but there would be no argument. "Anything less would be an insult." She squeezed his arm. "Stop scowling. Besides, I need you."

That declaration hadn't been easy for her. He nodded. Something had rattled her today and she wanted him to help her cope. Why hadn't she called him? As often as he'd checked in on her, how the hell had anything significant happened? Wouldn't her daughter have sounded an alert? Casey had been with her mother the entirety of the day.

The way Cecelia looked at him, waiting for his answer, a surge of protectiveness shot through him, and he patted her hand, warming her cold fingers. "I'm here."

"Thank you." She nodded toward others finding seats at the other end of the long table. "Let me introduce you."

"I look forward to it," he lied with an easy smile.

He could feel Camp's eyes boring into his back and the urge to turn around or roll his shoulders was overwhelming. He resisted, thanks to the years of practice at controlling or denying his physical responses for the sake of the job at hand.

Bring on the overcooked chicken and speeches so he could retreat, he thought. With her. His instincts were prickling and he kept an eye on the shadows for any sign of Isely's thugs or Thomas's Specialists.

He supposed he should add Colby's agents to the list

of possible party crashers. Unfortunately, he hadn't done his homework on them.

Well, there were worse things than winging it, and as soon as he had her out of this hotel, he'd have the advantage once more.

CECELIA HAD BEEN more than a little relieved when Emmett had finally joined her at the door. She'd worried all day that somehow Isely had uncovered his betrayal and taken action.

Keeping the unexpected encounter with Isely to herself had been the right thing to do. That monster intended not only to destroy Thomas but also to destroy Emmett. She had to stop him. Neither her brother nor the man beside her would want her to act on her own instincts. After all, she had no real training to speak of. But she suspected that was the only way to help both of them.

She had to do this. Yet she was no fool. Her daughter had her back. Cecelia was reasonably sure she had half convinced Casey that Emmett really was trying to protect her.

He was far closer to being that white knight than he realized.

She'd known the moment he'd joined the cocktail reception. Something in the air changed when he was near, when she felt his gaze on her. It was a sensation she'd never thought to experience with anyone but William. While he had done his habitual reconnaissance, she'd been swamped by guilt. She barely knew Emmett, yet her feelings for him were so strong, so vivid.

Now that she was touching him, she never wanted to let go. She introduced him to the others who shared the head table. It was a wonder watching him show such charm and relaxed polish when she knew the rough edges and constant vigilance lurking underneath.

As everyone took their seats, her daughter came up behind the head table. "Mom?"

"Is there a problem?"

"No. We were just hoping you'd come say hi." She tipped her head toward the table where Cecelia spotted Thomas glaring at Emmett.

"I'll be over once the formalities are done."

"Thanks," Casey looked relieved. "Uncle Thomas is twitchy."

"You can tell him I'm fine," Cecelia said, smiling as her daughter walked away.

Emmett leaned close to her. "What was that about?"

"That would be my overprotective detail." She patted his knee under the table, resisted the urge to leave her hand there. They weren't lovers, no matter how much she wanted him. They were hardly partners, though it had felt that way when he'd been sharing information this morning. "I had to tell her a bit more about you."

After the meeting in the café, Cecelia had been forced to give her daughter a detailed report of last night's altercations with Isely's men. It was the smart thing to do, if only so Casey could be better prepared for any more trouble.

She'd painted Emmett as the hero he'd been and Casey had been smart enough not to argue or imply her mother's perception was warped by circumstance.

"I've asked Casey to run interference for us tonight, so they won't hassle you. Much."

"Gee, thanks."

"She promised not to show them the picture."

"The picture?" He set his fork down carefully and blotted his mouth. "From last night?"

She nodded.

"Dancing at the marina?"

"That's the one."

She'd tried leaving out last night's more personal details until Casey had admitted getting a call from Heather. Even then, Cecelia tried to pin the girl's claims on a drunken stupor, but Casey had pulled out her phone and shown her the picture of the kiss.

Cecelia had nearly asked for a copy, but made the better choice and asked if her brother had seen it. Casey's denial had been sincere and full of concern, and nothing Cecelia said eased that worried look in her daughter's eyes.

Her throat went dry now just thinking about the picture, remembering how alive—how absolutely exhilarated—she'd felt in that moment when he'd kissed her in the middle of a party they hadn't been invited to.

"Nice effort, but it won't help." His eyes darted to the table in question. "They all know me."

"Know whatever you've led them to believe, anyway." She winked when he glared at her. "Let Casey handle them."

"If you say so."

"Lighten up. The salad isn't so bad." She took a bite and encouraged him to do the same. "It's the chicken you're likely to choke on."

"You're making chicken jokes. Why not just tell me about what happened while I was gone? Obviously something did."

"Nothing too dreadful."

"What exactly falls into that category?"

"We can discuss it later. I got the impression we'd have some time, just the two of us, this evening."

His silence was enough confirmation. Not that she needed it. When Isely's men grabbed her, she trusted him not to leave her with them for long. The idea had her shuddering inside. Having that monster touch her was enough to have her choking without a single bite of the chicken.

A waiter passed with a tray of champagne flutes, but Cecelia declined. Going tipsy on champagne wouldn't help her get through what she knew was coming.

She'd ignored the speculative looks Thomas aimed her way through the speeches and awards. Had even tried provoking him a bit by holding Emmett's hand in full view once she'd delivered her gratitude to everyone who'd supported the cause. Yes, she was moving on, personally and professionally, and it was time for the world to adjust.

William was no doubt giving her a standing ovation from the place good men like him went.

For the first time since she'd said a final goodbye to her husband, she truly felt as if she was where she was meant to be.

No one, not that evil man Isely or anyone else, was going to take this from her.

When the orchestra started up, Thomas wasted no time in claiming her for the first dance. She nearly laughed at the complete lack of subtlety when Casey and Levi and Lucas and Victoria flanked them on the dance floor.

"I told you to stay away from him," Thomas said through a tight smile.

"In case you missed it, I'm a grown woman. I've had a husband and daughter and a whole life, Thomas."

"This is different. He's dangerous."

"I think I like that about him," she replied with shocking honesty. It was the rough edges under Emmett's polish that made him so appealing. She'd been raised to expect certain manners and behaviors from the men in her social sphere. While he could fit in anywhere the job demanded, she liked the man he was when they were alone best of all.

"That isn't funny, Lia. I've traced the leaks to his computer. He's a traitor."

"Of course he is." She laughed lightly just to keep up appearances. "I don't believe that. I know you have your pick of talented agents and would never snap up a dud."

"He sold secrets to a black-market weapons dealer."

She shook her head. "Take another look. He's only been a picture-perfect gentleman around me." She was ready for Thomas to call her on the lie, or the reference, but he was lost in his own gloomy thoughts.

"He wasn't an agent when I recruited him. Clearly I misjudged his abilities."

"Not from my perspective." She pinched his shoulder when he ignored her. "Listen to me. We were in real danger last night and he protected me. You should trust your first instincts where he is concerned."

"Where's your wedding band?"

She sighed. He wouldn't hear reason from her. Not on this. If he needed a gift for Jo or ideas for a brunch menu, she'd be his first call, but she'd never have his ear when it came to agents, business or covert operations.

"It's in the safe at the house," she replied. "Where it has been since Casey's wedding." She was more pleased than she should have been by the shock on his face. "Where's your wife?"

"Working."

"Is that a politically correct way of saying she's in protective custody?"

"I should be so lucky."

Cecelia smiled. "So she refused, too?"

"She pointed out there wasn't an active threat on her."

Cecelia's mind leaped to the logical conclusion. "You have her looking for the mole." She hoped Jo would be objective enough to see what Emmett was really up to.

"Fresh eyes never hurt anything."

"True." Cecelia looked up into her big brother's face, studied every line he'd earned from the burdens and victories of his job. Why couldn't he see she wanted the same sense of accomplishment and purpose for her own life?

A not-so-small part of her wanted to tell him everything. To pull him aside and explain that she and Emmett had this whole threat under control. Or as much control as possible when the enemy was a madman bent on revenge.

"Thank you for being here," she said, kissing him lightly on the cheek. "I love you both. Tell Jo I said hello." She gave his hand a squeeze as the song ended. "That's my cue to mingle."

She stepped away before she did anything that could dilute the effect of tonight's looming drama. Whatever Isely had planned, she knew Emmett wouldn't let anything terrible happen to her or the people they both loved.

She grinned, thinking how adamantly he'd deny it if he'd heard her make such a statement. But she knew it was true. A man didn't do the things Emmett had done without love. For country, team or Thomas, there would be the logical, analytical reasons on the surface. But courage and conviction came from a noble place in the heart, and it took both to complete the lonely mission he'd taken on.

Chapter Thirteen

Emmett found her a few moments later and drew her out onto the floor for a waltz.

"A lie by omission is still a lie," she said.

His eyes were clouded as he met her gaze. "Whatever your brother said, you're stuck with me until this is over."

She was happy to hear it. "Not him. You. There was no mention of dancing on your profile, and yet you're quite talented."

"You're determined to be cheerful tonight." He flexed his fingers on her back and her body warmed to his touch. "You know I lie to everyone. That profile was geared to attract you."

"It worked." Too well, in fact. She was keeping it light, the epitome of a society matron reigning over a successful event, but she wanted some sign that what she was feeling for him wasn't one-sided. "Though a mention of dancing wouldn't have hurt."

She thought about the forest of untruths that made up the landscape Emmett, her daughter and brother worked in. William had surely lied to her a thousand times by necessity through the course of their marriage. The mission-related untruths and alibis had never been an issue before, and she could only rationalize that it was now because she barely knew Emmett.

Except she felt like she knew him better than he knew himself.

They moved across the dance floor with the rest of the crowd, waltzing and smiling in a swirl of color and light.

Since discreet inquiries hadn't worked on him, she went for a direct approach. "So tell me what's true."

"This." He held her a bit too close through a turn and her breath caught with anticipation as her body met his from breast to thigh.

She gave him the smile the world would expect her to show and saw that he recognized the ploy.

"Now who's lying?"

"Part of the job, right?" She let the music carry her, embolden her. "What do you want most from me?"

He hesitated, but she gripped his shoulder and gave him a look warning him to shoot straight with her on this.

"More than you want to give, I'm sure."

The words, the husky voice gave her hope. She cocked an eyebrow. "Mission parameters first, please."

"First?"

She didn't dignify that with an explanation, simply waited for him to make his decision.

"Nothing has changed. Isely intends to kidnap you as leverage against your brother."

"And you're the kidnapper?"

"Would you prefer someone else? I can introduce you to the man in the corner who infiltrated hotel security for tonight."

When he turned her on the floor as gracefully as any contestant on that dancing reality show, she spotted the hulking brute he meant. He probably expected her to collapse in some fluttery, feminine panic. She didn't, though she wouldn't want to run up against that man in a dark alley, or anywhere else for that matter.

Emmett Holt was her only protection.

"How do you know?"

"I got him in."

She gasped and he drew her tight against him again as they swirled through another turn.

"You wanted the truth," he said.

She nodded. "If my kidnapping's on the schedule—" she met his gaze "—I'd rather go with you."

"Good choice."

She wasn't so sure. After kissing him last night for the sole purpose of surviving, she was all too aware that this man presented more than a few other dangers. Many of them far beyond physical.

Yes, she wanted to dance with him all night, to soak up the sensual delight she found in his embrace. It had been so long since anyone had held her like she mattered purely as a woman, since she'd been able to hold someone the same way.

William had traveled often for work, but those absences had given her just the briefest taste of loneliness. There'd been time for girlfriends, movie marathons or quiet nights with a good book and a bottle of wine.

She'd quickly learned none of those nights with friends, movies or books replaced the very real need for affectionate contact. For kisses, for…

"You're not listening."

She blinked several times, bringing his face into focus. "My apologies."

"First lesson for ops is to maintain your focus."

"Duly noted, thank you." She found it odd he was the only person of her acquaintance showing any acceptance of her career change. "I appreciate your support of my career plans," she said. "I know it's not your priority here."

The last strains of the music drifted away and they came

to a stop with it, but he didn't quite release her. "Your life is my highest priority."

She felt something in her heart click as she looked into his eyes. The man just twisted her up inside. He'd lied, by all accounts was more than ready to use her without any remorse, but she couldn't seem to hold it against him. Knew she would never hold it against him.

People she'd known for far longer, her friends and family, said stay away, but she just couldn't. Especially not if a successful mission meant she had to spend time with that brute glowering at her from the corner.

"He just gave me the sign to move."

She hadn't seen a sign, but she was trying not to look that direction.

"Are you ready?" Emmett whispered.

She nodded, her throat too dry for words.

"Follow my lead."

Anywhere. She trusted him that much. He'd worked with her brother. He possessed more skills that she might ever learn.

He tucked her hand inside his elbow and steered her toward the head table. "Is there anyone else you need to speak with before we go?"

"Seriously?"

"Yes. I'm trying to make this as stress-free as possible for you."

"In that case, I should greet Lucas Camp and—"

"No." His muscles tensed—a physical emphasis of the quiet, stern refusal. "Anyone but him."

She gave a slight shake of her head. "Someone else will announce the silent auction winners when they can't find me."

"You have the gun with you as well as your phone?"

"GPS on as instructed."

"Good. We're done here."

She glanced up, saw his smile, but the warmth in it was suspect. Every move he made was calculated for their audience. She wondered if he realized they had that in common tonight.

She retrieved her purse and followed his lead as they aimed for an open bar station and the conversation area beyond.

They stepped out to the balcony area, where cocktails had been served. Trees planted in the lobby garden sparkled with holiday lights, branches reached toward the skylight above. The glass elevator serving the first five floors was wrapped with a bow like a present as it zipped up and down.

When they'd booked the Plaza for the gala, she'd seen the beauty and gracefulness of the design. She'd envisioned the perfect layout and the space full of guests eager to open their wallets for the chance to honor William's memory.

Tonight she saw shadows and threats where she should have only seen friends and donors.

"You need to brace yourself, Cecelia."

"You mean we can't just waltz all the way up to the suite and hide out with the convenience of room service?"

"Nope."

Those few minutes on the dance floor, wrapped in his embrace as the orchestra played, were so different from the heat and flash of last night's salsa. But the lingering result had been just as magical. Just as enticing.

"We can't show off more of our talent on the dance floor before disappearing?" she teased, mostly to quiet her nerves.

"It would make more of a scene," he agreed.

She grinned, just imagining the reaction. The poor, lonely Mrs. Manning never did anything as spontaneous as dance without the guide of music. What had happened to her, they would all wonder. They'd whisper behind their hands that she'd had some sort of breakdown. After last night's public display of heat—if not exactly affection with a virtual stranger—a similar uncharacteristic demonstration tonight might be enough to snap her perfectly respectable reputation in two.

She kind of liked the idea of being a wicked widow.

But that wasn't to be. She would simply vanish from the festivities, and those in attendance would speculate. She knew enough to understand how a report of her disappearance might go. Though for obvious reasons she didn't expect Thomas to report her missing. He had his own way of handling the situation. If there was trouble, any witnesses might call for security or the authorities. All the more reason they had to be discreet.

She could do this. For Thomas and Casey. For Emmett.

The men she assumed were Isely's crew had taken up stations on either end of their section of the balcony. She leaned closer to Emmett. No one but him would get a chance to do the kidnapping tonight.

She dug in her heels and drew them to a stop near the corner. Not at all out of sight of the crowd in the ballroom, but not as front and center as they'd been at last night's party. "Kiss me."

"Later. If you ask nicely," he said, his eyes locked on her lips.

She tugged his lapels. "Three o'clock and nine o'clock. You know they're there." This wasn't the time for nice. "Now kiss me."

Pressing her lips to his, she prayed he understood what she was after. She needed to leave no doubt that she was involved, willingly, with this man. Maybe he didn't care about his reputation, but she did.

He understood how to kiss; no room for doubt on that score. What she'd meant to be for show, to give the gossips something to chew on, turned into a banquet of sensations. Pinned between the wall and his equally unyielding body, she thrilled at the fascinating rush sizzling through her veins.

His wide palm cupped her cheek as he drew back a fraction of an inch. His breath was warm against her lips. She turned her face, pressing a kiss into his palm as she gauged the progress Isely's men had made.

"Once you're trained and in the field, no one will know you well enough to judge you," he murmured in her ear as he guided her past the elevator, around the balcony, toward the top of the wide staircase.

She wanted to ask how he'd guessed her earlier thoughts, but conversation, like kisses, would have to wait for later.

A door marked as a fire exit opened and the burly man from the ballroom waved them closer. Emmett deftly stepped around her, putting himself between her and Isely's man.

"This way," the man said, stepping into Emmett's path.

Emmett plowed a fist deep into the man's belly and pushed him back into the stairwell, yanking the door shut.

On the other side of the balcony, Cecelia's brother paused at the ballroom doors, his head swiveling from side to side. He was already searching for her.

She'd be hard to miss in this bold red gown. Next time she had kidnapping on the agenda, she'd wear something less flashy.

They reached the stairs and rushed down, and the fresh scent of the seasonal evergreens draped along the rails tickled her nose. The soft needles brushed her hand and caught at her wide skirt, but she kept moving forward. Oh, yes. Next time, a discreet gown and ballet flats. At this pace she'd be lucky if she didn't break an ankle and completely derail their plan.

"He hassled you, didn't he?" There had been a moment between dances when she'd lost sight of her brother. She suspected he'd had a word with Emmett. This wasn't exactly the time to carry on a casual conversation, but it kept her steady. "Thomas, I mean."

"If your brother had decided to act against me, I wouldn't be here."

She shivered at the thought. "Then what makes you so sure I'm worried about public opinion?" She was. Or always had been. But she was changing…slowly.

"You shouldn't be," he said. "The only opinion that ever matters is your own."

"A universal truth."

"That's me." He chuckled, checked behind them for trouble. "Moving to ops is a good call for you."

"You're probably still the only one who thinks so," she said under her breath. Would these stairs never end?

Why was it those who loved her couldn't see how desperately she needed to change things up? Everyone thought they knew what she wanted, what she needed. Yet no one listened when she tried to explain her new goals and the catalyst behind them. Maybe that was part of the reason she needed to see this through rather than hide in protective custody.

Finally they reached the lobby. "What about my things?"

She'd packed a bag and left it in the suite, according to his instructions.

"Handled." He took her hand. "Stay close."

She should have known that would be all the warning he'd give.

A muffled pop sounded above them, followed by the

startled shrieks of the crowd in the ballroom. Smoke poured from the center doorway.

"What did you do?"

"Diversion. No injuries."

"Lia!" Thomas shouted. Or maybe she just thought she heard her brother as Emmett ushered her out the front doors and into the cold night. Her heart sank just a little at the fear and worry she'd heard in those two syllables.

Stay alert, she ordered herself. No mistakes. No missteps. A front had moved in and rain with a chance of snow was expected over the weekend. She added a shrug or shawl to her mental list of things to wear at her next kidnapping. Her nerves calmed a bit with the mundane and totally ludicrous thoughts.

A gray sedan idled at the end of the Plaza's circular drive, as anonymous in this area as the black SUVs that escorted officials everywhere in DC.

Emmett opened the passenger door and helped her gather her dress inside. The only outward sign of his urgency was the way he raced around to the driver's side. She glanced to the hotel, spotted her brother and two men dressed in hotel uniforms. Specialists. It seemed several uninvited guests had joined the festivities. She wished she could call to Thomas and let him know she was okay.

"Where'd you get the car?" she asked, working hard to keep her voice steady.

"Courtesy of Isely." He pulled away from the Plaza. "Buckle up. We'll have a tail in no time."

"Which team?"

"Both, the way my night's been going. I'm sure each of them will believe they're an escort."

"What can I do?"

"Send your brother a text message. Tell him you're all right."

She pulled out her phone and sent more than one text message, hoping after that kiss one of her friends or family would assume what she wanted them to assume: that she was having a holiday affair.

Emmett cruised north through Old Town, toward the Beltway into Washington, D.C.

"We're not hiding in the marina, are we?"

"No." He slipped a phone out of his jacket and placed it on the console between them. "Let me know if any messages come through."

"Of course," she said, fishing her gun out of her purse.

"Ah, here we go."

A black car pulled up beside them and a voice ordered them to pull over. She sank back into the seat as Emmett floored it. He slipped in and out of traffic like he'd been raised by a pack of race-car drivers. That sense of danger she'd felt last night returned, bigger and more tempting than ever.

As did her brother's voice in her head telling her Holt was the problem child. She looked at her phone, wondering what message she could send to change his opinion.

"Ah, here comes the cavalry now."

She twisted in her seat and saw they were leading a parade of sorts. The black car was followed by a black SUV with blue-and-red flashing emergency lights.

"You want the police involved?" She thought police involvement was a bad thing.

"I don't much care as long as we lose the extra personnel. If Mission Recovery intervenes tonight, I won't be able to stop Isely's endgame."

She came up hard against the door as he jerked the car around slower traffic. As she reached to steady herself, she bumped the handle and the door flew open.

"Cecelia!" He slowed down and reached over to grab her arm.

"I'm okay! Drive!" As he accelerated, the momentum helped her get the door closed, but there was no hope for the hem of her dress. "Damn it."

"Are you hurt?"

"No. I dropped the phone."

"No problem." He jerked them in front of the shelter of a semi-truck and then took the first available exit. It was the airport.

"Thought you wanted them to track it?"

"It's not the end of the world."

He suddenly slowed to the posted speed limit, causing her to lean forward against the seat. He circled the terminal.

"Please don't tell me I have to get this dress and a gun through security."

"It would be a good training exercise."

"Funny. I can't believe I dropped the phone."

"Really, it's okay. It was some amount of insurance, but not essential. Isely knows how to contact me. He'll tell me where he wants you to end up."

She was starting to get antsy about that. "I thought you made other arrangements."

"I did." He reached over and covered her hand with his. "We'll be fine. It appears he still trusts me."

"How can you be sure? He's tried a hostile takeover on your kidnapping assignment two nights running."

"I can't be certain. But I have what he wants. That's always the key, Cecelia. Always."

Her throat felt dry at the thought. She dismissed her fears. She trusted Emmett. "So what now?"

He pulled into a rental car lot and parked in the return

lane. "Now we disappear for the evening. Should we go dancing?"

A smile spread across her lips. "Tempting as that is, I could really use a drink."

"Then drinks it is."

He took her hand as they left the car and hurried across the lot to the reservations side. With a swipe of a card, they were on their way again.

"Are you getting the hang of it?" he asked as they left the airport, heading into the heart of DC.

"You did part of this for my benefit."

"Two birds, one stone," he replied.

"I'm starting to realize just how much I have to learn."

"But you still *want* to learn?"

She paused, thinking over the past twenty-four hours, comparing those hours to the entirety of her life up to this point. It might not have been a fair comparison, since the months of fighting an unwinnable battle against cancer was foremost in her mind. Still, she knew she had it in her to do more—to be more—than a face for various charities.

"More than ever," she admitted.

Chapter Fourteen

Holt had never heard sweeter words. "Then let's get some more practice."

"What do you have in mind?"

He checked the burner phone Isely had provided. "I want to know why he's not giving me an address."

"We still have that location just off the coast."

"I know. I researched the wharfs and docks near Alexandria and on the Atlantic and came up with nothing I could tie to Isely."

"What about known associates with shipping or import interests here?"

He liked that they'd been thinking along the same lines. "Nada. He doesn't have any."

"Everyone has someone."

Not me. True or not, even in the privacy of his head the thought sounded pathetic.

"The only people I can put with him are his own crew. This job is personal. You as a target proves that."

"Maybe he forgot to send you the memo that he wants to kidnap me personally. Maybe it really has nothing to do with Thomas or Mission Recovery."

He shook his head. "Unless your husband left something crucial in your care that neither I nor Mission Recovery has learned of, that's not possible."

"But you can't know for sure," she argued.

"That's the one thing I am sure about," he guaranteed.

He drove in silence the rest of the way. Arguing with her would be a distraction he didn't need. This was about Isely and his need for vengeance against Thomas Casey and Mission Recovery. End of story.

When he reached the destination, he braced for the next part in his plan. He'd never had such trouble staying in the right frame of mind on a mission.

He started to get out of the car, but she stopped him with a soft touch on his sleeve. "What's the story here?"

"No story. Just another party. Smile," he said as the valet opened her door.

Outside the car he handed over the keys and wrapped his arm around her trim waist.

She followed his instruction to the letter. Somehow that made his heart glad, and there simply was no explanation why. She was a marvel, he decided. An uncommon blend of tenacity and bravery with a hearty lust for adventure. And her body… Well, he'd be better off if he put that out of his mind.

He paused in the lobby for a quick kiss. "This is an office party of sorts. You'll recognize a few faces from Casey's wedding."

"You're taking me into a room full of Specialists?"

"Well, a few folks are from the CIA, too."

She paled. "Why take the risk?"

"Because I need to get some rather sensitive information and showing up here as a couple supports the torrid affair gossip you started last night."

Her eyes narrowed, the blue spheres full of fire. It was an immediate turn-on. "That wasn't all my fault."

"I was perfectly respectable before we met," he lied

with a wink. "We won't stay long. Can't stay long," he corrected. "No matter who asks, do not leave my side."

"Yes, sir."

He studied her face, gave her a glimpse of the raw need she stirred in him. "I could get used to that."

"Don't count on it."

Damn, he admired her spunk. He wanted to laugh, wanted to see just how far he could tease her before one of them gave in. But that wasn't on the agenda, no matter how hot and inspired he felt when she kissed him. The woman deserved a far better man than he was. She deserved her shot at ops, too, and he meant to see that she got it.

"Ready?"

She nodded, but her smile wobbled. Not acceptable. He stroked his hand across the bare skin of her shoulders and praised her dress designer. When she looked up at him again, he dropped a featherlight kiss on those perfect, rosy lips. "For courage," he said, then he turned toward the private reception taking up the entirety of the Irish-themed hotel bar.

More than half of the gathering was connected to Mission Recovery, and the hush that fell across the room when they saw him was palpable.

No, he didn't do social events and they all knew it. To arrive at all was unprecedented. To arrive with a date might be a portent of doom. For him in particular, if Director Casey had shared his suspicions with any one of the Specialists in attendance.

Since this was a party to celebrate the recent marriage of Specialist Jason Grant and his CIA wife, Gin Olin, he wasn't surprised when several people also recognized Cecelia.

"Stay with me," he reminded her behind a tense smile.

If the way she was gripping his arm was any indicator, she had no intention of leaving his side.

The crowd parted for Jason and Gin as they welcomed Holt and Cecelia, drawing them inside toward the bar.

Gin called for champagne, shot Holt a curious look over Cecelia's head then the women were immediately engrossed in conversation.

Holt made a mental note to ask Cecelia how she knew Gin. He'd long ago given up trying to understand women, but even he recognized that kind of bonding was too quick under the circumstances.

He accepted the champagne Grant offered, though he was ready for something with more bite and less fizz. Ah, well, that's why he had a bottle of Scotch on his boat waiting for a victory toast the moment he buried Isely.

"You said you had something?"

"The man credited with the virus is dead." Grant said this as if he'd given the newest weather report.

"How?"

"Self-inflicted gunshot wound. Five years ago."

Holt sipped, ignoring the annoying bubbles in the wine. "Guilt after the sale?"

"Or designed to look that way."

"What about his lab, notes, apprentices?"

"As far as I've been able to dig, all of his work is just gone."

"A targeted strike?"

Jason nodded. "That's my guess. But it wasn't our team, as you well know."

Then why wasn't Isely trying to get more money for a limited-edition bioweapon? The vial Isely had given to Holt was worth millions, assuming the virus was still potent.

"I came across something I believe you and your lovely wife will appreciate," Holt said. "Forgive the lack of wrapping." He withdrew a long, slim box from his inner pocket and handed it to Jason. "Congratulations. You and your wife should open it later. It's one of a kind."

Jason pocketed the box and raised his glass in salute. "We'll enjoy it, I'm sure."

Using the mirror, Holt eyed the crowded bar in an attempt to pinpoint which Specialists weren't here and which ones were watching him too closely. He gave up after a moment. It wasn't worth the effort. Any one of them, if not all of those present, had likely notified the director of his arrival already. The moment he and Cecelia walked out of here, he'd be a target again.

"Everything okay, sir?"

"A word of advice, Grant?"

"Please."

"Always make time for two things: your wife and a hobby." It was the only tip he could offer and the only attempt he'd make to clear his name.

If Grant understood, Holt might have a job to return to once Isely was contained. If the man didn't understand the message…well that's why he had the boat.

Holt turned to Cecelia, couldn't resist running his fingers down the back of her arm. "Time to go," he said.

She gave Gin a quick hug and then put her hand in his. "Lead on."

He wanted to go out the back but figured their odds were better in the lobby. The more people who saw them take the elevator upstairs, the better.

She was quiet as they waited.

"How do you know Grant's wife?" he asked as the car arrived and they stepped inside. He pressed the button for the seventh floor.

"It's a vague acquaintance."

Her eyes were clouded and he knew she was a bit lost

in her past. A kiss wouldn't snap her out of it, though he was willing to try, but he thought she needed something. He rubbed her hand between his. For her, he told himself. Not because he felt the strange urge to comfort and soothe.

He didn't do the tender emotions. Until he'd met her, he didn't think he'd ever want to try. He tried to look at her objectively, but just couldn't anymore.

The doors parted on the seventh floor and he stepped out, only to get blindsided by a fist to the face. He reeled back into Cecelia's soft body, knocking her into the safety of the elevator.

He lunged at his attacker, taking the fight away from her. They hadn't discussed it, but with her brother's team downstairs, surely she'd go to them for help.

The man tried to sweep his foot in a takedown, but Holt twisted and blocked, gaining a brief advantage with an elbow strike that separated them. It was a relief to see his opponent was one of Isely's men, but the relief faded swiftly when he recognized which one.

The crew called him Thor for his long blond hair, broad build and hands as big as hammers. "Hand her over."

Holt spread his hands wide. "Who?"

Thor looked over Holt's shoulder, then ripped off what must have been an inspired combination of curses in German. But it wasn't enough to distract Holt from the fists racing toward his face.

He bobbed and weaved, ducking under one swing to bounce a jab off of Thor's sternum. Not much effect. He jerked back so Thor's next punch glanced off his jaw, but even that was enough to knock him off balance.

He staggered, then gave in and somersaulted backwards, bouncing back up to his feet. Thor closed in again. "She's mine to deliver," Holt said, hoping to goad Thor into sharing pertinent details. "I need the bonus."

He jabbed, ready to follow with a hook and left himself open to a devastating punch to the ribcage. Thor's cocky smile was worth the pain. Sort of.

The elevator chimed and both men turned. Cecelia stepped out into the hallway. "Leave him alone," she said, raising the revolver.

"Feisty," Thor said with an approving grimace. Grabbing Holt by the shirt, he turned, using him as a shield. "I see why you don't want to let her go."

Holt didn't bother explaining that Isely hadn't yet told him where to take her. "Downstairs," he snarled over his shoulder at Cecelia.

"Not without you," she replied, pulling the trigger.

The shot went wide, plowing into a framed print on the wall, but it was enough to startle Thor, who ducked away from the exploding glass.

Holt thrust his arms up and out, breaking Thor's hold. Rushing to Cecelia, he caught her at the waist and propelled her down the hall.

Another gunshot sounded, and chunks of wall exploded near his hip as they tumbled through the door into the stairwell.

"Down," he barked.

"Which floor?"

"Just keep going," he answered. There was a bridge to the parking garage on four. Her heels clattered against the cement stairs and he couldn't tell if there was anyone following or not. With every landing they passed without the assault of more bullets, a flicker of hope spurred him on.

"Here," he said when they reached the fourth-floor landing. He paused only long enough to see the way was clear, then he took her hand. "Breathe. The car is close by."

Her eyes were wide and a little wild, but she nodded, her skirt rustling as she rushed to keep up with him.

Holt prayed he wasn't leading her into another trap, but the car he'd parked here last week was registered with a member of the hotel staff. He'd bribed a bartender, who needed both a car and extra cash to cover a gambling debt.

As much as he'd coached her to stay calm, Holt didn't take an easy breath until they were back on the parkway and headed to the grungy little motel he'd booked under yet another alias.

"I'm sorry."

He glanced over when he heard the quiver in her voice. "For what? You saved us."

"I should have hit him."

"Rookie mistake. It happens."

"Oh, Emmett. You really didn't look up everything, did you?"

He'd looked up plenty, nearly picked apart her life. But then as a CIA family, she would know how to hide plenty. "What do you mean?"

"My husband and I used to go shooting for fun. Casey was three when she made her first trip with us. I'm no sharpshooter, but I'm pretty darned good."

He wasn't sure he wanted to hear about her husband, though he realized he'd made a critical error by not digging deeper into their married life. He wanted to classify it as irrelevant, but he knew now it had just been too uncomfortable.

"So why didn't you take Thor out?"

"He was moving erratically. I was worried about hitting you. I mean, I'm a pretty good shot, but not that good."

"Real life isn't the same as a paper target."

"Thanks, I hadn't noticed."

He reached for her, but she drew her hand away. "I'm not trying to patronize you, Cecelia. You have what it takes, but for the record, I can take care of myself."

"That's obvious." She shifted, staring out the window.

"You could have gone downstairs for help."

"I thought about it. But Isely sends men in pairs."

"You noticed. Good job."

"Hard to miss," she muttered. "I was terrified to think what might happen if they caught me first."

"You have everything the CIA wants in an agent."

"Right."

"You do." He reached over and covered her hand. "First of all, I wouldn't have let him take you. Second, that was my mistake back there for not clearing the hallway at the elevator. Learn from my mistake."

"Okay."

He didn't think she was convinced. "As for what you'd do if captured by Isely, I'm sure he'd be unhappy with your determination and resourcefulness."

"Maybe."

"Believe me. I've been at this longer than you."

She was quiet for a long time, and he hoped she was processing his praise while she replayed the last hour.

"Where are we going?"

"I have a reservation they shouldn't be able to track down," he replied. "We need some time to rest and regroup."

"Neither side will be pleased with our disappearance."

"Nope. But only one will get nasty about it."

"Isely."

"Yup."

Chapter Fifteen

As he pulled into the parking lot, he regretted choosing a cut-rate place like this one. She'd been through an ordeal and she deserved finer things than he would offer her tonight.

"Are we here?"

He nodded, wishing they were anywhere else. "Cash works here."

"And cash is untraceable." She reached out and caught his hand. "It's smart. Contrary to popular opinion, I don't need five-star accommodations all the time. Thank you for protecting me."

When she looked at him that way, protection wasn't what he wanted to give her. He leashed his unruly desire and led her through the back door and up to their room for tonight.

The door closed and her warm scent filled the small space. "Your things are by the dresser."

"Thanks. I'd like to change."

"In a minute." He had to focus on business. The mission. Anything but the thought of being near her when she removed that dress. "Now that we're alone, you need to tell me what happened today." He knew there was something, and she'd asked that question about this being about her instead of her brother.

"Do we have to do that now?" She reached up and removed the elegant jeweled choker. "You said rest and regroup. Surely it can wait a few hours."

He inhaled and shoved his hands into his pockets before he grabbed her and tossed that voluminous skirt up over her head. She needed his respect on a professional level, and somehow he couldn't not give it. "Does whatever happened pose an immediate threat?"

"Not unless they can find us."

"They being?"

"Isely."

"He has no idea where we are and I've sent him a message that I want to meet tomorrow."

"To turn me over."

"Of course, but—"

"I trust you to have a plan. Tell me later. Let's rest. And regroup."

Any argument he might have offered fled as she raised her hands to her hair, her full breasts testing the limits of her strapless gown. It was an entirely underrated form of torture to watch her free those long blond locks from the sleek, upswept style she'd worn all night. And she had a point. They were both mentally and physically exhausted.

He might have fantasized about the elegant stretch of her neck a little longer, but suddenly his fingers itched to fist in her hair.

Beware was right, he thought, staring at her. Isely had given the warning for an entirely different purpose, but it couldn't be more appropriate than right here in this room.

She gave him her back, drawing her hair forward over her shoulder. "A little help?" she asked, glancing over one bare shoulder.

Her lashes lowered, but her blue eyes smoldered. She

was clearly daring him to help her out of the gown. He wasn't strong enough to resist.

He found the small hook at the top and released it, but the line of tiny buttons down her back posed a new temptation. He swallowed.

She was a siren and he'd willingly dash himself against the rocks for this moment with her. His fingers trembled as he loosened each button, revealing her skin one slow, beautiful inch at a time.

She was the most delectable present he'd ever had the pleasure of unwrapping.

His cynical arguments about holiday attire turned into an instant appreciation as the festive red of her lingerie against her creamy skin stoked the fire already raging inside him.

His fingers brushed along her spine, resting at the curve of her bottom as the last button popped free.

Desire slid through his system in a warm rush as she let the dress fall to the floor. She turned to face him and his knees threatened to buckle. She was a vision beyond his ability to imagine, her breasts barely contained in those hot red cups of shimmering fabric, the matching panties a wonderful target dividing the creamy skin of her midriff and thighs. But the lace-topped stockings in lethal black nearly stopped his heart.

Who would've guessed the prim, perfectly coiffed Widow Manning had an arsenal like this?

Of all the pictures he'd used to export hidden data, this would have been his favorite.

But definitely the least effective. He nearly laughed thinking of how the director would delete this one immediately—or kill him for having it at all.

Didn't matter. This image of her was burned into Holt's

mind and would be there the rest of his days—no matter how few or how many remained.

"You're frowning," she said, taking a step closer.

He smiled, but it took work. "You're so damned beautiful." He drew back a step, cursed himself for being a coward. "We shouldn't do this."

"I disagree."

Of course she would. But it was a mistake, more on her part than his. He just needed to redirect enough blood flow to his brain to think of it. Raw need for her was riding him too hard. His control was nearly shredded. He knew he couldn't hold out. Better she had informed consent here.

"I don't want to be gentle with you." He wanted to scare her a bit, wanted to back her off so he could regain his balance. But it wasn't fear or worry he saw in her eyes, it was…anticipation.

God help him.

"So don't be gentle." She took another step and her red bra brushed against the white of his tuxedo shirt, making his pulse jump. She tugged the ends of his bow tie and slid it out of his collar.

"Cecelia." It was the only coherent word he could get past his lips.

"I'm right here."

He knew that. Her fragrance crashed over him in vivid, sensual waves. The things he wanted to do to that body… the things he wanted her to do to him.

Her hands gripped his shirt and she tugged, popping the studs free. Her white-tipped fingernails scraped lightly across his chest. Her gasp proved plenty of reward for all those hard workouts.

"I'm not that white knight you're looking for," he said with an ache that almost undid him.

"I don't care." She flatted her hands on his skin and smoothed those silky palms over his chest.

He groaned. She was killing him, but a woman like Cecelia deserved tenderness from a gentleman with an Ivy League degree and the manners to match. Not the hot, rough, fast kind of sex he craved tonight. His hands hovered at her waist to set her away. His mind told him to behave but his body argued just the opposite.

She took his hands in hers and pressed the palms down against her soft flesh. He stopped breathing as she dragged them up her sides to cup her full breasts. Her nipples peaked under his palms and she used his hands to squeeze and caress them as she arched into his touch.

Keeping one of his hands trapped between hers and one full breast, she raised the other to her face and drew his thumb into her mouth, sucking hard then giving the sensitive pad a light nip.

He wasn't sure his heart could take much more.

"I'm not fragile, Emmett."

He hoped she meant it. He bent his head to kiss her. Hard. Her lips parted and her tongue tangled with his. She tasted of champagne and a shocking dark desire that matched his.

Reaching lower, he palmed her bottom and then hitched her up, beyond pleased when she wrapped her legs around his waist. She rocked her hips, grinding herself against him. As if he wasn't aroused enough, she gave a sigh of sheer pleasure.

No turning back now.

He'd be lucky if he could find his way to the bed. The world with all its complications and consequences just didn't exist beyond the woman in his arms. He dropped her to the bed and her laughter spurred him on as he stripped away his shirt and slacks. The view of her in that sexy lingerie made him as hard as he'd ever been.

"No," he rasped as she started to push off one of her strappy high-heel shoes. "Leave them on."

Her blue eyes sparkled and the curve of her lips was nothing short of wicked. "As you wish."

He watched her eyes travel over his body, enjoying her obvious appreciation of the view he presented. One she liked, apparently. The idea spurred his confidence—something he'd never needed before.

He knelt between her parted legs, then traced the lacy tops of her stockings. First with his fingers, then his mouth. He planted hot kisses across her bare belly, taking his time as he freed her lush breasts from that bra. She speared her hands into his hair, holding him close. He made a study out of the curve of her throat until finally claiming her mouth. She opened under him, her tongue stroking his as her hands explored his body.

He was so close to the edge already. He tore her panties aside and found her wet and ready. When he pressed his fingers deep inside her, she bucked against his hand and her body arched. Moments later she cried out with a hard climax.

His eyes locked with hers as he gripped her hips. She rose to meet him and he drove himself into her with one swift thrust. Her body clutched around him as he gave in to the heavy rhythm pushing him. Those sexy heels dug into his hips as she tightened her legs around him. Her hands fisted in the linen; her eyes were dark with passion.

She moaned his name and he felt like a god at the sound. Her body strung tight as she reached her next climax. This one dragged him over the edge with her, and he thrust deep one last time before he sagged against the mattress.

He was way better than some fantasy about a white knight, Cecelia thought as she drew the sheet up over her body. The cool air chilled her skin as her heart rate returned to normal. She wanted to burrow closer to Emmett's warmth, but he wasn't giving off an inviting vibe. She settled for resting her fingers lightly on his arm.

It wasn't as though she expected a declaration of love. She didn't think she was capable of giving him one. They were two consenting adults who'd given in to a mutually intense attraction and need. Simple. Straightforward.

Stockholm syndrome.

The idea made her giggle. She wasn't his prisoner any more than he was hers. Maybe the intensity of the whole situation had rendered her helpless. She just wanted to laugh at it all. She'd just made love with a man besides the one she'd been married to for twenty-five years. She had lost the shadow of widowhood just now…somehow. Kind of like losing her virginity with William. The whole idea had her shaking with the need to laugh. Tears welled in the corners of her eyes. Dear God, she was hysterical.

"That's not what a man wants to hear about now," he murmured, rolling to his side, stretching his arm under her pillow. His eyes sparkled in the light of the lamp by the table, but a darkness still shadowed his face.

"It's not you, it's me. Is that better?"

"Not really." He smoothed her hair away from her face. "What were you thinking that made you laugh?"

She sighed into his touch even as she sent her fingers roaming across that magnificent chest. "I was thinking about rapid-onset Stockholm syndrome."

"You know you're free to go anytime," he reminded her unnecessarily.

She smoothed her fingertips across his brow, easing the frown. Going might be a viable option, but it wouldn't be the prudent choice. Not just because she wasn't done with him, but because she didn't think she could outwit the enemy on her own. And she wasn't leaving him to do that on his own, either.

Tonight's adventure proved once more he was caught in a vise, and she refused to leave him to deal with it alone. Despite being chased by both her brother's team and Isely's men, the biggest obstacle she could see was Emmett himself. When would he open up and give her enough information to help?

He shocked her, bringing his face close and rubbing her nose with his. It was an unexpected tenderness from a man who claimed with body and words he wasn't capable of such things.

"You're still thinking." His thumb caressed the furrow between her brows.

No amount of wrinkle cream would ever completely erase the tiny lines there. She was well into forty…middle-aged. Was this part of her crisis?

"I am."

"That may be worse than the giggles."

He rolled to his back again and she immediately missed the heat of his body, the hard planes and thick ropes of his muscles against her more pliant frame. No matter what happened in the coming hours, she wouldn't have traded this stunning, sexy moment for any amount of caution or safety.

"Don't worry. I was just thinking that *this* was worth all the rumors we've no doubt started. But I'm not in the mood for pillow talk." Not yet. She shifted closer to him, pressed her lips to the crisp hair of his chest.

"You're not?"

"Nope," she whispered against his skin, and was rewarded when he trembled as she worked her way down to his navel, and lower still. "Not even close."

Chapter Sixteen

The Senate Inn
Saturday, December 20, 7:05 a.m.

Holt slipped out of Cecelia's warm embrace and peered around in the darkness until he found his discarded tuxedo pants on the floor. Pulling them on, he went and turned on his laptop, hoping to find some good news to share with her when she woke up.

Sometime after their third round, they'd managed to turn off the lights and sleep. He hadn't felt this rested in months. It should have been a comfort, but it worried him. Cecelia wasn't meant to be part of his future. And right now he couldn't imagine her not in it.

He turned his back to her so he could focus on the mission instead of the glorious temptation of her body. He logged into the email account he used only for Isely. Judging by the messages, the bastard had had a grand time watching Thomas angst over Cecelia's disappearance. A terse acceptance was his only acknowledgement of the meeting Emmett had requested.

He scanned local news headlines online rather than risk waking her with the television. No one had reported her disappearance as a kidnapping, but it was hardly a victory. After months of behaving with a single-minded, ruthless efficiency, now Isely was unpredictable, changing the rules of the game at the last minute.

The bastard had been thinking it over for months and had finally come to the conclusion that something was wrong with the virus. Now that Holt knew the biologist was dead, it only added to the mystery. A bioweapon was a powerful thing, and Isely was just too damned casual about it. The man had thrown a fit and promised retribution when the CIA had grabbed one of the two remaining vials in Vegas last month, but Holt didn't believe the performance.

"Working already?"

He hadn't heard her leave the bed, more proof he was far too comfortable with her.

"Yeah."

"I'll make coffee." Her hands rested lightly on his shoulders and her hair teased the bare skin of his shoulders when she leaned forward to kiss his cheek. "Did he agree to the meeting?"

"Yes." He realized he didn't want to lie to her. "But he's not happy about it."

"No surprise."

"Yeah." He watched her walk toward the little niche where the coffeemaker, microwave and minifridge were clustered together. She was wearing his tuxedo shirt and nothing else. He was instantly hard for her, all too ready to forget enemy plans, betrayals and furious brothers who knew a dozen ways to kill a man without leaving trace evidence.

"Would you please tell me more about Isely? So I'm ready for the meet," she coaxed.

"Why? Having sex doesn't make us a team." He said this as coldly as possible.

She turned, crossed her arms and made that shirt ride up a bit higher on her thighs. "I asked you to stop doing that."

He stood up, stretching his arms over his head, his eyes never leaving hers. "I shouldn't have to push you away. You should have the good sense to run."

She licked her lips. "I know who's who in this little drama."

"You do?"

She nodded. "I ran from the bad guys last night." She blatantly looked him over from head to toe and back again. "And right into your arms." She walked over and wound her arms around him. It wasn't anything like yesterday's hug, as they were both wearing considerably less this time. "You're beautiful."

"Flattery? That's your next tactic? Sweetheart, it's no use. I know I'm gorgeous."

"Keep it up," she said, giving the back of his arm a hard pinch.

"Ow!" But he couldn't help laughing, then he stopped short, trying to recall the last time he'd really laughed. He couldn't bring a recent memory to mind, not to mention a moment of shared laughter with a woman. "Why does it matter? As long as you're safe and I get the job done, you don't need to worry about Isely."

"Thomas said something last night."

"About Isely?" *Please let it be about Isely.*

"More about teamwork. He said fresh eyes never hurt."

Couldn't argue that adage. "He's right. Maybe you can find a reason for Isely's abrupt change of behavior."

She poured them both a cup of coffee and joined him at the small table. "So talk."

"This is all still classified—"

"My clearance is current and this place isn't bugged." She shuddered. "Unless they're bed bugs."

"Ease up," he said, patting her knee. "I'm going down regardless. I just want you to know what not to say when you're rescued."

She rolled her eyes at him. "Just talk. Tell me about Isely. And maybe I'll tell you some things."

"Five years ago, Thomas infiltrated the Isely group and interrupted the first scheduled sale of a lethal new virus. Isely's father got killed in the crossfire when the deal was blown. The vials Thomas turned in when he got back to the States weren't any deadlier than a saline solution."

She frowned. "But Thomas would never have kept a deadly bioweapon."

"When the deal went sideways, everyone assumed Isely had planned to double-cross his original buyer all along. The reports Thomas filed on the operation were verified, and nothing more came of it until a few months ago when a deadly strain of flu wiped out a remote village in the Middle East."

"That was on the Pakistan border, right?"

"Good guess."

She shrugged. "I heard about it through other channels."

"Other channels," he echoed.

She leaned forward and her shirt gaped, giving him a distracting view of her cleavage. "You know exactly where I've spent my low-profile career. And knowing that along with who my husband was, you find it surprising I've made a few connections through the years? Please."

"I didn't give that much thought." When this had started, he hadn't thought about her husband because he wasn't relevant to the situation. After spending time with her online and especially after last night, Holt didn't want to think about her husband at all.

It was a double standard considering his storied and colorful past, but a relationship wasn't in their future. No way would she stick by him if he survived long enough to be charged with working for Isely. She was accustomed to heroes and good guys, not that gray place he represented.

His possessiveness for her was irrational and unexpected. It wasn't even based in reality. He'd started an online relationship as a means to an end. But he didn't want it to end.

"Hey."

He glanced down to where her palm gently covered his knee. His whole body reacted, zeroing in on that small point of contact. His pulse kicked, his breath hitched and his hands warmed with the urge to touch and take. He shook his head and gulped air deep into his lungs.

"Sorry. Wandering thoughts," he muttered.

"You've been working undercover for too long. Who else knows about your mission?"

"No one. That's just it. No one else in Mission Recovery was cleared on the Germany job. Despite that, no one could know or Isely would never have taken the bait."

She sat back, taking her warmth with her, and he knew she was doubting his story. And why shouldn't she? It was his word against the evidence. Evidence he'd purposely stacked against himself to keep Isely on the hook.

"Then why did we meet with Jason and Gin?"

"He doesn't know how far I've gone," Holt insisted. "I only asked him to look up the biologist who created the virus. And I handed over the last vial of the virus Isely gave me weeks ago."

She stared at him but he couldn't read her at all. "You'd better tell me everything. And fast," she warned.

Somehow he found himself answering to her demand. Way, way outside his normal protocol. "I wasn't supposed to see him again ever. It was kidnap you, deliver you to the address he chose and I'd be out."

"But you went on the offensive and demanded a meeting instead."

"Correct."

"And you don't have any idea what he was going to do with me?"

"The way I put it together, kidnapping you puts me in the rogue-agent category, which embarrasses the director and jeopardizes his career. Isely can also use your capture to further expose and antagonize your brother."

"Right." She sipped her coffee. "What about the virus?"

"I dispersed that last night at the gala."

"You did what?"

The flash of horror on her face proved he'd finally found the one thing to push her away. He regretted it instantly. "Isely wanted the virus dispersed at the gala so it would cause more blowback for Thomas. I arranged it so a couple of his guys were on the security detail, remember?"

"Yes." Her horrified reaction had already reverted back to what he considered her crisis face. The still, serene expression effectively concealed how fast her mind was working through the problem at hand. He wondered when she'd act on the disgust and fury she must be feeling.

"One of his men was supposed to contaminate someone or something. If the virus works as advertised, later tonight people will show symptoms and eventually a good many of them will die."

"And pathology will show it was a designer strain of the flu and call it a terrorist attack."

"Yes. The people who matter in the intelligence community will link it back to your brother and blame him because it happened on his watch."

"Isely gave this a great deal of thought."

"He's been working it out for years. Colorado, Vegas, those were just building blocks for last night."

"But…"

"Why do you assume there's a 'but'?"

She simply stared at him, waited him out. He supposed it was a dumb question. For whatever reason, she didn't view him the way the rest of the world viewed him—as a spook too quiet and withdrawn for his own good.

"I met the courier, let him inject me with the virus and then returned to the party. I danced and mingled and they reported it to Isely. Later I sent the remaining product and a blood sample to the lab."

"How?"

"My assistant was close by."

"But you never left the gala."

He smiled. "Only for a moment. I'm quick and I have good hands."

"Yes, you do." She traced the rim of her coffee cup with her fingertip. "What did you inject instead of the virus?"

"I used one of the bogus vials Thomas originally brought back." He waved his hands in the air. "Hand is quicker than the eye."

"Apparently." She uncurled from the chair and poured more coffee into her cup. "Sounds like you've got this under control."

"Everything but Isely's sudden urgency."

"He tried to jump the gun on the kidnapping but didn't succeed, so you're back on schedule, right?"

He shook his head. "It will fall apart when no one gets sick. And that possible exchange at sea is all wrong." He paced away from her.

"Talk to me, Emmett. Let me help. You're not giving me everything."

What the hell was he doing? But he couldn't not tell her everything. "He knows the virus is useless. He has to. He just doesn't care about it enough."

"But it wiped out those villagers."

"I can't explain that. Maybe it breaks down. Maybe they used a different formula."

"Is there anyone here in the States who can help him with the virus?"

"Probably, but he hasn't made contact. My gut is telling me we're in serious trouble here. If I leave you alone to go to the meet, either Mission Recovery or Isely's crew will find you. Isely will learn this quickly, and then we'll never know what he's up to."

"So take me along."

"What, like a date?"

"No, like a partner who has your back."

"You're not trained for that."

"My fresh eyes see it as your only option. You go alone, you walk into a trap and I'm stuck dealing with him."

He shook his head.

"Emmett, are you this good at everything you do?"

"What do you mean?"

"You purposely painted yourself into a corner. Who were you going to hand over to Isely in my place? What was your exit strategy?"

He scrubbed at his face and braced for her shock and righteous indignation. "Originally, I'd planned to hand you over, but with a GPS tag so I could follow you. Everything the director needed to clear himself and protect the team is scheduled to automatically dump into his inbox after the exchange. A precaution in case I lost your trail. You probably don't believe me, but I wouldn't have let them hurt you."

"I believe you."

He wanted to believe her, but anything might be going on behind her crisis face. "But now, with Isely shifting the plan…"

"You don't trust your own instincts or your own decisions."

"Something like that."

"Well, the man has reason to hate Thomas, and it's obvious he wants him to suffer. How did you get yourself between them?"

"Just doing my job."

"Emmett, if you don't start sharing what's really on your mind, I can't help you sort out the solution."

"The best solution is for you to go into protective custody with Mission Recovery while I take down Isely at the meet. The evidence will show up on schedule. Combined with what I've told you, Thomas will be satisfied and safe."

"That sounds like the easiest and prettiest solution, but it might not be the best."

CECELIA STRUGGLED NOT to flinch under the weight of that iron stare. She wasn't about to let him take the fall for this, not when he'd so selflessly given himself to protect her and her brother.

Her feelings were a tangled mess of guilt, expectations, lust and fragile new hope, but one thing was clear. Emmett needed her. Even more astounding, she knew she could be helpful, even if he didn't give her more insight.

Isely thought she knew something. She just had to figure out how to use that to help Emmett. If she dared tell him about that meet, he would definitely lock her away just as Thomas had wanted to. How could she help anyone then?

While the work she did for the CIA was straightforward and boring, she'd been honest with Emmett about making connections.

She should probably consult her daughter, but that would only negate the text message she'd sent last night declaring she was fine and wishing her and Levi a Merry Christmas.

"How old is Isely?" she asked, trying hard to reconcile anything Emmett knew with something she might know and not realize the importance of.

"Thirty-four in January."

She did the math. "So his father's death hit him at a prime point in his career development. Is he married?"

"No."

Too bad. The man had nothing to lose, no serious distraction from planning this detailed revenge. It made him more dangerous. "Other family?"

"His mother and a few cousins."

"Religious at all?"

"Catholic," Emmett snapped, glaring at her. "Stop grasping at straws. The man's been profiled already."

"You said he's breaking behavior patterns. I'm trying to find the angle."

"You're trying to find the place where he recruited me."

The way he saw through her was a bit unnerving, but she took comfort that he wasn't discounting her ability to analyze and assess a complex situation. "Wouldn't have to go fishing if you'd just tell me."

She smiled, but his eyes went flat and cold and his jaw tensed. The man could put up brick walls faster than anyone she'd ever met. Well, maybe except for Thomas. How could she convince him he wasn't alone in this anymore?

She wanted to believe they'd started something last night, long before that, really. Foolish as it might be, she wanted more than a wild, brief affair.

After William, she hadn't thought she'd bother with anything lasting again. Hot and thrilling had been the plan. But maybe she wasn't wired that way after all. Or maybe she was one of the lucky women who bumped into two good men in one lifetime.

It was abundantly clear Emmett didn't see himself as good guy or keeper material. There were skeletons in his closet, she was sure, but everyone had a past. She didn't have any desire to go digging them up, but she'd be more than willing to help him clear them out if and when he felt so inclined.

When his profile had popped on the online dating site, she'd had the option to dig and had refrained. Sometimes too much information was just that—too much information.

She'd wanted a bit of mystery in the men who'd expressed interest in her profile. Wanted the fun of discovery that came with meeting someone new.

Well, she'd gotten plenty of both with Emmett Holt. And now they were at a standoff.

"About yesterday." If she expected him to provide full disclosure, she had to do the same no matter if he attempted to get her into protective custody. She'd stood her ground with Thomas and she would stand it with him.

Emmett pierced her with a sharp gaze.

"Isely came to see me at the hotel."

"You didn't call." He stalked closer, leaned forward and caged her in the chair.

"I had the phone on and I was ready to press the number." Her voice cracked. "Casey was watching the whole time." She chose not to mention Isely's threat against her daughter. Or the stupid choice he'd asked her to make.

"What did he want?"

"He asked me for the formula."

Emmett reared back. "You don't have it!"

"Of course not. I told him I didn't know what he was talking about."

"For the love of God!"

"What?"

"Thomas stopped the sale while the CIA took down the biologist." He pounded a fist into the opposite palm. "I should have put that together sooner. Isely must think your husband was somehow involved and left you the formula."

"He didn't. Trust me, I've been through everything. William would never have kept anything that sensitive. He'd have destroyed it first. I do remember him mentioning some big scientist who was off the market after a mission, but he never elaborated."

"That's it." Emmett shook his head. "Isely must have learned that loose connection and now he believes the formula is in your possession." Pacing now, he was clearly turning over the implications of this new information. He wasn't willingly shutting her out this time, but it was just as effective. "No wonder he pushed the idea of getting info on the director's family. That's what Isely wanted from the beginning. How did I miss this?"

Before Cecelia could think what to say, he wheeled on her. "Why the hell didn't you tell me this hours ago?"

"I knew you'd try to take me out of the equation." She stood, planted her hands on her hips. "That's all there is to discuss about that. Now, I'm going to take a shower," she said, falling back on a tried and true approach. Men talked more when their hands were busy. She hoped he was serious about the risks of leaving her alone and would join her rather than leave her here. "Then we should get breakfast."

Feeling his hot gaze following her, she unbuttoned his shirt as she walked toward the bathroom and let it fall at the doorway. She paused, giving him a tempting eyeful of her nude body before she stepped behind the door to start the shower.

She was under the hot spray, letting it beat at her scalp,

convinced she'd made a tactical error, when the curtain went flying to the side. It required supreme effort to maintain her composure when faced with his sculpted body and obvious desire.

He was lean, but so well-defined an artist would never lack for inspiration. There was a balance to his form, an inherent strength that went far beyond the honed muscles.

She gave up the effort and licked her lips in anticipation. It saved her from smothering him with more flattery. Extending her hand, she would have testified sparks flew when he took it and joined her.

"Nice trick," he said, crowding her under the spray.

"I have more." She ran her hands up and over his chest.

"Prove it."

She proceeded to do just that.

Chapter Seventeen

Holt's legs were weak and he had the vague thought that he might embarrass himself and collapse in a satisfied heap right here in the dingy little bathtub.

She'd had tricks all right. Enough to surprise him, and he thought he'd seen it all. The woman was so much more than a first glance would suggest.

He had the absurd urge to ask if it had been like that with her husband. The question was taboo, and not at all the topic she wanted him to bring up, he felt certain.

Turning off the taps, he pushed the curtain aside and just enjoyed the view of her wrapped in a towel. This one was shorter than yesterday, and after what they'd shared, he figured ogling her was a compliment rather than overstepping.

"Like what you see?"

"You know I do." More than he should. They had a few more hours today, then it was over. He'd go his way and she'd go hers. It was for the best, but it put a sick feeling in his gut.

He pulled a towel off the rack and rubbed it across his hair, working his way down his body, pleased to catch her watching him, too.

Reluctantly, he put them back on task. "Isely approached me eight months ago in Monaco."

"Indebted gamblers make great marks."

He nodded, securing the towel at his waist. "Especially those of us with security clearances."

"No one on the outside knows about your team. How did Isely put it together?"

"I approached him. Or at least that's the way he made it seem. After what you told me I'm not so sure. I was on a mission to prove my worth to the great Thomas Casey."

Her pale eyebrows arched toward her hairline. "Well played either way. You wanted to get him and he needed something. Everyone lies and who wins?"

"Going on the offense is what I do. I lost brilliantly, on purpose, of course, then offered to sell him what I'd heard he was looking for."

"The agent who'd killed his father."

Holt nodded once more.

"He didn't bother to dig into your claims?"

"Of course he did. And I made sure he found what he needed to find."

"You lied." Her radiant smile made him want to confess the sordid details.

He reached into his bag for his razor and stopped. "Will it bug you if I don't shave?"

Her fingertips danced lightly along his jaw. "I like you a little scruffy."

He dipped his head for a kiss, needing another dose of her sweet taste. This one didn't burn as a prelude to seduction. No, it rocked him with something warmer, more real and far more dangerous to his sanity.

She dropped her towel across the edge of the tub and sauntered out to the bedroom to dress. He couldn't follow her and indulge in another sexual romp. They had to finish this thing.

He told himself this wasn't the woman to care about.

She was so far out of his league, but damned if he didn't want to go for it anyway.

He was only a few minutes behind her, but when he emerged from the bathroom, she'd dressed and had her bag packed and her tablet in her lap. Her efficiency was disappointing.

"You're leaving the dress here?" It was still hanging in the closet.

"It's a bit bulky."

She was being practical. But he was going to miss it. "And it's something for your brother to find."

"He's not supposed to be looking."

"You can't believe he's just ignoring your disappearance."

"A girl can hope." She set the tablet aside. "Where is the meet?"

Holt tossed the towel to the side in favor of clothes more suitable for the day's events. He felt her eyes on him as he tugged on jeans and drew a shirt over his head. It seemed in one area at least—passion—they were well matched.

"I'll explain on the way."

"Tell me there's time to eat something."

"Jittery?"

She smiled, slow and wicked. "No. Just famished from so much exertion."

"There are a couple of meal bars in my bag."

"There has to be another choice."

He grinned when her stomach growled. "There's a decent diner a few blocks away."

"Great." She popped to her feet. "We can plan how to take him down. I have some ideas churning."

"Sure." He felt her staring as he packed up his computer. When he looked up, he realized his plan to keep her out of harm's way would never work. "Relax. I have some gear in the car. You can be my backup while Isely tries to sweat me for you."

She pumped her fist and turned a quick circle. "Good answer."

AN HOUR LATER, they'd demolished a hearty breakfast and finalized their plan. She'd used her tablet to review a few documents related to her husband's estate, but so far hadn't found anything about the formula Isely wanted.

That was good news from his perspective.

As he topped off her coffee, he realized he had to tell her the whole truth. Only an idiot would keep playing the role that would never come true. Call him an idiot.

He scrubbed at his face and tried to smile when she shot him a concerned look.

"You okay?"

"I'll be fine." Maybe the better play was to see how far they could get, to wait until he knew she loved him. Then maybe she'd be too attached to dump him and hold him accountable for all the lies.

Strange as it was, he couldn't imagine his life without her in it. Staying with her would only make the pain worse when she left him a week, a month or a decade from now.

And she would leave. Women like her didn't stay with men like him.

It boiled down to one critical question. Did he love her enough not to hurt her? The answer was obvious.

"Are you always nervous before a meet?"

"Nerves keep you on your toes," he said. "But this meet is the most important of my life."

"It will work out, Emmett."

"You've contacted your brother?"

"And his wife, just in case Thomas blows off my message."

"After this, he'll see what I've known all along. You and ops are a perfect fit." He laced his hand with hers. "He'll try to recruit you away."

"Not a chance."

If she went into ops, they'd never work together. He pulled himself away from that slippery slope. First he had to survive today, and then he had to convince her he could leave his past behind.

The past. He didn't want her to hear it from a third party and Isely would know she was close, would try to use it against him. She deserved better than that.

"About that New York job." The words stuck in his throat.

"The one that caught Thomas's attention?"

"Yeah." He swallowed, searching for the right words. He couldn't believe how much he wanted her to understand.

"Emmett, you don't have to tell me. I don't want you breaching security after everything else you've managed to protect during this sting operation."

"The things I've leaked, even to protect myself, are punishable offenses. But the one I regret, the one I should have found a way to tweak, is revealing the director's family. Revealing your existence to a monster."

"Thomas won't punish the hero who single-handedly stopped his nemesis and protected the secret of Mission Recovery. Besides, I think we both know now that getting to me was Isely's intent all along."

Hero? She was making this so tough. He knew Thomas wouldn't see him as a hero, even if things worked out the way she hoped. When she learned the truth, he'd be lucky if she could look at him at all. "Cecelia, just listen a minute. Isely knows things about my past. I'd rather you heard them from me first."

Even if she hated him for seducing her, for having the

audacity to think he loved her, he knew she wouldn't abandon Thomas's cause. Whatever Isely said or did at this meet, she was strong enough to take over and finish what he'd started.

"When your brother found me, I was about to do a second stretch in prison for theft."

She didn't flinch at the news. Her calm blue gaze held his with a depth of compassion he didn't expect or deserve.

"Someone already told you. Who?"

"You." She covered his hands with hers. "Just now."

That was impossible. Maybe it was shock. "Did you hear me? Did you understand what I meant?" He rubbed the back of her hand with his thumb. "I've served time for theft. I'm a thief and a liar. Take away the cool job and fancy office and I still am."

"Only because the mission required it. And even now you're still trying to prove yourself to my brother when you wouldn't be in the position you're in if he hadn't been convinced from the beginning."

"Cecelia, be reasonable here."

She reached up and those soft, pampered fingers caressed his cheek. "What were you expecting? I haven't had a temper tantrum since I was thirteen."

"Then have at it. You're long overdue." He stared out the window, not wanting to see the disappointment on her face when she accepted the truth.

"No, thanks."

"I'm sorry for—"

"For what?"

Her voice had a definite edge now. He met her gaze, leaned back a bit from the intensity.

"Don't you dare apologize for the past two days or the actions that brought us together."

"But—"

"I thought you were the one person who understood I don't scare easy. Was that a lie?"

"No, that was true."

"Well, here's some more truth for you. I'm a big girl and I know everyone comes with baggage. I don't care who you were or what you did. I love the man you turned yourself into."

She loved him? Had to be a figure of speech, although he supposed she would know more about it, having sustained a marriage from "I do" all the way to her husband's untimely death.

Maybe he wasn't just the short-term guy filling the holiday void for a society matron eager to explore a latent bad-boy fixation. He'd never been more frightened of what that might mean.

"I know we have to go our separate ways when this is over, but I wanted you to know where I came from."

"Please." She gave a little snort. "You wanted me to run away."

"No." *Maybe a little.*

"You're stuck with me, Emmett Holt, and I think you're warming up to the idea."

"You can't be serious."

"As a heart attack." Under the table, she rubbed her calf against his. "I wasn't raised to view people as disposable."

"Ops training will cure you of that," he said, checking his watch. He needed to get into position so Isely wouldn't have reason to suspect anything had changed.

"I doubt that."

"How can you be so sure?"

"I've learned a few things by watching you." She ticked the list of names on her fingers, "Casey, Thomas and William. Integrity and honor are honed—not dulled—

by doing what's right and making the hard choices that protect others."

Holt wanted to believe her. With everything inside him, he wanted to believe in a pretty future where all the things she implied were possible. "You and I are worlds apart, Cecelia."

"But we don't have to be," she said softly.

"We should go." He tossed a few bills on the table to cover the check, then started scooting out of the booth. "Remember to chatter nonsense. It'll annoy whoever's listening on Isely's end, make them think you're flighty."

"One thing first."

He froze, hoping she'd give him another "I love you," another chance to say the words back.

"I have a secret, too."

Whatever it was couldn't be as bad as his. She was just trying to make him feel better, but he listened anyway. "Go on."

"I didn't cry when William died."

He didn't see the relevance, but he saw her lower lip tremble and knew there was more.

"I've never told anyone." Her breath stuttered, then she gathered herself. "It happened about two months before he died. His last good day."

"That's when you cried."

Her chin jerked twice. "No more tears after that day. And I vowed never to care that much for another man again."

Talk about brutal honesty. He didn't know what to say, couldn't have said anything anyway. The vicious ache in his chest made it impossible. Now he knew why he lied, why he pushed people—women—away. Because love hurt.

And he was looking at a woman who'd loved and lost

in a tragic fashion. She'd accepted his secret, he'd accept hers. "Understandable," he managed after a moment.

"Is it?"

"Yeah."

"I used to think so."

He wanted to pounce on that ray of hope, but they were out of time. "Come on. We have to go."

They walked to the car in silence, but as he reached to open her door, he changed his mind. He couldn't give her the words, but he could damn well show her how he felt, whether she could reciprocate or not. Maybe his emotion could help her rediscover her own.

He grabbed her close and kissed her, pouring out all the feelings he'd imprisoned inside.

Chapter Eighteen

The National Mall, Washington, D.C.
10:45 a.m.

Cecelia couldn't believe she'd told him her darkest secret. She was still reeling from the fierce kiss he'd planted on her in reply. It took everything she had to think up some inane chatter to irritate Isely's crew.

Emmett had located her at the perfect vantage point for watching the meet through binoculars. She wasn't happy about it, but she was here, overlooking his position at a small café. He'd told her it was to watch his back, but she knew it was another of those moves to protect her.

"Are you done with your shopping?" she asked, feigning excitement for the benefit of those listening in on their communications link.

"Never started."

"Did you make a list for Santa?" she teased, trying to pull him out of the shell he'd withdrawn into since the diner.

"No point. I'm always on the naughty list," he said.

Even through the earpiece, she caught the sensual undertone in that comment. After last night, she should expect her share of coal in the stocking, too. Thank goodness he couldn't see her blushing at the memory of how good they'd been. Together.

"Then what are your plans for Christmas?" She couldn't quite believe she was going to ask him to join her in the Caribbean. This probably wasn't an appropriate discussion under the circumstances, but she wasn't sure she'd get another chance to tell him what he meant to her.

"I don't make holiday plans."

"No family to visit?" She watched the slow shake of his head through the binoculars. "Not everyone is like you and yours."

"So that part of your profile was real?"

"Yes."

Hearing the edge in his voice, she knew his patience with the topic was about to snap.

"You should join me. I have a ticket—"

"This conversation could be monitored," he grumbled from behind his coffee cup.

"Yes, sir." Where was Isely? Had he gotten close enough to see that she wasn't with Emmett and walked away? Part of her couldn't help but hope…but then they might never get him and be able to clear Emmett's name.

"Why won't you be with family?" he asked, drawing her attention back to where it was supposed to be.

She sighed. "We've had enough togetherness for one season. I need a change of scenery."

"To get ready for your next phase."

She didn't like the implication behind that comment. He wasn't a phase to her. Although what else could he conclude after she'd said what she had about not loving anyone again?

"It's easier my way," he said. "No family. No plans. No problems. I'm spending the holiday on my boat."

"Sailing away into the sunset?" a male voice asked.

Cecelia jumped at the voice, even as she watched Isely sit down at the table with Emmett. "Sounds positively romantic. At least it will be when the women realize you are wealthy."

"Can't wait," Emmett said.

Isely looked at his jaw, still swollen from the fight in the hotel. "Did you run into something?"

"I tripped on a box of hammers."

"How unfortunate. Where is my new friend?" He glanced around. "She is supposed to be here, no?"

"Safe. I'm happy to make the introduction if you'll tell me when and where."

"Mr. Holt, it is a cold day. I would like to know that my investments have not been in vain. I fear you are playing games with me now, and I have no patience for games, my friend."

"I've delivered everything you've asked for," Emmett ground out between clenched teeth.

Cecelia swore. If this conversation wound up in the wrong hands, it was just more evidence on the growing heap against him. It was as if he wanted every agent to swarm in and bury him for life. He was better than this, but the breadcrumbs he'd left would only help if someone cared enough to go looking. At this point, she was his last chance.

She couldn't make a mistake.

"And I have shown the agreed-upon appreciation," Isely said. "You have not cooperated with your new team. This is not a good sign."

"We had an understanding. I don't answer to your team."

Isely sighed. "You caused many injuries."

"You should have told me directly about a change in plans."

"I'm telling you now." Isely looked around the park once more. "I think you have developed an affection for the woman."

"She's business. You assured me you wouldn't harm her."

"And I will not. But you, I think, is another matter altogether."

Cecelia's lips tightened to prevent telling the monster he wasn't harming a hair on Emmett's head while she still had breath.

"Then why bother with any of the rest of it?" Emmett demanded. "I've done all you ask. When guests from last night's gala start dying, you'll have won."

"That was for my own entertainment," the bastard said with a laugh. "Besides, I've heard no reports of this. Perhaps you've double-crossed me."

"What is it you want me to do, Isely?"

"Bring me the woman. She is useful in other ways. More useful than you."

Through the binoculars, Cecelia saw the other man approach, but her warning to Emmett came half a second too late. The man appeared to slap Emmett on the side of the neck. Emmett jerked. Was there something in his hand? Fear tightened around her heart. She watched the shock on his face and knew she was right. Tears welled in her eyes. She wanted to race to his side but he had made her swear she wouldn't move until he said the word.

Damn him! What was she supposed to do?

"Deliver her to this warehouse and you'll have the antidote in plenty of time to enjoy the wealth I showered upon you."

Antidote? Had he poisoned Emmett? Oh, dear God! She watched the monster tuck a card into Emmett's pocket.

"What did you give me?" Emmett demanded, his words slurred.

"Sometimes the old ways are better." Isely leaned close. "Don't worry. It is not contagious. Keep cooperating, Holt, and all will be well."

She watched in horror as Emmett's head lolled to the side. From this distance she couldn't shoot the bastard who'd done this. She couldn't reach him in time if she rushed toward them… She needed help.

Isely leaned over Emmett and his voice sounded in her ear. Cultured and slick, it made her want to take a shower. "Are you listening, Mrs. Manning? I do believe I might have given your lover too much. But perhaps he will survive until you get him to the warehouse for the antidote. The address is on the card in his pocket."

She wished she could put a bullet straight through his brain, to hell with his endgame.

Cecelia clenched her teeth and held her scathing reply as well as her position until Isely walked away. It required a measure of strength she didn't know she still possessed.

"Faster," she muttered, hoping she could hasten his departure by sheer force of will. If she bolted to Emmett's side too quickly, Isely would have them both in a snare.

She couldn't let that happen.

As soon as Isely and his cohort were long gone, Cecelia rushed to Emmett.

"Hang on," he mumbled, lurching to his feet. "I'm coming to you."

"I'm here," she assured him as she tucked herself under his sagging weight. "What did he give you?" She practically dragged him toward the car. It was hardly a block away and it felt like miles.

"I was hoping you'd know," he slurred. "…says there's an antidote."

"I heard. Let's go get it."

"No. He'll make me hurt you."

"Too late," she muttered.

"What?"

"I'm already hurt, Emmett." She turned her face up to his face. "Just because you're hurting."

"Forget about me. Call the authorities." His words were scarcely intelligible now. "You deserve better."

"You're right." She deserved a man who treated her as an equal. As he'd done from the start. A man who trusted her to watch his back while he tried to keep her safe from a criminal like Isely. She deserved a man who accepted his personal worth and shouldered her darkest secret. "When this is over and you're feeling better, we'll hammer out new terms."

He didn't say anything. He'd passed out.

Cecelia waved down a taxi and got him into the back seat while explaining her friend had drunk too much. No way she could get him all the way to where they had parked the car. She dug the card from his pocket and checked the address, then provided it to the driver. She couldn't believe it had come down to this. Her against an international crime boss, the lives of two men she loved on the line.

Her whole body shook as she moved around to the other side of the car. She had to keep it together. Isely wanted Thomas to suffer. He had a flair for the dramatic, and based on what she'd learned from Emmett, he had impeccable timing. A dead man would have less impact on a man like her brother than a dying friend. This was just another part of the plan.

Isely would know that, would try to use that to rip Mission Recovery apart.

Well, he was in for a shock.

If Isely said the antidote was at the warehouse, that's

where she had to go. And she'd arrive just as he expected: a weepy, worried mess. "Just like you taught me," she whispered to herself as she climbed in next to Emmett. "Give them what they need to see."

Her vision blurred and she realized she was crying. She swiped away tears, oddly relieved that she still had that depth of emotion inside her.

As she reached to close her door, a male voice interrupted. "Need a hand?"

She gave a startled cry when the square face of the burly security guard from the gala filled her window. "Go!" she shouted to the taxi driver.

"Wait." He flashed a badge. Real or fake, she didn't care at this point.

The taxi rushed away. She didn't have time to examine credentials or to verify a story. A plan was coming together in her mind. While it was dicey, it was hers, and she knew she could trust the players.

All she had to do was get word to them. Thomas would never question her need for help. He might not trust Emmett but he would do what needed to be done.

Failure wasn't an option.

She made the necessary call to Jo, Thomas's wife, instead of calling him. Jo promised to take care of everything. She said Thomas was already on it. Cecelia didn't know what that meant, but she was relieved to hear it. Thank God. She dragged a bottle of water from her bag and gave Emmett's shoulder a shove. "Come on, wake up."

His eyelids fluttered. "Where are we?"

"Doesn't matter. Drink this."

He shook his head. "No, thanks."

"Cooperate, Emmett." There wasn't much she could do without knowing the exact toxin in his system, but with something this fast acting, she knew his kidneys would need the help.

And who knew what dangers waited. She couldn't think about that or she'd freeze up. One step at a time.

Beside her Emmett muttered, but he kept sipping the water when prompted. Maybe Isely had done her a favor by incapacitating Emmett; now she wouldn't have to lie or hide what she was doing. In his condition he'd never remember her moves this afternoon—assuming they both survived Isely's final showdown.

She closed her eyes, thinking of the tropical paradise where she intended to spend Christmas day. They would all get through this.

Steadier, she called the marina and used her considerable influence as Mrs. Manning to arrange for Emmett's boat to be prepped, launched and moved around to the launch on the river.

A phone in his pocket rang and she knew the blocked number could only be Isely.

"Hello?"

"Ah, Mrs. Manning. It seems you've drifted off course."

"I—I know," she said, letting him hear her fear. Not of him or his petty plots, but that she might not be able to do what she knew it would take to eliminate him. "We had some car tr-trouble. The engine was acting funny. I had to get a cab. We're on our way."

"Now, now. I know this is overwhelming. Just bring him to me."

"We're on our way now. I swear."

"Good. Your brother is getting impatient."

"Thomas is with you?" Now she was panicked. Did Jo not know he'd been captured?

"What can I say? He insisted on crashing our party."

"Let me talk with him. Please?"

"Oh, we'll have plenty of time to chat in person when you arrive, Mrs. Manning."

The line went dead and Cecelia muttered a curse she'd learned from Emmett. The cab driver glanced at her in his rearview mirror. "Is everything all right?"

"Yes. Thank you." She shoved the burner phone deep into the seat cushion. It was only marginally better than tossing it out the window. No sense adding littering to the charges looming against Emmett. And her.

Beside her, Emmett's body shook with tremors.

Fear closed her throat. "Hang in there. It's almost over."

"Drop me off and go," he said, surprisingly coherent and with less slurring.

Was that good or bad?

"Absolutely not. I'm your backup."

"I can handle this."

"I believe you." No point arguing with a professional—particularly a man.

"Then let me do it alone."

"You'd like that, wouldn't you?" she argued. "Glory hound. I'm going in with you."

Emmett shifted, reaching for her face. She held his palm to her cheek when he didn't have the strength. This would not be their last moment. She refused to accept a future that didn't include him.

"Cecelia," he rasped. "Don't—"

"Shh," she interrupted, taking the water bottle. "Rest while you can."

His eyes drifted shut once more and Cecelia launched into a string of silent prayers. A few pleas for Emmett and Thomas mixed in, but what she begged for most was the courage to see this through.

Alexandria warehouse, 6:32 p.m.

HOLT WISHED HE'D been strong enough to shake off Cecelia when she'd refused to leave his side as they exited the cab at the warehouse. He wished he'd found a way to shield her from all of this.

Most of all he wished he'd told her he loved her when he'd had the chance. Falling in love hadn't been on the agenda for this op, but it had happened anyway. Ironic to come to terms with that now, when he was about to die.

His wrists burned where the cuffs bit into his skin, and the ache in his shoulders was too awful to contemplate. He'd been cuffed to a pipe above his head and the toe of his boot scraped the floor, but not enough to relieve the strain of his body weight.

Whatever Isely had given him was wearing off, but he didn't recall being dosed with an antidote.

"Wake up," a male voice hissed from nearby.

"Director Casey?" Holt tried to clear his dry throat. "That you?"

"Yeah."

"Cecelia?"

"I'm certain she's here…just not with us."

Holt's heart plummeted. What freakish use did Isely have planned for her? She didn't have what he was looking for. "Told her to go."

"Isely would have dragged her back. Whatever his endgame, she was part of it, I think before you were even involved. He's been plotting this revenge for years."

Holt wasn't so sure. She'd shown some interesting talents over the past days. Of all the things he'd done to protect Mission Recovery, he couldn't let the director believe he would have sacrificed Cecelia. "Never would've hurt her. You…must know…that."

"Shut up. Save your strength."

"What'd they give me?"

"A sedative, if it's what they gave me. Doesn't really matter. Keep breathing until we can find a way out of here."

"Never betrayed you." There were other things he should probably tell the director, but now wasn't exactly the time.

"You damn well blurred some lines," Thomas muttered.

If Thomas knew that, then he knew exactly what Holt had done. A glimmer of something close to hope flared in his chest. "If we get out of here, I'll get glasses," Holt joked despite the bleak circumstances.

"If we all get out of here, I'm going to beat the hell out of you and then I'll pat you on the back for getting that bastard."

"Anything." Anything but a resignation. He'd been ready to defect, to die if necessary to protect Thomas and Mission Recovery, until he'd met Cecelia. She made him want more than the solitary existence he'd been living long before going undercover to stop Isely. Two days with her and he believed in dreams again. With her.

Even if she couldn't feel as much as he did, he wanted her. Whatever she could give.

He peered up at his cuffed wrists. There had to be a way to get out of this.

A high-pitched cry ripped through the thin corrugated-metal walls, derailing his thoughts.

Holt jerked against his restraints even as Thomas ordered him to calm down.

"He's testing us."

"It's not her fight," Holt growled. He was done playing opossum. Drawing his knees up to his chest, he growled in frustration. There was no foothold he could find, no weakness he could exploit.

"Be still. You're going to need your strength when it'll actually do some good."

"Only when I'm dead."

The door opened and Holt squinted against the bright light. "You should listen to your boss," Isely said, stepping into the room.

Holt's vision was clear enough to see Thomas attached to a chair in the corner.

"Give it up. You won't get away with this," Holt warned.

"Just as I suspected." Isely stayed just out of reach of Holt's legs. "You were too weak to choose the right side."

"It's my underdog complex," he said through gritted teeth. "Let the woman go."

"But she is the whole reason we are here. Have you learned nothing through our talks?"

"Only that you're an—"

"Ah, yes. Vulgarity suits you well, Mr. Holt. Much better than a tuxedo, or the fine lifestyle my payoffs would have funded."

"Might want to invest your money in a better chemist, Isely. That dose of poison seems to have worn off." He kept Isely distracted, hoping to give Thomas an opening. They had to get Cecelia out of here.

Isely revealed a Taser and Holt jerked with the force of the electricity coursing through his body. He should have seen that coming. But it'd be worth it when Thomas made his move. *Come on, man,* he urged silently. *I'm waiting for the big bad Thomas Casey to rescue me.*

"Aren't you the prince of deception?" Isely taunted. "Or is it thieves? It's no concern of mine. I only gave you enough sedative to cause panic and make the woman cooperate."

Holt swore. His instincts had warned him she'd been holding back, but just how much? What information could a CIA admin have that Isely needed?

"She cares for you," Isely said, zapping him again. "Pathetic, but I found it quite useful. I have everything I need now. Except the ending to this story."

"Enough," Thomas shouted.

They both knew that when Isely was done posturing he'd kill all three of them. Whatever he thought Cecelia had given him, it would never save them.

"Willing to talk at last, Director Casey?"

"Your father built his business and reputation on intelligence, not cruelty."

"You weren't his son," Isely said with a dreadful calm. "But your family will soon know the pain and bitterness of defeat."

"You've kidnapped three American citizens. You have to know that won't go unanswered."

"Really?" Isely crossed the room to tower over Thomas. "Who will act on your behalf? Who knows to ride to your rescue? Not your government. You don't even exist! Not your precious secret team. They think that one of you is a traitor and they don't yet realize you are gone!"

"I can tell you who really ruined that sale of the virus in Oberammergau," Thomas offered.

Isely jerked his chin toward Holt. "He has already told me."

Holt sensed defeat closing in around them. "I lied."

Isely crossed the room and shot him with the Taser again. "I know that! And by your omission, I have found the truth."

"If you let them walk out of here alive, I'll answer any question," Thomas offered with admirable calm.

Holt struggled to breathe. Thomas couldn't roll over like this. "Not for me," he challenged.

"Oh, is there honor among liars and thieves after all?" Isely's bitter laughter clanged against the metal walls of their prison. "Not in my experience. No matter. I have a better surprise. Load her up," he shouted.

The door opened and Thor pushed Cecelia, hands bound and feet chained, into the open doorway. "We're going far away now," Isely promised. "And there is nothing either of you can do except enjoy the ride."

Holt flexed and kicked, but Isely fired the Taser again. His mind drifted away from the pain and he blacked out with Thomas's fury and Cecelia's tears ringing in his ears.

Chapter Nineteen

The boat rocked gently under Cecelia as the yacht motored down the Potomac toward Chesapeake Bay. She was cuffed to a door in the engine room, and the sound and fumes were making her dizzy.

Isely crouched beside her, flipping through files on her tablet. Jo had come up with the plan. A Specialist, the burly man who'd tried to show her some ID before she got into that taxi, had located the car where Cecelia and Emmett had left their things. They had loaded the necessary notes and fake formulas on her tablet. Everything Cecelia needed to make Isely believe that her own husband had stolen the formula from the biologist he'd scarcely known other than on paper.

Cecelia prayed it would work long enough for help to get to them. As soon as she'd told Isely where the formula was, he'd sent two of his men to retrieve her tablet. Mission Recovery was watching the car. Hopefully backup was able to follow the goons here.

Isely was too smart to wait around for the tablet. He'd loaded them onboard his yacht and headed out to sea, hoping to reach international waters before he was intercepted. They were barely out of port when his goons had arrived with the tablet Cecelia had claimed was her husband's.

Now, if only Isely bought the credibility of the formula.

"I thank you, dear," Isely said as he studied the photos and diagrams. He gave a pleased nod and closed the device. He handed the tablet to one of his men. "Lock this in my estate room."

The man hurried to do his bidding. To the other man, he asked, "Is everything ready?"

A nod gave him the answer he wanted.

"Then we go." He unhooked Cecelia's cuffs and hauled her to her feet.

"You're a monster," she said as Isely pushed her up the narrow stairs toward the stern of the boat. "That formula should stay buried." Didn't take much to make her indignation sound real.

"So a few million people die. A vaccination will be discovered." The bastard shrugged. "This world is overdue for a cleansing."

She gasped when she saw Emmett and Thomas on their knees at the edge of the deck. Two more of Isely's crew stood behind them. Isely removed the chain at her feet and then her handcuffs.

"You can help with that effort, starting today."

"What?"

He handed her a gun and she immediately aimed it at him. "Good riddance."

"Now, now." He smiled at her. "You can't shoot me, my dear. My men will kill yours and then you. Everyone loses."

Her hands trembled. "Why are you doing this?"

"Because it needs to be done," he barked. "I've read the reports, spoken with the survivors. I know how my father suffered. Now your family will suffer."

"I gave you what you wanted," she cried, her heart pounding for real. Where the hell was backup? They had to be close.

"You're a woman. You weren't raised to know how men conduct their business. This is something you cannot possibly understand."

Her finger twitched on the trigger at the insult, but this wasn't about her. This was about inflicting lasting pain. Isely wanted her brother to suffer a loss as deep as he'd suffered. She and Emmett were merely a means to that end. It was obvious to her he intended to make this confrontation very personal and agonizing for Thomas, and then he would kill her anyway.

"Call off your men. Stop this nonsense."

"You lovely, sentimental woman." Isely threw back his head and laughed. "The time for begging has passed." In three quick strides he was beside her. "Remember our previous meeting. Have you made a final decision? Who survives? The clock is ticking, Mrs. Manning."

His taunting snapped her out of the red haze blurring her vision. She wasn't Mrs. Manning anymore. Those days were long gone. She was the woman who loved her brother with all her heart and Emmett Holt just as much.

"Come now. The final decision can't be that difficult. You only have to shoot one. Your brother or your lover?" He smiled patronizingly at her.

"Either way, you won't let me live."

"Not true. Someone must explain the mess to the authorities. It won't be me." His smile evaporated and all of his slick charm dissolved into so much cold hatred. "Someone must bear the consequences and someone must take the blame."

"I'll only tell the truth," she said, keeping her gun trained on Isely.

"Oh, but the truth is nothing more than smoke and fog without the right evidence."

And according to what Emmett had been feeding him,

Isely believed the evidence condemned the man she loved, destroyed her brother's reputation and exposed the entire Mission Recovery team to what would surely be a media frenzy.

She looked at Emmett and knew what he wanted her to do: get out alive, with or without him. Worse, she knew what he expected her to do: walk away from his corpse.

Well, if the past forty-eight hours had taught her anything, it was the utter folly of expectations.

Two days ago his doubt in her fortitude might have stung her pride; now she understood the value of being underestimated, though they would damn sure have a long talk about the importance of sharing honest feelings when this was over.

"Choose, Mrs. Manning…"

Ignoring Isely's continued gloating, she looked to her brother and said a prayer that he could somehow give her a sign as to what she should do.

"Brother or lover," Isely prompted with that faint urbane European accent. "It is a difficult choice."

"Lia, you know what to do," Thomas said quietly.

She looked into his eyes for a long moment and she realized he was right. She did know what to do.

The boat rocked under her feet. Couldn't they have done this on land and increased her odds of success?

"Not a tough choice at all," she said to Isely, pulling the trigger as she spoke and firing at her brother. He toppled over.

In their shock, the remaining men gaped while she sent another bullet into the knee of the man holding a gun on Emmett.

The man went down with a violent scream. The boat rocked and Cecelia stumbled backward, a stupid grin splitting her face as she watched Emmett launch himself at Isely.

Her brother quickly subdued and cuffed Isely's other lieutenant.

Cecelia took aim at the fight but couldn't get a clear shot, so she ran for the cockpit, holding the man at the controls at gunpoint until Thomas told her to do otherwise. With his help, they cuffed the man at the wheel and she reduced speed until they were idling.

"Sorry I shot you." She'd barely grazed his shoulder, but he'd toppled over before anyone realized she hadn't gotten him right in the heart.

"That's what you were supposed to do." He pulled her into a fast hug. "And you did good."

"Thomas!"

They both smiled at the familiar voice of Thomas's wife, Jo.

"I think that's my cue," Thomas said.

They both hurried to the deck. Specialists were securing all the bad guys. Jo was hugging Thomas. Cecelia searched through the crowd for Emmett.

"Are you injured, ma'am?" the man who'd tried to help her at the National Mall asked.

Cecelia shook her head, not trusting her voice, trying her best not to burst into tears. It was over. It was really over. She looked around to see Emmett and Thomas talking quietly off to the side.

When the two men she loved most shook hands, she knew it was really over.

Chapter Twenty

Holt ached from head to toe, but nothing was sweeter than having Cecelia in his arms. He wanted to spin her around, but opted for pulling her into his lap while they motored back up the river. He couldn't deny that having Specialist Grant at the control of Isely's yacht gave him immense pleasure. The whole lot, Isely and his goons, were secured and under watch in the engine room.

"Your brother's going to punch me as soon as you're out of range. He's already warned me that he intended to beat the hell out of me. I think in all the excitement he just forgot. Or maybe being shot by his own sister has distracted him."

"Funny," she groused. "I think Thomas is too pleased with how things turned out to hold any grudges."

"Hope so." So far it seemed he still had a job. He tipped his head back and let the cool air wash over them for a moment. "You lied to me," he said, smiling with open admiration. "Thomas was already in place and backup was en route."

"I could lie to anyone," she replied. "I learned from the best. Besides, you were incapacitated."

"Hmm," he groaned.

"Hmm?"

"If you're so good at the lies, how will I know what's true?"

She walked her fingers up the torn front of his shirt, then fisted her hand in the fabric, pulling herself close for another hot, hard kiss.

"That is true," she said. "I never expected to love again, not like this. Thank you."

He tugged at her ponytail and gently tipped her head back so he could kiss the spot under her jaw that made her shiver. "I love you, too."

He smiled against her skin as her hands clutched at his shirt. "Say it again," she whispered.

He obliged, knew he always would where she was concerned. Her arms were chilled, so he hugged her closer. "You were magnificent today."

Her proud grin sliced right through his heart.

"Thanks. You did well yourself."

He shrugged. "CIA will be lucky to have you."

"If what happened here had actually 'happened'—" she used air quotes "—you'd be right."

"What're you saying?" He wasn't sure he could trust the hope that wanted to come to life.

"I'm looking at all of my options. Word is you're a hero. Got any pull at your place?"

"The boss might owe me a favor," he teased. He rubbed his nose against hers. "After he knocks me out. Still, I saved his sister."

She scoffed and pushed at his chest. "She saved herself."

"And me. You definitely saved me." He turned her in his arms and drew her back against his chest while they watched the shoreline of Alexandria approaching. "Is that my boat?" he asked as they neared the marina.

"I made a call," she said, "while you were fighting the sedative. We can cast off whenever you're ready."

"We?"

"If you'll have me."

She sounded nervous, but he didn't think it could possibly compare to the jitters he was fighting. He turned her around, made her look into his eyes so she would see the truth.

No matter what it cost him, he had to be completely truthful with her. "You're all I've ever wanted. My first and only Christmas wish. Say you'll marry me, Cecelia."

"Oh, yes! I will definitely marry you."

Before he could kiss her, they had moored the yacht and were calling for everyone to report and clear the premises.

As he guided Cecelia off the vessel, Thomas Casey stopped him.

Before Holt could react, Thomas gave him a soft cuff to the jaw. "I don't know what you two have in mind for Christmas, but Jo and I would be happy to have you over for the holiday."

"I'm afraid we have plans," Cecelia piped up. "We're setting sail right now and wherever we end up on Christmas, we're going ashore and getting married."

Thomas frowned. Jo rushed up just then. "How romantic." She slugged her husband on the shoulder. "Isn't that romantic, honey?"

Thomas nodded and shrugged at the same time. "Absolutely. What about Casey?" He blinked, clearly startled.

"I'll send pics!" Cecelia wrapped her arm around Holt's. "We can all celebrate when we get back."

As they parted ways with the others, Holt drew her close and kissed her silky hair. "Is that really what you want to do? We can do this any way you want."

"This is perfect." She turned her face up to his. "I can't imagine celebrating Christmas any better way than saying 'I do' to the man I love."

He grinned. "Merry Christmas to me."

He kissed his bride to be, and less than an hour later they were making love on his boat with nothing but time and the sea in front of them.

* * * * *